Why do People Suck?

K.A. Meng

The Three Pens

The Three Pens Publishing

Blurb

Cobie Meine, the world's top singer, is abandoned by her manager who stole her money, fans, and stage name, Cam, after she decided to remove her mask. Left with nothing but her clothes on her back, she no longer sings until she saves a well-known musician from a horde of teenage girl fans.

Jordan Space leads Solar Harmony as its singer and songwriter. He'll always remember the woman who saved him from his fans, even if she doesn't like his music anymore. He follows her advice in only releasing songs he's happy with. Someday, he hopes to thank her.

However, fate, overzealous fans, lawsuits, Cam's impersonator, and the music industry continually drive Cobie and Jordan apart, leaving them questioning why they can't find happiness?

Amazon
Playlist

Spotify
Playlist

To the true fans.

Contents

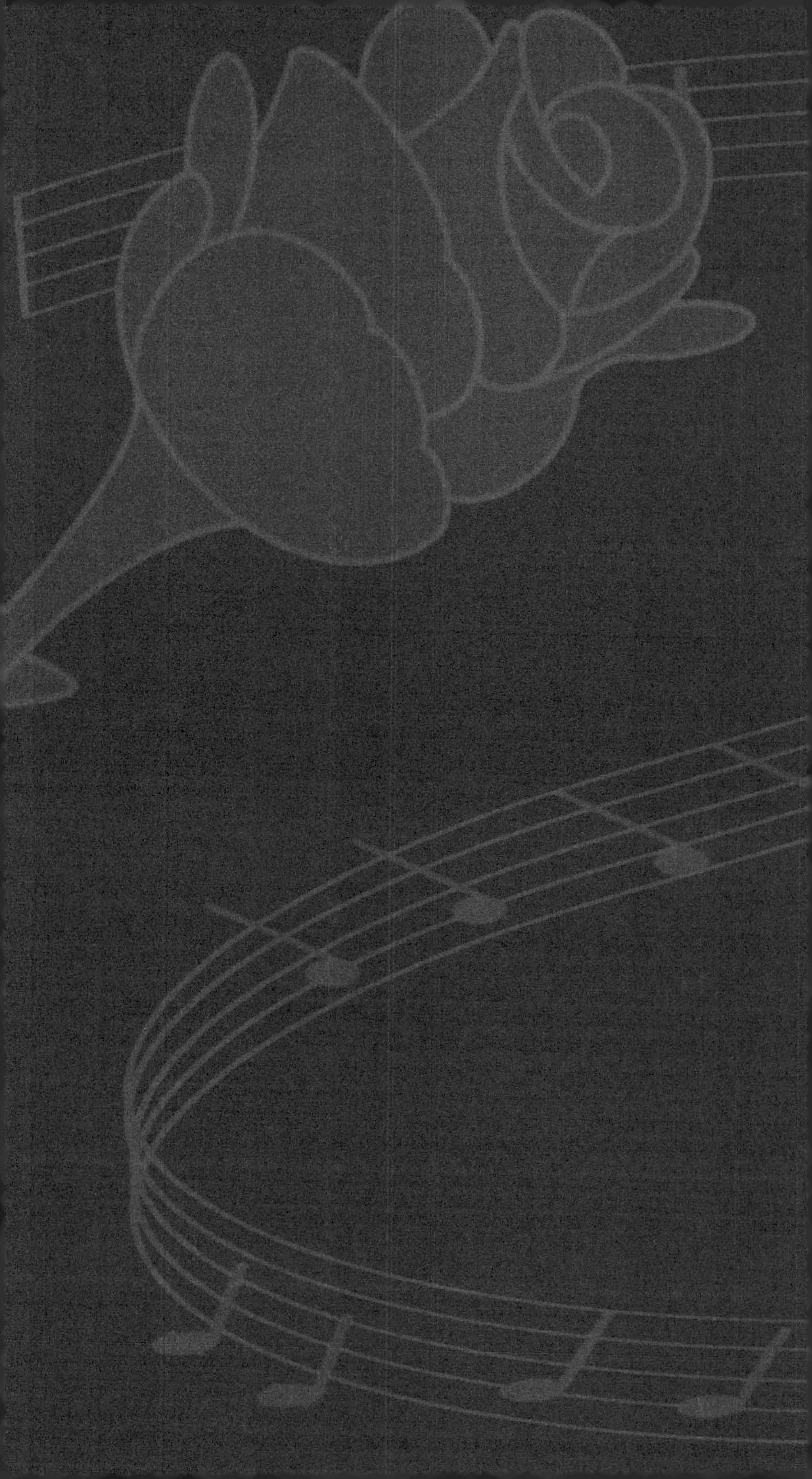

Chapter One

Cobie

S hrieks from the most frightening monsters pierced the air.
My heart hammered, sweat beaded on my forehead as I
searched for them. They headed in my direction, chasing their next
prey.

I retreated to the grass to let them pass. Those barbarians had
once stripped the clothes off a boy band's lead singer, scaring him
into leaving the entertainment industry forever. I couldn't afford
a bodyguard to protect me from the Sol fans, Solar Harmony's
fanbase name, because my manager had stolen my money.

The famous person rollerblading would never lose the teenage
girls chasing him without help. Pity rose inside me, and I rolled
across the bridge, waiting for them. The bridge blocked my view.
They had nowhere to go unless he turned around to face them. I
doubted he would.

The guy arrived at the top of the bridge. He kept the brim of his baseball cap low, as if it did anything to disguise himself.

"Under the bridge," I called to the lead singer of Solar Harmony.

Jordan Space glanced at me and then behind him. He had less than a minute to decide to follow me or not.

"You'll never lose your fans," I told him. Maybe he thought I was worse than them, but I had never acted like them, and I never would after experiencing it.

Jordan hesitated and asked, "Which way?"

I gestured for him to follow me, then carefully descended the small dead grass next to the bridge, using the side as support.

He hurried behind me, and we hid underneath the bridge.

The screams from the teenage girls sounded closer.

I missed them at my concerts, and jealousy rose inside of me. I had trusted the wrong person, and he took my stage name, Cam. Jordan had fans loving his music. Well, I had nothing, but I didn't want them chasing me.

Footsteps thudded on the wooden planks.

Jordan pulled me against the underside of the bridge, pressed his body close to mine, and placed a hand over my mouth. His scent of overpriced cologne wafted into my nose.

"Jordan!" one girl screamed.

"Marry me!"

"I'm marrying Jordan!"

They argued until someone announced, "We can all marry Jordan." They cheered as they finished running across the bridge and hurried away, chasing after nothing.

I didn't have the heart to tell them that they all couldn't marry him. If I did, I would reveal our location. Not like I needed to hide.

Jordan took his hand off my mouth and muttered, "Sorry."

"Yeah, you didn't need to cover my mouth," I told him. Annoyance built inside of me, and I pushed it back down. Faced with overzealous fans, he did what any celebrity would: run, hide, or confront them.

"Sorry," he said again. From the sound of the word, I could tell he didn't mean it.

"Are you?" I asked.

Jordan opened his mouth and closed it again. "No. I had to get away. Didn't want to lose my clothes." He looked down at the ground, bringing his sunglasses to the tip of his nose and tilting his head as he looked up at me in his classic smoldering style.

I rolled my eyes. "Where are your bodyguards?"

"I'm not famous enough for them."

I told him, "Surely a man consistently ranked among the top five sexiest men since eighteen doesn't require fan protection." My voice dripped with sarcasm. If the magazine lacked principles, it would've listed him much sooner.

"You know who I am." His words weren't a question.

"And I would like some personal space." I motioned with my hands for him to move away from me. He didn't need to stand so close that I could touch him. His scent gave me a headache.

Jordan inched closer, twisting his body to gather momentum before rolling backward. His loose designer gray shirt rustled in his wake. "Most of my fans can't wait to be near me."

"Who said I was a fan?"

"You don't like my music?" Jordan asked. His smile faded from his handsome face. He pushed his sunglasses back up, but not before the hurt expression passed through his brown eyes.

I hesitated. Critics' negative comments about my work always stung, but I had a grown thicker skin. I wished someone would've told me the truth. "I preferred your earlier work," I answered.

"Not now?"

"Sounds like you're trying too hard. Please don't make a Christmas album."

"What do you mean?" He leaned against the wall.

My legs ached, and I did the same on my side. "Singers make a Christmas album to make money or because they fear their careers are dying," I answered.

"Not about the Christmas songs. Why don't you like my recent music?" Jordan asked.

I took a moment to answer him. His latest song missed something, and it was like everything else out there.

"With your latest song, *Best of Me,* someone has sung it before. Why can't women succeed alone? Why must you tie her to you? Or any guy, for that matter?" I answered. My cheeks heated. My intention included every love song, not solely Jordan's. He wrote his own music according to the magazine *Music Right Now.*

"My song didn't sound quite right, and I couldn't figure out why. I didn't want to release it, but I got outvoted by my band." Jordan ripped off his hat, running a hand through his brown hair. He sported the classic swept back hairstyle popular among boy band members and actors. "Honestly, I should've changed the lyrics to something more like *Best of You.* Do you write music? What's your name?"

The urge to escape flowed through me, but my exhaustion prevented me from running away. I hated discussing myself after everything that had happened. "You don't need to know my name." Like he would remember my name, Cobie Meine, anyway.

"Why not?"

"You won't remember me, and we live in different worlds. We should go. Your fans will notice they lost you and circle back to find you."

Jordan frowned. "You're right, we should leave, but I'll remember what you did for me, mystery girl. We live on one world unless you've discovered another? Should we go together or separately?"

I laughed and rubbed the back of my neck as a plan formed. "I realize you may not be keen on the idea, but we should depart the park together, holding hands. No one will suspect you're on a date with me."

"Why not?" Jordan asked me.

"You're you and I am me," I answered him.

"You're beautiful."

I plastered on a fake smile. "Thanks. We should go."

Jordan rolled toward me and held out his hand.

I took his hand, and my heart picked up speed a little. Yes, I could verify that Jordan was a heartthrob.

We glided out of the tunnel and followed the path. His clammy hand had calluses on his fingertips from playing guitar. He worked hard. I shouldn't have told him his songs sucked. I really was a fan of his earlier music.

"Can't believe this is working," Jordan whispered.

"I told you no one would believe you were on a date with me," I reminded him.

"Why wouldn't they? You're totally my type." His hand clenched mine, and his body stiffened as we glided past a group of teenage girls searching. Probably for him.

I half laughed at his statement.

Jordan glanced down at me and motioned with his head.

We steered away from a rather large pack of hyenas. They shrieked and laughed so loud that everyone nearby covered their ears. A few had broken off, making me suspect there might be others.

"This way," I told Jordan. I tugged on his hand. We needed to find the exit.

Near it, more teenage girls waited. Another group joined them. Had they told others Jordan was at the park? They'd have swarmed him if they had.

Jordan released my hand and braked. He must've spotted his fans, too. After I stopped next to him, he pulled me into his arms.

I protested until he touched my face.

"They're looking over here," Jordan told me. Of course, he wouldn't actually want to kiss me. "Thank you for saving me."

"Thank me when we leave the park," I whispered.

"Is there another way out?"

"Yes, your fans are probably there, but I may have another way." I had snuck inside this park a few times after needing a break from touring. Someone might've fixed the board. If they had, I would leave him and tell his fans he was somewhere else.

"You don't need anyone to rescue you." Jordan smiled at me, and I bet his eyes twinkled underneath his sunglasses.

"I'm my own knight in shining armor." I had to be after my parents kicked me out. They wanted my money, and since I was no longer their meal ticket, they had no use for me.

"Not me. I'll rely on you. Why won't you tell me your name?" Jordan asked.

I stared up at him. "Because I don't want to be another notch on your belt. Let's go when your fans aren't looking."

"You could never." He touched the small of my back and pressed me against his chest. "We have an opening; however, I'm reluctant to mention it. I enjoy holding you." Despite his words, he released me.

I guided him until we ended up behind the bathrooms. I took the overgrown path. We got lucky with the board being loose there. I peeled it back.

"I don't want to leave you like this," Jordan said as he bent. He had a hole near the knee of his blue jeans.

"Like what?" I asked, confused. I hunkered next to him.

"Not being able to thank you."

"You did earlier."

"Yeah, but I want to give you tickets to my concert or your favorite handbag, or something."

"I need nothing," I told him.

"I like you," Jordan said.

My breath caught in my throat. "Sure, you do. Why didn't you kiss me?" He had the chance more than once.

"I will on our first date."

"You should go."

"You're not coming with me?" Jordan asked.

"Who else will lead your fans away from you?" I asked him.

"Again, you saved me, and I can't do anything for you?"

"You can do something for me." I realized I wanted something else. "Actually, two things."

"What?"

"Don't make a Christmas album," I answered.

"Why not? You don't like my music," Jordan pointed out.

"Not now, but I did before."

Jordan sat up straighter, and he brushed his knee against mine. "What if I make the album for money and never quit making music?"

"Then you're doing it for the right reason."

"What's the second thing?" Jordan asked.

"Only release music you're happy with," I answered.

"I had already planned it after our talk. Goodbye, mystery girl."

"Goodbye, Jordan."

He squeezed my knee before he climbed through the hole. I was a bit surprised he fit through it, since his shoulders were so broad.

I waited for a minute and stood with my knees cracking. My feet ached, and I needed to remove the rollerblades, but I kept my promises. I rolled toward the center of the park. After getting there, I screamed Jordan's full name and took off.

He had given me a new perspective on life. I could either stay angry or I could sing like he did, but I wouldn't forget.

Once I got home, I tore off the eviction notice on my door. It would wait. I searched online for a talent show, any talent show, to perform. One happened next week, and I had enough money for the tram fare. The repo company repossessed my vehicle after I missed a few payments.

Chapter Two

Jordan

The mystery girl invaded my thoughts as I headed to my car. Why wouldn't she tell me her name? My frustration mounted. I was more upset with her not telling me her name than with her not liking my music. I'd survive without the latter. She was the woman of my dreams.

My sports car had another ding on the door. Poor Stella. To best care for her, I should park farther away and never double-park. I apologized to her as I climbed inside, placing my rollerblades on the seat next to me.

Stella roared to life. I headed home to capture the swirling lyrics inside my head, inspired by my muse. *Best of You* would become a hit.

I got stuck in traffic. I should've avoided the park, but my current energy levels wouldn't be so high. Sometimes getting out of my head was the best way to combat writer's block.

I parked next to Royal Earth's Jaguar, and my body filled with dread. He had pestered me to collaborate with another singer for our album, coming out before the tour next year. We had many offers, and none of them were from my idols, except for one. Her influence launched my career, yet her elusive nature hindered her working relationships. I had once enjoyed the mask as a child, but not so much now. What did she look like? How would combining our talents work if she never showed me her face? I had to see my cowriter's expressions.

Royal called me the moment I entered our mansion, technically our label's mansion, "Jordan?"

Inside my head, I groaned. "Yeah?" I turned to face him.

"Where were you?" Royal glared at me with his black eyes.

"Out blading."

"Why did you leave? We have a deadline?"

"We don't have a deadline. I do," I reminded him. I wrote every song for our band, and when Royal tried to, I reworked every line into something cohesive to the point everyone in our group said it was my song except for him. His idea, my words. Although I changed most of the ideas too, since they were stupid.

"You shouldn't do anything else but write. How many new songs have you written?" Royal asked.

"A few." The lie rolled off my tongue and tasted fine. Royal was my least favorite person in the universe, even more so than the fans who stalked me. I'd never join a band alone with him.

"When will you play the songs for us?" Jay Sun asked. I hadn't realized the rest of the band hung by the entrance to the living room until he spoke.

"Soon. Once I nail down the lyrics some more." I ran a hand through my hair.

"You know you touch your hair when you're lying?" Danny Star asked me. He sat on the couch and tapped the button to open the doors, revealing the infinity pool and skyline.

"Do I really?" I asked. The urge to touch my hair again swept through me, and I balled my hands into fists at my side.

"Yep, or nervous," Danny answered.

"You caught me. I swear if I don't have something, we can do the Christmas album," I said. The view outside our home was breathtaking, while it resembled a jail. The record executive who gave us permission to live here said it was modern.

"Seriously?" Royal asked.

"Yeah. I have a deadline, and if I can't meet it—" I started.

"You don't want to disappoint our fans," Royal cut me off. He remembered my speech, and he rolled his eyes. The girl I had met was much cuter when she did it than he was.

"Hey, I met someone," I told my friends and Royal to switch the topic.

"Already?" Jay sat next to Danny and stretched his arms out. He wore a similar outfit to mine with straight blue jeans and a long-sleeve gray shirt instead of short. The tabloids loved to comment on it. We had similar styles, and he was like a younger brother to me.

"Bree and I are over," I answered.

"Like yesterday," Royal scuffed.

"Yeah, she hated our fans hassling her. Man, we gotta do something about them," I said. Our record label loved us single and available. We sold more records. I envisioned a future with love, marriage, and children, with a picket fence and bodyguards.

"Or you date someone who can handle them," Royal suggested.

"Hmm." I thought about the girl I had met. "She may."

"Why don't you write a song with Cam? You were gaga over her for years," Royal said.

"You'll have one less song to write alone," Baylee Moon pointed out. He had been quiet until now. He usually was.

"Fine. Let her label know." I never denied Baylee. He was more the studious boy to Royal's bad boy. I was a player, even though I only dated one girl at a time. Jay was the baby, and Danny was the jock. He excelled at any sport without trying. I envied him.

Royal had already called before I finished my sentence.

"I found my muse," I said.

"What's her name?" Jay asked.

"Not sure." I shrugged, took the open spot next to Danny, and across from Royal. Behind him sat the cement fireplace.

"How can someone be your muse, and you don't know their name?" Royal asked me. He was a royal pain in my ass.

"She wouldn't tell me." I hung my head.

Royal laughed and resumed speaking to our manager. He would talk to our label; our label would talk to Cam's, and then come to some type of agreement if we wrote a song together. Many suited professionals took part in a lengthy procedure. I expected to see her in one month.

"What's your muse like?" Jay asked me.

"Beautiful. Kind. She saved me from my fans." I opened the hidden mini-fridge next to me, dressed as a side table, pulled out a soda, and downed half of it in one gulp. My nose twitched. I also stank and needed a shower. I had worked up a sweat running from my fans.

"We saw your social media going off and bet if you'd lose your clothes." Danny held out his hand, demanding a drink.

I handed him a diet, since he hated it.

"Not me," Baylee said. He stared at his phone, reading a book as always.

"Thanks, man. At least you have my back." I tipped my can at him.

Baylee didn't acknowledge me as he continued to read.

"I wouldn't make bets if you'd stay home to blade instead of running off somewhere," Royal pointed out. He had already finished his call.

"Where? The concrete forest?" I asked him.

"We don't have a tree." Royal shook his head before taking off toward his room. In the sole rollerblading area, all we had was concrete, so I left for a more pleasant view.

"Is there any other soda?" Danny asked me.

"Nope, the label knows Royal likes it, so they stock more." I took a sip of mine and kept my hand away from my hair. I had pulled off my exceptional disguise in my car, not sure how my fans spotted me. Might need to try glasses next time. The man whose chest was adorned with an "S" presented a straightforward, effective concept.

Danny didn't believe me and checked for himself, saying to me, "You're a liar."

"Don't make bets you'll lose against me." I ground my teeth together.

"I said you wouldn't," Danny said.

Jay stated to me, "I did, too, and Royal went against you."

"Figures he would. I hope he has to strip somewhere." I finished my soda and stood.

Danny grinned. "He'll lend us his Jag for a week."

"Ha, make sure you park near Historical Park," I said.

"Why?" Danny asked.

"Stella got dinged there," I answered.

"Does the park host food trucks?" Danny rubbed his jaw, clearly not bothered by the stubble. While on tour, he kept himself clean-shaven.

"Borrow the Jag on Saturday," I answered.

"You two are so mean," Jay said. Although he couldn't hide the amusement in his eyes.

"Hardly. I'll be locking myself away to write music. Let me know when Cam is available to meet." I headed to my side of the prison. Our home had a strange U shape, with Royal and me on either end. Despite being uncomfortably close, we needed to pass through two doors and step outside to reunite or walk down the long hallway.

Four days later, Royal forced open the door to my studio, and it banged against the wall. He chipped the soundproof black tile. "Let's go, dickhead," he told me.

I faced him, asking, "What the hell, man? What do you want?"

"We need to meet Cam."

"Now?"

"Yeah, dipshit. You told me to set up the meeting, so I did."

"Why didn't you tell me sooner?" Three days ago, I finished *Best of You* and two other songs.

"Rather not. This is more fun." Royal shrugged. He wore a leather trench coat to complete the bad boy image. I hoped he sweated his ass off in the seventy-plus degree weather. Would serve him right.

Since I had agreed to meet with Cam, I had to go. She toured until Thanksgiving, then resumed after with a week off in December, followed by a break in January until March. When did she plan to write an album and record it?

"Where's your Jag?" I asked Royal after following him outside. One good thing about the U-shaped mansion design, we had several doors to enter our courtyard. Bodyguards hated it, but we had a security fence to keep the fans out. They easily located us during the celebrity tour bus stop, although they only saw the road to our cul-de-sac. They happily took pictures at the first gate. Sometimes I stopped and said hi.

"It's at the shop. We need to take your ugly vehicle," Royal answered in a lie. He maintained his own vehicle, only seeking a mechanic's help for major repairs beyond his capabilities, such as tire changes. Which of our bandmates had his vehicle?

"Stella isn't ugly. She's been here for a while, but she's still a reliable car." I didn't mention the ladies loved my Lambo more than his Jag. I pressed on the rubber pad and the door popped open before unlocking the passenger side. After grabbing my rollerblades, I set them inside the boot for another day. My wheels barely fit. I didn't require this vehicle for errands or essential needs. Someone bought and brought everything for me.

Royal told me where to meet Cam when I climbed inside.

I turned up the music and pressed the button to turn on the engine. We rode silently to the city's—or the planet's—most exclusive recording studio. Figures someone of Cam's caliber would work here. Although we weren't laying tracks today. I needed my entire band. Since only Royal was with me, he didn't exactly constitute the whole band.

Royal said nothing as we headed toward the front door.

The renowned recording studio sat next to an adult theater. The tan bricks were painted red around the entrance. All the greatest artists had seen the Old Recording Studio sign before they stepped through the threshold.

I trudged behind Royal with my belly tied in knots. Not every day I got to meet my idol. What Cam had done for her fans and the world amazed me. Some celebrities gave money to natural disasters. She assisted in the cleanup. If asked, she'd hold a concert to help with donations. Whatever the victims of the tragedy needed. She hadn't gotten a chance this past year because of her tour dates.

The front door opened up to a leather couch with Cam and her manager, Dick Bronson. Off to the side sat a desk with a mixing console, a mixing board, an audio interface, a musical instrument digital interface, and a couple of computer screens.

"Hello, Jordan," Cam said. Her tone sounded higher than her sultry singer's voice. She held out her hand.

I took it and noticed she appeared much shorter than she looked on TV. She must wear high heels a lot, unlike today. "Hi, Cam. It's nice to meet you. I love your work," I gushed like a nervous fool. I shifted my weight from one foot to the other.

Her pale blue eyes brightened behind her mask. Didn't she have brown eyes like mine? I swore she did. Did she wear contacts?

"I'm Royal," my band member said. He took Cam's hand, giving it a squeeze.

She giggled as she took her hand away. "I understand you're the gentleman in your band."

"Also, the leader," Royal said smoothly.

A nasty taste filled my mouth. "Co-leader," I told Cam.

She smiled at me. "How does this work? I've never co-written a song before with anyone."

I swore she had. Maybe she was being nice. "We can discuss the theme and lyrics for our song together," I answered.

"Why is Royal here then? I won't be working with both of you?" Cam asked.

"He's here to meet you," I answered. Why was he here? He should've just told me where to go instead of tagging along.

"Yeah, but I don't have a crush on you, unlike this guy." Royal squeezed my shoulder.

The air grew heavy, as though I wore the trench coat instead of Royal. I tugged at my collar, saying, "We should get to work. I have a deadline."

"I do, too," Cam said. Her voice worked on my nerves like my nails on a chalkboard. People said never to meet their heroes, and now I understood why.

"Jordan, I'll leave Cam in your capable hands," Dick said.

I nodded, not liking his words. He always rubbed me the wrong way whenever we met, and today was no different. Cam was a woman like my mystery girl. She should not be relying on anyone, especially since she wrote better music than I did.

"Later, Cam. We should do dinner or something," Royal told her.

Cam nodded.

Dick and Royal left together, probably why my bandmate wanted to come with today. He was meeting with another manager, which suggested trouble. I had loyalty to ours. I was also still pretty sore over the fact Dick had told Royal to lose me when we first started out. Solar Harmony wasn't Solar Harmony without me as part of the harmony. I had to alter my voice when a member got off-pitch.

"What do we do now?" Cam sat on the couch again.

"We write a message. Is there anything you want to say?" I answered her. I was pretty sure she knew that.

"No." Cam sighed and tucked her legs underneath her butt.

"Do you have writer's block?"

"Writer's block?"

"When you're stuck without a lyric or an idea. I got over my block recently," I answered.

"No, I lack the motivation to write. I hoped you would write a song and put my name on it. All your music is great." Cam touched my hand.

"What's your plan while I work?" I moved my arm so her hand fell away and shifted further back like I needed space.

"Shop. I get no alone time. The fashion district's one mile away. This was why I picked this studio. Can you believe they told me they were booked? I'm Cam. I told them to bump someone so we could work."

"But *we* wouldn't work. Only me."

"Yeah, you know what I'm saying. Someone told me this place was awesome, and I figured you'd like it." Cam adjusted, her knee skimming mine.

"You want me to write the song and allow you to take the credit?" I found her words unbelievable.

"Won't you do it for me? I'm so tired from the tour, and I'm not done yet." Cam leaned into me, her mouth hovered close to mine, and she placed her hand on the couch between my legs.

I hurried off the couch. "That's not how I work. I love making music and singing. When I'm on the road, I look forward to getting back in the studio, and vice versa."

"Not the same for me. I guess when you've been singing as long as me, everything gets old."

"You should take a break then. Find your love for the music again," I suggested. I imagined singing for as long as my voice allowed. After that, I'd at least write music.

"I never loved it. I wanted the money," Cam said.

"How can you write the songs you do?" Her words inspired me to sing, and many others.

Cam shrugged and pouted her lip. She patted the chair next to her. "Let's skip talking and make out instead."

"Nah. I like my woman without a mask."

Cam touched the white with gold swirls mask that covered her face and said, "I'll take it off for you."

"Leave it on. I prefer you to keep it on." I had initially hoped to see beyond her mask, but meeting her changed my perspective. With no one coming to my rescue, I told her, "This has been fun. We'll talk later." Let Royal find his own ride home. He had placed me in a very awkward position.

"Why are you leaving? Am I not pretty enough for you?"

"Your mask hides all but your eyes and lips, so I can't say."

The door opened up, and Royal and Dick stepped inside.

"How is everything?" Dick asked Cam and me. He glanced between us. Our placement looked weird with Cam still in her predatory stance on the couch, and me standing by the door.

I shifted my weight from one foot to the other.

Cam repositioned herself, explaining, "Jordan and I were becoming acquainted."

"Oh, yeah, totally. Thank you, Cam. It was nice meeting you. I have to get back. Sorry to cut this short," I said.

Royal stared at me and pressed his lips together.

"I hope you'll take me up on my offer, Jordan." Cam blinked at me, acting innocent.

"We'll be in touch soon," I told her.

Not, I thought.

"Ready to go?" I asked Royal.

"Sure, man. Thanks for the advice," Royal told Dick. They shook hands.

Dick offered me his hand. "I hope you will treat Cam well. She's like a daughter to me."

"I will." I gave him my smoldering smile and pumped his hand once. The child he ignored from being away with Cam.

Inside my vehicle, Royal asked, "How did it go with Cam?"

"We're not recording a song with her," I answered him.

"Why not? She'll get us in the top ten for weeks."

"I didn't vibe with her." I hated her work ethic. A song's creation presented challenges unrelated to shopping. She wanted to claim my work. I already had Royal trying and didn't need anyone else doing the same.

"Why do vibes matter? I don't connect with you. A new album launch is key to a successful tour."

"If I can't get the songs ready a day before the deadline, I'll rework Christmas songs for an album," I decided, much to my dismay.

"You can rework thirteen songs in a day?" Royal stared at me in disbelief.

"The songs are there. I have to add who will sing what part and adjust the melody. Besides, you'll finally get your wish."

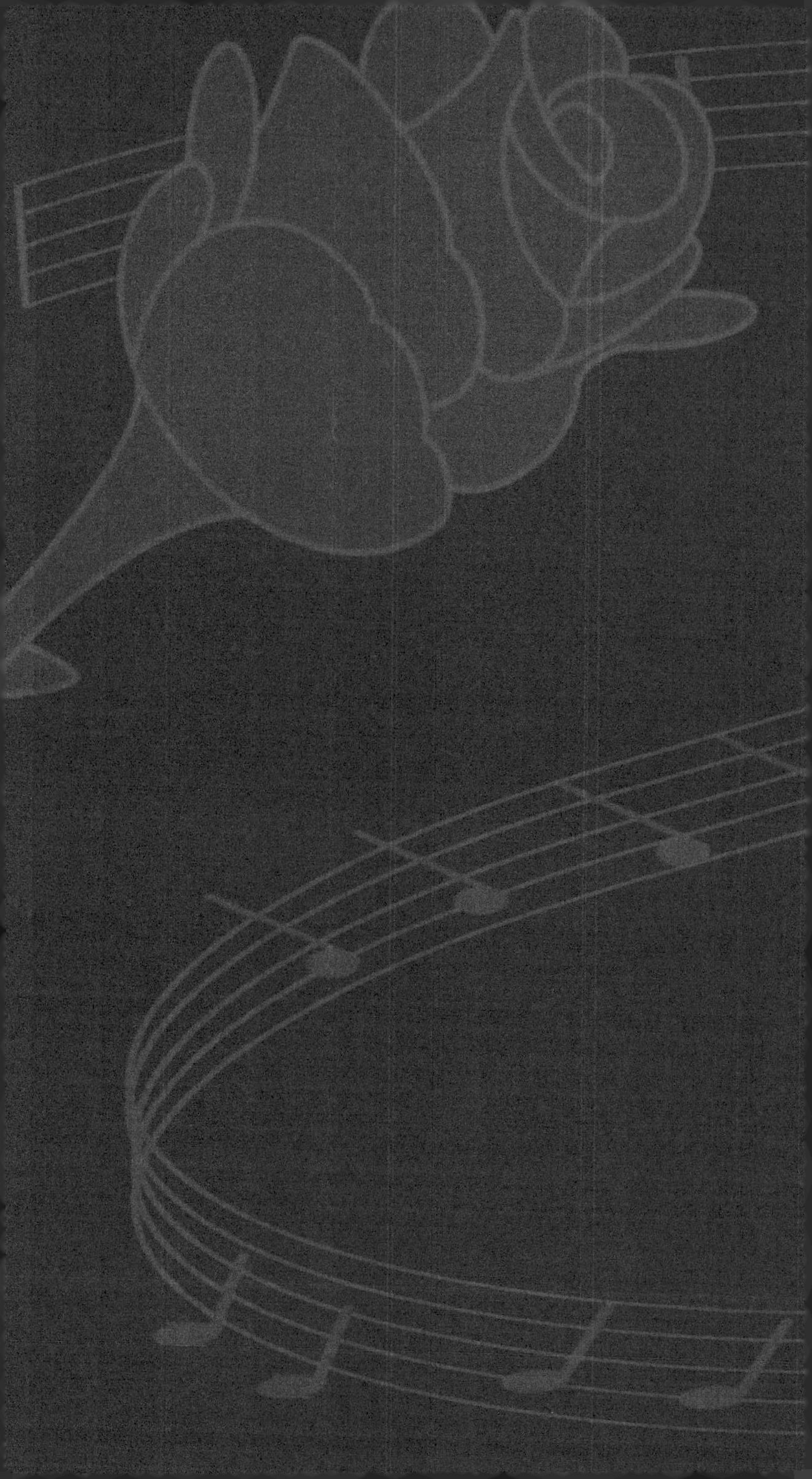

Chapter Three

Cobie

Same Day

The audition hall for *America's Next Big Star* vibrated with energy from the contestants.

A chill gave way to heat, and a tightness formed in my chest. The weight of not making it and failing rested on my shoulders. Could I do this again and again? What if I was not good enough?

The casting member called my number.

"Good luck," a friendly face said.

"You too. I know you'll make it," I told her. From her practicing, she would come in the top ten and possibly win if she controlled her nerves.

She smiled at me with dull eyes.

"Please hand me the paperwork," the worker said. After I did, she asked me for my name.

"Cobie Meine," I answered. I finally stood singing as me, but not really, since someone had stolen my name. That was my past; this was my present.

"ID, please."

I handed it to her, and she confirmed my information, including my old job as a server. My manager fired me after I switched shifts to be here. He didn't care that I had someone to cover for me. He had made the schedule, so every worker should follow it.

"What are you singing?" she asked.

"*I Don't Know Why* by Cam," I answered. Yeah, I didn't leave myself behind, not yet. I figured singing what I knew would get me past the preliminaries.

"Good choice. Sing when you're ready."

The person next to me voice squeaked. The dividers between the five casting sections did nothing to hide the noise, the triumph, and the rejection from the contestants.

Did Jordan get stage fright? I had it bad when I was younger, hence why I wore a mask. Years later, I felt like I no longer needed it, at least not on my face. Did he use anything to help him cope with performing? Why was I thinking about him? I hadn't seen him since last weekend.

"Everyone's nervous. Please sing. We must move on to the next contestant." The worker adjusted her chair closer to the folding table and swirled her pen between her fingers.

I touched the outside of my pocket where I had shoved the first mask I wore as Cam. After taking a deep breath, I sang, "I don't know why I told you I loved you, but the feeling inside was just so great." I persisted, reliving the pain and rejection from my first boyfriend. He told me I wasn't good enough after we slept together.

He never learned I was Cam, and he wouldn't say those words today if he knew. I figured out he wasn't good enough for me.

"Wow," the worker said after I ended. She cleared her throat. "I mean you pass." She scribbled something on my sheet, handing it to me along with my identification. "Follow the gold arrows and give your paperwork to the worker there. They'll tell you where to go next. Pay attention to your number being called. They won't call it more than twice."

"Thank you." My starred sheet prompted me to turn to the friend behind me.

She gave me a thumbs-up.

I took a deep breath, letting it out and pointing at her before returning her gesture. Hopefully, she would listen. I would wait and see after following the gold arrows. White arrows led to the exit.

A worker with a headset requested my sheet, reviewed it, then motioned, "Follow me. I assume our talent agents told you to listen closely for your number to be called." He hurried forward.

I ran to keep up with him. "Yeah, they did."

"You won't be called three times, so make quick bathroom trips. Good luck." A room brimming with chairs and wildly dressed individuals greeted us. "68789," he told someone my number before the door closed.

I rubbed my hands on my jeans and found an open chair near the back. The memories of sitting with other hopefuls from my youth to audition for open manager calls flooded back to me. Back then, I believed Dick had my best interests at heart when I signed with him. I was young and trusting. Too trusting.

"Hey, girl, are you a singer or a dancer or something else?" a guy next to me asked. He wore a blue top with a hot pink cardigan, and his makeup was subtle and perfect. I had a dollar twenty-five store products, enough said.

"Singer. You?" I asked him.

"Same, and you're my biggest competition."

"What makes you say those words?" My heart hammered in my chest. Had I given something away?

He waved his paper at me, showing the smiley face drawn on the corner. Why did I have a star? "Keep your sheet close and do not show it to anyone."

"Why?" I whispered.

"You have talent, and this acknowledges it." He nodded his head in front of us.

Two rows ahead, a man grinned, waving a smiley-faced paper at his companion. She wore a similar outfit to him, but I couldn't see her sheet.

An artist near them displayed a doodle on her paperwork, and the corner featured an identical sketch to the one by the guy beside me.

Two chairs down from her, a guy with a red and blue checkered flannel shirt and gray beret had a smiley face on his paper too. He spoke to the girl next to him.

She giggled and touched his arms.

I flipped my paperwork over in my lap. "Thanks. I'm Cobie."

"Nice to meet you. I'm Blaire Gunn. Remember my name, since I will be famous someday." Blaire adjusted an imaginary hat.

"I will."

"What are you singing?"

"You shouldn't tell anyone your choices. I figure you have the song you love, your backup, and a second backup, right?"

"Why shouldn't I share my songs?" Blaire asked.

"Another person will take it," I replied. Happened at every audition I had gone to.

"I swear over half this room is planning to sing *Best Heart*."

"People pick the top pop song of the year a lot."

"Good to know."

"Along with songs from the top three pop singers, and I bet you know who they are. The group. The queen for this year. And the hit soloist." I didn't mention my old name, but I was second after releasing my album ten months ago, and a week before my dismissal.

Blaire swore under his breath.

"Do something not from this year, and you'll be fine," I told him. I assumed he had picked one of my choices.

"Thanks for the tip. You've done this before?" he asked.

"A few times." I had done twelve auditions before Dick had signed me. I threw up either during or after each one.

"So, you can spot talent. Who else has the star?" Blaire leaned into me and scanned our competition.

"The girl after me would if she tamed her nerves." I closed my eyes and listened to the voices as others warmed up. Among the crowd of at least a hundred, I found her. She had a unique style. Finding her with everyone talking was tricky. "Third row, fourth from the column near the windows. The girl with the green shirt and pants."

"Why her?" Blaire asked.

"She has a raspy voice, and if she picked the right song, she'd be on the radio," I answered.

"Miss Perfect over there has my vote." He inclined his head toward the girl warming up near the door.

She had big blue eyes and pale hair. She shook her body out before she picked up her paper, revealing a smiley face.

My pick read her sheet with the same scribble as me.

"Hmm," Blaire said as he side-eyed me.

We chatted until his number was called.

He blew me a kiss, promising to see me next round before following the worker out of the room.

Numbers continued being called until only I remained. Had they forgotten about me? Night had fallen hours ago, and my stomach growled. I should've remembered to bring a snack.

"68789?" a guy called, despite me being alone.

I joined him and showed him my paperwork.

He took it, telling me, "Follow me. You close tonight's audition."

A flutter of guilt filled me. The girl with the number after me hadn't made it. She was great and should audition again next year.

"Sit here. I'll signal your stage entrance. When you do, stand in the white box and answer the judges' questions. Got it?" the guy asked.

"Yep." I repeated back to him in an abbreviated version.

He nodded and then touched his headset.

The crowd booed, and I assumed the contestant before me hadn't made it through.

"The judges are ready for you, 68789," the worker said.

"One more," someone called from the room I was about to enter.

"Can't wait to call it a night," another person said. They sounded familiar.

The first person inquired, "Are we prepared to finish this night? With one last contestant?"

The crowd cheered.

The worker ushered me onto the stage.

I did as he instructed earlier, and panic rose inside of me. In my haste to find the next open auditions, I forgot to check who the judges were. I had met three of the four seated behind a large table. One of them, I had cried when I met her.

"Hi, what's your name, sweetie?" Charlene Roane asked.

I said my name, and my voice squeaked. "Sorry, I'm nervous." I was afraid she would figure out my secret. If she did, the contest would eliminate me, and I would miss out on the three hundred-thousand-dollar prize money. I planned on using the cash to make an album.

"You're fine, sweetie. What's your talent?" Charlene asked me.

"Singing," I answered. Maybe I should let slip who I was. Charlene consistently supported women exploited by men in the industry.

"I figured with the jeans," Charlene said.

The other contestants laughed behind her.

"How old are you?" Charlene paid the crowd no attention, and I did the same.

"I'm twenty-two," I answered.

"You're young," Judge Edvard Forman, a record executive for Talent Records, said. He wasn't at my old label.

"I was young when I started," Charlene pointed out.

"When dinosaurs existed," Edvard said.

"Bah. Ignore the no-talent, sweetie. What is your dream?" Charlene asked me.

"For my voice to connect with my audience," I answered.

"And after?" Charlene placed her hands on top of what I assumed was my sheet.

"To touch the hearts of everyone," I answered.

"I like that. I've heard many times about being number one on the radio and filling stadiums. To truly desire to sing in order to connect is a first. Dazzle us," Charlene told me. Her clunky, pricey jewelry was as big as I remembered.

The music played through the speakers, and I grabbed the microphone. The first time I sang to a crowd of five, I fell in love with performing. I had thrown up afterward, but the rush wasn't something I forgot. Charlene had told me the size of the audience didn't matter, only the music. Keep my mask on or rip it off. This time I would prove to her I didn't need anyone else and shed Cam forever. I was much stronger than my manager, my parents, and everyone who wronged me, like the song I sang.

After the music stopped, sweat fell from my brow, and I wiped it away.

The judges stared at me, and the audience did nothing.

Emptiness settled in my stomach, and I regretted my song choice. I should've done something safer.

Edvard startled, leaned into his mic, and said, "Where have you been?"

The crowd climbed to their feet and screamed. They clapped.

"Ah, I'm from Garfo, North Dakota," I answered once the applause died down. Glad I didn't spill the actual truth.

"Not what I meant. Why are you auditioning? Radio's your place. You have already touched everyone's heart here, including myself." Charlene pushed her glasses up and placed her hand on her heart.

"I'd buy your album tomorrow," Mandy Mamana said as she wiped tears out of her eyes. She probably did already.

"Is there any point in voting?" Edvard asked his fellow judges. He faced the crowd.

"Send her through," they cheered.

Charlene picked up the pass sign and held it out for me. "Hell, no. Cobie, come get it, and America, remember this girl's name." She shuffled the papers in front of her. "Cobie Meine."

"Thank you," I told them. Tears prickled my eyes. I had a chance again to sing in front of a crowd.

"Sweetie, why are you crying?" Charlene asked me.

"My manager fired me for going to this audition. My apartment has an eviction notice, and my parents kicked me out last year," I answered.

Charlene got out of her chair, walked to me, and embraced me. She whispered to me, "Your life will change from this moment on. Hold on for one month."

Edvard squeezed my shoulder.

Mandy and Sam also hugged me. They both told me something similar to Charlene.

I returned home with their words echoing in my mind.

Almost a month later, the radio announced a record company contest to find a band's opening act. If I took it, I wouldn't owe *America's Next Big Star* money if I won and they learned my true identity. This contest never announced the band's name. They could be an up-and-coming band, an established band, or something in between. I had to make another important decision since I couldn't do both. Earning the only spot would mean a quicker return to the stage.

Chapter Four

Jordan

Almost a Month Later

The Christmas album recording took longer because Royal wanted more solo singing. I'd given each member two songs to sing lead and split the rest of the lyrics between us, which would harmonize best. In the end, I had fewer lines than Royal, and he got a third song. Now I had to promote with him, and I wasn't in the mood.

"I have an idea," Royal said as our driver pulled away from the curb.

"What now?" I asked, not bothering to hide the annoyance in my voice. His last suggestion had us doing this late-night show before we filmed our Christmas video. They squeezed us in for today only, and we needed to catch a red-eye tonight to make it back to the studio in California to film tomorrow morning.

"We asked Cam to sing with us a few times on stage before she starts her tour," Royal answered.

"No, thanks," I told him.

"Why don't you want to work with Cam?" Danny asked me. I had never told them why I refused.

"Why does Royal desire to collaborate with her?" I countered.

"She has an enormous fanbase, even bigger than ours," Royal answered.

"Your turn to answer my previous question," Danny said to me.

A stiffness settled in my jaw, and I rubbed it away. I'd been avoiding anything to do with Cam since I met her. I even tossed away her CDs. Royal would never drop the idea until I told the band why. Finally, I answered, "She wanted me to write the music, and she'd take the credit. Also, make out."

Royal inquired, "Your dream girl wanted a kiss, yet you refused?" His voice rose.

"She wanted to steal my work. You know that is the biggest turnoff," I answered.

"She wasn't stealing it, just taking credit," Royal said.

"That is the definition of stealing," Baylee pointed out. He covered his mouth with his sweatshirt.

"So, let's drop the idea of working with Cam. We have other requests, and I swear I'll pick one," I decided. What if my mystery girl wrote songs? We might get together, get married, and have kids. The chances of that happening were slim to none. They were even less that I'd meet her again.

"I'm with Jordan. No Cam," Jay said.

"You always side with Jordan." Royal shook his head and adjusted his seat back to rest on Jay's knees.

"Because we don't want another legal battle like the one we had after someone stole our song last time." Jay pressed his lips into a line as his eyes flickered. He worked on choosing his next words carefully. "I don't always side with Jordan."

"I'm with no Cam, too," Danny said.

"Vote?" I called. The rest of the band members agreed, even Royal. To keep from fighting each other, we would vote on anything we disagreed on.

"Who doesn't want to work with Cam?" Danny asked. He, Jay, and I raised our hands.

"Who is for?" Royal asked. He alone raised his hand.

"Majority wins," I said. The weight of misleading my bandmates lifted off my shoulders. I never spoke badly about other performers unless warranted.

"Baylee hasn't voted," Royal pointed out.

"Doesn't matter. We agreed not to collaborate with Cam. Don't we need to decide who's opening up for us?" I asked.

We spent the ride deciding on our top three picks. I wanted a new band, Royal wanted a pretty chick, and the rest of our mates didn't care, as long as whoever opened for us sang well.

Our manager, Cole Benson, met us and ushered us into makeup at the late-night show. "Thank you for doing the show tonight and getting your picks for the opening band. Love the idea. I'll call our driver when your segment ends. When you're done, you can head to your flight," he said.

"No problem," I told Cole.

"I can always count on you, Jordan." Cole clapped me on the back.

"I'm the one who sent the text," Royal muttered.

"Thanks for stepping up. Glad to see you're being a great co-leader." Cole patted his shoulder, then let the makeup artists begin.

We changed into our slacks and Christmas sweaters. Our faces had enough concealer to keep the shine off our foreheads.

The host called, "Solar Harmony doesn't need any introduction."

The audience cheered.

Royal and I bumped shoulders as we came onto the set. He moved ahead, waving.

I bobbed my head to the beat playing and smiled at everyone, pretending his actions didn't bother me and acting like the bigger person.

The rest of our band filed in behind us.

Royal sat on the couch, right next to the host.

I sat at the back, distant from him. He and I were supposed to sit next to each other.

Jay sat next to me.

"Welcome, Solar Harmony. Honestly, do we even need to say your names? The world knows you," the host said.

The audience screamed and clapped.

Once they died down, Royal said, "Royal Earth, leader." He nodded his head at them.

They screamed.

Once they stopped, Danny said, "Danny Star, drummer." He below them a kiss.

The audience shrieked, and someone almost fainted.

Baylee said nothing, and I tapped him on the shoulder. Confused for a moment, he then uttered his full name and instrument.

"We love you, Baylee!" someone shouted. The audience reacted identically to Royal's performance.

"Jordan Space, guitar, and co-leader," I said when they died down.

The crowd shrieked and clapped.

"Jay Sun, rapper," he said. He displayed the peace sign, and he got them to scream as loud as I had, if not louder. Royal would hate that.

"Thank you for having us," I told the audience and the host.

"Thank you for coming." The host brought out our Christmas album and placed it on the table. "This is amazing. How can you release an album while getting ready for a tour?"

"Jordan doesn't sleep," Jay joked.

Everyone laughed.

"We stay busy for our fans." Royal winked at everyone.

The audience screamed and clapped. They would do this after anything we said, and I loved it.

"I heard Solar Harmony might collaborate with someone soon," the host said.

"With Cam," Royal answered the non-question.

My anger rose. I had to fix the situation, or I would have to work with her despite our vote against it. If I could strangle Royal and get away with it, I would.

"We won't because she steals," Baylee said. His face scrunched up, and his lips curled.

"She steals?" the host asked.

My mind drew a blank for a second and then I said, "Our hearts. We can't work with Cam because she'd steal our hearts, and our hearts belong to our fans." I made a heart symbol with my fingers.

The audience aahed.

"You have our hearts too!" someone yelled.

"We know they love you. Are you dating anyone? I want to know as well," the host said.

"Jordan is," Danny answered. He turned around and grinned at me.

"Who? I thought you and Bree broke up a month ago," the host said.

"We did. I don't have anyone else in my life," I answered.

"What about mystery girl?" Jay asked. He didn't look at me, but I knew he was smiling.

The host repeated his question.

I sighed and sat up straighter. "I met a woman who helped me out of my writer's block. She didn't tell me her name."

"Didn't stop you from pining for her," Jay said.

"Unfortunately, I'm single," I said.

"Are you looking?" the host asked.

"I can't with the coming tour. Road life makes relationships difficult," I replied.

"Thank you for visiting us, and I hope you will sing us a song," the host said.

"Sure, we can," Royal said, much to my dismay. We had recorded the Christmas carols and needed further harmonizing before we performed them on stage.

"Do you all want to hear Solar Harmony?" the host asked. After he got their answer, he continued. "What will you sing for us?"

"Last Christmas," I answered before Royal did. I felt most comfortable with it.

Someone handed us some mics, and Royal sang. I had to change my pitch to match my band a few times and take over when Baylee forgot his line twice. We ended the song with the audience clapping. We promised the host a return visit and a great time during our tour.

Six hours after the flight home, I was still upset. I needed to clear the air before sleeping. "Why the hell did you say we'd work with Cam?" I asked Royal.

"Baylee said she stole," Royal said.

I said, "If you hadn't brought her up, Baylee would've stayed quiet." After the video shoot, I planned on chatting with him about the mix-up. Hopefully, my quick explanation kept it from going viral.

"Baylee shouldn't have said Cam stole," Royal said.

"You know how Baylee gets." I turned to my bandmate. "Sorry, Baylee." I didn't enjoy discussing him in front of him.

"I messed up, didn't I?" Baylee asked. His shoulders dropped, and tears flashed into his eyes.

"You did. I'm not sure if we can fix it." I ran a hand through my hair.

Royal desired collaboration with Cam again.

"We voted on it, and we're not. Stop bringing her up. You've already made a mess of everything," I said.

"We're working with Cam," Royal said. His face flushed red, and he kicked the couch.

"You don't have veto power. No one does. I can't deal with you for the rest of the night. I'll be seeing you on the way to the video shoot, and you better forget about working with Cam." I stormed out of the room, heading toward mine.

When I arrived, my belly growled, and I had cooled down. I turned around, peeking inside the living room. Everyone had left. I headed to the kitchen to make myself a sandwich.

Danny was already there, pulling out the ingredients. "Royal messed up royally tonight, didn't he?"

"He sure did. He may need dismissal from the band." I spread mayo onto two pieces of bread and added peppered turkey to both sides. The best sandwich had meat in every bite.

Danny stared at me for a moment. "Are you serious?"

"Royal's putting our band at risk. We need to do what's best for us, and I can't keep fighting with him. I let go of the song I didn't want to release. He should do the same for Cam."

"Maybe he has a crush on her? She might vary from his usual sleeping companions." Royal only did one-night stands.

"Doubtful. He came with me to meet her and never stayed. I doubt he's into her." I took a bite of my sandwich, and the bread to meat ratio was perfect.

"Did Royal accompany you? He told me you went alone," Danny said.

"I drove him there since you or Jay had his car."

"We never got it because it's in the shop."

I scuffed.

"What?" Danny set a water bottle next to me.

"Royal's lying to you. He doesn't like it when anyone touches his car, and he also met with Cam's manager."

"He completed the details of the collaboration?" Danny's words sounded as unsure as I felt.

"I'll ask Royal and find out. Secrets destroy bands."

"Will you tell him you're considering dismissing him from the band?"

"I'll have to if I consider it."

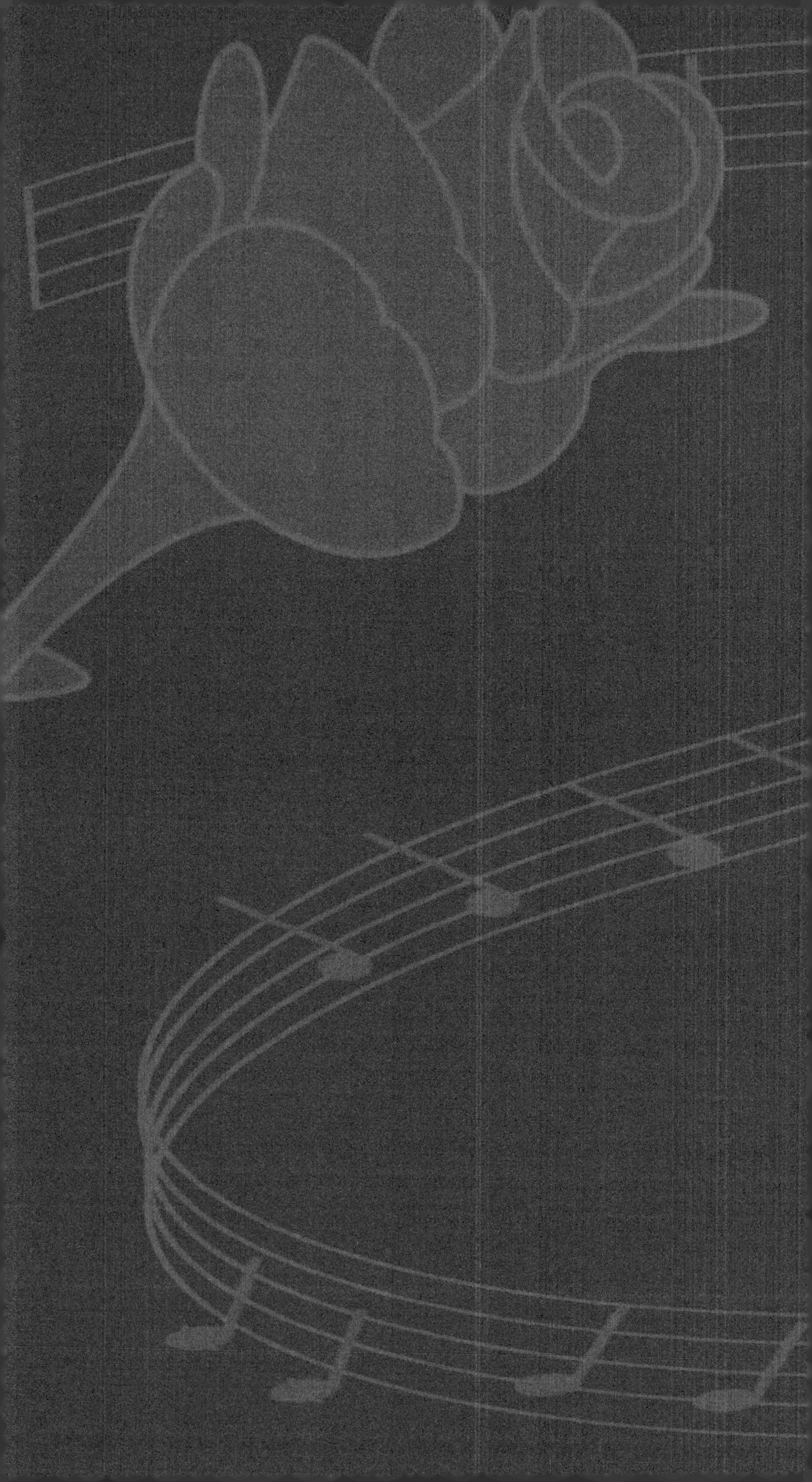

Chapter Five

Cobie

Four Weeks Later

After completing the contract, the worker departed, advising me, "Wait here. We'll get the band and their manager. I'll bring back your copy of the contract before you leave today."

I thanked them and sat on the couch. My mouth ran dry, and I needed a drink of water or something. Two tan couches faced each other, their ends toward a large TV, and a small kitchenette sat near the entrance I used. I pulled a glass from the cabinet, filled it with water and gulped it down. Had I chosen wisely, selecting this band?

The contest heavily publicized my victory, which would eventually get back to my ex-manager. They had filmed me blindfolded as they drove me here, and I bet they planned on getting my reaction to the band. Did all this mean it was someone big? What did my new contract signing mean, considering I was still under contract with Dick's management company and my old record label? This was a legal mess waiting to happen. Not like my former manager would admit I was Cam, not with the scandal surrounding her and Jordan right now.

I didn't believe he had called her a thief. Although I barely knew him from the chance encounter, he didn't seem the type.

Cam is a thief. He had seen right through her, and most of it was my fault. I should've tucked my contract into a bank or something. Dick had left me at a curb, no joke, and when I returned to the record label's mansion, security denied me entry. I had used the few bills in my pocket for a bus ticket home for my parent's copy. They had moved and lost my paperwork. I had stayed with them until they no longer received a payment a week later. They had kicked me out, and I worked odd jobs until I made it back here. My desire to sing led me to this city. I'd given up until I met Jordan.

I kicked and crawled my way, one year to the day I had told Dick I wanted to remove my mask. Did he regret the decision now? Cam had released nothing new since he forced me out.

After filling my cup again, I sat on the couch. To avoid issues, I slowed my drinking of water, so I wouldn't ask to use the bathroom.

The door opened, and my chest tightened. In walked a cameraman. His face, half-hidden, remained unseen as he turned. "Ready," he called.

I had been right.

Royal from Solar Harmony sauntered into the room. He glared, annoyed at me. He demanded, "Why are you here?"

My jaw had dropped without me realizing, and I snapped it shut. "I...I won the contest," I stammered. I had somehow become the opening act for Jordan's band. What did I say to him? Would he even recognize me?

"What contest?" Royal asked me. Didn't the band know?

"What's going on?" one of his band members asked behind him.

Royal moved further into the room and folded his arms. He glared at me.

"Hey, I'm Jay Sun, and you won the contest?" He sat on the couch near me and offered me his hand.

Jordan and someone else arrived after the band.

I stared at him as I shook Jay's hand. My tongue got tied, and I couldn't speak.

Jordan spotted me, and his eyes widened. "Mystery girl?" He quickly sat beside me.

Jay dropped my hand.

"Hey," I said to Jordan.

"You won the contest?" he asked me. His tone sounded excited and happy.

"I did," I answered. Some words he had told me gave me an idea. "Reuniting with you felt easier than exploring a new world."

He laughed, and his eyes twinkled. "Do I finally get to learn your name?"

"Cobie. Cobie Meine," I answered.

"Nice to meet you, Cobie." Jordan smiled at me.

My heart fluttered, and I cursed him inside my mind.

Damn heartthrob.

"You know our contest winner?" a guy, who came in with Jordan, asked. I guessed he was their manager.

"She's the mystery girl," Baylee answered as he sat on the couch. What did his last two words mean?

"The contest winner isn't supposed to know the band," the manager said. He dropped his head and closed his eyes.

"I don't know her, though. Cobie saved me from a group of fans almost two months ago. She didn't tell me her name," Jordan explained.

"But she changed you. You told everyone on live TV," Royal pointed out. He leaned against the wall next to the other couch. I sensed he wanted to look cool, and he did.

"I did?" I faced Jordan.

"Yeah, I had writer's block, and you telling me *Best of Me* sucked gave me a new perspective." Jordan stretched his arm across the back of the couch, and his thumb skimmed my shoulder. His small touch sent a tiny shiver down my body.

"You changed me, too," I told him. My face heated, and I tucked a strand of my hair off my face.

"How?" Jordan asked.

"You inspired me to let go of my past and pursue my music passion again. I asked myself how would Jordan handle the competition? I figured you would give it your all, so I followed suit," I answered. My face heated. I wanted to run and hide from the embarrassment of my confession.

"I would." Jordan drummed his fingers on the back of the couch.

Royal scoffed and faced his manager, questioning, "They met only a few minutes, and that happened? You can't buy this crap and accept it. Jordan and the girl know each other."

"Cobie," Jordan corrected him. Him saying my name sounded good.

The manager hesitated.

I stated, "In life, we sometimes receive only one moment."

"And I plan on not wasting a single moment of it." Jordan kissed my hand. "I still like you."

"I feel the same for you," I told him. The giddiness inside me rose, and I pushed it back down. I wouldn't go fangirl. He might differ from my imagination of him. I had to at least give him a chance.

"They're in love. We can't work with her. The competition should've been a contest. Everyone will think we picked a favorite," Royal said.

"I like her," Baylee said.

"Same," Jay said.

"I agree with Baylee and Jay." Danny walked to me from the other couch and placed his hand on my shoulder. The sleeve of his suit jacket pulled back. "You be good to my boy."

"I will try." I didn't know what I was to Jordan. We liked each other and had only met twice now.

"Let's put working with this chick to a vote," Royal said.

"Why? One vote against four means you'll never win," Baylee said. He flipped the hood of a mustard-colored hoodie, hiding his blond hair.

Danny sat next to Baylee on the couch with a smug look on his face.

"I don't want to mess up your band. I should go," I said. Why didn't Royal like me? I had done nothing to him except wait in this room for him. Had I taken his favorite spot on the couch or something else?

"Please don't leave." Jordan squeezed my hand.

"Stop recording and only use the footage up to Royal scuffing and not liking the situation," the manager said.

The cameraman removed the camera and then departed.

Jordan suggested, "We should release up to Cobie, saying we only have one life."

"Yeah, that would sound better. I'll review the footage and decide." The manager rubbed the back of his neck and turned to me. "You already signed the contract, right?"

"I did. Who are you?" I glanced at the door and back.

"Sorry, I'm Cole Benson, manager of Solar Harmony. Okay, if I understand everything, Jordan and you met once and have never spoken since then, correct?" the manager asked me.

"Yes," I answered.

Cole faced Jordan next.

"Met once before this." Jordan squeezed my hand before he let it go. He stretched his arm along the top of the couch again, and his leg touched mine.

"Okay, and who learned about the mystery girl thing?" Cole asked.

"The entire world." Royal plopped onto the couch next to Danny. An author's fantasy centered on him and the others on the couch with him. The order transitioned from him with the dark hair to light. Those desirable men possessed toned waists, broad shoulders, and impeccable attire. Their appearance was CD cover-worthy.

Cole looked at Jordan for an answer and bent in front of us.

"I told the late-night show host after someone spilled, I liked someone. I never thought I'd meet Cobie again," Jordan answered.

"Okay. I can manage those terms, and I hoped you'd keep yourself out of the news after the Cam fiasco." Cole broke eye contact, and a pinched expression crossed his face.

"I'm sorry." Jordan set his head in his hands.

I wanted to tell him I was Cam. He had exposed her deception. No way would they believe me, though. I had my first mask, but I didn't bring it with me. I also desired to step away from the shadow of my former life.

"All of your actions are being watched. Every band member's actions." Cole stood and rubbed his hands against the suit pants. "Even Cobie will learn she's a celebrity and will also have to follow strict rules. One mess-up can end your career. If you make a mistake, I'll assist everyone in this room. Unfortunately, some things are irreversible."

This lecture seemed familiar to the ones Dick liked to give, but he had never promised to save me from myself. He had repeatedly dictated my limitations, which involved not attending after parties, not mingling with celebrities or fans, and not sitting among the audience at award shows. His threat of someone finding the truth kept me from doing many things.

"You're not her manager," Royal said.

"If you continue with this attitude, I might not be yours. Cobie is new to the business, and I vowed if the winner won to show them the ropes until they gained proper representation. Why do you care, Royal? You suggested the competition, so why are you complaining?" Cole asked.

"Wait, Royal wanted the competition. We agreed to ask three different bands instead." Danny moved away from his bandmate on the couch.

"I didn't like any of them," Royal said.

"So, you changed what we agreed upon? This isn't your band only," Danny said.

"I'm the leader and want what's best for us." Royal stormed toward a door, and he kicked the rug out of his way.

"Where are you going? Jordan and you are co-leaders, but we should remove you, since we can't trust you," Danny called after Royal.

"What do you mean?" Royal stopped, and his hand hovered on the doorknob.

"I'm calling a vote for our leader," Danny answered.

"What did I do? You're picking some new chick over me?" Royal asked.

"This has nothing to do with Cobie. You keep on making unilateral decisions and ignoring the band. We're supposed to be a cohesive unit," Danny answered. His face was red, and the magazines saying he was more laid back weren't true. Although Royal had decided without him, I didn't blame him. I would be angry too.

"Sorry, our band is having some issues," Jordan whispered in my ear.

"I should give you space," I whispered back.

"Stay. We must complete the tour details." Jordan moved closer to me and took my hand.

"You need to fix your band first, and I'll be available tomorrow," I told him. I gave his hand a squeeze. I would also be around up to the tour, since I'd gotten a payment for showing up today. Careful budgeting allowed for a short hotel stay. I had left my apartment shortly after the eviction notice.

"Knock it off, you two. We'll discuss the band after the tour logistics," Jordan said. Danny and Royal had been arguing the whole time.

We discussed what songs I should and shouldn't do. Everyone agreed, even Royal, against any songs by Cam. This proved liberating, a first step toward my complete freedom from her.

Chapter Six

Jordan

After Cobie left, dread filled me. I wished to return to the moment before encountering her on the couch, to relive confessing to her, and to forget the Royal situation. She had brought a joy to music that I didn't know I missed, and she knew her vocal range like she'd done it for years. Where had she come from?

"We need to vote," Danny said. He appeared calmer discussing the tour, yet glared intensely at Royal now. He had taken Cobie's spot on the couch once she left. He probably wanted to avoid the troublemaker.

"Why? My actions prioritized the band." Royal shifted in his spot on the other couch. Was he uncomfortable? He should be after the stunt he pulled. "We should vote for me, being the only leader."

"Yeah, that will never happen," I muttered.

"Hold up, what has Royal done?" Cole asked. He was good at negotiating deals for us and dealing with us. He had been our manager since the beginning, eight years ago.

"Where do we begin? Royal suggested a contest instead of picking from the three bands we had agreed on," I answered.

"Which worked well for you. You met Corie," Royal said.

"Cobie," I corrected him for the last time. He intentionally said her name wrong again.

"What if she didn't win?" Danny asked.

Jay criticized Royal for not following the band's wishes. He trembled with rage next to Danny.

"Got us good publicity for the tour." Royal averted his gaze, fixing it on the wall.

"Yes, it did. We needed it after the mess up on TV." Cole ran a hand against his face. He looked like he hadn't slept in a week, despite appearing refreshed when he picked us up this morning.

"We wouldn't need a fix if Royal hadn't suggested we do the broadcast," Danny pointed out.

"We needed the publicity for our Christmas album," Royal said.

"And singing the song when we had rehearsed nowhere near enough?" I asked. My mom had taught me to walk a mile in someone else's shoes before I said or did anything. After speaking with Royal, I understood his motive. He cared deeply for the band, but he couldn't overrule us.

"We did fine. We've been doing interviews and shows for years." Royal picked at a rock stuck on the bottom of his size fourteen dress shoes. I couldn't fit into them without resembling a clown.

Jay inquired, "So, everything worked out and you don't see any problem with making all the decisions for us?"

"I don't," Royal answered with a shrug.

"Actually, it didn't turn out great. Cam's fans still hate Jordan," Baylee pointed out.

"Because of you. You need to watch what you say on live TV," Royal told him.

Tears welled in Baylee's eyes. He pulled his sweatshirt over his face and lifted his hood to cover his face.

"Hey, leave Baylee alone. He's not the problem. You are," I said to Royal. Baylee barely spoke; now, he might remain silent forever.

"You caused the problem to begin with by dissing Cam. We don't discuss other people in show business." Royal put his foot on the ground with a stomp, and he planted his legs wide apart.

"I say what I mean, and I won't take back my words. I won't apologize," I said.

"We should vote if you should apologize," Royal said. A smug look crossed his face.

"You can't force me to," I said. Cam had tried to do one of the four things I found inexcusable: stealing. The rest were lying, cheating, and being immoral.

"Who prioritizes themselves over the band?" Royal leaned back.

"Asks the guy who willingly admitted he had done something wrong." Danny raised his hand and asked, "Who thinks we should demote Royal and make Jordan the only leader?"

Baylee and Jay raised their hands.

"Whatever," Royal said.

"Jordan, what do you vote?" Jay asked me.

"We have the majority," Danny said.

"I...I actually don't vote for Royal to stop being the leader," I answered. I didn't believe my own words.

"Why not?" Royal lifted a single eyebrow and cocked his head to the side.

I paused, then responded, "You desire our band's success. However, collaboration requires open communication, not unilateral decisions. I say you're on probation. All in favor?"

Danny, plus our two bandmates, raised their hands, not Royal.

I joined them. Grown men raising their hands looked ridiculous, but the four of us had strong personalities. I excluded Baylee, as he conformed or remained unresponsive. His vote today surprised me.

"What does this probation mean?" Royal asked.

"You won't be telling our decisions to Cole to start," Danny answered.

"I will as the leader. Royal will also say what he thinks is best for the band at all our votes," I said. He couldn't claim later, when he did something wrong, that he was helping us. Part of me believed he had made it up.

Royal curled his lip and took off. He slammed the entrance door in his wake.

"I'm glad you worked it out," Cole said.

"Did we?" Baylee sniffed and hid his head with his hoodie.

"For now. Unless someone does something we can't forgive, I can't see us removing them from the band," I answered.

"Royal loves you guys. He just doesn't know how to show it," Cole said.

Was I being an asshole for always hating on Royal? He had helped me out a few times during our careers, such as when the bouncer confronted me for flirting with his girl. I'd never pursue another man's woman. She hadn't acted like she had a boyfriend.

The rest of the band left, leaving Baylee and me alone. I wanted to talk to him after the Cam incident. He had become even more withdrawn. "Why did you vote for Royal on probation? You never vote on any of our votes."

"The band either supports you or Royal, making my vote mostly irrelevant. I'm sorry I told the world you think Cam steals. I messed up, didn't I?" Baylee took off his hood and rubbed at his red eyes.

"You did, but the news will blow over when something else happens. Always does."

"I wished it wouldn't."

I frowned. "You want Cam and my feud to continue?"

"No, no, no. I want to stop with the drama surrounding celebrities. Every day there is something. Why do people care about what we wear or who we date?" Baylee asked.

"My mom didn't like the death hoax last year of me," I answered.

"I haven't had one. Does that mean I haven't made it?"

"You made it. The way you play different instruments and sing in different ranges is insane. I'm glad I found you, and I'm surprised other bands haven't tried to poach you."

"Wait, you wanted me? Didn't Royal choose me?" Baylee ran a hand through his hair. Did he also do it when he was nervous too?

"Nah, Royal didn't. I saw your potential when you played the piano at the mall," I answered. Those days were much easier. No one knew us, and we had to prove we existed by performing at theme parks or whoever would have us.

"But I didn't audition. My friend did." Baylee didn't sound too happy, and he rolled up the sleeve of his yellow sweatshirt. His sweatshirt and leather coat combo didn't clash with his blond hair.

"I didn't want your friend, and I asked you to perform for a reason. You had immense potential and achieved superstardom. How is your friend now?" I suspected I already knew the answer.

"He ignores me, and when we booked the charity gala, he threw food in my face."

"I'm sorry. He's jealous of your success. A real friend would want you to succeed and cheer you on."

"You defend Royal because of your friendship?"

Why did my band members always make me think? Because they challenged me and cared for me, I told Baylee my exact thoughts.

The door swung open, revealing Danny, who asked, "Done with your chick moment? Ready to go? We're heading home."

"I enjoy being your friend," Baylee said.

"We do, too," Danny told Baylee. He patted the other guy's back.

I followed behind them, noticing on the door our record label had removed our band's name, so the contest winner wouldn't figure out who they were working with. I doubted anyone accepted Cobie and my surprise reaction at seeing each other again.

I contemplated what to text her as I trailed behind my bandmates. Should I even? Would she think I was too pushy? Everything I had come up with sounded lame. I settled on something basic.

> Me: Hey, Cobie. I'm sorry about today. I hope for a second chance.

The little notification of her answering my text made my heart soar.

> Cobie: Will your band fight again?

> Me: I hope not.

> Cobie: Did you work everything out? I don't want to cause you any trouble.

I asked Cobie to meet me at my mansion tomorrow, and she agreed. Happiness filled me like my band had won our first award.

"What are you grinning about?" Danny asked me. He knocked me on the shoulder. We consistently sat together during car rides.

"I have a date," I answered.

"Already?" He leaned in closer to me. "With Cobie?"

"Yeah, shh. Don't tell anyone. What am I going to wear?" I didn't want the band teasing Cobie and me. Baylee was back to reading his book in front of me. Jay sat next to him, but he would never tell. Our manager was next, taking up a seat and getting on the phone. Royal was in the front seat, next to the driver. Even with his big ears, he couldn't hear us in the back. He supposedly got carsick and had to ride up front. I never believed him.

"I'd be more worried about your room than your clothes. Housekeeping already serviced our home except for your room with the 'Do Not Disturb' sign," Danny said.

"We're not entering my bedroom." I experienced a minor annoyance at his words and ground my teeth together. We had played a New Year's show and returned the next morning to plan the set list.

Because of Royal, we had to finish the rest today, and we hurried to meet the contest winner. I hadn't gone through my notes. What if I lost them?

"Your studio is worse. Why did you mention your bed?" Danny grinned at me.

Excessive heat flashed through me, and I tugged at my shirt's collar. "Because you implied it. My studio is cleaner." I didn't keep any drinks near the expensive equipment or dirty clothes on the floor.

"Are we discussing the same studio?"

"Can it. I need to get ready for tomorrow." My head buzzed with a list to get my space presentable, and I could sleep for a week.

"When is Cobie coming?"

I gave him the direst look in my arsenal.

"I meant to visit. While you finish cleaning, I'll whisk her to your studio before Royal sees her. He won't be happy with her at our home," Danny whispered.

"Thanks, man." I told him the time and shook his hand. Royal should take his judgmental ass somewhere else. Many women had visited him at the mansion over the years. Cobie would be my first. The annoying voice nagged at me, saying she was opening the show for us, and he had never crossed that line. He did afterward, repeatedly. I had to comfort multiple girls, sometimes simultaneously.

"I'm glad you and Bree ended. She got on my nerves with her constant complaining. I dig Cobie. Does she have a sister?"

I shrugged. Cobie had told me nothing about herself, and I resolved to learn more, beginning immediately. I asked her favorite color, and she answered, purple. Mine was blue. Those colors worked well together. I hoped that meant we would too.

Chapter Seven

Cobie

During my first practice the next morning, every cell in my body vibrated with excitement. I would finally sing on a stage filled with an audience soon. I hadn't written a new song yet. Dick hadn't let me learn the guitar until I convinced him I needed to learn to write music. He never allowed me to perform with it and scheduled consecutive tours to increase his earnings. He allowed the new Cam to take a two-month break for reasons unknown.

I pushed down the jealousy, needing to leave her in the past. Nothing else mattered except hyping up the crowd for Solar Harmony's performance.

The song flowed through me, and the guitar player riffed. I bobbed my head, dancing across the stage to him. The music captivated me, and I experienced every word I sang. I planned at some point to let the crowd sing for me because they'd know the headliners' song.

After the music ended, I wiped the sweat off my brow and needed a drink of water. I was out of shape. One year off without exercising didn't do me any good. I needed to build up my endurance again, especially if I wanted to dance.

"You're awesome. Are you sure you haven't sung before?" the lead guitarist, Derek, asked.

"Yeah," I answered. Someone handed me an unopened bottle of water, and I thanked them for it.

"No, before this. You know your range like a master." Derek checked his phone after it beeped with an incoming message. His wife probably sent another adorable toddler picture.

I shrugged. Maybe I should keep leaving breadcrumbs to my old life, or I should play the wide-eyed girl who had never sung in front of an audience? As the opening act, I recalled I had asked tons of questions and thanked everyone, much to Dick's annoyance.

"Are you ready to do one more set? We're ready," Derek said.

"Definitely, I love to sing." I took one last gulp before tossing the empty bottle into the recycling container.

The lead guitarist and the bass player exchanged glances.

I paid them no mind and readied myself in the center of the stage. I opted for a more relaxed approach this time, staying in the middle. Once the songs ended, I didn't move. I desired more, but time ran out.

"What are you thinking?" Derek asked, as he handed me another bottle of water. Performing for fifteen minutes was a lot of work.

"Thanks. I want to see those adorable toddler pictures you got first," I answered.

"What's second?" He eagerly showed me his phone, and his child didn't like the green food she ate.

"I was curious about your thoughts on my performance. Everyone here," I answered.

"I preferred when you danced around the stage more," Derek said.

"Same here. It felt much more energized," stated the bass player.

"Sorry, I ran out of steam. I'll dance in the performance." I made a mental note.

The drummer wrote something on a card and gave it to me. "This trainer offers great rates. You'll need to build your stamina up for when you're the headliner soon."

I thanked him and glanced around for anyone else's input. What if they hated my performance and were being nice to me?

"We stopped to watch you," a crew member answered.

"You captivated me," another one said.

"Thank you. Is there something I can do better?" I asked.

"Why are you asking us?" a crew member asked.

"How many years have you been in the industry? I would be a fool not to take your advice," I answered. Especially the concert band. Solar Harmony had employed them for years.

"You're dancing is too precise. You should let loose. Have you had professional training?" another crew member asked.

"Some. Can you show me what you mean?" I shifted out of the way to give her the floor.

"Seriously?" she asked. Before I answered, she squealed and ran up the stairs. We reviewed a routine based on my prior dances. I had learned to strive for perfection and steer clear of anything less. Her way let me be more real. She ended our session, and we hugged before exchanging our phone numbers.

I thanked everyone for their help and promised to work on everything they had mentioned in practice the next week. My text alert sounded from Jordan, messaging me, asking when I would meet him. I sniffed myself and realized I needed a shower first. I told Jordan to give me an hour. Gym memberships offered cheaper showers than other accommodations.

"You can stop here," I told the rideshare. The amount clicked too close to the remaining number on my bank account. After Jordan and I finished, I needed to get to the closest shelter. I doubted this rich area had one.

I exited when the driver stopped, and he departed immediately. The climb to Jordan's street exhausted me. At the gate, I said my name.

The guard checked a list and asked me, "Where's your car?"

"I don't have one," I answered.

He pressed his lips into a tight line. "You'll have to walk a quarter of a mile."

"I'll be fine."

He granted me access, and the distance he mentioned was correct. Next time, I would ask Jordan to meet me somewhere less fancy.

If he wants to meet with you again. I stank, like I hadn't taken a shower. I spritzed my clothes with the remaining fabric refresher before buzzing the second gate. If I had to walk another quarter mile, I would turn around.

This guard smiled at me when I said my name and handed me a badge. "For after hours," she told me.

I took it and slipped it into the back pocket of my jeans. Why would I need it? Their shift ended at 11 p.m. and resumed at 6 a.m. according to the sign.

The gate slid open, and I silently groaned. Why did Jordan have a long driveway, fitting ten cars plus an enormous courtyard? The concrete structure didn't match his character. He was warm and kind. He had told me to break a leg before my rehearsal because of the superstition around wishing a brilliant performance.

I rang the doorbell, and I second-guessed myself why I was here.

Danny opened the door, pulling me inside. "Come on, this way." He hurried to me past the entrance, the living room, the theater room, and kept going. We passed by door after door, finally stopping outside one. "Jordan's waiting for you inside."

I knocked on the door before entering.

"Hey, Cobie," Jordan said. He had a big smile on his face, and he held up a red rose.

"Hi," I told him. I rubbed my wrist where Danny had tugged me a little too hard. Why had he forced me through the mansion? Did he and Jordan live together?

"Are you okay?" Jordan took my hand and winced. "I'll get you some ice."

"I'll be fine in a minute or two."

"Who hurt you?" He brushed the hair out of my face.

"Danny, but not on purpose. My wrist is a little sore from when he pulled me through your place."

Jordan cursed under his breath. "Sorry, Danny doesn't realize his strength."

I rotated my wrist, feeling already better. "I'm not hurt."

Jordan checked my wrist, and his fingers brushed along my skin.

The sensation sent tiny shivers down my body.

He threaded his fingers between mine and kissed the back of my hand. He held up the rose with his free hand, saying, "I got this for you."

"Thank you," I told him.

"You're welcome. I wanted you to listen to my new song." He turned around and led me to the open computer chair.

I took the one next to him.

In a few seconds, he had the computer playing a track with him singing softly on it. "Imagine my band members joining in on the chorus."

I closed my eyes, letting his words sink in. He had bared his soul to me. Tears sprang to my eyes, and I swept them away. I'd never encountered a Solar Harmony song like this.

Following the song, Jordan asked, "What do you think?"

"The song is perfect. I sensed your desire to excel for the girl. I love it. What's the name?" I asked.

"*Best of You.*"

I cringed and gripped the rose. The thorns bit into my hand. He revised *Best of Me* to a level that fell short of its deserved greatness.

"You don't like the title?" Jordan asked. My hand had slipped from his as I heard the music.

I hesitated.

"Cobie, don't stop telling me the truth, please. I need someone like you in my life," he said. Like I had needed him when I was Cam and now.

"I hate it. The title sounds like you're trying to redo *Best of You,*" I answered.

"What do you suggest?"

I set the rose on the stand in front of me, next to the mixing console. "*Best for You.*"

Jordan rubbed his clean-shaved face and tapped his chin. "I love it. You're a genius."

"When will you release it?" I asked.

"Doing the tour, possibly. I'll suggest replacing it with *Best of Me*," he answered.

"Suggest?"

"My band and I vote on every major decision, including the set list. We have strong personalities." Jordan rolled his chair closer to me and played with a knob on the musical instrument digital interface.

I laughed. "Strong personalities? I'd say nuclear personalities, but you work well together. I wished I had someone to lean on like you do."

"What do you mean?" Jordan stared at me.

"My parents kicked me out last year when I returned home," I answered. I hadn't meant to tell him anything about my past, but he was easy to talk to.

"Where's back home?"

"Garfo, North Dakota."

His eyes widened, and he jerked his head back. "Why does that city sound familiar?"

"We had a flood almost thirty years ago, made national news," I answered. Everyone had heard of my hometown from me, Cam. I should tell Jordan the truth. He might believe me. I opened my mouth, but he was already asking me another question.

"Will you go out with me?"

"Yeah, um." I stumbled on my words and my mind raced. I liked Jordan, but a backup singer had dated my keyboardist. Once their relationship had ended, everything was uncomfortable until Dick fired one. "Can we wait until after your tour? What if I mess up?"

"What would you mess up?"

"If we broke up, being your opening act could get awkward."
I signed up for the tour's first month, with a potential extension
contingent on performance. The tour manager had allowed plenty
of time to find a replacement if necessary. I'd gotten lucky with
them wanting to wait to announce me as the winner until before
the show. Dick had lacked the power to halt me during my performance.

"What if we didn't?" Jordan asked.

I took a moment to choose my next words. "I have feelings for
you and would enjoy going on a date, but I can't risk jeopardizing
the tour. Everyone works so hard to get ready. I don't want to be the
one who causes issues."

Jordan studied me for a moment. "I'm willing to wait, but can
we at least be friends?"

"Yeah, I would like that." I loved discussing music more than
anything else.

"Do you have a sister?"

"Yes, but she's a brat. Why?" I asked. His question shocked me.

"Danny wanted me to ask you." Jordan flashed me an apologetic
smile, and yet again, my heart throbbed.

Damn him.

"You're good friends. He doesn't want to date my sister. She's the
golden child, spoiled rotten," I said. My words were not a question.

"He's my best friend. Honestly, living apart from him will be
strange. We've lived together since we signed with Cole," Jordan
said.

"Is this your mansion?" He lifted an eyebrow, and I continued.
"Not your style."

"The record label owns this baby. I believe I'm in prison."

"This room is surprisingly homey for a prison."

"It's my favorite part."

We discussed music, and he played three more songs he wrote. I answered him truthfully, and we worked on the changes. He produced music fast. I never had his ability since it took me longer to write the melody.

At midnight, I barely kept my eyes open. "I need sleep," I told him as I stifled a yawn.

Jordan insisted on dropping me off at my home. I told him about an apartment a block away from the shelter. I would stay on the street again unless it weren't full. Tomorrow, I needed to take odd jobs to pay for my meals and fare to practice.

Chapter Eight

Jordan

I texted Cobie the next morning.

Me: Good morning, beautiful. Thirty-four more sleeps until our concert. Are you excited?

Cobie: I couldn't sleep. I can't wait to see you.

Cobie: And sing.

Me: I can't wait to see you, too. We should do something.

Cobie: Like what?

Me: Something. Talk?

My heart pounded as I watched her send something, and then she stopped. My stomach plummeted. Had I pushed her too far?

When my phone rang, I almost dropped it. Cobie's name appeared. I answered, "Hello." I sounded lame.

"Hey," Cobie said. She paused before she spoke again. "I figured this would be easier. What do you have to do today? I have work."

Disappointment filled me, but I could at least text her. "I'm not sure."

"What do you mean? Don't you have a schedule?"

I groaned and rolled onto my stomach. I wanted nothing more than to stay in my king-size bed, speaking to her. "Let me see." After checking, I sat up. "Dammit, I have practice and a talk show."

She inquired, "Nothing planned for today either?" Her tone teased.

"Looks like I can't do anything with you. Can we skip?" I asked.

"Well, I need to pay bills, and you have obligations."

"Are you content with your wages for the concert?" I hoped the money wouldn't set her back financially. Opening for a band boosted a performer's career, provided a powerful performance. Cobie would get a manager and a record deal soon.

"I'll be fine. I may need to cut back on expensive morning coffee."

"We can't have that. I'll get you a coffee maker and the best coffee in the world." I climbed out of my bed, searching for my boxers. After finding a clean pair, I put them on, along with a pair of shorts.

"You don't need to buy me anything. Which coffee do you like?" Cobie asked.

"I need a cup of paradise blend in the morning."

"Aren't the beans from animal dung?"

"Ah, no. I tried it once and thought it was amazing, but I couldn't overlook its animal-based origin," I replied.

"Me, either, and I wouldn't drink it unless I had to," Cobie said.

"What situations would make you?" I headed to breakfast, skipping a shower for now.

"Hmm. Diplomatic." I imagined her tapping her chin before she answered.

"Oh, yeah. You don't want to upset anyone. Might start a war unintentionally."

Cobie laughed, and I loved the sound of it.

Danny held out his hand like a phone, pointing at it. He clearly wanted to know who I talked to.

I ignored him and dished myself up. Since the band and I were busting our asses with shows, practices, and whatever else, a chef prepared our food until the second night of our concert in our hometown. We then took a bus to the next city to perform.

"What would you bring with you to a deserted island?" I asked Cobie.

"A guitar," she answered without hesitating.

"Not a phone to call for help?"

"Nah, I'd get some sunshine and sleep first. What would you bring?"

"A phone."

"Of course you would," Cobie said.

"How else can I call you?" I wanted to switch over to video calling.

"How could I rescue you from a deserted island?"

"Who says you would get me off it? Why wouldn't you join me?"

"We'll see."

Jay asked rather loudly, "Who is Jordan talking to?" Our band sat down to eat breakfast together, even Royal.

Danny made a kissy face.

"The girl from yesterday?" Jay asked.

Danny shrugged.

I bit into my food and thought about what to ask Cobie next.

"Was being a singer always your dream?" she asked.

I paused and thought about it. "I cannot envision my life without my band or singing. When I wake up, I can't wait to play music or discuss music. I have the best job ever."

"Why did you want to skip?"

My face heated. "I want to see you."

"Yep, it's her," Danny said with a smug look on his face.

"Or Jordan's mom," Baylee pointed out.

I grabbed my food and headed toward my room. "Have you always desired a singing career?" I asked her.

"Hey, don't leave. We'll behave," Danny called after me.

I ignored him and continued to walk away, waiting for her response. She always had an answer I didn't expect.

"Since I first sang, I did. I love connecting with people," Cobie answered.

"Nothing else is like the rush," I said. She didn't disappoint me with her answer. I set my plate on my side table in my room and noticed it needed cleaning. Between touring and a hectic schedule, free time was scarce.

"Who do you admire the most? Did any singer influence you?"

"I had one person, but they weren't who I imagined." I had lost all respect for Cam.

"They never are," Cobie said.

"Who do you admire? I mean, when you were younger, who did you admire?" I suspected she would say Cam. Most female musicians in pop and country loved her.

"Many talented singers make selecting difficult. I can't pick just one. Everyone did their part to shape me and influence my music."

I should've said her answer when asked. "Will you release a song soon?" I asked.

"I'm working on one," Cobie answered.

"Can I hear it?"

"The Jordan from Solar Harmony wants to hear my music?"

"Why did you call me 'The Jordan'? We're friends. I showed you my songs, and I want to hear yours."

"When I'm ready to share, I will," Cobie said.

"Okay, I am waiting patiently. You should record it and release it when you open for my band. Publicity would improve sales, potentially leading to a record deal," I said.

"I will. Thanks for the tip."

"I know someone with a recording studio you may use."

"Danny?"

I chuckled and realized she probably heard my band teasing me. I would kill them later.

Someone knocked on my door, and I opened it.

"We leave in ten minutes," Danny said.

"Thanks, I'll be right there." I closed the door and spoke to Cobie. "Sorry to cut our conversation short. I have practice."

"Okay, I'll talk to you later."

"Bye, Cobie."

"Bye, Jordan."

I hung up, chowed down my food, tossed my dirty clothes into the hamper, and took a shower in record time. Tomorrow I planned to stack my papers of song ideas. If I kept on doing one portion a day, even with my busy schedule, I'd have a clean room soon.

"How is Cobie?" Danny asked next to me in the van. We headed to the venue with the rest of our band and Cole.

"She's good. Sucks I can't see her today," I answered.

"Are you asking her out again? Women dislike clingy men," Danny stated. I had told him about Cobie's aversion to dating me, and he had agreed with her, much to my dismay. They made a good point.

"Don't take love advice from Danny. If you like her, ask her out. If she says no, get over her and find someone else," Cole said.

"Hey, I give expert advice," Danny objected.

"Who's the only person married in the vehicle?" Cole held up his hand. "Jordan, you're still young."

"She hasn't said no. We're both busy with the concert," I said.

"Our driver is also married," Baylee pointed out.

"Noah is on my side," Cole said.

"I'm actually not. My wife said no, and I told her I'd ask her again in a week. It took a year for her to agree," Noah said.

"Your example is different," Cole said.

"No, I won her over by telling her I knew she would be the woman I married. We've been together for over thirty years now," Noah said.

"Jordan shouldn't date anyone related to the concert," Royal said, much to my announce.

"You shouldn't date or screw anyone, either," I said. He had interacted with multiple women, causing them either to leave or to avoid him.

Everyone laughed except for Royal and me.

"Jordan has you there," Danny said.

Royal scoffed and looked out the window. He shouldn't make a comment if he couldn't handle someone returning the favor.

I should follow Cole and Noah's advice, or at least work out when Cobie and I would get together again. My schedule before the concert was full. I had a few afternoons off to check whether she had plans. I really liked her since she loved music and didn't go crazy about me. She also gave me advice when I needed it the most.

The concert band had already set themselves up and were waiting for us. Derek had stated we ought to arrive half an hour beforehand for all events. I understood for a live show but not every day.

"How are your daughter and Deedee?" I asked Derek.

"My girl is trouble, and my wife is amazing. I wouldn't change anything." Derek smiled at me.

"When's Deedee due?"

"In two months. I can't wait, and I hope it's the week during our break."

"Hey, we have a backup plan ready to go. Schedule extra time off."

"Always appreciate you and the rest of the band," Derek said.

"You've done so much for us." I couldn't mention how many song changes we did the day the concert started, and he made sure his band did it. I asked them all about their families. They'd been with us since we made it big five years ago.

Staff handed my band and me our microphones. Many were long-term employees. Did they make enough money to live? We toured for nine months, taking abrupt breaks, except in April. We performed only twice that month. They did something for the remaining three. The venue helped get additional staff when necessary. I hoped they paid well since we brought in a lot of revenue.

The upbeat melody played, and I sang our biggest hit song. My band joined in for the chorus.

Some of the staff stopped to watch and dance. When they did, I knew we didn't have to change anything.

Royal took center stage for the next song I had jokingly written for him when he'd pissed me off one too many times. He acted like a total ass, so I worked my magic. He was thrilled, and I didn't tell him what the words actually meant.

We took a break after the fourth song until we would at our concert. I enjoyed resting my voice between sets and relaxing. At the concert, we'd get our clothes handed to us since we had minutes to change and dry off the sweat.

I couldn't wait to practice my latest song until we got it right. In a few days, we'd record it, and the day after we sang it, our record company would release it. I sensed it surpassing our first song's performance.

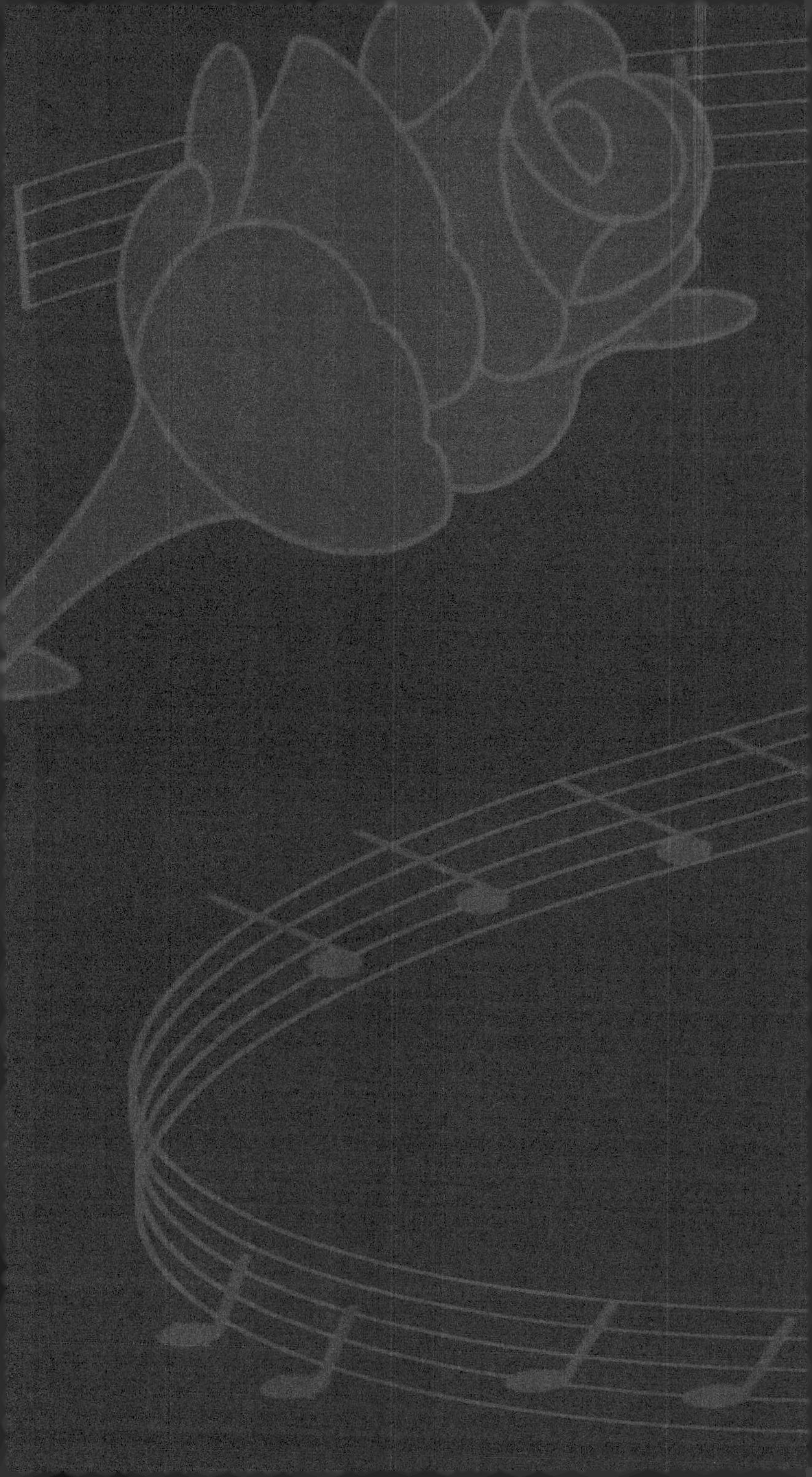

Chapter Nine

Cobie

The Following Week

Jordan texted me every morning, counting down to our tour and wishing me a good day. I never had the impression anyone cared for me until he messaged me for the last seven days. I hated avoiding him whenever he asked to hang out, not date. Hang out. Today, I had planned on telling him why I never agreed.

My phone rang after I hadn't texted him for close to an hour. Now was a better time than never. "Hey, Jordan," I said after I answered.

"Is everything okay?" he asked. His tone filled with worry.

"Yes, I'm working on what to tell you next." I chewed on my bottom lip and folded the blanket I had used last night.

"Is it bad?"

"I hope not. Okay, I like you, and if I see you, I'll want to date you. We can't date because of the tour."

Silence came from the other end.

My mouth ran dry, and I wished I had waited to say something.

"Why can't we?" he finally asked.

"What if one of us can't perform? I've seen what happens when singers have a messy breakup." His lack of singing ability would hurt me more than anything my previous manager ever did. This past week we'd spent talking and texting gave me more hope in the future than I had ever had in the last year.

"I need to go." Jordan hung up.

Tears fell from my face, and I prayed I'd done the right thing. I'd seen the videos of him after his previous girlfriends dumped him. Their actions had devastated him, and his concerts would flop for a few days. I wouldn't cause him to fail.

I brushed away my tears before shoving my blanket into a bag and then into the space between a crumbled wall. If someone else was homeless and found it again, at least they'd get a warm night's sleep. I couldn't take it with me to work; it was simply too heavy.

Jordan sent me a text, and a rush of relief washed over me.

> Jordan: I'll agree not to date while you're our opening act, but I have a condition.

> Me: Okay.

> Jordan: We should continue to talk and text like we do now. If I can't be with you, I don't want to lose you.

> Me: I feel the same. What are you doing today?

> Jordan: My band and I are finishing recording my song. You?

> Me: Heading to work.

My heart seemed lighter, and I breathed again. Post-tour, we would be together. Jordan could focus on his new song and the fallout from Cam until then. My fans loved her. How was she able to impersonate me? And why didn't anyone else notice?

Jordan had. His pure love of music shouldn't surprise me. What had she said to make him dislike her?

> Me: What is a big turnoff for you in music?

My phone rang with Jordan's reply, and a second later, my work alarm rang off.

I jumped up, running toward the bus. I had already skipped the first alarm to contemplate what to say to him. After swiping my card, I settled in a spot near the back to read his message.

> Jordan: I dislike pretenders.

> Me: Have you met a lot?

> Jordan: More than I care to admit.

> Jordan: Can we do each other a favor?

Me: Sure.

Jordan: Never be a phony. If we can't sing or no longer love it, admit it to our fans.

Me: You have fans. I don't.

Jordan: You have me.

Me: Then I'll admit it to you if I no longer want to sing.

I wanted to hug and thank him, but my decision to stay away from him prevented it. Jordan was a fan of mine. Wait, how did he know I could sing? I asked him, and he responded, saying he had watched my audition performance and two of my three rehearsals. He regretted not seeing the last.

We texted about nothing and everything until I headed into the building for my temp job. They would pay me for the nine hours I worked next Friday. Once I paid my taxes, I should have enough for a hotel the night of the concert.

"Hi, I'm Cobie from the temp agency," I told the front desk worker.

She glanced at the clock behind me. "You're on time."

"I was told you liked punctuality."

"I do. Come this way." She stood and then guided me into a file room where my coworkers waited. "We're digitizing our paperwork. You'll have to scan them onto the computer and send them to my email. I assume you know how to work a scanner." She handed me her card.

"Email scanning is familiar."

"Use box and folder names when you name the files. These other girls can show you how." She waved her hand in the air before she took off.

Boxes filled shelves from floor to ceiling in a room that occupied a quarter of the operating floor. With three of us working, it would still take days. I could actually spring for a hot meal once or twice after getting paid.

"What have you done so far?" I asked the two.

"We got through one shelf already." She pointed to the first one against the wall. No wonder the agency called me in.

"I'm Bella," the other girl said.

"Amy," the girl who had answered my question said.

"Cobie," I told them.

Bella giggled and said, "Our names start with A, B, and C."

We shared a laugh, getting to work. Chatting with other women who had never met me was liberating.

A worker retrieved a box, and another returned with one.

"How are you keeping what you did straight?" I inquired regarding additional returned boxes' departures.

"We added a mark in the upper-right corner." Amy tapped her box.

I checked the box. I was about halfway done and continued removing paper clips and staples from the corners.

We worked until lunch and ate together at a nearby food truck. I ordered the cheapest thing on the menu.

"Did you see Solar Harmony's performance on the daytime talk show? I can't wait for their concert," Bella said. She was a fellow temp agency worker like Amy. Spotting us among the real staff wasn't hard. Those paid by the company glared at us as if we were encroaching on their territory.

"You have tickets?" Amy asked her.

Bella nodded. "I didn't sleep a wink, fearing the tickets would go on sale early."

"I wish I could go. Tickets are so expensive." Amy blew a strand of her dark hair out of her face.

"This job is paying for the bobbleheads," Bella said.

I preferred a light stick.

They turned to me with tilted heads and raised eyebrows.

"I would love to go, but I'm not," I answered their unasked question. How much would they freak when they realized the girl they worked with actually was the show opener? I messaged Jordan, telling him I had met two of his fans.

He responded with a happy-face emoji. He used way more emoticons than my teenage girl fans.

"Who are you texting?" Bella asked me.

"I bet your boyfriend. You have a smile on your face," Amy said.

"He's a friend," I answered. They would die if they found out I had messaged Jordan.

Despite my aching feet from the hard floor, I energetically searched for a music store after work. Unfortunately, no guitar called to me. Maybe not so unfortunate, since they were all out of my price range.

I happily walked to the next store. The town's music scene offered abundant choices, in contrast with my previous hometown's limited options. This place's ratings didn't match up to the others. They displayed many instruments on their walls and stands.

"Can I help you?" the worker asked me.

"I need a guitar," I answered.

He looked me up and down before telling me to follow him. "These are in your price range." He stopped in the beginner section.

I stared at each one and strummed a string on a few of them. None of them belonged to me. "What else do you have?"

He rolled his eyes and showed me the next price range.

These weren't what I searched for either. I pointed at one and said, "You wound the string in the wrong direction on this one." I touched the composite wood. "Why are you selling a knockoff at this price range?"

"I can assure you nothing in my store is a knockoff," the man answered.

"You'd better check with your distributor then. The composite wood is peeling."

He inspected and swore. After he took the guitar down, he checked the others. His face had turned bright red, and he breathed heavily through his nose. "I'm sorry for this mistake."

"Happens more than it should."

"Thank you, miss. I was mistaken. Can you string a guitar?" he asked.

"I can. Why?" I asked.

"Are you looking for a job?"

I hesitated, since I wasn't sure when it would end. "I could be soon."

"Whatever your job is paying now, I'll double it."

"They also pay me on Friday for the previous week," I said.

"We can work that out. Please follow me." He entered the back room, illuminating it with a single light. The table had a guitar on its missing strings. More hung on racks in different states of damage.

"You want me to string these guitars?"

"Along with receiving shipments from the vendor when I'm not available. The previous person accepted the knockoffs."

"I have a complicated schedule."

"Don't we all?" he asked.

"I'm only available to work for you for a couple of weeks," I said.

"Perfect. I have inventory coming soon, and I need someone I can trust. I have other obligations. You can also string the guitars I finished fixing. You'll at least get me caught up. On-site staff assisting customers boost sales."

"Why would you hire me? You didn't like me when I walked into your store."

"You were a customer, and I can spot money. Honey, you don't have any." He held up his fingers, displaying perfectly manicured nails.

I glanced at mine, and he was right. When I got ready for a concert, someone always did my nails and makeup. He was a jerk to me earlier, and I should walk away, but I needed the money. "I want a discount on a guitar that sings to me."

"Deal." He held out his hand, and we shook on it.

"When can I start?"

"I'm open until 7 p.m. Can you work until then?"

"Sure. Where can I put my bag?" I asked.

He showed me a locker in the corner and returned with paperwork. "Complete this form to work here."

I strung the guitar, since it was the easiest. After I finished the paperwork, I headed to the front. I lacked an address, a problem while applying for jobs. I used my old apartment, figuring by the time he checked I'd be opening the concert.

"Done already?" he asked.

"Yeah, you didn't even tell me your name." I handed him the sheets.

"Neither did you, Cobie. I'm Murray, like the store name says." He read my name on the sheet.

"What guitar do you want me to string next?"

He showed me the next one and the next. "Begin work on this rack, should you have time."

I spotted a case on the bottom shelf. "What's wrong with this guitar?"

"The owner pawned it for cash years ago and never returned for it. The agreement says it's mine. I can't throw away an instrument. The fake guitars you found I plan on donating," Murray answered.

I unzipped the case and felt a pull from the guitar. It didn't sound right as I strummed it. The strings frayed. "How much for this one?"

"One hundred dollars after you restring it."

"Why so cheap?"

"It's been collecting dust for years. What's your plan for the bag?"

"I'll keep it." After I cleaned it and replaced the strap, it would look much better.

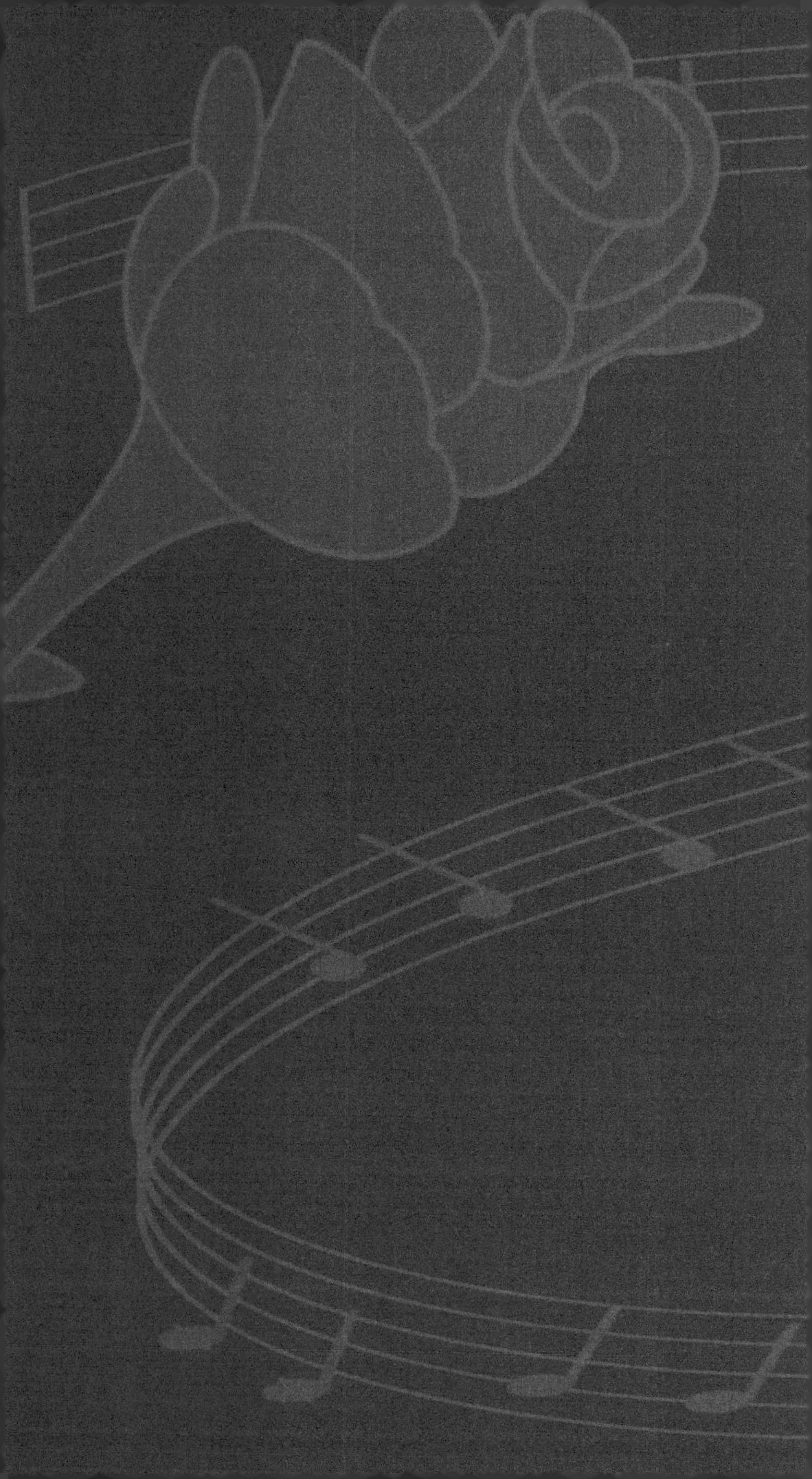

Chapter Ten

Jordan

The Day Before the Concert

The anticipation of seeing Cobie tomorrow for the start of the tour killed me. I had made a promise, and I intended to keep it. Danny had nagged me about my moping more than once. I no longer counted her rejected me and waited eagerly for the day we would date.

My door flung open, and Royal entered. Without a hello, he said, "We need to change the set."

"Why?" I asked. Any happiness I had faded into anger as heat flushed through my skin. Royal was a joy sucker.

"I'm not feeling the setup. Everything is wrong." He flashed the paper in front of my face.

"What exactly is wrong? We settled on the set weeks ago."

The rest of the band stood outside my room, and the cowards must've sent him to me. At least Jay didn't look at me.

"You said you'd let me decide," Royal pointed out.

My cheek twitched, and I had the urge to strangle him. Instead, I said, "We agreed to hear you out. Calm down, and describe the changes you desire and their purpose."

"To begin, let's kick off by calming the crowd with *I'll Be There* instead of *Hey, Girl*. We can switch the latter with the last song before our show closure." Royal waved the sheet of paper in my face again.

I wanted to grab it from him and shove it down his throat. My tone sounded calm. "Our opening act is amping our crowd for us. We can't force her to change her set the day before the concert." *Hey, Girl* was our number one partying song.

"You mean your girl can't change it," Royal corrected me.

"Cobie isn't my girlfriend. She is our opener, and we can't ask anyone to change their set list the day before a show," I said. She and I agreed to postpone dating until after her performance—and evidently for this very reason.

Royal glared at me for a moment and then continued with his unhelpful suggestions. "I want to move *Best for You* to second instead of a first place in the main set closer." He had argued to be the lead singer, but I wouldn't let it go. The song belonged to me.

I reviewed Royal's paper. "We may move my song with a vote. Why do you want to move it?"

"We should wrap it around our other songs for our fans to feel what you're trying to say," Royal answered. He explained more of the parts of the songs that I knew damn well since I had written them.

"Who is in favor of moving *Best for You* after Royal's suggestion?" I started the voting.

The band and I concurred.

"What else do you want to change?" I asked Royal. We reviewed his multiple suggestions and chose one. I vetoed our tour band learning a new song for him to get the lead. I conceded by promising to add it later on our tour.

My call to Cole about the new set list left me utterly drained, and my mind raced with chaotic thoughts. I needed to leave the mansion, work up a sweat, and crash. My usual method was to end the endless debate in my head before it consumed me.

I drove around until I recognized Cobie's neighborhood. I needed to speak to her in person rather than through a text exchange, and I hoped she would understand. Her voice would calm me.

Every single apartment except the couple vacant didn't have her last name on the mailboxes. Had I gotten the address wrong? I doubted it.

I sighed and trudged to my car, slipping my hands into my pants pockets. Cobie and I had met at one place. No way she would be there. If she weren't, I'd call her and ask her for advice.

I tightened my rollerblades, so I wouldn't break my ankles. My band would never let me live down hurting myself before the tour started. I should've been home, resting. Instead, I stuck on the glasses I bought, and messed up my hair. I fiddled with it more in my side mirror. Yep, this was the look. No one would recognize me.

The park was hopping on a Thursday. A group of teenage girls passed by me, and my heart stilled. They kept glancing back at me, so I hurried off.

Before I decide to buy a hat or head back, I spotted Cobie. My anger disappeared, and my thoughts calmed. She skated toward the same bridge where we had first met. I followed her, but by the time I arrived, she had disappeared. I searched for her before retracing my steps and noticing the familiar path we had used to go under the bridge.

Once I descended, I tapped on the bridge, hoping not to startle her. "Can I join you?" I asked her. She strummed a guitar.

"Jordan? Why are you here?" she asked. Her eyebrows furrowed together.

"Needed a break. Royal's been on a warpath ever since we put him on probation." I pointed at the spot next to her, and she nodded. I sat, brushing against her. Someday she would be in my arms, and I couldn't wait.

"Probation?" She eyed me.

"He broke the band code, so he has to be on his best behavior."

"Doesn't sound like he is," she said.

"He's trying. We had a civilized conversation this time." I grew tired of discussing Royal and asked her, "What are you working on?"

She had her notebook open in front of her. "A song."

"When you finish, can I hear it?"

"Why would a famous musician listen to my music?"

"Because you should be the superstar. I'm buying your first album and asking for your autograph before anyone else can."

Cobie's face flushed, and she glanced down at her guitar in her lap. The item had scratches and required polishing. I could buy her a kit, but I dismissed the idea as soon as I had it. Women liked expensive things like perfume or handbags. Which gave me an idea to congratulate her on her performance tomorrow.

"I'm glad I ran into you. I wanted to talk to you before the tour begins," Cobie told me. Her face reddened even more.

"Oh, what about?" I asked. Had she missed seeing me in person as I had with her?

"Does the crew get gifts? I'm not sure of the process, and I want to thank them for their help."

"They do, but if you want to give them something personal, we'll figure something out together."

"Thank you." She smiled at me.

"You're welcome. Do you mind if I sit here and close my eyes? I need to do nothing for a bit," I told her.

"Are you okay?" Cobie asked.

"I'm stressed, but your presence is calming."

"Sorry you're having issues."

"Comes with the territory. Tell me if I'm hindering your work, and I can leave." I lacked the desire to go, but I had no wish to trouble her.

"You can stay. Although, your disguise won't stop your fans from finding you, and this time you're on your own," she joked.

I laughed. "This doesn't surpass my previous attempt?" I pushed my glasses back onto my face.

"Stay here, and I'll get you something better. Can you watch my stuff?"

I agreed, and she hurried away. Her work tempted me to read it, but I dismissed the idea as soon as I had it. I hated sharing until I was ready. Each time I had, my band voted to release my song early.

Cobie returned with a blond wig and a hat. "Try this."

"A wig?" I asked her.

"Considering you've never gone blond or had long hair, no one should suspect you're you." How did she know I had done neither?

Happiness rose inside as I placed the wig on and then the hat. She had either looked me up or at least thought about me. "How do I look?"

She adjusted the hair in front of my face, and I noticed her beautiful brown eyes had a ring of lime-green in them. "Better now."

"Take my picture, so I can see myself."

She did and showed it to me.

The man differed from me. His long hair was messy, and the hat didn't help. With my glasses, I had only the lower portion of my face visible. If a fan identified me, I could never leave home. "Thank you for the better disguise."

She smiled at me.

I closed my eyes and listened to Cobie play. She had an amazing vocal range, probably the best in the business. If she sang louder, she would draw a crowd, and they would stop to watch her.

She played until almost nightfall. "I needed to rest my voice for tomorrow," she explained as she put away her guitar.

"Best thing to do is take a vocal nap," I told her. The next second, I cursed myself. I wanted to continue speaking with her.

Cobie raised her eyebrow, and she cocked her head to the side. I figured she didn't understand the terminology, since she was new to singing.

"No singing, talking or whispering for the rest of the night," I explained.

She pointed at me and giggled. "You lose."

"You're so cute." She had messed with me. "Let's rollerblade out of the park together. I'd like to take you home."

Cobie gave me the okay sign. Why was it necessary for me to instruct her to start now?

I tried to stand, but my legs had fallen asleep. I held my hand out to her.

She helped me to stand.

I pulled her in close to me, and when she didn't move away, I lifted her chin, pressing my lips against hers. This was a nonverbal cue we understood.

She placed her hands around my neck and deepened our kiss.

I touched the back of her head.

We pulled apart, and she kissed me again.

My heart raced. I could spend the rest of the night kissing her. She had soft lips. I regretted not kissing her on our first day, but I promised myself no more regrets about her.

I pulled away and took her hand in mine. She needed sleep. I needed space because all I wanted was to spend the night making love to her. If we hadn't stopped, I would've wanted to take her home. Our relationship deserved time, not to be rushed.

Cobie released my hand to pick up her things.

I grabbed her heavy backpack from her and took her hand again. We glided slowly toward the park entrance. This seemed different from the previous occasion, not the losing fans part. I hesitated to release her, but we had to wait until after the tour.

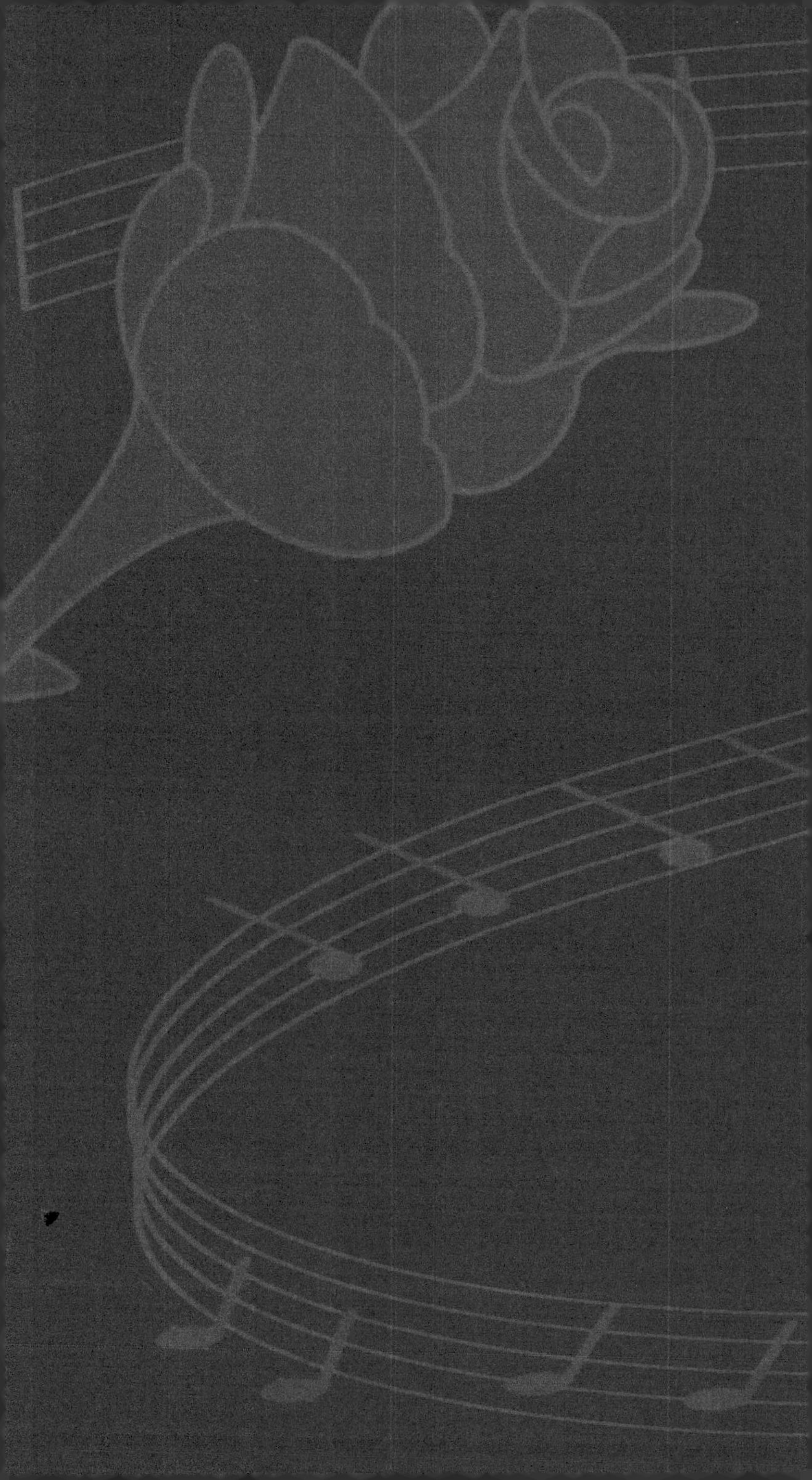

Chapter Eleven

Cobie

No one came to my soundcheck, and I figured because I was an unknown artist. Despite my thoughts, it still stung. I had hoped someone was interested in my music.

I thanked the band and headed off stage to watch Solar Harmony's soundcheck.

The room filled when the doors opened.

A very pregnant lady came over to me and asked, "You're Cobie, right?"

"Yeah." I showed her my badge.

"Come with me." She headed toward the staff entrance.

I followed behind her, and a security guard stopped me. I flashed my staff badge.

He ushered me through.

After we passed through, the woman urged, "Let's go."

Our fellow workers moved out of her way, like she parted the sea or something. Probably because she was pregnant. To avoid being swallowed up, I walked a step behind her. Unlike others, I felt lost.

"Where are we going?" I asked her.

"Hair and makeup. Brittany will get your outfit, and I'll make you look magical."

"We'll make you look magical," Brittany corrected. We had already arrived in the dressing room. How did we get here so fast?

The woman who escorted me sat in an open chair. "I'm resting for a moment."

"I'm sorry you had to come get me," I told her. If someone would've told me I got hair and makeup, I would've met her there.

"I am not. I hoped to watch your performance, since my husband said you're amazing. He was right. Why the hell are you working as the show opener?" she asked.

I replied with a partial truth, saying, "No one gave me a chance. Auditions are harsh. Who is your husband?"

"Derek." Her face brightened at the mention of his name.

"You're Deedee and your toddler is Daliah?" I had assumed his wife was at home looking after their child, considering all the pictures he shared with me.

Deedee inquired about the number of images I saw.

"So many. He loves you and her so much." I hoped to have a relationship similar to theirs one day.

Brittany laughed. "Yeah, Derek loves Deedee." She faced me and held up a yellow pleated blouse, shaking her head. "You probably won him over by looking at those pictures. Oh, I have the perfect thing for you, and I've been dying for someone to wear it."

While Brittany searched through the rack, Deedee inquired, "Is this your debut concert performance?"

I didn't want to lie to her and Brittany, since they were being so nice to me, but no one would believe I was the real Cam. The sooner I realized it; the sooner I could get over her. "Yeah, and everything is overwhelming," I answered.

"We got you, girl. Come to us with any problem and we'll fix it," Deedee said. I believed every word she said.

"Let's start with this." Brittany held up the most beautiful top I had ever seen.

Tears welled up in my eyes as I took it from her. The cotton had a swirly floral design with sequins sewn in, overlaying a dark blue shimmering top. I changed into it and sparkled.

"What do you think?" Brittany asked me.

"I love it. This is so pretty." I checked myself out in the full-length mirror.

"One of your originals brought the girl to tears," Deedee said to Brittany.

"You made this?" I asked Brittany.

"Yeah, I make several of Solar Harmony's clothes, fitting the look they want. They tell me and I get it ready. You didn't fill out my sheet, so I had to guess what you would like," she answered.

"What sheet?" I asked.

She handed a pair of dark blue jeans. "Figures our tour manager didn't tell you. He'll say he told his assistant, and he didn't."

"I bet he omitted mentioning that your soundcheck was closed to the public. He wants your name revealed right before you hit the stage, so everyone searches for you online," Deedee said. She rolled her big brown eyes.

I hadn't made new social media accounts. I messed up big time again. Someone took my old domain name, Cam (short for camera), for adult content. Dick had a fit when they wouldn't relinquish the name.

Brittany handed me some two-inch heels. "I'll set your clothes in your dressing room."

"No, I can take them there. I don't want to trouble you," I told her.

"You are not, sugar. I love women who cry when they see my clothes." She gave me a hug before turning to Deedee. "When are you having the baby?" Brittany asked her.

"In a month," Deedee answered.

"And you're still working?" Brittany asked.

"I love the work." Deedee held out her hand for me to take, and I helped her off the chair. For a pregnant woman, she moved pretty well. I loved the comfortable-looking, baby blue, cotton, and knee-length dress she wore.

"Same," Brittany said. She put the shirt she dismissed for me on a rack filled with women's clothes. She had style, with her pixie cut and black ruffle top. Her jeans hugged her trim waist.

"I'm loving it," I told them. I had thought I'd be wearing my jeans and T-shirt.

Deedee and I strolled to her room, which wasn't too far. By the time she finished, Jordan had entered the stage for Solar Harmony's soundcheck.

A worker told me to follow them to a dressing room with my name on it.

I sent Jordan a quick text message, telling him to rock out. I spent my time joining the major social media accounts and posted an old image of myself.

Jordan texted me to rock out after I finished claiming my name as a website domain, and a smile broke out on my face. We had eight concerts until we could be together.

Someone knocked on my door and opened it. "Ready?" she asked.

My mouth ran dry, and I thought she would tell me the concert no longer needed me or Dick had found me. When she didn't, I mumbled, "I need one last drink."

I finished my water and shoved my mask into my pocket. I almost got rid of it, but it would be hard to explain its presence if someone found it at the concert.

"Cobie?" the worker called.

"Sorry, I'm nervous," I told her.

"You'll do great." She flashed me a fake smile.

We walked toward the stage, prompting others to clear a path. Not as fast with Deedee, but quick enough we didn't stop. The worker gave me instructions, but I heard none of them. Blood pounded in my ears.

My eyes adjusted to the darkened stage, and I fumbled my way to the center.

The announcer called the city's name and mine.

I took a deep breath as the band played and sang my heart out.

The crowd cheered.

I missed singing, my band, and the audience watching me perform. I vowed to find my way back to them as the song ended. This moment surpassed everything else.

The lights dimmed, and the piano player played four bars.

I sang a classic about my love removing me from their life and being overwhelmed without them. Neither was true for me, since I had no love yet, but the chorus fit my fans. I loved them, and I'd do anything for them. I promised not to let them down again.

The audience had the lights on the phones, swaying in the air.

The band played the rest of the three songs perfectly. I had let the audience mainly sing *Hey, Girl* from Solar Harmony, since I wanted to honor them.

After my set ended, Jordan came onto the stage and said, "Thank you, Cobie!" He turned to the crowd. "Remember the name Cobie Meine, and Solar Harmony found her first." He gave me a quick hug and a kiss on the cheek.

The lights when out.

"Sorry, I had to tell everyone about you," Jordan said to me. His hand rested on my lower back.

"Thank you for your kind words." I looked up at him, and the urge to kiss him flowed through me.

Jordan's hot breath tickled my face. "I want to do nothing more than kiss you."

I pecked his cheek to let him know I felt the same. He had become my rock, and now my life was incomplete without him.

The audience cheered the band's name.

Jordan kissed my hand and told me, "After the show?"

"I'll see you then." I left before the lights resumed with me on the stage and hurried to my dressing room for something to drink, but I kept getting stuck behind the stage crew. The humming back here faded. I missed the first song, and I contemplated watching Jordan and his band sing instead. When I coughed, I changed my mind.

I ran to my dressing room, dodging workers. I drank from the water bottle and noticed another big change. A bouquet of red roses and a shopping bag from a designer who had wanted to sign me in my past sat on the coffee table. I plopped onto the black leather couch, reading the card and smiling.

To the mystery girl who won't be no longer. You killed it tonight.
-Jordan

Jordan was sweet. I took out the silver sequined designer bag—ideal for evenings out or fashion shows. What would I do with this?

I carefully stuck the bag inside my backpack and set it next to my guitar case. A chill overcame me despite the comfortable room temperature. What would I get Jordan after his thoughtful gift?

An idea came to me, and I scribbled a note on a sheet of paper. The other day, he shared with me his struggles in finding the right lyrics for a song he wrote. Man, he could write. By the time I finished one, he had done three. I envied him.

I kicked off the heels that hurt my feet and folded up my attire neatly on the chair to bring to Brittany. Witnessing Solar Harmony's performance backstage wasn't something I imagined doing since I had no time. Now, I wanted to do nothing else.

They were midway through their third song. They would either sing one, maybe two more, or take a break. Would they do a set change?

I swayed to the next song along with their fans. They relaxed the crowd before they exited the stage momentarily. I had done the opposite to amp the audience up.

After the song ended, the lights dimmed, and the band came off the stage.

Jordan smiled at me while Brittany handed him a fresh shirt. He and the rest of his bandmates were all sweaty from singing under the intense spotlights. They pulled off two shirts, not caring that everyone fluttered around them. Jordan had abs like I assumed.

Someone handed him a washcloth.

He dried off and drank some water. He rubbed deodorant onto his pits before sliding on an undershirt.

Brittany handed Jordan a new pair of shoes and pants.

He took off his pants and shoes, tugging the first one on before sitting down to put on his second. They looked the same as the old one.

I suspected someone would help him into a new pair of underwear if he needed it. Watching everyone get ready was crazy. They worked in sync.

A worker called five minutes. He checked his watch and spoke into his headset.

The band couldn't reach their dressing room quickly enough because of the rapid change. Security kept fans out of this section. They would go crazy over Solar Harmony with their shirts and pants off.

The guy with the timer walked up to them, and I glanced at my phone. Time was up. He held on to his mic as he spoke.

Jordan stood first and waited for the others. As if he sensed me watching him, he looked my way and waved.

I waved back and then gave him the rock sign.

He laughed, taking off with his band.

Jay sang their hit *I'll be There*, and I loved the mix of rap with the song. Jordan had done well with the lyrics to blend them just right.

My phone dinged with a notification of Cam being used somewhere in the world. I had not removed my notice, deciding now was suitable. I opened my email and read the caption.

Holy shit!

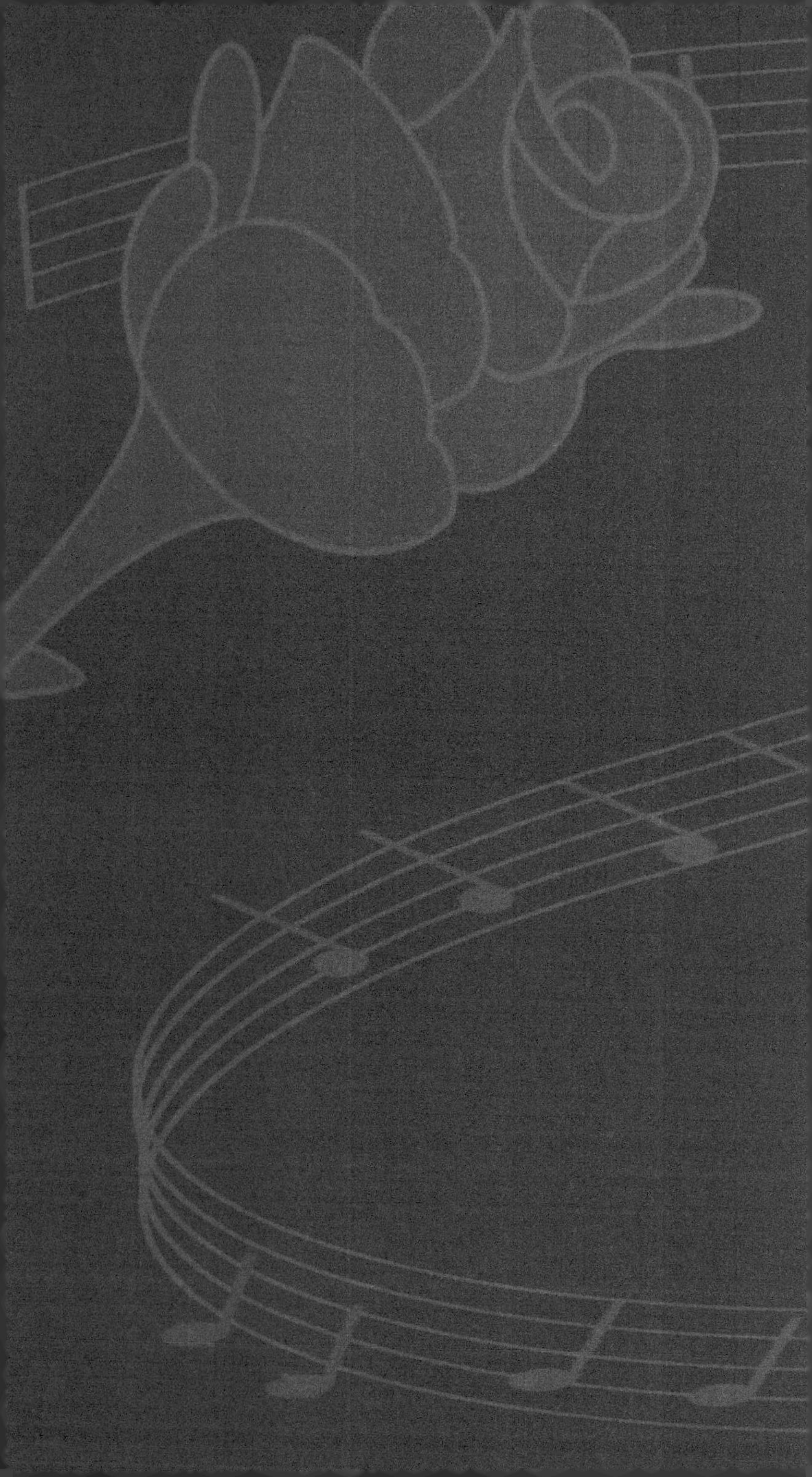

Chapter Twelve

Jordan

Royal sang, and the rest of us backed him up with the chorus.

I didn't care he got the lead on this song I had fixed for him as long as he didn't touch the next. I would announce it, and it would appear for sale tomorrow morning. The world would listen. Our band was on the verge of creating the most downloaded song ever, surpassing our top track.

I planned to express my feelings to Cobie after the show. The idea sent me into a panic. Not because I didn't want to date her. We needed to keep our relationship secret because of my fans. Who would desire such a life? She wouldn't agree to it because I knew she deserved something better.

Danny nudged me for not joining in on the final chorus.

I did, and the song ended.

Royal stepped forward, and for a second, I thought he would announce my song, but he tapped the stage with his shoe. His cheek twitched.

I would never allow him to have it. "Thank you for being here tonight. As a special treat, I wrote the next song to thank you for all the support you've given us over the years. This is *Best for You*, our newest hit," I called out at center stage.

The fans went crazy, screaming our band's name.

The concert band played.

I sang, and halfway through the song, someone tossed something onto the stage. I side-stepped it, not wanting to trip over it. Women had the habit of throwing their bras and underwear at me. Security would find the person, warn them about the danger, and eject the repeat offenders. Someone would clear it out when an opening presented itself.

The boos started and then grew louder and louder until I couldn't hear the band playing behind me. How could they hate my song?

My thoughts raced, and I urged myself to focus on the song. I would bring my fans back if I kept singing.

My band took a cue from me and harmonized.

When we reached the chorus, the lights turned off, and the concert band stopped playing.

Danny looked at me, shrugging his shoulders.

I nodded toward backstage and rushed off. My band followed me as I tried to understand the situation.

Fans screamed insults at me.

My stomach fluttered, and my nervousness threatened to make me vomit. What had I done? Tears stung my eyes.

Cole directed us, "Follow me."

We trailed behind him along with the tour manager, and the workers glared at us as we passed. What had I done to gain such animosity from them?

Danny, next to me, had his lips in a tight line. I had never seen him so grim.

Cole opened the door to our dressing room, ushering inside. Once we sat on the couch and chairs, he said, "There's a video."

Those three words—never good—brought bile to my throat. Between sex tapes and fans recording everything, social media managers had a ton of work to cover up the scandals. I had made none in the past few months. Tour work and songwriting consumed me.

"Watch this," Cole said. He pulled up a video and tossed it onto the smart TV. Cam had addressed her fans during a live.

"Last night, Jordan Space from Solar Harmony sexually assaulted me," she said. Tears brimmed in her eyes and slid down her mask. Her upper lip had a cut on it. "I know I shouldn't have invited him over, and I asked him to leave, but he refused to go. He forced me onto the ground and pulled off my clothes."

I puked in the garbage can as Cam continued on with her lies. I had never exploited a woman. Before we slept together, I got confirmation before, during, and after. Our first date didn't give me the right to sleep with her, not even if I paid.

Once the video ended, Cole asked me, "Where were you last night?"

Danny handed me a napkin.

"I stayed at the mansion," I answered as I wiped my face.

"Not the whole time," Royal said. His upper lip curled, and he moved away from me to sit further back on the couch.

"Yeah, I'd gone out for a few hours, not to rape Cam. I hadn't seen her since before Thanksgiving. She sent me a couple of texts, and I ignored most of them," I said. My mind raced, making it impossible to find another alibi except for Cobie. I wouldn't let her get involved in this mess.

"You can't believe Jordan did this," Danny came to my aid.

"He isn't the type," Jay added.

"I believe nothing when one woman mentions a celebrity, but Cam has fans. They'll want justice." Cole looked down at his shoes.

"What are you saying?" I asked him. Why wouldn't he look at me?

"Cole's saying you're out of the band," Royal explained. Did he sound a little too happy?

"Only until the police investigation proves Jordan is innocent. He's not leaving the band," Danny said.

Royal rubbed his face and sat forward, stippling his hands. "We agreed that if we ever did anything to hurt our band, we would leave of our own accord."

"He can't. I caused this, not Jordan," Baylee said. His eyes were red from crying.

"How did you cause Jordan to rape Cam?" Royal yelled.

"She's doing it because I told everyone Jordan badmouthed her. This is retaliation," Baylee answered.

I had no choice. "Royal is right. I have to be on hiatus, and Baylee, you did nothing wrong. This is between Cam and me."

Baylee said, "If I had kept quiet—"

"Someone else would've said something, eventually. I mean what I said, and I didn't harm her," I cut him off. Saying rape or sexual assault was too distasteful for me to utter.

"Should we vote?" Danny asked.

"No point. As the leader, I'm calling it. Danny is in charge while Royal is on probation. The band still has a show to do," I answered before anyone else could.

Royal scoffed and sat back in his spot again.

"So, what do we do?" Jay asked.

"I'll announce Jordan is taking a hiatus while the allegations are being investigated. We'll tell them we take this seriously," Danny answered after a few seconds, proving I had made the right decision by putting him in charge.

"What do we do about the concert?" Baylee sniffed. He needed to visit the makeup again. I hoped he could hold it together for the rest of the show.

"We'll cancel the rest of tonight and figure everything out tomorrow." Cole had brought out his phone, and it rang in his hand.

"Ask the fans instead," I said.

"What?" Danny asked. He blinked at me and looked at Cole.

"Ask the fans if you should sing. They'll let you know," I answered.

Someone knocked on our door, and Cole moved to answer.

"Whatever happens, I'll support you any way I can," the tour manager said.

"Okay, you have a show to finish," I said to my band. I needed to consult a lawyer about how to proceed with Cam.

"You can't come in here," Cole told the person who interrupted.

"Jordan is innocent. I have proof," Cobie said. I would recognize her voice anywhere.

"Let her in. If she can save Jordan, let her in." Danny rushed forward and headed for the door, but Cole had already allowed Cobie inside.

"I'm sorry. You don't deserve this," she said to me.

"What proof do you have?" Cole asked. His tone rose with his annoyance.

"I was with Jordan last night. We were texting all morning and night after we met. He didn't have time to hurt Cam," Cobie said.

"Cobie, please don't." I stood in front of her.

"A sexual assault accusation could ruin you," Cobie said.

"My fans could ruin you," I pointed out.

"What do you mean?" Cobie searched for something in my eyes.

"My relationships end badly because my fans harass my girl-friends. I won't let you become another victim of theirs." I reached up to touch Cobie's face, but pulled my hand back instead. She had to distance herself from me for the sake of her career.

"You spent a couple of hours with me last night. Right when Cam accused you. How can I help you?" Cobie asked me.

"Cobie, no." I shook my head.

"Where did you go afterward? Where were you before you met me?" Cobie asked me.

"Please stay out of this," I said.

Danny ignored me, checking the footage from our surveillance cameras. "Jordan got in at 6:38 p.m. What time was he with you?"

Cobie answered, "We stayed together until after sunset, around five thirty, and then he drove me home, so five forty-five."

"Where were you?" Danny asked her.

"At Historical Park," Cobie answered.

"Jordan could've taken an hour to get home." Cole scratched his jaw and sent a phone call to his voicemail. He'd get a lot more soon with the shitstorm.

"Trust me, I know he did. He messaged me when he got in." Cobie showed the text of me, saying I had arrived home.

"What time did you meet up?" Danny asked. He played with his phone again.

"I'm not sure. Wait, I know." Cobie checked something on her cell and answered, "I took a picture of Jordan at 3:02 p.m., so not too long before that."

Danny stated I exited the mansion at 2 p.m.

"Jordan had a one-hour window to rape Cam," Royal pointed out.

"He couldn't have sexually assaulted Cam then since he left during rush hour. Plus, she said last night. 2 p.m. is not last night," Baylee said. The sadness and blame on his face vanished.

"You don't know when rush hour is," Royal said.

"Every hour is rush hour. Besides Cam lives in Gold Lake, which is well over an hour from our home," Baylee said.

"Thanks everyone. We should let the police handle this. You should get on stage," I told my band.

Danny clapped my shoulder, and Jay gave me a hug.

I stopped Baylee before he could leave. "Go see Brittany for a second and do me a huge favor?"

"Anything," he said.

"Stop blaming yourself for my mistake, and sing tonight," I told him.

"You told me one favor," Baylee said.

I stated my desire, "Do both."

He promised he would before he left.

Had our fans stayed? Everyone would wait, since they had front-row seats for the drama.

I faced Cobie next. "I can't let you be my alibi," I told her.

"You're not letting me do anything. I'll speak to the police with or without you," she said. She stood taller, and defiance ran through her pretty eyes.

"I'll need a lawyer to see if I have to turn myself in," I told my manager.

Cole moved his phone away from his face, saying, "I'm already speaking with the best." He ended the call and then displayed the stage on the big screen.

The fans wanted the band to play, saying they still loved them.

"What do I do? Do I turn myself in or wait for the police to come get me?" I asked to break the awkward silence.

Cobie had sat next to me, not touching me.

I ached for her comfort.

Cole glanced at Cobie and said, "We'll talk when we're alone."

"I'm leaving. Inform me when I may speak with law enforcement." Cobie wobbled as she stood.

"Cobie, no. Your career is starting, and you need to distance yourself from me," I said.

"Listen to Jordan, and we'll get to the truth without you," Cole said to her.

Sadness crossed Cobie's face as she left.

Once Cole and I were alone, he said, "Your lawyer will bring you to the police station for questioning. Seeing you plastered on the news in handcuffs will tank your trial, especially if you refuse to use Cobie's testimony. The only reason I sent her away. I should prioritize your best interest, but I've always followed your desires."

"I can't hurt her career. She has so much potential," I said. Tears spilled from my eyes, and I set my head in my hands. My career was over, and I had lost the woman I loved. The latter hurt more than the first.

Chapter Thirteen

Cobie

Jordan wouldn't let me save him, much to my frustration, but I wouldn't let him take the fall for something he didn't do. What could I do, though?

"You were with Jordan last night?" Deedee asked me.

I jumped, for she had scared me, not expecting her there. "He's refusing to use my statement. Why doesn't he want my help?"

"Sounds like him. He knows everyone will want to know why you were with him." She took my hand. "Come this way."

Yet again, our coworkers parted as she walked us to her makeup room. She shut the door.

"What can I do?" I asked her.

"You will go to the police and tell them what you know," she answered.

"What if he denies it?"

"I hadn't thought of that." She sat in her chair and rubbed her belly.

I took the spot next to her. What could I do to force his hand and make him accept my help? He had written his newest song about being the best in a relationship, and he certainly wasn't acting like it now. He was infuriating.

The idea popped into my head. I had one way Jordan couldn't deny me, and the wheels in my head spun as the plan formed. "I have an idea that requires your help. Your husband and his band's help too," I said.

"What?" Deedee asked.

"I'm telling the world I was with Jordan last night during a break."

"Why involve my husband?"

The wheel stopped churning. Why use a band when I spoke on stage? "Because I'll sing Jordan's latest song. No one has heard it except those involved and everyone tonight. His fans will believe me then." Royal had sung it after Danny asked their fans to continue singing.

"This can work. I'll be right back," Deedee said.

I stated, "I also need to get something."

Deedee checked the wall clock. "The band is in the middle of its second song."

"They'll take a break for their show closer after the next song."

"We'll meet back here in five, otherwise you'll miss your chance. Unless you want to do it after they sing again."

"We need to go now." I ran to my room, apologizing to anyone I collided with along the way. Once inside my dressing room, the adrenaline in my veins vanished, and I cried out in anguish. The outfit I had on earlier with my mask in the pocket had vanished. I scanned the room quickly but couldn't find it. Brittany had grabbed it. I hoped she wouldn't wash the pants.

At record speed, I was at her door, knocking. When she didn't answer, I opened it and called, "Brittany?"

She wasn't here.

I stepped inside anyway and searched for my pants among the clothes on the ground. I moved a pile of stench-filled Solar Harmony shirts.

"Are you looking for something?" Brittany asked as she twirled my gold mask around her finger.

I placed a hand on my chest to still the beating. "Yes, you found it."

"What is this?"

"My mask. I had it for years as a safety blanket." I preferred honesty; however, lacked sufficient time for an explanation.

"Cam would be upset you have this." Brittany had realized where it came from.

"I'll tell you everything later." I held out my hand for it.

She hesitated.

"I need it to save Jordan. He didn't rape Cam, since he was with me last night and I'm the real Cam. I'm sorry, and I'll explain after," I told her in a rush. My words probably jumbled together.

She handed me the mask and asked, "How are we saving Jordan? What? He has helped me a few times with my ex-boyfriends, who couldn't take the hint. I owe him more than one."

I told her the plan.

"Olivia won't turn on the lights, but I'll convince her to. She has a thing for me." Brittany grinned at me.

"Thank you," I said.

"Don't thank me. Save Jordan, but I'm doing your makeup." Brittany handed me a removal towel, and she shushed me when I tried to object. "I've always wanted to try makeup that stays put, and we'll make time just in case you take your mask off, Cam."

After she finished, I rushed out the door, thankful she believed me and did not question why.

Deedee waited for me in her room. "My man has gotten the message."

"How?" I asked. He was onstage.

"I have my ways. My hubby will instruct the band to remain onstage until your appearance. They'll take their cue from you. We need to get you there after Solar Harmony exits. Preferably away from anyone who can stop you. I haven't figured out how to turn on the lights yet. Olivia will not be down for this."

"Brittany will talk to her."

"Good. I swear they would make the cutest couple ever. I am so excited." Deedee tried to hop up and down, but her arms moved instead.

"Please don't break your water."

"I have little choice in the matter. He'll stay inside. Won't you?" Deedee rubbed her belly and placed my hand on it.

Her baby kicked me.

"Your baby is a fighter," I said.

"Like his mom," Deedee said. She stopped in front of a worker with her hand out. "Can I borrow your hat?"

"Sure, you can have it." The guy took off the cap and handed it to her before returning to work.

She gave it to me with a smile.

I stuck it on and tried to figure out why she wanted me to have it. The next second, the realization dawned on me. Jordan's band would recognize me the second they stepped off stage.

We set up right where Solar Harmony would hand off their microphones.

My nerves were shot, and I contemplated my situation. Should I rip off the mask or go with the original plan with proof?

The stage lights turned off, and Solar Harmony approached Deedee and me.

I pulled my cap down, waiting with an open hand for a mic.

The men greeted her, and one of them gave me their microphone.

Deedee wished me luck as I stepped onto the stage. When my eyes adjusted, I kept going until I came to Derek. I whispered to him, "Follow my lead, please."

"Will do," he said. He looked back at the others, and they nodded; they were ready.

One person could save Jordan, and she wasn't a newbie to the music scene. I pulled on my mask, straightening it so I could see. I turned on the mic and sang, "I don't know why I told you I loved you."

The band played Cam's song instead of Jordan's new one.

I sang, "But the feeling inside was just so great."

The crowd quieted.

When I got to the next verse, the lights popped on, and the spotlight turned onto me.

The fans started chanting my name. Some screamed at me their apologies like they had a part in the lies that would end tonight.

I completed my song, and they became ecstatic. "I'm sorry," I told them. Everything appeared too slow, affording me time to think.

They quieted. What could I tell them about the crazy scenario they would believe?

"Cam, you did nothing wrong," someone said.

"I did everything wrong, and this is all my fault. Jordan didn't rape me. I'm not sure who that person was in my live, but they're not me." I took a deep breath and continued, "Dick Bronson, my former manager, stole my identity and paraded someone else around as me. I'm not sure why they're making these accusations against Jordan, but he didn't do what they're accusing him of, since I was with him. He is innocent."

The crowd stared at me, stunned into silence.

"Please forgive me for allowing them to use my name. I won't allow it anymore." I yanked off my mask and declared, "I'm Cobie Meine, and I am Cam. I'm sorry for the trouble I caused." I bowed, seeking forgiveness from the crowd.

They chanted my real name.

Tears streamed down my face, and I wiped them away. I had saved Jordan's career. Even if RAB Management pursued me and seized all my possessions, including my guitar, rollerblades, and everything in my backpack, I'd be content. I wouldn't abandon a good man.

"I'm sorry, but this is Solar Harmony's concert, and I hijacked it to set the record straight. Jordan is innocent," I said. After I apologized, I turned to the concert band and bowed before them. "Thank you for playing my song."

Danny walked across the stage, followed by the rest of the band. "Actually, we hoped you could sing a song with us," he said to me.

Royal rolled his eyes and plastered a smile on his face before he faced the crowd. "Who would love to hear Cam sing with us?"

Their fans cheered.

"Say you will," Danny whispered to me.

"I will. I'm sorry for stealing the stage," I whispered back. My heart beat faster, and my hands trembled as I turned my mic back on.

"Glad you did. We'll talk later." Danny winked at me as the song started. An old Solar Harmony song called *What I do for You*.

Royal took over Jordan's parts, which was unsettling.

Next to me, Danny signaled for me to sing.

I complied with him, and we harmonized for his parts. I remembered listening to the song when it first came out. Each member had their own part.

After the song ended, I expressed my gratitude before walking off stage toward the employee's only section. Was I allowed back here after the stunt I had just pulled?

The staff stared at me, and no one said a word. They should start preparing for when the band finishes its performance soon.

"I'm sorry," I told them. Fresh tears prickled my eyes.

Deedee squealed and came to me. She hugged me tight, saying, "I knew something was special about you."

"We knew," Brittany corrected her. She embraced me after Deedee let me go.

Our fellow workers came forward, clapping me on the back or giving me a quick hug. Despite attending fan meet and greets, I had never interacted with so many people in such a brief period before.

"Get back to work! We'll speak to our darling Cam more after the show," Deedee said.

Everyone scattered except for her and Brittany.

Deedee reminded the girl, "Go prepare clothes for the encore."

Brittany squeezed my shoulder, telling me, "I'm here whenever you need me." She barked orders and took off.

"Thank you for coming to my rescue," I told Deedee.

"Hun, you'll need some bodyguards," Deedee said to me.

"I can't afford it."

"Don't tell me you're the celebrity who wasted their money instead of investing it." Her smile faded, and she shook her head.

"I wish I had. Dick cut me off when he left me by the side of the road, and my parents burned through my money. They had emptied my bank accounts by the time I tried to get back into them." If I had spent my money, I wouldn't feel bitter.

Deedee embraced me again. "I need to sit and calm down, child. If I ever meet your parents, I'm giving them a stern talking to." Despite her calling me a kid, I wasn't much younger than her.

I helped her to her makeup studio. "Won't the guys need some touch ups?" I asked.

"My assistants can do that. Hand me a bottle of water in the mini-fridge, please."

"Where's Jordan?"

"I'm not sure. He left before your performance."

Chapter Fourteen

Jordan

A dark SUV pulled onto the street outside of the back entrance. Cole had done what he promised and called my lawyer.

Paparazzi and anti-fans hung out, trying to throw something at me or get a picture. The venue security guards worked to keep them at bay.

I should've had the disguise Cobie bought for me. I doubted it would do much good with the media circus brewing. My neck hairs prickled, and I regretted the trouble I'd caused. I hadn't done it. This was Cam's doing.

Cole handed me a baseball cap. "Ready to go?" he asked.

"You're coming with me? The rest of the band needs you," I told him.

"You need me more, and our band has done many shows, so they can handle themselves." Cole signaled to something behind us.

More security guards came, and no expression crossed their faces.

I bet they blamed me, like the rest of the world did. Some rich celebrity needed help to leave after their actions caught up with them. I still didn't regret leaving Cobie's name out of this.

Two guards opened the metal doors, and the rest flanked Cole and me.

Once the onlookers saw movement, they rushed forward. Those stopping them didn't stand a chance.

We pushed our way forward, and my lawyer opened the back door of the SUV. He glanced at his watch.

Cole pushed my head down as he forced me inside. He climbed in after me.

"Jordan has no comment," Gabriel Hoffman, my lawyer, said. He adjusted the sleeve on his tailored suit jacket and glided into the front seat. The man wouldn't climb into anything in the outfit he wore.

The driver slowly departed, using his horn to disperse the crowd.

Turning the corner, Gabriel glanced back at me and inquired, "What trouble have you found now? I expect things like this to happen with Royal, but not you. You should be above this."

"I am. I never touched Cam," I answered. My mouth ran dry.

"Keep saying those words whenever asked, and you'll sound like a politician." Gabriel switched on the radio and heard a breaking report about Cam's slander.

I squirmed in my seat, and I didn't want to hear it again.

"Please turn off the radio," Cole said after noticing my discomfort.

"No," Gabriel said.

"We've already heard Cam's accusations," Cole said.

"We'll keep hearing it until we get all the facts. Where was Jordan yesterday? Did he leave the mansion or not?" Gabriel hung onto the grab handle as we drove down a steep hill.

"I left," I answered. The air in the SUV became heavy, and I removed my cap, running my hands through my hair. I wondered where I'd been, other than hunting for Cobie.

"Where did you go?" Gabriel asked me.

"Jordan didn't do this," Cole said in my defense.

"Okay," Gabriel said. His tone reflected nothing. If he believed Cole, I would never find out.

"What is Jordan's defense?" Cole asked.

"I'm my client's defense. Let me handle everything. The media. Whether to remain in the band is my decision. Everything," Gabriel answered.

Cole opened his mouth to object, but another special news report stopped him.

"This is Honey V, adding another story involving the accusations from our beloved Cam and leader of the band Solar Harmony, Jordan Space. Cam showed up at the venue his band played tonight. Videos of her singing live on stage minutes ago have already circulated online." Honey paused and continued, *"Here is the speech Cam gave after her performance, and this is shocking news."*
"Dick Bronson, my former manager, stole my identity and paraded someone else around as me," Cam said.

Cobie? I listened to the rest of her confession. Anger rose inside of me at the man she had trusted. She sang for years, only to be discarded as if she meant nothing. To me and her fans, she meant everything. She had saved us in our darkest hours and brought joy and comfort.

"Cam is Cobie?" Cole asked, shocked when he heard my girl say her name.

I had missed the signs. Cobie's experience surpassed that of a novice singer. She sang as if she had done it for years. Why didn't I see it? Because I wanted to make her dreams come true.

"How do you know Cobie?" Gabriel asked. He turned the radio down to the level of background noise.

"She's Jordan's alibi, and Cam, I guess," Cole answered.

"You guess?" Gabriel asked.

"On her being Cam, yes. She's Jordan's alibi and has proof she was with him last night. He remained at the mansion for the rest of the day yesterday." Cole turned to me. "Did you know she was Cam?"

"No, I should have." I hung my head. Every time I watched her sing, flashed before my eyes, and I compared her to my idol. They sounded alike. "I need to return to the venue."

"You'll give your statement to the police first, and I'll ask for all charges to be dropped immediately because of the news from Cobie," Gabriel told me.

"After that, I need to see her. I mean Cam," I said.

"You won't be meeting with the girl who accused you of a crime," Gabriel said. His tone sounded final.

"Not her. The real Cam," I said to him. The thought of how to achieve my goal came to mind. "She'll need an excellent lawyer."

"Why?" he asked.

"Haven't you figured it out yet? Cobie is Cam. Someone stole her money and her life. She'll need a lawyer to sue everyone to get it back," I answered.

Gabriel's eyes widened, and I saw dollar signs reflecting. He made a phone call.

"Can I go back to the venue?" I asked.

"Statement first, and then we'll return. I can't work on the real Cam's case while I am representing you," Gabriel answered.

"Who are you sending for Cobie?" I asked.

"Someone better than me," Gabriel answered. He had never spoken like that before. If he valued the person, they could help Cobie.

"No way, you're using her?" Cole asked Gabriel. His question made no sense to me. His eyes bugged out of his head, and he fidgeted with his phone in his hand.

"When money is involved, we send the best." Gabriel turned up the volume on the radio as the DJs played Cam, singing with Solar Harmony except for me again. It was already their most requested song.

Jealously rose inside of me. Now that Cobie was Cam, I wanted to sing with her. She and Danny had harmonized beautifully. For a second, I contemplated her being part of the band, but she had done fine on her own. She didn't need me.

We drove to the police station with the radio playing. Everyone was quiet, including the driver. Gabriel spoke freely in front of him, so I doubted he would say anything to the tabloids.

The driver pulled up to the curb, and reporters waited for me. Clearly, they realized where we had headed after abruptly leaving the venue. Several probably camped near the mansion. I doubted the guard there would take a bribe. I'd find out later tonight if they had.

"I'll open the door, and Cole will get out, followed by Jordan. We'll flank him, rushing him inside. I'll speak to the reporters, and no one else will." Gabriel did the lower button of his jacket, since he must've loosened it before getting inside.

Cole raked a hand through his black hair speckled with gray. He and Gabriel made an odd pair. They had clearly been friends for years and argued at work openly. They planned a post-crisis beer to discuss everything. My manager had told me once after I complained about Gabriel and his relationship. Work and friendship were separate. I doubted I could have the same connection with anyone.

"Let the show begin," Gabriel said as he glided out. He must've been around the same age as Cole, but with his dark brown hair, no one would suspect it. He also didn't have the start of crow's feet like my manager. The other man probably used something.

Gabriel opened my door, and Cole slid out, followed by me.

The flashes of cameras blinded me for a second. Someone placed their hand on my back and the other on my shoulder as they guided me through the rung of reporters. Why hadn't the police come out to help dispatch them? They might love the media circus and attention. Everything about my case would become political, or it would've if Cobie hadn't made her declaration.

Once inside, a line of police officers and detectives waited. One stepped forward.

"No handcuffs. My client is here of his own accord and is more than willing to make a statement. No one has issued an arrest warrant," Gabriel said. He made big bucks for this reason.

"You can't be certain if we did," the detective said. He had on a dark brown suit jacket over the same-colored jeans. His jacket was open, revealing a gun in its holster and a light blue dress shirt. His whole outfit cost less than the leather on my gifted wallet. What a shame it did because he had to deal with criminals. Not me.

"I am, actually. Have you issued a warrant?" Gabriel asked.

The detective sneered at him.

"Stop wasting my time and my client's. Shall I conduct the interview myself?" Gabriel asked. Despite his superior attitude, I liked him, especially when he was on my side.

The detective grumbled and told us to follow him. His partner kept a neutral look on her face.

"Wait here. I'll have Jordan out in a few minutes," Gabriel said to Cole.

Cole sat and used his phone. Any phone calls involving me, he would forward to Gabriel's law firm to answer.

I trailed Gabriel, who walked with the detectives, and the police officers followed behind me. My lawyer knew where to go.

Four of us sat at a table. With any movement, we'd be touching knees. A camera hung on the wall, pointing at me.

"I'm Detective Brady Venma, and this is my partner, Brooke Reyers. We're investigating the sexual assault of Cam. Where were you yesterday between 3 and 6 p.m.?" the detective asked me.

I checked with Gabriel, and he remained silent, prompting me to explain Cobie and Danny's findings.

Detective Venma inquired, "Who's Cobie Meine? Will she collaborate on your story?" He didn't sound like he believed me, and he scribbled a note on his notepad.

"Like you haven't heard of Cobie. Turn on your radio," I answered.

"How do we get in touch with Cobie?" Detective Reyers asked.

"Give me your card, and I'll make sure she gets it," Gabriel answered for me.

"You're representing both Mr. Space and Ms. Meine?" Detective Venma shifted his chair closer to the table.

"My firm might. I am representing Mr. Space, and I will make sure she gets your card even if my firm doesn't." Gabriel picked up the cards and stuck them in the chest pocket of his suit next to his white pocket square. The color matched his dress shirt.

"We'll need confirmation of when you left the mansion and returned," Venma said to me.

"You should receive it soon by email. Is there anything else?" Gabriel asked.

"We'd liked to search Mr. Space's car," Venma said.

"You'll need a warrant for Jordan's vehicle, since it wasn't involved in the crime. You should also get the information from the onboard computer to prove he wasn't near the accuser's home at the time of the supposed crime," Gabriel said. Why had he given the police the information? He had to have a plan. He always did.

The detectives asked us a few more questions before they dismissed us. I was told not to leave town. I wouldn't re-join the tour until they resolved the situation.

Chapter Fifteen

Cobie

I considered texting Jordan an apology, but decided a face-to-face would be better. I pressed one rose into my music book, since I couldn't take them all with me. His note found a home in the zip-up portion of my backpack for safekeeping. After swinging my guitar onto my shoulder, I stepped out of my dressing room and almost bumped into Brittany.

"Deedee asked me to tell you to wait here," Brittany said. Her voice and face held no emotion.

"Why? Is Deedee alright?" I asked. What if her water broke, and she went through early labor because of me?

"She's eight months pregnant and needed a break. She shouldn't be running around at a concert right now."

"Sorry." I winced at causing another person more issues.

"You're not to blame. Jordan's lawyer knows he can trust Deedee. Everyone does."

"What does Jordan's lawyer want with me?" I asked, confused.

"No clue," Brittany answered. Did they want me to give a statement?

"Can you stay longer, or do you still have to coordinate switching clothes?"

"Already gave them their last clothes change. I'll gather their things from their dressing rooms after the concert."

"Pretty flowers," Brittany said as she took a seat next to me on the couch.

I set my belongs on the ground next to me and asked her, "Do you want them?"

"Can I? These are pretty. Are you sure you don't want to take them home?"

"I can't take flowers on a bus."

Brittany raised a perfectly trimmed eyebrow.

"My ride got repossessed last year," I explained. Happened after Dick stopped making the payments. It had been in my name, and I couldn't afford the luxury vehicle. He had said I needed it for appearances.

"How are you still standing? I'd be a mess after going through everything you had," Brittany said. Sadness filled her eyes, and she sniffed.

"I cried and screamed in the beginning, but when a gnaw in your belly forms, you get up and eat. Besides, I'm not the type to just sit around. I could afford the bus fare home."

"Where are your parents? Why didn't they help you with the situation?"

"They drained my bank accounts and kicked me out since they no longer got a paycheck. I didn't realize Dick had been paying them even after I turned eighteen." I rested my cheek against the backrest, facing Brittany.

"Why?" Brittany asked.

"That's a good question. I doubt I'll ever find out," I answered. Why had he? He kept me working and singing to make him money. Why give my parents any of it? He should've pocketed the money for himself.

"I hate your old manager. Met him once on a tour, and I'm glad I landed this gig with Solar Harmony. They don't let me experiment too much, but the job pays well."

"Meeting you and Deedee has been a godsend. Okay, enough about me. Tell me about yourself." I had to change the subject, or I would become depressed again.

"We haven't explored your situation, but after your experience, talking about it must be painful." Brittany patted my hand and gave it a squeeze.

I nodded, wiping the tears off my face.

"We'll discuss you slowly, and you're lucky. I love talking about myself. I was born and raised in this city. I lived here until I started dressing celebrities for worldwide gigs," Brittany said.

"Who's been your favorite celebrity to dress?" I asked.

"Besides you?" I must've given her a strange look, for she continued. "You let me put you in my original shirt. No one has ever allowed me to do that, so you're my favorite. My dream is to have my clothes as part of Paris Fashion Week."

"What's stopping you?"

"Being recognized, for starters. What's Paris like? You walked the runway two years ago, right?" Brittany would remember I had.

"I didn't see Paris. After I landed from a country hours away, I went to my hotel, and four people got me ready. They ushered me into the show. After I walked, Dick had me on the next flight to resume my tour."

"Did you ever get a break?" Brittany asked.

"Not really. Why are we back on me? I'm sorry I took over the conversation again," I answered.

"Stop apologizing. We're having a talk. Sharing stories about your life happens, and you've had an interesting one."

We spoke for a few more minutes before someone knocked on my door.

"Time for me to leave," Brittany said.

I opened the door to a beautiful, short woman.

Brittany said goodbye to me as she hurried out.

"I'm Megan Adams with Adams Hoffman Law Firm." Megan held out her hand for me to take.

"Did Jordan send you?" I asked, unsure. I had trusted the wrong people, and I planned on never making that mistake again.

"He didn't, but his lawyer, Mr. Hoffman, told me to come and talk to you." She barged into the room, setting her briefcase on the glass coffee table. She pulled out paperwork for me to sign.

"What is this?"

"My paperwork to have a conversation with you. My time costs money."

"I don't have any money," I pointed out.

"You won't get any back with your attitude. You should tell me the truth," Megan said.

"Which is?"

"Someone stole everything you own, and I plan to recover it for you—for a fee, of course." She handed me a pen.

"What if you can't?"

"I will." Megan sounded too sure of herself, and her suit was high end, so she must've won some cases.

After taking the pen, I hesitated, saying, "I don't trust many people." My list comprised of Jordan, Brittany, and Deedee. He wanted nothing from me except my opinion, and I probably ruined it. The other two desired friendship.

"Good."

"Why would I sign with you, then?"

"Trust when I say I love money, and I'll do everything in my power to get some for you. More money for you means more money for me."

I studied her for a moment. Despite her words and smugness, I kind of liked her. I would never understand why. Why did I hesitate then? I signed her damn sheet and handed it back to her.

"First mistake not reading your contract over," Megan said.

"Like I could understand the lawyer jargon you put on the paperwork to confuse clients anyway," I said.

Megan gave me a little smile. "This says I'll hear you out and decide whether or not I'll take your case. Tell me why you're Cam."

"Besides having the first mask she ever wore?" I pulled it out of my pocket and set it in front of me. The material had stretched thin over the years.

"Anyone can get this." Megan took the mask and set it inside her briefcase. Did she want to use it in court? Should I let her have it?

Annoyance built inside of me, and I pushed it back down. "They could, but they couldn't sing like me. I had spent ten years honing my voice. Run my song tonight against any voice identification software, and you'll see."

"I already have. You and Cam exhibit strong compatibility, though not a perfect match. What else makes you her?"

What made me Cam? I never had an ID under my professional name. No one knew who I was except for Dick, and I had worn a mask for my therapy appointments. Besides my voice, what made me Cam? The stories and life I lived, but those weren't tangible.

"Nothing. Dick made sure no one could tie me to Cam," I finally answered Megan.

"Like I thought. I've met and won against men like him. They take advantage of young girls like you. Sweetie, you're a victim. Are you ready to reclaim your life?" Megan touched my hand, and I hadn't realized I made a fist.

"I don't care about the life I had. I want him to stop lying to my fans." Half-moons blossomed across my palm as I released my fists. Punching Dick would make me feel better.

"Tell no one else those words except for me." She grinned at me and pulled out her official contract. She went over it, line by line.

I signed with her. "Why are you working with me?" Like I had said, Dick made sure no one could tie me to Cam, and Megan liked money. She'd receive nothing without proof of me being the singer.

"I've been a big fan of yours for years. I planned on signing you as soon as I heard your story, but I wanted you to be ready to sign with me. You're amazing."

"You are too."

She blushed and brushed her dark brown hair out of her face. Her bright red lipstick complemented her fair complexion.

"When should I talk with law enforcement?" I asked.

"Tomorrow morning, when you're nice and fresh." She continued to read over everything I signed and filled out. "What's your address?"

"Tonight, a hotel off of West Road. Tomorrow, I will be on the tour, either staying at a hotel or on the bus. When I said I had no money, I meant it. Dick abandoned me on the roadside with only the money in my pocket and the clothes on my back. He kept my identification on him just in case it fell into the wrong hands."

Megan studied me.

My thoughts raced, mostly fearing rejection because of my perceived inadequacy. A man I had known for years deceived me and took everything from me. How could I meet the standard to be her representative?

She gave an address.

"Whose place is that?" I asked her. Was there a universal address everyone used when they were homeless, like the 555-phone number?

"My place. Write it on the sheet, since you're now living with me. What better way can I keep you safe than to have you under my roof?" Megan corrected me after I made a mistake writing her address down. Put me in front of sheet music and I jotted every note, anything else, nope.

"Now what?"

"I bring you to my house and give you a key. Should you collect your belongings from the hotel?" She placed the paperwork into her briefcase, saying she'd make me a copy at her home.

"Everything is right here." I picked up my bag and guitar case.

"The more you tell me, the more I want to sue your ex-manager. He's for sure your former. I'll find you a better one and get you the best rate in the industry."

This time, I smiled at her comment. After I settled into her expensive SUV, I wrote a message to Jordan explaining everything.

"Who are you texting?" she asked me.

"Jordan," I answered.

"You can't contact him until the police dismiss his case."

My muscles quivered, and I took a moment to plan my next words because on the inside I seethed. My parents had dictated what I did, and then Dick had. No one would again. If the detectives didn't believe me, Jordan's case could take months, if not years. "I can't live with those terms."

"Why not? I don't want the police believing you're in cahoots. I'm giving you the best legal advice to protect yourself."

After changing my text message to an apology, I also explained why I couldn't contact him again. I showed Megan my phone, asking her, "Will this work? I need to apologize to him for keeping who I am a secret."

She read it over and answered, "Change the ending to on my lawyer's advice, then you can send it. I listen to the needs of my clients as well. He's a friend, isn't he?"

"First one in my life." I also counted Deedee and Brittany. Being famous was lonely.

I canceled my hotel next and showed Megan the proof I did nothing else. Since the time read after 10 p.m., I had lost my money, and I wouldn't fight the hotel for it. They needed to keep the lights on, like everyone else.

The driver left the road, entering a long driveway. The gate opened as we approached the large courtyard with a tall tree in the middle. Megan lived in a mansion. Did everyone here? At least I suspected she owed it instead of staying at it like Jordan and his band.

"Thank you, Fred," Megan said as she slid out of the vehicle.

I followed her, and the doors opened.

"Wilma, are they here?" Megan asked the older lady.

"Yes, ma'am," Wilma said.

"Wilma, this is my guest, Cobie. She'll intermittently stay with us," Megan said.

"Hi," I said to Wilma.

She looked me up and down before saying, "Cobie, I'll get you a set of keys." She left, glancing back at me.

"The world all knows you said you were Cam. I suspect you'll get a lawsuit from your ex-manager in the morning." Megan told me to follow her past the grand entrance with a beautiful bouquet of red flowers, not roses, but something else. I must've stopped to stare at them, for she added, "Wilma changes them everyone morning. Come on, follow me. Pick a bodyguard."

"Bodyguard?" I asked. Everything appeared to move too quickly, and I questioned the imminent end.

"Henceforth, you require protection. The world knows you're Cam. How many times have fans or the paparazzi tried to expose you?"

"More times than I can count."

"I'm expecting them getting worst."

The thought made me weak. After the debate, I had four guys constantly looking out for me. Why did I need so much protection?

Chapter Sixteen

Jordan

The Next Morning

My message last night to Cobie was still unread the next day. I had told her I understood why she hadn't told me and why she couldn't talk to me now, but this sucked.

"If you keep sighing, I'm banishing you to your room," Danny told me. He sat next to me on the couch.

"You can help us find a new show opener with the mess you and your girlfriend caused," Royal said.

"Why are you looking? Cobie's performing tonight," I said.

"She's claiming to be Cam. No way should she open for us tonight," Royal said.

"Cobie signed the contract. She will." I didn't think he'd believe me, and I couldn't call her for confirmation.

"Do you think so?" Danny asked me.

"Why wouldn't she?" I asked.

"She's a megastar." Danny side-eyed me like I was an idiot.

I opened my mouth to tell him why I knew Cobie would be before he got a phone call.

"Cole." Danny answered the call, "Hey, Cole." He listened for a moment and nodded his head.

I hated being sidelined, but that was my situation. I had spoken badly about the fake Cam, and she paid me back in the biggest way she knew how by trying to end my career. Hopefully, the police would drop the charges soon. My vehicle never went to her house. I didn't even know where she lived.

"Let me put you on speaker. Jordan is here too." Danny set his phone on the coffee table.

The rest of the band sat up straighter and moved in closer, including me.

"Good news. Cobie will open for us tonight. Her security will inspect the venue beforehand. Jordan, you need to stay in the mansion," Cole said.

"My lawyer already advised me," I said unhappily. I wanted to see Cobie sing. Would someone record it for me? Some fans would upload the video. Would they go live?

The rest of Cole's statement finally dawned on me. Why did Cobie need bodyguards? I asked my manager for a reason.

"Not sure," he answered.

"She thinks she's big." Royal rolled her eyes and leaned back.

"She is big. If she proves to be Cam, our world will change," Cole said.

"What do you mean?" Royal asked.

"Record companies will scrutinize everything managers do. If they targeted Cam, why not everyone else?" Cole asked. He didn't sound too worried, and he shouldn't be. He was good to us.

"Because we're not stupid. We didn't hide our identities," Royal answered.

"Cam isn't stupid. She trusted the wrong people," I told him.

"You know a lot about that, don't you?" Royal asked me.

"What do you mean?" I asked him.

"Figure it out, or you're an idiot, too." Royal left the room, and I hoped he headed to his bedroom to die.

"You're on probation," Danny called after him.

"Gratitude in all caps," I whispered to Danny. He should become our co-leader after Royal failed.

The doorbell rang.

"Who's here?" Baylee stretched out on the couch Royal had vacated and looked at his phone.

"Is anyone expecting anything?" I asked. Few visitors came before concerts.

The rest of the guys shook their heads.

I went to answer, and Danny pushed past me. "Let me get the door. You don't want the paparazzi photographing you in your outfit."

"Did they go over two fences or scale the cliff?" I asked skeptically. His second sentence finally hit me. "Do I look bad?"

"You look sad, missing Cobie," Danny answered. He grinned at me before standing.

"Whatever." I slumped onto the couch.

Danny conversed with the individual at the door before opening it. "Um, the police have a warrant."

Two officers entered.

"What's it for?" Baylee set his phone into his lap.

"Jordan's phone," Danny answered.

"Why?" I asked.

The police officers showed me their paperwork, and I told them I had to contact my lawyer first. They let me call Gabriel in front of them before I handed it over with his approval. Why were the police interested in my phone? It didn't hold any evidence besides my ignoring the fake Cam and my one response to her. I only answered her not to be a complete asshole. How had she gotten my number? Royal probably gave it to her manager.

Once the police left, my bandmates, except for Royal, helped me search online for the cause. We quickly found it. Cam, the fake one, had posted our sex text messages. They had to be fake as well. I would never text those awful things to a woman.

"Wow, Jordan. You can write some steamy messages," Jay said.

"I didn't write these. You believed I didn't, right?" I asked.

"We do. The police can easily figure out they didn't come from you," Danny answered.

"Cam didn't block your number when she released the fake texting," Baylee pointed out.

Words couldn't describe the anger I felt. The world now knew my phone number, but I was angrier at her for getting my phone confiscated. Cobie's number was on there, and I had yet to learn it since I had a freakin' phone. The police had to give me my phone back after the investigation. Would they? Those messages would prove the fake Cam's allegations were false.

"What will I do?" I asked my friends. My lawyer told me not to log into my account because the cops would assume I deleted text messages.

"You didn't send the texts. Fake Cam had made them, probably to get her story straight," Baylee answered.

"Will anyone ever believe me?" I showed off the worst message in the fake Cam debacle. She had promised her fans more to come.

My career was over. Following the fake Cam narrative, helplessness overwhelmed me. Tears filled my eyes. "I...I need space, guys."

Seeing my face, Danny wrapped his arms around me and squeezed. Men didn't hug according to him, yet he did for me. Once he finished, he asked me, "Did your lawyer say you could have a phone? Your mom will freak out soon."

"He did," I answered.

"I'm getting you one now. We should leave Jordan alone," Danny said.

Baylee gave me a quick hug.

Jay questioned the necessity of their departure before he hugged me.

Danny tugged the youngest out of the room, saying, "Come on, you're coming with me to buy Jordan a phone."

Jay questioned, "Why do I have to go? This is our living room. We're supposed to share it."

"Jordan needs space, and you both are coming with me to get him a phone." Danny grabbed Jay by his collar and pulled him outside.

Baylee followed them, not saying anything.

"Thank you," I called to Danny before I headed to my bedroom. I sat on my bed and let the tears fall. I doubted even the great Gabriel Hoffman could save me.

After I allowed myself to grieve, I got angry. Thankfully, by then, Danny had bought me another phone. I activated it and looked up my lawyer's phone number. Convincing the administrative assistant of who I was took longer than I'd like.

"Hey, Jordan. What do you need?" Gabriel asked.

"You ask what I need? Have you not seen the news?" I asked. My anger rose again, and I gripped my phone.

"I have, and we'll do nothing. You have nothing on your phone, right?"

"I don't, but you've seen the messages fake Cam has posted online, haven't you?"

"I have."

"She posted my real number," I said.

"You'll get a new one," Gabriel said.

"What are we doing?"

"Nothing. The police need to make their case, and according to you, they don't have one."

"They won't find anything except me rejecting fake Cam's request to work together."

"Did you delete any of her messages?" Gabriel asked.

"Not a single one. I hoped she'd leave me alone if I left her unread." I switched my phone with my hands. A red mark stretched across my palm, and I waved it in the air.

"I'm debating whether I should get access to your texting to Cam."

"Fake Cam."

"Fake Cam then." Gabriel didn't sound impressed with me, correcting him.

"How can you access my information? You told me not to," I reminded him.

"I have my ways. Do you think I should?" Gabriel asked.

"Honestly, yes. My career is over if we don't prove she is lying." Anyone could've gotten into my phone, since I had the habit of leaving it behind, but I didn't share this information with my lawyer. He probably already thought I was a dumbass.

"Okay."

"Do you need my password?" I asked.

"Nope," Gabriel answered.

"Do I want to know how you're doing it?"

"You'll hear from me afterward."

"Thank you."

Gabriel hung up before he heard my gratitude.

A few hours later, I got a text from my lawyer. I had done nothing except toss a ball against the wall. I didn't feel like writing music or doing anything.

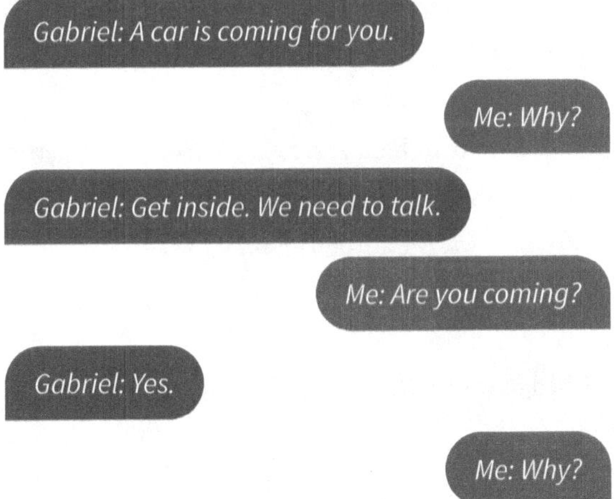

I groaned when he didn't answer. Bad thoughts passed through my head like what if he got rid of me? What if the police pursued charges against me? I called the guards to put him on the permanent guest list. With the sexual assault charge pending, I would meet with him a lot over the coming weeks.

Darkness filled the rest of the house. The band had already taken off for their concert. Singing without them proved peculiar and agonizing. I had never missed an event with my band, even singing ill.

"I'm heading out to meet my lawyer," I told no one. We had a camera pointed at the front door and behind me aimed at the patio, as well as every entrance. My record label had yet to dismiss me. If Gabriel wanted me to turn myself in to the police, they would soon. I should call my manager, but I had put it off.

A black SUV pulled into the courtyard.

I breathed the incredibly satisfying fresh air for the first time that day. I wouldn't do well in prison. What would happen if the other prisoners liked fake Cam? I dismissed the thought as soon as I had it. I never touched her, and I didn't deserve this treatment.

The passenger door of the SUV opened, and Gabriel ordered, "Get in."

I slid inside next to him, and he moved over. His getting me seemed suspicious; his later actions even more dubious. He likely had important news. A wave of nausea hit me.

"You texted fake Cam," Gabriel said. His words weren't a question.

"I refused to work with her once," I answered his unasked question.

"No, you texted more." He reached into his briefcase, pulling out sheets of paper.

I read the first exchange and then the next. When I got to my admitting I had harmed her, the bile in my throat rose. I opened the door, puking onto the ground and barely missing the inside of the SUV. Once I finished, I protested.

Gabriel asked me after I stopped talking, "If this were anyone else, I wouldn't believe them, and I would drop them as a client."

"Then why are you here with me?" I assumed that since he wanted to meet with me, he would keep me on.

"Call me sentimental." He was never the word.

"Why Gabriel? Why?" In that moment, I needed someone else who wasn't my best friends to believe me. Would Cobie after she read those texts?

"I remained hesitant, since I follow the evidence. Everything points to you, but when I saw your face pale and you puked after reading the messages, I'm on your side. Your actions confirmed what I already knew. My partner is telling me to drop you."

"Why aren't you?" I leaned back and closed my eyes. My tears were gone.

"I do what I want, and your case is interesting. Who had access to your phone?" Gabriel asked.

"Huh?"

"Who had access to your phone?"

"Why?" I stared at him.

"Someone texted the fake Cam and deleted them," Gabriel answered.

His words clicked inside my mind, and I explained, "My bandmates. I live with them, and I leave it in my dressing room during concerts or on my chair during filming." I left it anywhere.

"Too many chances for someone to get a hold of it." Gabriel held his clean-shaven chin. "That explains her statement about your visit three days before the texts. What happened that day and the next?"

I gave him the rundown, most of which he already knew, since I had given the police my statement.

"Your phone was in several places. Your bandmates and any of the concert staff could've taken it," Gabriel said once I finished. He narrowed his eyes and counted to rub his chin.

"My band didn't," I insisted.

"The confusing part is the person knew your phone's password." He paid me no attention.

My face heated. I had committed an unforgivable act. "About that."

"Tell me."

I winced and said, "My password is my name."

"Dammit, Jordan," Gabriel cursed.

"I know I'm not supposed to, but no one stole my phone."

"They just sent nasty texts to frame you. Who knows your password?"

"Danny for sure. Likely, my entire band plus several staff members. If they needed a phone, I would let them use mine."

Gabriel glared at me hard enough to force a confession. "You're taking a cybersecurity course tomorrow. I'll have my assistant come by and give it to you. You need to continue taking it every day until you understand the importance of keeping your information private."

"I'm understanding now." I promised to set a new code, and I would start with my new phone. He didn't need to know.

"What is your new password?"

"I'm changing it."

"You will do at least two sessions of cybersecurity training. Hurry and change your password."

"In front of you?" I asked.

Gabriel gave me another one of his dagger looks. Yeah, he would make me and any criminal admit things we didn't want to confess.

I did what he told me. "Happy?" I asked him.

"I would be happier if you stopped doing stupid things," Gabriel answered.

"What do we do next?" I had to change the subject because I had no excuse. Cole had told the band about the importance of not losing their phones or letting photos leak.

"We do nothing. My security team will go check everyone you spoke with during those two days. I'll call you when I have more information. You get me more suspect names to check."

"Okay, okay."

"Is there anything else, or will you sleep in my vehicle tonight?" Gabriel asked, obviously done with me. The worst thing I did was disappoint him, and I felt the burn and humiliation of it.

"Did Cobie make a statement?" I asked.

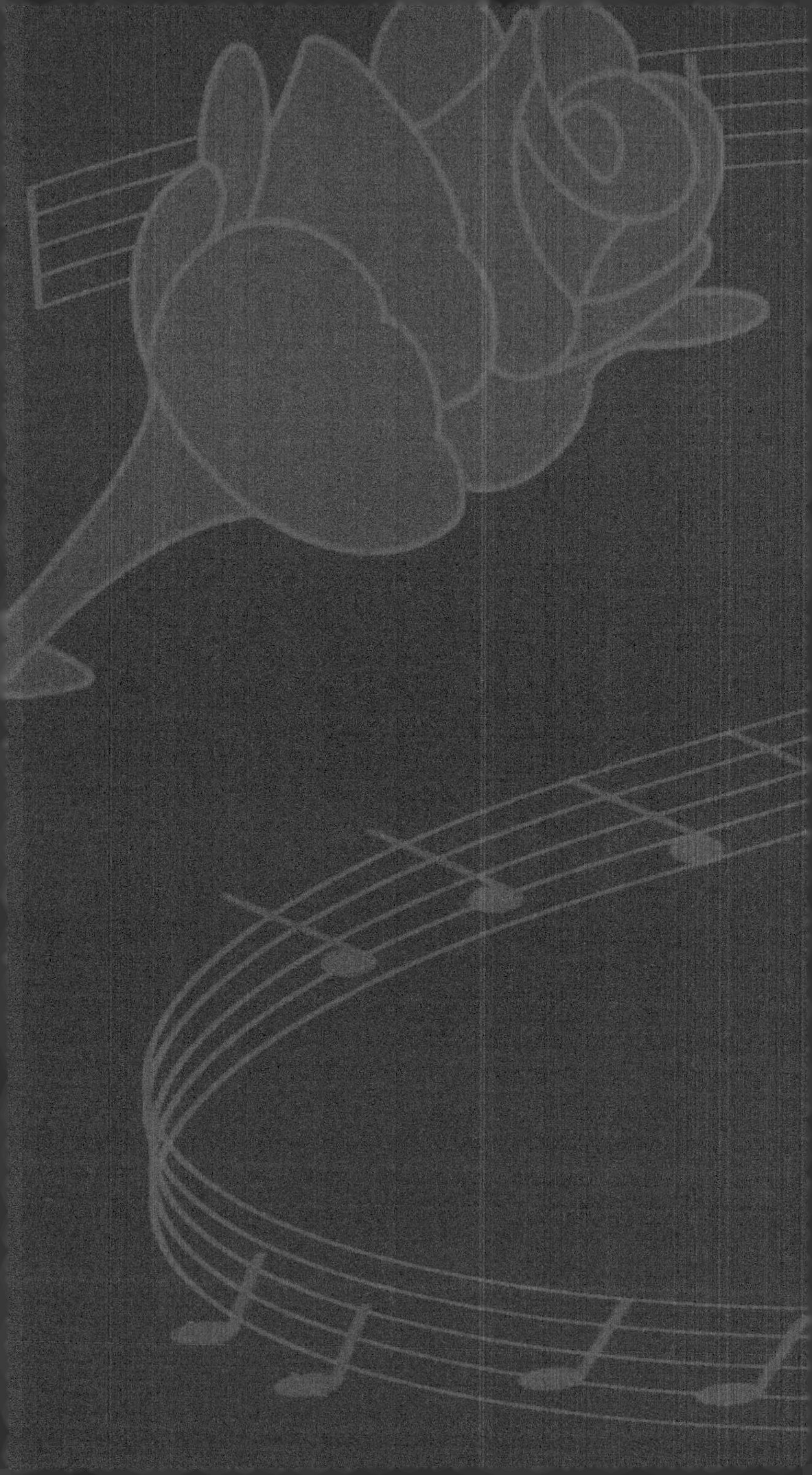

Chapter Seventeen

Cobie

The Same Morning

Sleeping on the ridiculously expensive sheets and mattress was something I missed about being rich. Although any bed was wonderful, since I had spent most of the nights on a bench, a cot, or a cardboard box. The shelter offered minimal provisions, like a lukewarm meal and shelter. Their blankets were better than the one I owned. I never carried it around since people would ask questions. It was most likely stolen by now. Hiding it inside a wall wasn't Fort Knox.

"How did you sleep?" Megan asked me once I entered the kitchen for breakfast.

"Extremely well," I answered. My stomach rolled, and I didn't want to eat, but figured I should. Someone had left a spread out on the table, including different cooked eggs, bacon, toast, sausage, pancakes, waffles, and every fruit and juice imaginable. "Who lives with you?"

"Just Wilma and me. I swear I can't keep this place running without her."

"Why did you make so much food?" It surpassed our capacity, and Jordan's band couldn't finish it either.

"Wilma did, and we will feed your bodyguards. I also didn't know what you liked. Sit and eat."

I thanked her.

"You don't need to keep thanking me. Although I'm understanding why you do. You've never really had anyone to take care of you, have you?" Megan asked me.

I poured myself a glass of orange juice, contemplating my answer. "You're correct." Dick had stolen everything, and my parents the rest.

"I remember you on stage a few times, and you looked sick."

"Probably when Dick said I was too fat and made me fast. He used to tell me, 'No one buys music from fat chicks'."

"When?"

"Anytime I was above a size eight. He wanted me to drop to a size two, but I'm not petite." I slathered some butter on a piece of wheat toast.

"Cobie, I'm sorry." Megan came to me and embraced me.

"Why are you sorry?"

"What your ex-manager said and made you do is highly illegal. Fans buy music from artists we love. We don't care what you look like."

"That's not how the music industry works."

"In America, it is. Certain nations prioritize appearance over music in other countries, not here," Megan said.

"I knew nothing else." I hugged her back and wanted to thank her, but suspected she would yell at me.

Megan gave me one last squeeze before she sat. "You will learn from now on. I've already gotten offers to become your new manager."

"What? Why would they?"

"Because they realize you're Cam. I'll have my firm's investigators look over them. I won't let anyone else hurt you again, even if I have to become your damn manager myself. Sorry, I get a bit heated."

I still never understood why.

"Eat up, and we need to talk about our next steps. Plus, we don't want the food to get cold," Megan said.

I enjoyed fried eggs, sausage, and fruit.

"Eat more," Megan told me.

"I'm full, and I'm an adult," I said.

"Yes, you are. I keep forgetting. A show business career at such a young age hindered you." Megan must've seen anger cross my face, for she continued. "Every famous singer who starts early in life needs someone who they can trust. What Dick did to you and keeps doing will end soon. Let's leave the food to the bodyguards and speak in my office."

I followed her out of the room. An upscale magazine should photograph her office with the enormous oak desk, bookshelf behind her, and the three comfy chairs. I sat in the one across from her. "When will I give my statement to the police?"

Megan hesitated. "I'm advising you not to." She excelled at her job, but I couldn't collaborate with someone unwilling to let me decide about my life, especially not now. Did she have a reason?

"Why not? Jordan didn't rape the person pretending to be me. I was with him that day."

"My law firm got word of texts between the other Cam and Jordan. These are the less racy ones." Megan opened a folder and slid a paper over to me on the desk.

I read through the exchanges. Jordan possibly dated the other Cam while I flirted with him. We never said we were exclusive, so I couldn't get angry at him for it. Well, I could, but I never wanted to act like the jealous girlfriend when we weren't dating.

"Where are the worst ones?" I asked. My throat had thickened.

Megan handed them to me and said, "We should distance ourselves from Mr. Space."

I rejected the idea. What other Cam and he had done wasn't my business. I handed the papers back without looking them over.

"Are you sure?"

"Sexual assault isn't something anyone should lie about. The other Cam's actions undermine women's credibility, and she'll potentially imprison an innocent man. He's finished in the music industry if the truth doesn't come out."

Megan displayed the papers of their text messages, questioning, "You still believe he's innocent after this?"

"I've read hotter erotica," I answered. My face heated as soon as my brain realized what I had said. Any sex conversation seemed awkward. Megan acted like an older sister than a parent.

"I'm glad you're helping him out, but you're not making my job easy."

"Nothing is easy if it's truly worth it."

"Especially since Jordan's record label and management firm have been getting funeral flowers and death threats. The latter is stupid, but why wreaths?"

"They're calling for the death of his career," I explained.

"Oh," Megan said. Her eyes widened, and her mouth hung open.

"Almost as bad as a black ocean, where the audience isn't singing along with you or waving their light sticks. I feared disappointing my fans. One of the contributing factors in my wearing my mask for so long."

"What was it like when you took it off?"

"Amazing. I never thought I'd have the strength to do it. I chickened out every time until I told Dick I would. Those words empowered me to attempt it."

"Since I can't change your mind, your bodyguards should be ready. We can head out now."

"Why do I need them?" I had never before.

"Honey, you're Cam. You need them, trust me. Tim?" Megan called.

"Already ready, ma'am," my first bodyguard said in the doorway. He looked like his job with the bald head and stood at least six foot six. He could intimidate a honey badger, and he looked nothing like his name, Tim.

Tim drove Megan and me, along with another one of my bodyguards, to the police station. Two more followed behind me. "Get used to this," she told me.

"Get used to what?" I asked her.

"Everyone wants to photograph you." She nodded outside as we parked alongside the curb.

People surrounded the metal barricades on either side of the sidewalk. They held signs of hating Jordan, freeing him, believing me, or saying I was the devil. I gave the last one props, since that was an original. Police officers stationed themselves every five feet.

"People have photographed me for most of my career," I told her. Megan had given me expensive clothes to wear and added security.

The situation might turn deadly if it escalated. I had escaped some trouble before, though not without injury.

"We'll let you know if Cam can walk," Tim, the head bodyguard, said before he exited.

Another bodyguard approached from outside, scanning the crowd.

Cars passed by slowly as more people joined the rest.

Tim tapped the SUV's side.

The second bodyguard said, "I'm out first, followed by Cam and Ms. Adams." He turned around to face me. "We'll surround you and walk you to the entrance. When we say stop, you stop. When we tell you to go, you go."

I nodded, unable to speak. Did someone plant a bomb or threaten my life? Dick might want to kill me. Much harder to pay someone when they were dead.

"Wait," Megan said. She handed me her sunglasses, and I put them on. She whispered calming words as we walked. Inside, she told the desk officer, "My client, Cam, is here to make a statement regarding the accusations against Mr. Space."

Megan instructed me to go by my stage name, Cam, from last night on.

"We'll see if the detectives are ready for you," the desk officer said. He made a call and told us they would be out soon.

Upon their arrival, Tim told them, "We need to check the room before Cam enters it."

"Is this for real?" the detective asked.

"She's a superstar," his partner pointed out.

The first detective scoffed and allowed two of my bodyguards to follow him. Once they returned, we were guided the rest of the way through the halls.

Inside the small integration room, Megan and I sat across from the two detectives. My protectors waited outside. This was ridiculous.

"Cam, what is your real name?" the first detective, who spoke earlier, asked.

"Cobie Meine," I answered.

Megan set her hand on my arm to tell me I needed to answer only questions she didn't object to. She had told me this repeatedly earlier.

When I was nervous, I spoke without thinking or talked fast. Many times during an interview, I had to tell myself to slow down. It got so bad Dick would tug on his ear.

"May we call you Cobie?" the partner asked.

"You can. This is Detective Brooke Reyers, and her partner is Detective Brady Venma, Cobie," Megan answered for me. Her knowing their names didn't surprise me.

"Why is your client here today? And why does she have a lawyer?" Detective Venma asked.

Megan didn't object, so I answered, "I'm here because someone made a serious accusation against Jordan Space, and I have a lawyer because I do." They didn't need to know I planned on suing my former manager and label.

"Were you with Mr. Space two nights ago?" Detective Reyers asked.

"Yes," I answered.

The detectives kept asking questions like they wanted to trip me up, but Megan stopped them several times, and I only answered what she allowed me to. After we finished, I wasn't sure if I had helped Jordan or not.

"Before you go, can you explain these messages, then?" Venma handed me a piece of paper from a folder.

I reread it, and a sudden loss of warmth left my body feeling cold.

Megan checked the sheet and objected.

Venma tried again.

"How would my client explain a conversation between people when she wasn't involved?" Megan asked him.

Did Jordan know about the texts? His phone number was in the messages, and I double-checked it. Why did I believe he wasn't a part of this? I believed he was innocent, but I wasn't the best judge of character.

Megan asked the detectives, "Anything further?"

"We have nothing else." Venma inquired about contacting me.

"Through me." Megan handed them her card, and we left.

Inside the SUV, I asked Megan, "When will they drop the charges?"

"I'm not sure," she answered.

"Do Jordan and his lawyer know about the texts admitting the charge?"

Megan gave the same three-word answer.

"Will you ask them?" I asked.

"Why should I? Those messages have killed his career and might take yours too. We need to distance ourselves from Jordan," Megan answered.

Alternative explanations existed for those messages. I remembered an old TV show where a teenage detective proved anyone could borrow a phone and send anything. I kept my faith in Jordan, even as doubt nagged at me.

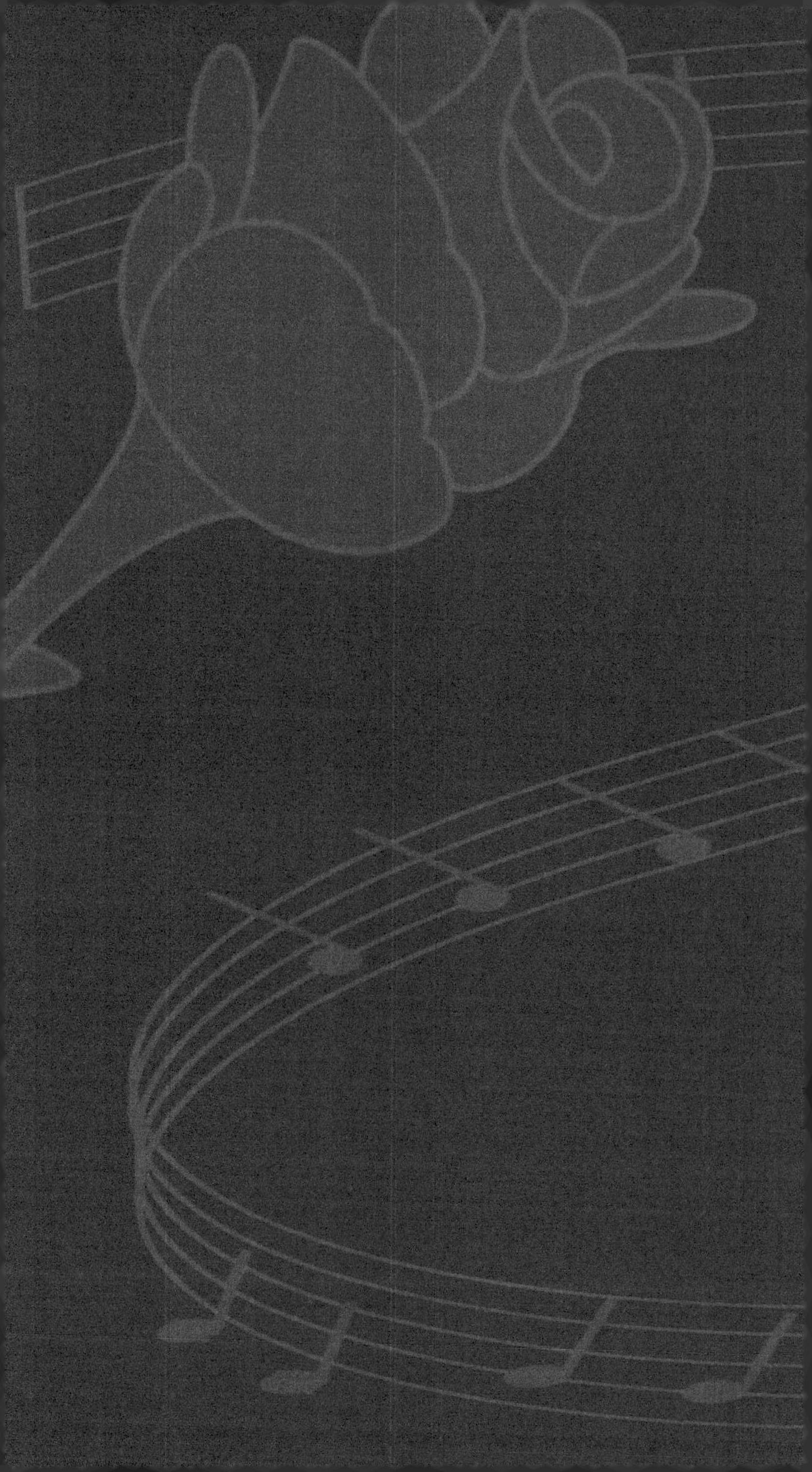

Chapter Eighteen

Jordan

The Next Morning

I spent the night tossing and turning over the recent development, giving up around 3 p.m. I trusted Danny completely, but someone had planted the messages on my phone. Bile rose into my mouth, and I threw up into the trash. Why would anyone think I was capable of this? Would my best mate?

I could find out.

Danny either relaxed or worked on the concerts for Friday and Saturday. He answered on the first ring. "About time you reached out to me," he told me.

"I needed space," I said.

"No, you don't. Why are we touring without you?"

"The band comes first, and I'm fine."

"Are you? Those messages are fake."

"You believe I didn't send them?" I asked.

"Come on. I've known you since elementary school, and I re-member you passed out during the sexual assault and consent health class. Of course, you didn't send those texts. You still leave the room when anything gets too rough sexually on fake TV," Danny answered. He sounded upset with me.

I experienced a lightness. "You don't understand how much I needed to hear you say those words."

"Now you did. Tell me what's happening."

I answered, "Someone used my phone to send those messages. I'm not sure who."

"Anybody could. You use your name as your password. Everyone knows it," Danny said.

"Gabriel made me change my new phone's password." I felt pride in my newly developed code.

"Did you use Jordan1?"

"How did you know?"

"Change your code to a phrase, and input numbers or symbols instead of letters. Do it now."

I did. "What should I do next?" I asked.

"Build your timeline. Have you seen Cobie's performance?" Danny asked.

"Not yet. How was she?" I didn't believe I should. No way would she believe I was innocent after reading those texts. I didn't deserve her.

"Watch it and see. I have to go. Here's a link with our band photos on the days of those texts. Use them to identify the culprit." Danny sent me a link to an encrypted file.

"Royal gave you his pictures, too?"

"Hell, no. He has a strike, and he's on probation. If he gets three, he's out."

"You surpass me as a leader." When had Danny gotten the images?

"Stop with that crap. You're getting back to the band pronto, and whoever the fake Cam is will send a public apology for framing you. I can't manage our band without you. Jay has been a pain in the ass."

"I'm not that bad," Jay said. He sounded louder, and he must've snatched the phone from Danny. "Hey, Jordan."

"Hey, Jay," I said.

"How are you holding up?"

"Not good."

"Danny told us to get our photographs to build your timeline, after Baylee came up with the idea. We know you didn't send those texts."

"Thanks man. Keep your mind on the concerts and don't worry about me," I said.

"How can I not? You're my idol. I admire you and want to be like you," Jay said to me.

"No, you don't. Put Danny back on."

"Hey, do you need something else?" Danny asked.

"Tell Baylee this isn't his fault," I answered.

"Why?"

"Watch him and you'll see."

"I will." Danny hung up without a goodbye.

On the table was a box with my name on it. Who had put this here and when? My goal of speaking to Gabriel had kept me from noticing anything last night. For a moment, my thoughts circulated to a stalker. They wouldn't get past the two guard stations unless they were incredibly skilled.

After lifting the lid, a note from Danny fell out. He didn't leave his name, but I recognized his handwriting.

Wait to log into your accounts until the police drop their investigation.
Use this instead. Also, eat.

I heated my burger and booted up the laptop Danny had given me. He got his favorite brand, which I disliked. At least he would finally get his wish of me switching over, even if it was just temporarily. I had to search the net on my phone to find the search engine. No way would I keep this computer.

Looking through my friends' everyday pictures was an invasion of privacy I didn't like, and not what I expected. Danny had a lot of selfies showing off his body. Okay, him, I believed. Now Jay had him and me. He also did pics with the staff more than anyone in the band. I doubted Royal ever did. Baylee had random images.

I took image by image, building my steps the last few days. The strict schedule was a blessing. By the time I finished, night had fallen. I called my lawyer.

His admin sent me straight to him, and he answered, "I told you once we have news, I'll get in touch."

"I'm tired of waiting, and I can prove I didn't send the texts. Give me the times and I can likely identify the saboteur," I said.

"How?"

"I built a timeline."

"I'll come get it."

"No, we'll go over the information together. I'm tired of being out of the loop," I said.

"Have you called your parents?" Gabriel asked. His sudden topic gave me whiplash.

"I can't." My mom had a history, and no way would she believe or forgive me. I couldn't bear finding out whether either were true. My dad worked, and we barely spoke. I hadn't forgiven him for cheating on my mom.

"We'll clear everything up then you will." Did he know my mom's past? He hung up.

While I waited for him to arrive, I cleaned up the mess I had made. The mansion had occupancy requirements, including upkeep and a connection to it. Charges filed would get me sacked and kicked out.

I opened the door for Gabriel.

He surveyed his surroundings and then inquired about the workplace.

"This way." I showed him to Royal's side of the mansion, since I needed the actual recording studio to make music on mine. He had attempted to take it, but the rest of the band voted against him each time.

I glanced around before heading inside, placing a few books on a shelf. Baylee had kept the area relatively tidy. I hadn't stepped over the threshold since I had searched for some music books and found none. Why didn't a record label have any at a home they owned?

Gabriel set his briefcase on the large dark wood desk. He handed me the papers.

I sat in front of him, looking it over. The system printed times and dates next to the messages, and none comprised the horrible ones. Despite being a hardass, my lawyer was thoughtful. I set my handwritten timeline on the copier and made him a copy.

We settled in to compare. The first message sent from my imposter was when I had done the final approval for my clothes at the show. Brittany had chosen black jeans with a white shirt and coat. I wanted a grown-up look instead of the usual crazy colored top like Danny loved to wear. He and Jay had also done their last check too.

I penned their names and Brittany's next to the message. I doubted she did this to me, and I would prove she hadn't.

After I filled names on the side of the messages, I noticed a pattern. Danny, Jay, and I spent considerable time together. Baylee flitted near us, unlike Royal, who remained distant. He disliked me and left me alone. I doubted he had the brains to pull this off.

Near the end of the texts, Royal and I had been at rehearsal. The little guilt I had for thinking he did this washed away. Unless he wasn't alone.

"Are you done?" Gabriel asked.

I replied, "I have a few more messages to go, but my band and key support staff were usually with me." What if more than one person worked with the fake Cam?

"Same with these messages. We must identify those with opportunity." Gabriel tapped his chin and swirled his pen between his fingers.

"Like who?"

"Someone who goes unnoticed, even at a venue." Gabriel's eyes widened for a second.

"Who does?"

He held out a finger and called someone. "Get me the names of the janitorial staff for the Solar Harmony concert." He hung up after a thank you.

"Why them?" I asked.

"No one would question them tidying up your dressing room," Gabriel answered.

"Also, Brittany and her staff."

Gabriel raised an eyebrow.

"They arrive to organize clothes before and after our show. We should look into who delivers the flowers and stocks the mini fridge, too," I answered his unasked question. Guilt rose inside me for accusing my friend.

Gabriel made another call, and after he finished, he checked something on his phone.

I returned to the last two messages on my list. Once I finished them, I had a strange thought. Should I check when the faker sent me a message against my location? I had been busy with her first text and then the next.

What the actual hell? How did fake Cam know when I was busy? This had to be a coincidence. The more I checked, the more I discovered she'd sent messages when I didn't have my phone on me, like during rehearsal. The impersonator and she had sent the sexts consecutively.

"I found something," I said.

"So have I. Have you heard of a Talia Bronson?" Gabriel asked.

"No, why?" The last name sounded familiar, but I had met a ton of famous people who used stage names instead of their real names.

"She's Dick Bronson's daughter. Why work with a famous dad?"

"Her dad might've cut her off. I never met her."

"Are you sure?" Gabriel asked.

"I'm busy writing and singing music. My friends are my band." I shrugged and told him what I had found.

"All of them?"

"Every text."

"Let me confirm mine, too." He worked on it, and a few minutes later, said, "This is interesting."

"Would the police even believe us?" I asked.

"They might. You're known for leaving your phone behind for specific reasons, like at practice and when you sing," Gabriel answered.

"Yeah, I got reamed for letting a text go off once during a concert in my early days. I also don't carry my cell with me for fittings. I've left it behind too many times."

Gabriel asked, "Where were you during these times?" He had to bring up the black holes in my timeline.

"If I had my phone, I would tell you," I told him instead.

"This list may persuade the police, perhaps diverting suspicion from you," he said.

"When will you tell them?" I suspected I would hate the answer.

"After they charge you. We'll get the official paperwork, and after a day, we'll prove to them you were on stage when they sent these messages." Gabriel lifted his work.

I'd been right about his answer. "Will I get my phone back then?"

"The police will return it after they recovered the text messages from your phone between you and Cam," Gabriel answered.

"Recovered?" I asked.

"Yeah, the person deleted it."

"Explains why I didn't see them. I often go back and reread my messages, worried about what I sent."

"They also deleted it from your phone."

"You can do that? Do I look like someone who could? Get me in front of any instrument or recording studio technology and I will show you how, but on a phone, I'm clueless."

"You worked the copier earlier," Gabriel pointed out.

"It has a picture. You should've seen me search how to run the laptop," I said.

"Don't you use a laptop for recording?"

"Not this kind. Do the police have a case against me? Give me the information straight." My mind buzzed enough, and I needed sleep.

"Cobie made a statement, and the police might drop charges against you because of that."

"Why did she?" I couldn't cause her career to go down.

"Her lawyer described her as determined. I can see why you like her."

"She saved me from fans."

"So, she's the girl who doesn't need a knight in shining armor?" Gabriel asked, referencing my song lyrics. He must've listened to Royal sing it. I doubted my record label released my version of it.

"Have you seen Cobie's performance from last night?" I asked.

"Everyone has. Have you?"

"I don't believe I earned the right to."

"You should watch it. She states yet again that you're innocent and explains a bit more about what happened to her. She also sang her songs."

"Won't the faker stop her?" I asked.

"The court doesn't open until Monday, so next week will be interesting." Gabriel gathered the sheets into his briefcase. He looked up at me and said, "Your cyber training will be here in an hour. Make sure you let them in."

I didn't complain. He took the paperwork since we weren't supposed to have it. "Will do. What's the faker's plan?"

"If I were their lawyer, I'd deny permission and file an injunction to stop Cobie. I'd sue the venue for any royalties. Determining whether ticket holders attended for Solar Harmony or her will be difficult to distinguish. Although your tickets are getting scalped. The outcry for her is incredible."

"What will her lawyer do?"

"Sue. If they can prove Cobie is Cam, she'll get a hefty payday," Gabriel answered.

"Can you pass along a message to her?" I asked.

"Maybe."

"Tell her what her manager doesn't know will hurt him." I had written a lot of songs, and some I trashed, but if I were in Cobie's position, I would use one not released against them.

"I'm not even sure what those words mean."

"She'll figure it out." I saw Gabriel out and watched Cobie's performance. Using one word to describe the way she sang didn't do her justice. She held a mini-concert, and the fans ate it up. At the end, she called the fake Cam out. Few people in the world sang like her.

Chapter Nineteen

Cobie

The Following Wednesda

Monday came with no lawsuit from Dick and the same thing on Tuesday. Today, Wednesday, I needed to be at the venue to practice. I came into the kitchen with the big breakfast and invited my bodyguards to eat with Megan and me.

I picked at my food and asked Megan, "When will we drop the lawsuit?"

"Soon," she answered, like she had the last two days. She glanced at my bodyguard, Tim, and then back to her paperwork.

"I feel waiting is a mistake," I said. Dick probably planned something major, and he'd sue. I could feel it in every fiber of my being. Didn't filing first matter?

"To achieve perfection takes time, especially given your losses. I'm going over the details, and you should focus on the show Friday and Saturday," Megan said.

"I can sing my songs in my sleep," I pointed out.

"Work on something new, then. Keep yourself busy, and we'll discuss when and who we'll sue. Have you figured out Jordan's message?"

I shook my head and ate some of the divine thick-cut bacon. The salt and black pepper worked well together.

"Why couldn't he spell it out?" Megan asked.

"He might not want anyone else to know," I answered. I figured I'd come up with an answer someday if I let my brain work it out. What did Dick not know? What did I do that he didn't know? I sang and wrote the music. He would never feel a connection between the fans and the artist. He saw only dollar signs.

I looked forward to seeing Deedee and Brittany again. We had texted a few times and shared a meme or two. We were at an awkward stage in a friendship just starting out. I didn't have the same experience with Jordan. Despite agreeing not to date, we discussed music and random topics easily. I missed him.

The police hadn't dropped his case or made charges yet. I asked Megan whether I should do anything to help him again.

Megan pressed her red lips into a thin line before she answered, "You shouldn't for a bit. If you keep protesting, people will think you're getting paid or something. Keep setting the record straight when you need to."

"I'm glad the other Cam ceased communication," I said. Every time she opened her damn mouth, she made Jordan's life worse. Danny had taken me aside the moment I arrived at the venue for the second day of the tour and explained to me why Jordan never texted her. His words made me believe in Jordan even more. He had the friends I wish I had.

"Worries me though. She should've released a statement debunking you. Why hasn't she?" Megan asked.

"Too busy keeping her lies straight?" I asked. Danny had also explained to me why the other Cam had attacked Jordan. He had figured out she wasn't me from one meeting. I doubted anyone else had.

"Not sure. Finish eating your food so we can go," Megan answered.

"Will you eat?" I asked. She barely ate anything, although I had every meal with her.

"I don't sing and dance like you or go to the gym regularly. We should call a dietitian for you," Megan answered.

"I work out so I can dance on stage. Taking lessons years ago doesn't keep me in shape, and I listen to my body for when I'm hungry," I said.

"What type of lessons?" Megan asked.

"Ballet, modern, hip-hop, contemporary, jazz, and ballroom. Never used the latter, despite Dick insisting," I answered.

"Every time we talk, I learn something new. Haven't you fainted on stage before?" Megan asked.

"Once or twice. After I was checked out, I returned to finish the show," I answered. Yeah, I'd be getting a dietitian soon.

"Why did you faint?" Megan asked.

"Both times my ex-manager had me on the ice chip diet," I answered.

"I don't want to know what that is."

"You don't."

Megan covered her mouth with one hand and muttered something about wanting to kill Dick under her breath.

"We need to leave in twenty to check the venue in time," Tim said.

"Thanks, Tim." Megan turned to me. "Finish your food or I'll find a dietitian who will start tomorrow."

She didn't need to tell me twice.

After we finished, we traveled to the venue in two vehicles. I sat next to Megan with Tim and another bodyguard in the front seat.

"What if I can't win my life back?" I asked Megan.

"You don't believe I can win?" Megan asked. She sounded upset, and she stared at me with her brown eyes.

"You will emerge as the winner, but what if I can't repay you? The constant four bodyguards must cost you a fortune." I played with a small sticky piece on the leather door.

"You're worth every penny." Megan took the paperwork out of her briefcase and read it. I swear she always did this.

"Why though?" I asked.

She lowered her glasses onto the bridge of her nose. "I'm a fan. A die-hard Camie. I had posters on my wall of you, and I promised to be your lawyer. You're fulfilling my dream. When I heard how your manager tossed you aside and your record label didn't recognize you, I got pissed. My dad did the same thing to my mom, Wilma."

"She's your mom?" I asked, confused. They didn't act like they're related.

"Yes, she helps me around the house and cooks. We have a great symbiotic relationship." Megan pushed her glasses back and held up two pieces of paper.

"You don't act like she's your mom," I pointed out.

"My mom's never been the maternal type. My dad destroyed her self-worth, and I'm helping her the best I can," Megan explained. She settled onto one of her sheets. "How does this sound? 'This is not a story. On January 2nd of last year, Cobie Meine told her manager Dick Bronson, owner of RAB Management, that she would remove her mask to reveal she is Cam at her first concert in March. Instead of fulfilling his duties as a manager, he dropped her, leaving her by the side of the road with little money and no identification.'"

"Very dull," I answered.

"All court documents are. We have to state the facts of why we're suing," Megan explained. She continued to read the documents, and I corrected the information where needed.

When she asked why we were suing, I hesitated before answering, "I am Cam. I want my life and fans back. I didn't dedicate a decade of my life to end up with nothing because of my inability to deceive my fans anymore."

"We understood why you wore the mask," Megan said.

"At the beginning, I wanted it. Whenever I opened my mouth to sing, I puked after. I had the mask on, and it helped me to calm my nerves. Years passed, and I grew to resent it," I said.

"Oh, you gave me a much better idea for the lawsuit." Megan wrote something on her phone.

We discussed our lives on the way to the venue, and the two bodyguards answered my questions. Tim had gotten divorced recently. Brad had a wife.

Megan woke me early Friday morning. "Read this," she said.

"Can it wait?" I needed coffee and to finish waking up.

"Not when you have to sing in less than ten hours."

"What's going on?" I sat up.

"You have an injunction from fake Cam to stop singing her songs tonight."

"And that means?" I asked.

"You can't sing your songs." Megan sat on the end of the bed dressed in black and white silk pajamas.

"Is there anything we can do?"

She shook her head. "You could sing them anyway, but you'd cause issues for the venue and Solar Harmony."

I swore. At least Dick had finally made a move. What could I do or sing? Sticking with the songs the band knew would make our lives easier. I had to get dressed and speak to them.

"By the time you shower and change, the hotel will have delivered our breakfast," Megan said.

I opened my mouth to object, but she stopped me.

"You need to eat, and the concert band won't arrive until after 9 a.m. anyway. Now go shower." Megan pointed to the bathroom door.

I listened to her reluctantly and cried in the shower. The water hid my tears. I felt like I was losing an enormous piece of me. I could no longer sing the songs I had written. The ones I fought with producers over the lyrics for. Producers? Jordan's cryptic advice made me realize something. I dried my tears and most of my hair.

Questions swirled around my head. Would the concert band go for my plan? Would Solar Harmony? What I planned was an enormous gamble. I never played things safe as Cam. Why should I start now as me?

"You're surprisingly upbeat for not being able to sing your music," Megan noted as I hummed to myself.

"I figured out what Jordan meant. He was right." I bit into my toast and pushed my plate aside to work while I ate.

"What did he mean?"

"You'll find out during my set, maybe before. I need to speak to the band."

"Which one?"

"Both. I need to do something." I wrote more notes on the blank music sheets.

"Will you tell me?"

I should keep her waiting, but she had been kind to me. I told her the rundown of my plan.

"Who knows about your song?" Megan asked.

"Only Rick Davis. He and I were arguing over lyrics the last time we met. Before I embarked on the tour, we were supposed to return to resolve it. I'm not sure why the fake Cam didn't release the song. It was mostly ready." I liked the new nickname Megan had given to the other me.

"Won't your label know the song?"

I shook my head. "Rick won't let any songs be released without his final say, and he'd rather see it die than have it go to someone he felt was not worthy of it. The record label never heard it." If they had, it would've been out already. Any song he co-wrote goes platinum. He held the title of world's most sought-after producer.

"Will singing the song anger him?"

"Most likely, he might never forgive me. Unless I make sure the song is perfect," I answered.

"How will you?" Megan asked. She had changed out of her PJs and now wore a suit. She had styled her hair perfectly.

I needed to brush my hair again and use the product she had bought me to help with the frizz. "Finish the music." I had not done this for a year, and now I planned to in a few hours. How crazy could I get?

Chapter Twenty

Jordan

The Same Day

I woke up before noon, in better spirits than I had been in a long time. Gabriel and I had at least proved a few days ago I didn't send the texts like the fake Cam claimed.

Another matter made my gut churn. My mom hadn't called me, and she wouldn't contact me until after the police dropped the charges. Our relationship would never recover.

I turned on the news as I made lunch. The kitchen had two of almost everything, including sinks, refrigerators, and stoves. I fought for a microwave and hid it each time after use since it didn't go with the tan gourmet style. Why was heating food on the stove fancy?

After I sat on the island to eat my mac and cheese, a special news report broke in with fake Cam filing an injunction against Cobie. The crazy part was that it worked. Singers did covers of songs all the time, and if they wanted to sell it, they needed a special license to ensure the original copyright holder received payment.

I couldn't call Cobie to tell her what my tip meant, so I decided on the next best thing.

Danny answered on the first ring, "Were you sleeping the day away or what? Your girl was in trouble."

"Was?" I asked him. Hope rose inside me.

"Yeah, she and the band are practicing the song she wrote. Royal isn't happy and is demanding we give her less time. I'm trying to find a solution to make him content. How do you deal with this bullshit?"

"For Royal, I play to his ego."

"How? Ow." Danny said something to someone on the other end.

"Hi, Jordan. We can't wait for you to return," Brittany said. She must've snatched the phone from Danny. I imagined her hitting him to get it.

"Thanks, Brittany. I hope to clear up the accusation soon," I said.

"Good. You need to get back. Your boy is losing too much weight, and I have to take in his clothes."

"Give me back my phone, woman," Danny demanded.

I laughed. Those two always bickered like a couple. I thought my boy had a thing for her, and she the same. They never made a move on their feelings. Dating and breaking up while working together could get awkward. Now I understood why Cobie wanted to wait.

"What do I do about Royal?" Danny asked after he got the phone back.

"Give Royal a lead on another song. You'll keep him happy and yourself sane," I answered.

"What song?"

"Any of the ones you don't feel like singing?"

"Is that why you sang less? Man, you need to stop babying him."

"I called it keeping the peace. Besides, you hate singing, *You're My One and Only*, and Royal will love it," I said.

"We're not singing that song tonight," Danny pointed out.

"Tell the band you would like to make a change because of Cobie. Some crap about how Royal is helping. He'll vote yes since you gave him a song. Baylee won't vote, and Jay will go with what you say." After he messaged me, but I didn't tell my best friend. Danny needed to find his way to run the band. Until he did, he would get stressed. They all had big personalities, and Baylee's was finally shining, which I was glad to witness.

"I still don't get how you do it."

"You'll figure it out. Stop trying to be like me."

"Then I shouldn't give Royal a song tonight?" Danny asked.

"Up to you," I answered. I did a lot of compromising to concentrate on the music.

"You're no help. At least tell me the police dropped the charges and you're coming back tonight."

"Not yet." I caught him up on what Gabriel and I discovered.

"Why would Dick's daughter work here?" Danny cried out in pain, probably from Brittany again.

"No clue. I was hoping someone with our concert would know," I answered.

"I'll check with Deedee and get back to you."

Man, I should've thought of Deedee. Between her and Brittany, they knew the gossip on set. "Please do. Break a leg tonight."

"I'll break both." Danny said goodbye and hung up.

I finished eating my food, figuring he would need to finish with Brittany before he spoke to Deedee. He might also meet with the band to stop Royal's complaining. Each time he appeared on stage in a bad mood, he ruined the mood of the audience. I should've warned Danny. Oh, well. He needed to figure things out on his own, anyway.

Ever since the debacle with fake Cam, I never tried to write music. She had zapped my creativity, and with the proof of me not texting her, I sensed my creative juices flowing. I washed my dishes and cleaned up after myself.

My studio needed a deep cleaning, and I settled on getting the papers I had scattered everywhere picked up. I should've let the cleaners come in here earlier this week. I needed to be tidier when I had a visitor. Only one person came to my mind, but I quickly brushed the idea away. She would be busy with her lawsuit soon. Why hadn't her attorney filed yet?

I sat in my comfy black egg chair and twirled my pen between my fingers. My music showed my emotions and experiences. *Hey, Girl* originated from my initial clubbing experience with the band. I had written *Sorry, I Can't Love You* after a stalker had broken into the last mansion the band and I stayed in. Why hadn't we gotten homes for ourselves? We could definitely afford mansions. If I didn't live with Royal, I would never see him unless we had a band meeting or something. Maybe Baylee too. Which reminded me I had to check on him.

He responded with his typical doing good.

I documented my emotions on paper, as I once had done. Anger at being accused of something I didn't do. I was sad about losing my relationship with my mom and not speaking to the woman I fell in love with. Did Cobie share the same feelings? Dick had thrown her away, yet she still smiled and carried on.

My phone rang, and I jumped at the sound. I checked the caller, answering, "Hey, man. What did you find out?"

"I need to make this quick. Deedee checked, and someone on the staff vouched for Dick's daughter. We're short staffed, so everyone got asked if they knew anyone who wanted a job," Danny answered.

"Is she still there?" The hair on the back of my neck stiffened, and I rubbed it to chase the feeling away.

"Nah, I checked and instructed Cole to issue her a permanent ban, preventing her from working for us ever again. He's keeping this a secret."

"Will Deedee and Brittany?"

"Totally, they're pretending to be amateur detectives and are excited to assist," Danny answered. I bet he rolled his eyes.

"Will Deedee tell Derek?" I asked. Spouses didn't keep things from each other.

"Do you think Derek invited Dick's daughter to work with us? We know Derek hasn't even looked at another woman ever since he met Deedee."

"You're right. I'm more concerned with everyone finding out someone sabotaged me."

"Why? We should let the betrayer sweat."

"Why do you keep answering your questions?" I asked.

"I'm running late, and I want to end our conversation sooner. Keep up," Danny answered.

"Whatever, jackass." I smiled. Danny's words weren't harsh, for he had a lot on his plate. Leading the band and now running an investigation wasn't easy.

"Deedee and Brittany will keep us updated on their progress. I gotta go."

Before I could say goodbye, he hung up. I looked at the time, and sadness filled me. We should hang out. Did he change the set or did he keep it the same? I would find out tomorrow when websites released the list.

Someone rang our doorbell.

Who was there? The band was gone, and I had put no one on the permanent list besides Cobie and my lawyer. She was at the show five hours away. He never visited unless he called first. I hoped the police wouldn't come to arrest me.

I glanced through the peephole.

Gabriel checked his expensive watch and rang the bell again.

I opened the door.

He handed me my phone and then pushed his way inside, saying, "Where can we watch the news?"

"What's going on?" I asked him. My mouth ran dry.

"You need to watch the news."

I showed him into the living and used the remote to reveal the hidden TV.

He snatched the remote from me, turning the channel to the local news.

"Captain William Skully is making a formal statement on the accusations from Cam with the lead singer of Solar Harmony," the reporter said.

The screen flipped to a much older man standing next to the two detectives who had interviewed me. "My name is William Skully, and I am the police captain. I'm here with my two detectives, Brady Venma and Brooke Reyers, the lead investigators in the alleged sexual assault of Cam. We take every accusation seriously and investigate thoroughly. We have found Jordan Space couldn't possibly have committed the crime on the night Cam said."

The reporters in the room freaked out and asked questions.

"Yes, we're aware of text messages between Cam and Mr. Space, but we do not believe the admission of guilt is relevant in this case because of the evidence. Mr. Space couldn't have committed the crime. He was with his band and someone else during the time of the allegations, and the GPS location from his sport vehicle proves it," Skully answered one question. He licked his lips and continued on. "We'll address wither or not we'll file charges against Cam in this matter at another time."

The screen cut back to the reporter. "You heard it here first. Jordan Space isn't guilty."

Gabriel turned off the TV and said, "Try not to get into trouble for a while."

"I won't," I told him. My body grew numb from anger, sadness, and now happiness.

"Doubt I could convince you to sue fake Cam, could I?"

"I'll let you know later." All I wanted was to watch Cobie's performance and join my band on set tonight.

"Make sure you don't hang around fake Cam alone, whoever she may be."

"I swear I won't." I held out my hand, and we shook.

"Cobie has been getting death threats, so keep her close," Gabriel said.

"What? Who would want to hurt her?" My mind raced at the possibilities, and the one that stuck out the most was Dick.

"Cobie said she is Cam. Cam's fans aren't too happy." I'd been wrong.

"Why can't they tell she's Cam?"

"Do you want your idol to have flaws? A lot of them are questioning everything, and what Cobie sings and says is making more sense to them that she is Cam," Gabriel answered.

"How are we protecting her?" I asked.

"My firm has hired bodyguards."

"Is her life in danger?"

"Yes, we have concerns." Gabriel parted.

I watched his car pull out of the long driveway, and I battle cried. Freedom never felt so damn good. I needed to call Cobie to make sure she was safe and my band. My old cell was dead, so I dialed Danny, since I didn't have her number memorized. I reached Danny's voicemail and informed him that the police had dropped their investigation.

The band might need to vote for me to return, but they couldn't keep me away from the venue. I needed to watch them and Cobie perform.

About thirty minutes into my drive, Danny called. I answered, saying, "Hey, man."

"Don't hey me. Are your flying down here or what?" Danny asked.

"Driving like a madman. I doubt I'll make soundcheck, but I should get to the stage before we sing if the band will let me."

"We already voted, and you're in."

"You better get your ass here," Jay said into the phone.

"I'm on the way. How is everything there?" I wanted to ask more about Cobie and the investigation.

"You mean Cobie? She's thrilled you're no longer canceled. You should call her," Danny said. He wouldn't discuss the other matter with our band in the room.

I didn't believe any of them had sabotaged me, but I couldn't take the chance. One week of being a celebrity pariah had made me much more cautious. I never wanted to go through something like this again. Royal was right about getting nondisclosures from the women he slept with.

"My phone is dead. I'm waiting until I have a better charge, and I also want to surprise her. Please don't tell her I'm on the way," I said.

"We'll keep the secret for you," Danny said.

"Why doesn't Jordan want to tell Cobie he's joining us?" Baylee asked. Danny must've placed me on speaker, and I wished he'd let me know. I didn't normally talk badly about my band except for Royal.

"I want to surprise her." I cleared my throat, and my heart overflowed with emotion. "Thank you for believing me. Few have, and you don't know what that means to me."

"You don't need to express gratitude to me. What I said was my fault. You shouldn't blame yourself for my mistake," Baylee said.

"No, Bay. Fake Cam did this. I learned a long time ago not to say anything I don't want repeated." I should have kept my thoughts to myself next time.

"You're welcome," Danny said.

Jay said the same thing, and Royal did, too. When push came to shove, we really were there for each other. We had each lived through something hard, like Jay losing his mother. Danny lost his brother. Royal lost his father. So far, only Baylee had been unaffected by such tragedy.

"No more chick moments, and get your ass here." Danny hung up before I could thank them again. They would be there for me when I had to go low contact with my mom.

I continued to drive with the words from my new song playing through my head. Once, I had a half battery I called Cobie. She picked up and sounded excited to hear from me. We spoke for thirty minutes before I lied to her, telling her I had to go. She needed to rest her voice for tonight.

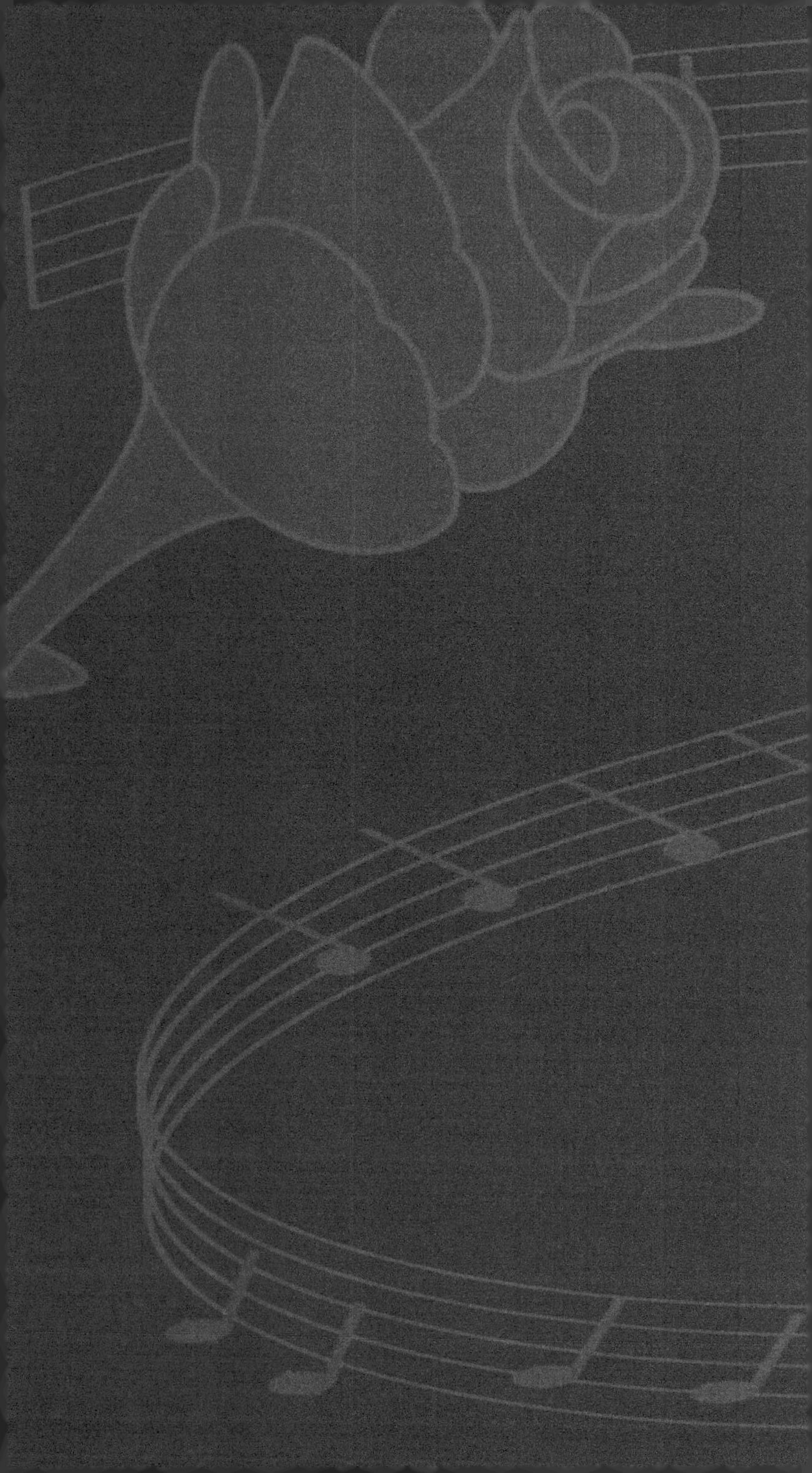

Chapter Twenty-One

Cobie

"**M**y last song tonight is called *Heart to Heart* by me. I worked on this song with Rick Davis, and I hope he can forgive me for releasing it without his permission." I figured out the hiccup we had and changed a few more lines to fit the melody better. After my life this past year, I had grown.

The piano played, and when it stopped, I sang. I had my heart on my sleeve and wanted to talk with those important to me. I cherished them.

After I finished, the crowd erupted in screams and applauds.

I had never bared my soul in a song before. My music was usually upbeat, fun, and relatable. This tested me, like Rick liked to do. After every session, I told Dick I never wanted to work with him again. A few days later, I scheduled another session after an idea came to me. Rick and I would hash it out, and I repeated the whole not working with him sentiment again.

"Thank you, Rick, for making me into a better singer, and thank you to my fans for supporting me. Solar Harmony, thank you for giving me my voice back." I bowed to everyone, and then the lights turned off. I headed off the stage after my eyes adjusted.

Jordan held roses, and tears streamed down his face. Had my song touched his heart, or was he happy to see me?

My bodyguards waited near him.

I signaled for them to move away as I ran to Jordan, wrapping him in my arms. I didn't think he had enough time to get here for his concert, let alone watch mine.

He held me and then lifted my head, kissing me.

I kissed him back. I broke us apart, realizing he had to go on stage. "You need to go. You have a concert," I told him.

"Don't remind me." Jordan pecked me.

"Your fans have waited long enough for your return."

He set his forehead on mine. "I care about one fan."

"Who says I am one?"

"You will once I release the next song. Two songs." Jordan smirked at me.

"Good, I can't wait to hear them," I said. Being this close to him made my heart beat faster.

"We agreed to wait until after the tour to date, but I can't wait that long. Not after everything. I missed you so much."

My throat thickened. "I don't want to wait either."

His face brightened, and he ran a hand down the back of my neck. "Will you be here once I'm done?"

"I will."

Someone cleared their throat next to us.

I jumped at the same time as Jordan pulled me in closer.

My bodyguards shifted the weight between their feet because I had told them earlier not to hurt the band.

Danny said, "Jordan, we need to go."

Jordan kissed me again.

I pulled away, and heat flushed through my face as everyone stared at us. Our relationship would definitely be out. "I'll be here when you're done. Rock on."

Jordan squeezed my hand one last time before he headed away with his band. He had worn a gray long sleeve shirt and light blue jeans. He looked good, and he needed to shave, but no one cared. Men could look rugged, and women couldn't in the industry.

"You and Jordan?" Megan asked. How long had she been standing there?

"Pretty much why I agreed to no contact. I didn't want to hurt his case," I answered.

"You should cool it for at least a month. The police will believe you're in cahoots."

"Cahoots? Like we're some mastermind cartoon criminals?"

"Always a possibility."

"Didn't they drop the charges because of my photograph and his vehicle's location?" I asked.

"Mostly your testimony. I have a feeling fake Cam will try something else, like she messed up the date or something." Megan folded her arms and strummed her biceps.

"That's why we should sue her, my old manager's label, and the record company." If I tarnished her name, she couldn't destroy anyone's career. I forgave a lot of things except for what she had tried to do. She had somehow picked the day Jordan left the mansion alone. I checked, and he hadn't left many times by himself with prepping and promoting for his tour.

"We're starting Monday."

"What will happen next?"

"We'll discuss the details this weekend. Your man is heading to the stage," Megan whispered to me.

Jordan stopped to get a microphone and waved it at me. He smiled big. Not being able to sing had devastated me. I couldn't comprehend what it had done to him, and I never wanted him to experience it again.

He stepped onto the stage, and his fans clapped so hard it sounded like thunder. "I'm sorry for any pain my absence has caused you. I am back, and I have no plans to leave," he told them.

"We love you, Jordan!" a fan called.

"I love you, too." He wiped away the tears from his eyes. "Thank you to Solar Harmony and our concert band for carrying on without me. Here is our first song of the night."

Jordan sang the song he had written after meeting me.

I closed my eyes and swayed to the music. If he sang more songs like this, I was a fan, his number one fan.

The song ended, and I clapped along with the fans.

Royal took over as lead for the next two songs.

I remembered Danny had sung most of the lyrics for the last time they sang. Why had they changed the lead singer? I preferred Danny, but I never got along with Royal since he acted hostile toward me every chance he got. A vote was called to let me play the song I wrote this morning, and he had lost. The concert band had wanted to try the song. They had accomplished the impossible.

Jay sang the next one after Royal stepped back. I should give Royal a chance, since he hung out with Jordan a lot.

Listening to the different styles made me realize how much experience Jordan had. He brought out the best in his fellow members. When Danny got too low, Jordan changed his tone to balance everyone out to harmonize.

The song concluded, and then someone plunged the stage into darkness.

I moved out of the way.

Megan followed me, asking me, "Why are we over here?"

"This is the real action," I answered her.

One by one, the workers swarmed the band members as they left the stage. The men removed their shirts. After wiping the sweat from their chests, workers gave them fresh shirts similar to their old ones.

Jordan looked around and caught me watching him. He smiled at me before I looked away.

"Wow, this is busy," Megan said once the band was back on stage. We had stayed in my dressing room the last time. I couldn't handle listening to Solar Harmony without Jordan.

"This is nothing. The staff had already put out everything the band needed for the next change. I've seen singers do full makeup, outfit, and stage in minutes for their performance," I said.

"Did you perform?"

"If the tour called for it. I miss planning everything and working with the coordinators." I at least changed in my room to keep my identity a secret.

"This explains how someone might have framed Jordan."

"What?" I asked. Had I missed something?

"He didn't tell you?" Megan asked. She held my gaze for a second and looked away. "I shouldn't say anything."

"You saw our first meeting. We barely had time to kiss, let alone talk. Please tell me."

"He should."

"I doubt he will." He had an annoying habit of sacrificing himself.

"You can ask someone else." Megan inclined her head toward the workers.

I searched for what she tried to tell me and spotted Brittany. Would she know about Jordan being framed? If she didn't, surely Deedee would.

"Come on, I need to speak to someone." I tried to hurry away, but my bodyguards stopped me. Okay, I understood them being around me at the police station, but no one cared what I did here, and I was more in the way.

"Where are you going?" Tim asked me.

"To speak to Deedee in makeup. You already checked her out earlier," I answered.

He studied me for a moment. "Let's go." He turned on his heel, and the crowd parted for him.

I trailed behind him with Brad and Megan on my side, with the two other bodyguards trailing behind me. "Isn't this overkill?" I whispered to Megan.

She shook her head.

I stopped in my tracks, and Brad pulled me to the side, out of the way. "What's going on?" I asked Megan.

Tim must've used his bodyguard sense to stop and turn around.

"What's going on?" I asked again.

Megan pressed her lips together.

"There has been a threat to your life," Brad answered.

"What threat? What happened?" I asked. Panic rose inside me. What if I were around Deedee and someone tried to kill me? What if they missed? She and the baby could die.

Megan glared at Brad and answered, "My firm has gotten death threats because of you claiming to be Cam. If they knew where you lived, your home would have them, too. The calling and mail have gotten less the more you perform. More people realize you're the real Cam."

"You can't keep these things from me," I said.

"I'm sorry. I didn't want to stress you out more. You have enough on your plate as it is," Megan said. Her face softened, and she shifted her weight from one foot to the other.

"Please don't keep things like this from me. I can't lose my trust in you," I said.

"I won't from now on," Megan promised.

I knocked on Deedee's door, and when she told us to enter, Tim did first.

"Wait out here," Brad said as he moved in front of me.

Another bodyguard joined Tim inside Deedee's room.

"Thank you for telling me the truth," I said to Brad.

"You deserve to know what's happening in your life," Brad said.

At least someone was looking out for me. If Tim or Megan tried to fire him, I'd be pissed.

"All clear," Tim said.

I entered the room.

"Give me a hug," Deedee said. I did, and she whispered in my ear, "Are you okay?"

"I'm good. The bodyguards are here to protect me from the fake Cam's fans," I whispered back.

"Why do I get the honor?" She rubbed her belly and shifted in her chair.

"Who framed Jordan?" I asked.

"He told you?" Deedee asked.

"No, I did. We need to tell Cobie the truth," Megan answered.

Deedee gave me the breakdown of the investigation. Brittany and she looked at their staff, those who handled deliveries, and were custodial. They had a suspect already with Dick's daughter.

"I met her once. She's a spoiled brat and only did what her father told her," I said.

"Did her father send her to work here?" Deedee asked.

"Maybe," I answered. Dick was capable of anything.

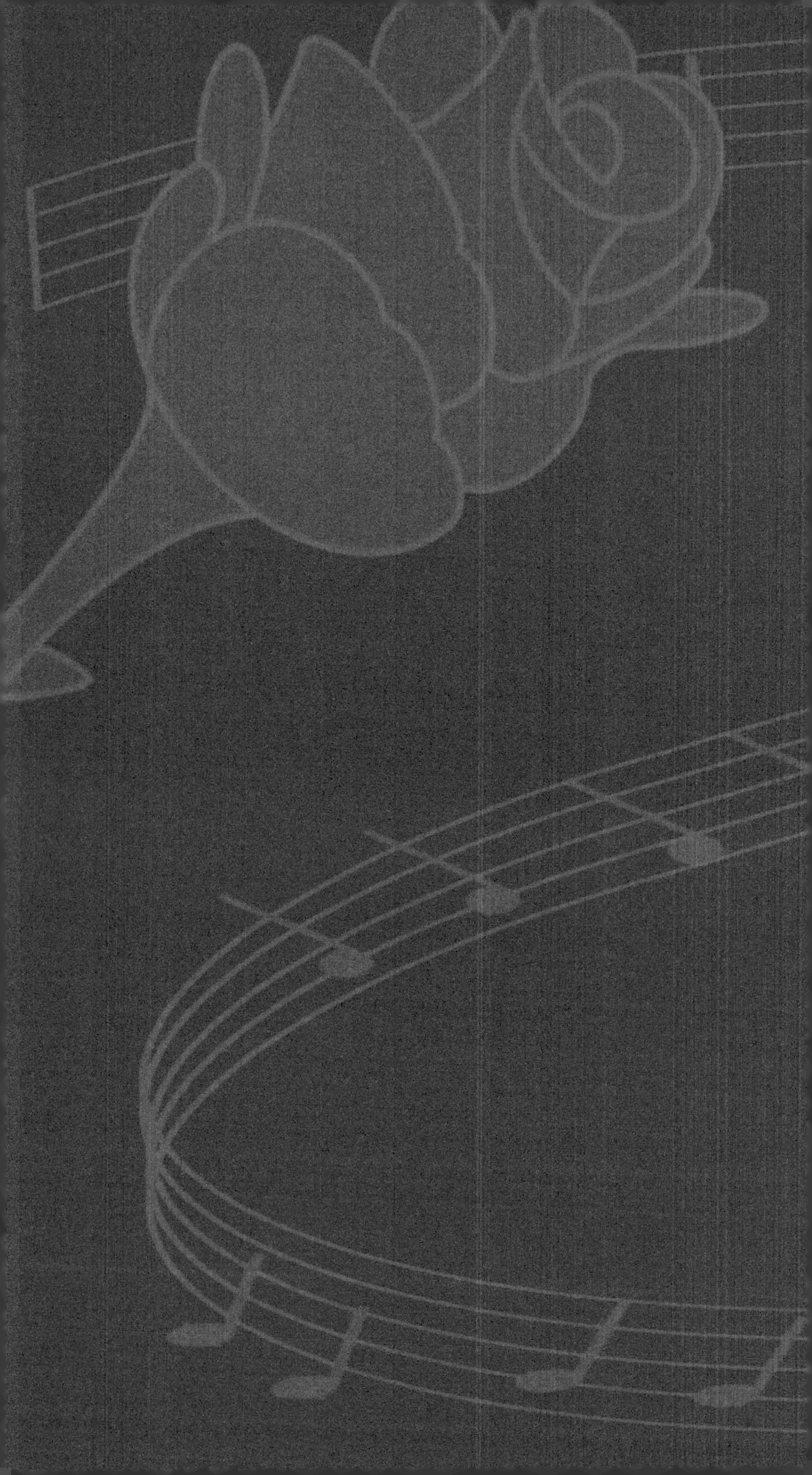

Chapter Twenty-Two

Jordan

Nothing compared to being on stage with my friends and in front of my fans. Sweat dripped from my hair, and I loved every minute, even the stinging in my eyes. I adjusted my voice when Danny got too low and when Royal changed the lyrics. He had an annoying habit of doing whatever he wanted.

We thanked the crowd, saying we'd be back. The three songs we played ended far too fast for me. I couldn't wait to return for the rest. I never wanted music to be stolen from me again.

Brittany handed me a towel to clean the sweat off my face and chest.

She kept on glancing over at Danny as one of her people got a little too close to him.

"Are you nipping the flirting in the bud?" I asked her as I unbuttoned my shirt. I had drenched my undershirt in the short time we sang.

"What?" Brittany asked as if she didn't see or understand.

I nodded in Danny's direction.

"He isn't my boyfriend. He can flirt with whomever he wants," Brittany said. Her lips twitched into a frown, and she handed me my clean shirts.

"You like him. Talk to him," I told her. I wouldn't tell her he liked her too, bro code.

"I can't date those I work with."

"What's wrong with it?"

Brittany tilted her head down, giving me a death glare. "How are you and Cobie doing? Will you date her?"

"I hope so," I answered. At the mention of her name, I searched for her. She hadn't been around when the set ended. Where did she go? Was she safe? What if the threat against her somehow worked backstage and got to her? I needed to keep her close to keep her safe. Even if she had four bodyguards watching her back.

"She's with Deedee and will return soon," Brittany said.

The tension in my shoulders released. No one messed with Deedee, and not because she dated Derek. She was on her own level.

"You like Cobie a lot, don't you?" Brittany whispered.

"I do," I admitted and experienced discomfort.

"Cobie does, too. I can tell, and Deedee is catching her up on the issue here." Brittany glanced around nervously.

I ground my teeth and kept my voice even. "I didn't want Cobie involved."

"Honey, you're too late."

"What do you mean?"

"If she hadn't risked her job, you'd be in jail. Who would've come forward against the other Cam?" Brittany asked.

"Fake Cam," I corrected Brittany. I took a moment to let her words sink in. Yeah, Cobie had believed me even as the evidence mounted against me. I bet those closest to me had already blocked me except for my band. Even after the police dropped my charges, my mom still hadn't called. I'd given Cole my phone, so she might've called me during the concert.

"How many women would take on fake Cam?" Brittany glanced over my shoulder. "Our stage manager is waving at everyone to get back. Answer my question before you go."

"No one." Not the last woman I dated. She had left me because of my overjealous fans, and I didn't blame her. They acted as if they owned me.

"Exactly. Cobie is one of us, and I can't believe she is Cam. I dressed her." Brittany squealed and jumped up and down.

I covered my ears. "Damn, girl. I need my hearing for my music."

"You'll lose a lot more than hearing if you don't get on stage. Someone is about to have a conniption." Brittany pushed me with one hand away and picked up the clothes I had discarded.

I hurried to the band. Someone placed a microphone in my hand, and I thanked them. "Sorry," I told our stage manager, Chris.

"Get out there then," Chris said.

"Jordan, rock on!" Cobie called from behind me. I knew her voice anywhere.

After spotting her near the back next to a woman in a suit, I followed behind Danny, catching up to him.

"Why do you have every woman?" he muttered as he passed me.

I caught up to him and whispered, "I want Cobie, and you should make a move on Brittany. She likes you." He and I had a bro code, not her and me.

"She likes our lighting gal." Danny sighed and took his spot.

I followed him. "Pretty sure Brittany doesn't and likes you."

"She doesn't date anyone she works with. Now get in your spot before you make us look like idiots."

"You two already are," Royal said behind us.

"Learned from the best." I flashed him a grin despite him not being able to see it.

The band played and Baylee sang.

The lights popped on, making our fans go wild. They loved it when he took the lead.

He flinched when he sang, "I am a sinner and I don't mean to be." His voice cracked and tears welled in his eyes.

I placed my hand on his shoulder during the chorus. "Sins we love and can't stop."

"I can't stop sinning," Baylee sang.

Danny moved to his other side and sang the next line with him. "I don't plan to stop."

Jay ended up next to me and Royal on the opposite side, near Danny. We weren't where we were supposed to be, but Baylee needed us. Our band sang together, "Sins we love and can't stop. We try, but everything we do is a sin."

The crowd joined in, swaying together.

I hugged Baylee after the song ended and sang the opening lines to *Hey, Girl*. No one could be in a bad mood after hearing it.

By the time the song ended, Baylee had a genuine smile on his face. He sang his lines for our next song without issue.

We exited the stage for a quick change of clothes.

"Wait, Bay," I said.

He handed his mic to a worker and told me, "I messed up."

"No, I did. I should've picked another song instead of the sinner one," Danny corrected him.

"Let us know when you're ready to sing it," I told Baylee. I clapped him on the back.

"Why have you forgiven me? I could've ruined your life," Baylee said.

"You did nothing needing forgiving. You need to forgive yourself," I pointed out.

"What if I can't? What if I make another mistake again?" Baylee sniffed and rubbed his nose.

"We'll find a solution together," I told him.

"We will," Danny agreed.

"Totally," Jay said.

"Whatever." Royal rolled his eyes before heading to change his clothes. His wearing a leather jacket had him sweating the most.

Our fans screamed for one more song, like they did after every concert. We always gave in to them once more before we had to go. Tonight was no different. I stepped off stage, feeling the best I had in a long while.

Cobie waved at me.

"I need to change my clothes. Can we talk after?" I asked her.

She nodded and glanced at the woman with her. Her lawyer, probably?

"I'll meet you in your dressing room in ten," I told Cobie. After kissing her on the forehead, I made my way to mine. I loved the post-show adrenaline rush the first night after a concert in the same town. Usually, I hit the gym at the hotel, but this time I wanted to do something with Cobie. Going for a walk in disguise would be great, even with her bodyguards following.

Danny had his shirt off and removed his jeans in our dressing room. "What are we doing tonight? I feel like hitting the casinos or something," he said.

"Put some clothes on before you make plans," Royal said as he exited the bathroom. The ends of his black hair dripped. Our fans would break into our dressing room more if they learned we showered at the venue after the concert. A few of us waited for the bus or at our hotels. Mostly because the bad boy prince always used up the hot water.

I wouldn't tonight. "I'm calling dibs on the next shower."

"Why? You got a date?" Danny asked. His blue eyes twinkled with mischief, and he grinned at me.

"You could too if you grew a pair," I answered.

Danny's smile vanished from his face.

"A pair of what?" Baylee glanced between the two of us.

"Brains. Between the two of them, they share one." Royal sat on the couch and had to readjust his spot, since he had put on his trench coat. I should tell him he looked like an idiot.

Before anyone objected, I took the next shower in record time. I would've gotten a medal in it if the Olympics had it.

Cole waited in the room, and a grave expression crossed his face.

I had to stop myself from groaning. Honestly, unless he smiled, he always had bad news. My heart pounded against my ribcage. Had the fake Cam tried to accuse me again?

"What's up?" I asked. My voice sounded raw.

"We need to talk. The whole band and me." Cole waited for us to sit and carried a chair to sit in front of us.

"Can I shower first?" Danny stole a glance at me. The bastard wanted me even later meeting with Cobie.

"You can," Cole answered.

"I have plans tonight, and we need sleep before tomorrow's show. If this is important, Danny can wait," I said.

"Glad to have you back." Cole took out a stack of papers and handed each one out. He set his briefcase on the floor. "If you have a date or start dating someone, ask them to sign this nondisclosure agreement. Otherwise, you shouldn't date them. We don't need another incident after the last one."

"Only a date?" Jay asked.

"Yes," Cole answered. He stared at Royal. "If you need more, let me know prior. I don't care who you date or screw as long as they're of age and willing to sign. You won't work alone with anyone without at least two of us in the room."

The new rule was because of me, and I was happy with it. No one could ever accuse me again.

"Why should we? We didn't cause any issues, and I already get NDAs," Royal said.

"The world has changed, and this will stop any damage before it happens. I never wanted to place restrictions on you like this, but we can't have incidents," Cole said as he chose his last word carefully.

"So, Jordan messes up, and we get punished?" Royal rolled his papers and tapped his leg with them.

"If you wrote our songs, fake Cam would've blamed you instead," Danny pointed out.

"I'm not stupid enough to allow that to happen," Royal said.

"First off, I'm not a complete idiot. Too trusting, I'd say. One meeting with fake Cam and she accused me. These new restrictions are a good idea." I hated the nondisclosure, but I had to protect myself and the band.

"Why are you calling her fake?" Royal asked.

"Because Cobie *is* Cam," I answered.

"You believe her? She's lying to get free publicity. Every year someone claims to be Cam." Royal shook his head.

"Listen to Cam's recording and Cobie's concert. She is Cam, and I was a fool for not realizing it when I first heard her sing," I said.

"Jordan knows music better than any of us. I believe she is Cam," Jay said.

"Cobie has another two weeks with us. So far, she hasn't damaged the tour and has helped Jordan. If she does the first, I'll ask her to leave," Cole said.

"We should look for someone new already," Royal said.

"What's your problem with her?" I asked him.

"Since she joined the tour, you demoted me," Royal answered.

"You being on probation has nothing to do with Cobie. The band decided, not her." Danny held out his hands with his palms up.

"Of course, you'd be on Jordan's side." Royal crossed his legs and his arms over his chest.

"You decided we should do a contest for our opener when we had three picks. You can't blame anyone but yourself for being demoted." Danny planted his feet.

Royal opened his mouth and then stormed out of the room.

"Did I take our conversation too far?" Danny glanced at everyone left for an answer.

"You did. Bands shouldn't fight," Cole answered.

"We shouldn't, but Royal has been extra lately. He needs someone to put him in his place." I was glad not to have to do it. Maybe Danny should stay on as co-leader or take over for me. I could work on the music. Although I would miss hanging out with Cole.

"Make sure you get signatures for anyone you date," Cole said.

"What if we don't date? Like only kissed?" Jay kept glancing at me.

"Will you get serious? Will you date?" Cole rubbed his face, and dark circles were around his eyes. His tan suit hung loose on him from his weight loss. My issues must've caused him more problems than I realized.

Jay shrugged and continued to look at me. He might want to know what Cobie and I were doing.

I wanted to also, and I should talk with her to find out.

"If my company has to release a statement stating you're with someone or not, get the damn contract signed." Cole set his head in his hands.

"You heard the man. Get in bed at a decent time since we have a concert tomorrow," I told my members.

Cole lifted his head. "I'm glad you're back. I'll send you the details of your hotel room reservations. Does anyone need a ride there?"

"I will, and I'll let you know when I'm ready." I told them goodbye before they stopped me.

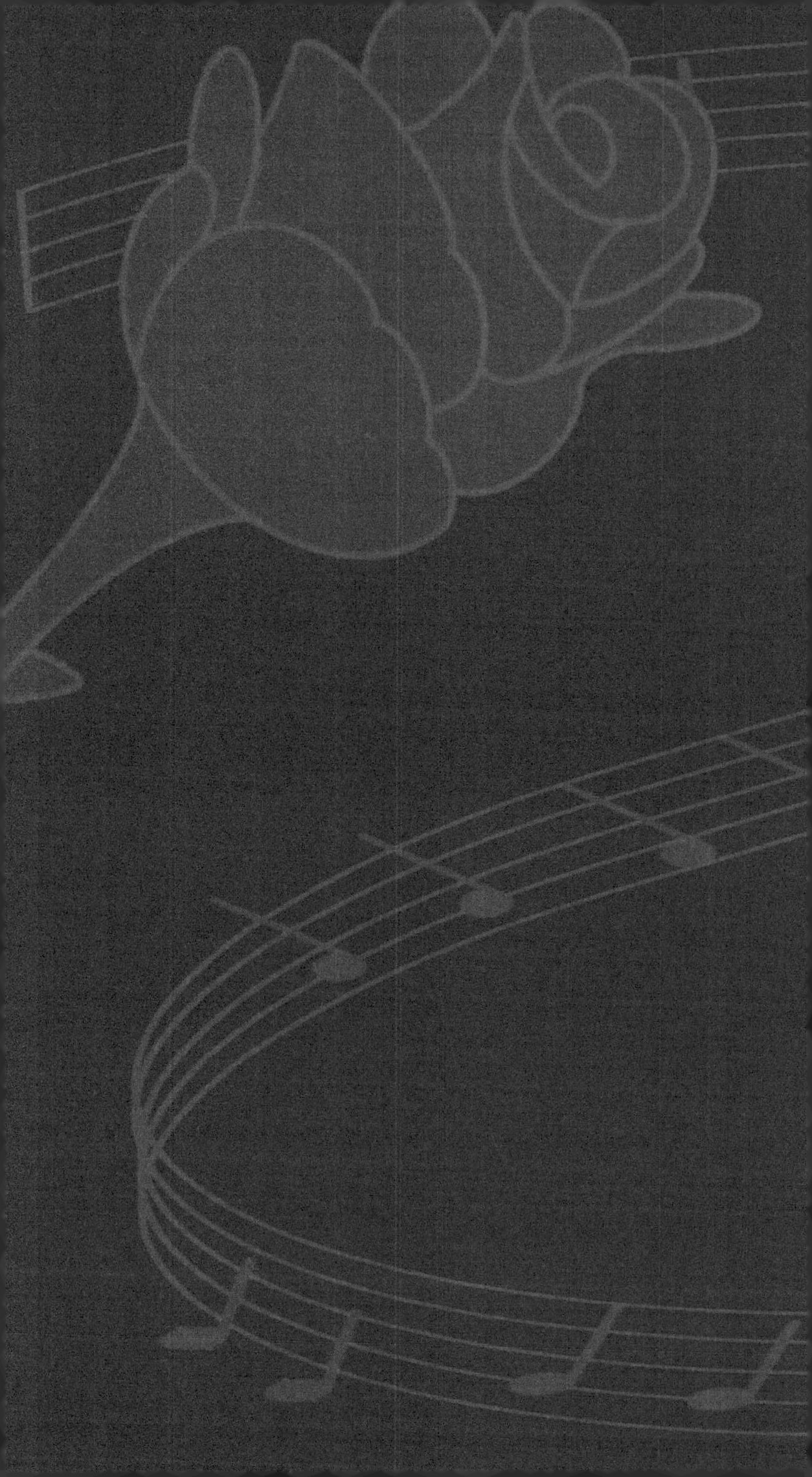

Chapter Twenty-Three

Cobie

"How long does it take to change clothes?" Megan kept glancing at her expensive watch.

"Depends on the band. For example, my manager would tell me what I did wrong and how to improve for the next show. Someone would then escort me to the hotel or bus. I'd wash up there and never in the dressing room." I adjusted the strap on my smartwatch, a knockoff of my old one. It needed replacing, but it had to wait until I had money. I had tagged my newer watch to my old phone with Cam, and I couldn't release it without Dick's permission.

"Ex-manager. Refer to him always in the past tense."

"Okay."

"We shouldn't give him legal standing once you're proven to be Cam."

"Will I be?" I asked.

"We're suing him and your record label on Monday. One excellent piece of evidence can break or make a case," Megan answered.

"Is that why you took my first mask?"

"Sorry. I didn't want it to get lost since we're using it as evidence. Do you have anything else?"

"My old phone and watch."

"Can I see them?" she asked.

I handed her them. They had died a while ago, and I never bought a charger for them. My new watch wasn't compatible with my old one. Dick had made me get a certain brand that I disliked. With it, I had to tap multiple times to do what took my cheap cell one tap.

Megan tried to turn on my phone. The dead battery light displayed. "What cell do you have now?"

I showed it to her.

"I'm getting you a new one for security and a new number." She typed something into her phone.

"My operating system, right?" I showed her my phone, not the expensive one.

"If you like it, yes. Tell me what you want, and I'll get it for you."

"I need nothing except—" I cut myself off. What I wanted seemed silly now, since I had bought one recently.

"What? Please tell me." Megan leaned closer to me, and her light perfume drifted into my nose.

"Dick has my guitar, and I want it back." I had bought it with my first paycheck.

"What kind and how much is it?"

I answered her questions, even though it wasn't worth anything except to me.

"We can sue for it, but you'll be able to afford a new one soon enough," Megan said.

"I want mine. I bought it, and I want it," I said. Like the guitar I had now. It sat next to my backpack.

"We will sue for it then."

"Also, can I borrow some money?"

Megan lifted a perfectly trimmed eyebrow and asked for what.

I explained I wanted to get the staff something when I ended as the opening act. I enjoyed doing it when I ended a tour and planned on keeping the tradition.

"Send me a list and I'll make sure you get it," Megan said.

"Thank you, I swear I'll pay you back," I said.

Someone knocked on the door.

Tim checked before I did. I had forgotten he and the other three bodyguards were there. I should get them something too.

Jordan glanced around the room, and when he spotted me, the smile on his handsome face brightened. "Hey."

"Hi," I said.

"We should give them some space," Megan told my bodyguards. At least she finally explained to me why I had them, and they should be gone once the hostility ended.

After Megan and my bodyguards left, Jordan sat next to me on the couch. "Hey," he said.

"Hi," I said. I giggled, for he was so cute.

"There is so much I want to say to you, but nothing is coming out except for the one word." His face flushed red, and he tightened his grip around a rolled paper.

"I get it, and I'm sorry for what you went through."

"If you hadn't stood up for me, I wouldn't be back. Thank you for telling the truth."

"You don't need to thank me. Celebrities are often targets for allegations like yours." I ran my hand through my hair.

"Not all accusations are false," he pointed out.

"Especially with the ones that come from multiple people." I shuddered at the notion, and he moved closer to me.

"I thought about how I almost lost everything, and you actually did. I hope you can get it back, too."

"If I can't, I can still sing."

"How are you not pissed? I rode a roller coaster of emotions this last week." Jordan set his papers down and took my hand, tracing the lines on my palm.

"I couldn't let go of my anger until I met you. You fight for what you love," I answered. Tears brimmed in my eyes. Every conversation I had with him played through my mind. He loved music as much as or more than I did.

"I'm fighting for you. Not being able to contact you for a week sucked."

"My lawyer, Megan, said not to date you for a month. The police will think I made up your being with me."

"Fuck that. They have the evidence even without you. I don't want to wait because something else will pop up, and I won't be with you again."

"I completely agree," I said.

"My manager asked me to have you sign this." Jordan held up the rolled paperwork he had brought with the words 'nondisclosure agreement' across the top.

"Okay." I held my hand out for it.

He ripped it up and threw it in the trash.

"You need to protect yourself," I told him.

Jordan kissed me, and any objection died on my lips. When we broke apart, he said, "I'm not in a relationship with you to hide anything. I'm in it because I trust you and want to be with you. We'll talk like adults and be open about what we want. Do you feel the same way about me?"

"Yes." I cleared my throat. "You should still protect yourself."

"From you? No, I need to save you from the corporate assholes who hurt you, probably my fans, and the rest of the world. When fake Cam accused me, everyone turned on me, except for you, my band, my lawyer, and Cole. I didn't even try to find out what my recording company said. My mom ignored me."

I gave him a hug and held him tighter.

"You'll never know how much I need this from you," Jordan said as he embraced me back.

I needed his touch, too.

Jordan let me go after a few minutes and wiped at the corner of his eyes. He had red rims around them.

"We need some good news. Do you have any?" I asked.

"I'm writing a song better than the last, and I can't wait for you to hear it," Jordan answered. His expression relaxed, and my spirits immediately improved.

"When you're ready, I'll listen. Might be difficult because of when I'll have court. I doubt Dick will settle. I've sued no one before, so I'm not sure how long that'll take."

"Wish I could help you. When we had a lawsuit, my lawyer handled it, and I only had to be at court for a few days. My attorney said yours is better than him. Trust her."

I set my head against his shoulder and let the final shred of doubt about Megan fall away. "Thank you for the roses tonight and on opening night." I couldn't remember if I had thanked him or not.

"You're welcome. I'm not sure what your favorite flower is," Jordan said.

"I like roses now." A tingling sensation crept up my nape and across my face. His good-smelling cologne wafted into my nose. Why did I ever think he smelled bad?

"I'll have to get you more." He intertwined our fingers and kissed the back of my hand.

We stayed like this until I wanted to do something more, like kiss him. I started by pecking his cheek.

Jordan moved his face, so our lips touched. We shifted to face each other on the couch.

I ran my hands down his back, feeling his toned muscles there. My fingers skimmed the dark navy shirt he wore, and I wanted to do nothing more than rip it off to touch his abs. After seeing them, I needed a better look.

He pulled away. "We'd better stop before we go too far."

Why shouldn't we sleep together? I liked him and no longer wanted to wait. What if something happened again and again? "I don't want to stop," I told him.

Jordan stared at me for a moment. "We need a hotel room. I won't sleep with you for the first time in a dressing room."

"Do you have one, or can you get one?" My lack of funds sucked.

"I do." He held up his phone with a name near here.

The realization of what we wanted to do dawned on me, and my face grew warm. "I have to tell my lawyer and my bodyguards we're leaving together."

"This seems like we have to ask for permission," Jordan said.

"Yeah, it does."

"I'll keep you safe." He kissed me on the forehead and then helped me to stand.

I picked up my backpack, but he grabbed it from me.

His eyebrow lifted as he struggled a little. Almost everything I owned was in there.

"Sorry. You're carrying most of my things. Well, besides this." I hadn't figured out what to leave behind at Megan's mansion yet. I swung my guitar case onto my back. I also had a gym with a locker to store my rollerblades near the park.

"Why? Where do you live? I tried going to your apartment and couldn't find it," Jordan said. When I didn't answer him after a few seconds, he backtracked. "You don't have to tell me if you don't want to."

"Sometimes I lived on the streets or in a shelter. I lost my apartment a few days after we first met." I looked at the floor, which had an interesting design on the carpet.

He gently lifted my face to stare into my eyes. "No more. I can't have you where I don't know you're safe."

"I'm staying with my attorney. She took me in."

"Do you want to stay with her or with me?" Jordan asked.

"We're too early for living together," I answered after a moment. Everything felt a bit rushed, so we needed to slow down. I reminded myself he had offered because I had no place to go. He wanted to help me.

"Nothing we do is too early or too late. We do everything at our pace, no one else's." He kissed me on the forehead.

"I'm fine staying at Megan's. With the lawsuit, I'll have to discuss everything with her."

"If you need a break, go to my place. You're on the permanent guest list, but stay on my side of the mansion. My bedroom is close to my studio. My roommates will have a fit if you sleep in their rooms."

"Thank you."

We left my dressing room to face the music. Everyone probably heard everything, since the walls weren't soundproof.

I pretended they didn't. "Jordan and I want to talk more alone."

"Talk, huh?" Megan asked. She didn't bother to hide a smile.

"Yes, we're hanging out after not being able to for a while," I answered. My heart pounded, and my face felt uncomfortably hot.

"I swear I'll keep her safe. She's the most important person to me." Jordan gripped my hand.

Tim looked him up and down before saying to me, "I can't force a client to take us with, but you can at least keep this on you." He handed me a gadget with a button.

"What does this do?" I took the object.

"It's a panic button that'll send me your location," Tim answered.

"Cobie, I'll send your hotel information if you want to sleep there," Megan said to me.

I thanked her before Jordan and I left.

Chapter Twenty-Four

Jordan

I stopped by my dressing room to grab my things and put on the disguise Cobie had gotten for me.

She giggled and said, "If the picture of you I took got leaked, you couldn't wear this anymore." She toyed with the ends of the long hair.

"Then I'll have to ask you, what else can I do." God, I loved her laugh. I handed her my baseball cap.

"I'm not sure, but I'll think of something." She put the cap on and retook my hand.

"I bet you will."

The cold air hit me when we left the venue. I pulled Cobie closer to me, heading to an SUV. Cole made sure I had a vehicle to take to the hotel. He would never treat me like Dick had treated my woman. The sheer fury inside me hadn't abated ever since I found out. My mind spun with ways to help her, and the one thing her former manager cared about stuck out. I had to hit him where it hurt the most—the money.

Noah asked where to go after Cobie and I settled in.

I gave him the hotel name.

"Do you have a key?" Cobie asked.

"Not yet. I'll have to get one from the front desk," I answered.

"You should get it on your own."

"Why?"

"I doubt your disguise will hold up."

"I don't care if the entire world knows we're dating. Do you?" I asked her.

She rested her head against my shoulder again, and I enjoyed it a lot. The simple touch from her meant a lot to me. "No, but my trial might bring you criticism."

"Doesn't matter to me. I'm more concerned about how my fans will act toward you, and I'll promise to keep you safe from them."

"Can anyone be safe?"

"What do you mean?"

"Scammers, fans, former managers, etc. steal money or turn on anyone in an instant. How can we keep ourselves safe from them?" she asked.

I intertwined our fingers. "We'll rely on each other, like we do now. We want to date, and we will. I'll be there for you as much as possible with your lawsuit."

"You have concerts."

"That's why people invented airplanes and phones."

"Smartass." She smiled at me, and this time her pretty eyes reflected her happiness. I could stare at them forever with the lime-green rims around her pupils.

Noah stopped near the back entrance to the hotel. "The front is worst," he said.

Fans lined up, and the police struggled to keep them at bay. They screamed when they saw the SUV.

"Ready?" I asked Cobie.

She nodded, and her face paled. Her palm was sweaty in my hand.

"Keep your head down, and no one will get a look at our faces. I'll protect you no matter what," I told her.

"Who will protect you?" Cobie stared at me.

"You can, since you're your own knight in shining armor." I had to give her the line she used on me.

She sat up straighter and gave my hand a quick squeeze. "We can protect each other."

The hotel staff ran out and lifted umbrellas, despite no rain.

I asked Noah to borrow his jacket, and he handed it over without question.

"Thank you," I told him. I wrapped it around Cobie, planning on pulling it over her head after we stepped out. "Are you ready?"

"Are you?" she asked. Her voice sounded raw. Hopefully, she didn't catch a cold.

I opened the door as my answer and helped her slip out. I shifted the jacket over her head, taking her hand.

The fans screamed and asked for Cobie and I to show our faces.

The staff hurried us inside the hotel while lights flashed. Someone would post those pictures online.

I thanked the workers for their help.

The manager stepped forward and led us to the front desk.

I took off my wig.

He didn't ask my name as he typed into the computer. He handed me a card that said suite. "I complimentary upgraded your room." Aka, his hotel, had fucked up with someone releasing the news my band stayed here, and he wished to make the situation go away.

"I appreciate it," I told him, even though I didn't feel it. All I wanted to do was keep Cobie safe, and this hotel almost jeopardized that.

The manager led us to the elevator and stuck a card on the floor for the penthouse. He left with a nod.

Once the door closed, Cobie relaxed near me. She set her guitar case on the floor, standing up.

I gently took the jacket off her and folded it before taking her hand again. "I'm sorry about our treatment."

"What do you mean? The staff ushered us inside, and the manager made sure we got to our hotel floor," Cobie said.

The elevator dinged, and we stepped out, walking to our room number three. I wanted every room in every hotel with that number on it from now on.

Once we were inside, I wanted her, but I wouldn't pressure into anything she didn't want. "Are you sure about this?"

Cobie answered in a calm tone, "I am."

I pulled off my hat, swept the hair out of her face, and kissed her. I set my other hand on her trim waist.

She touched the back of my neck, kissing me back.

I lifted her up, and she wrapped her legs around me. How did I never notice she was so thin?

We kept kissing as I carried her to what I assumed was the bedroom. I was wrong. I changed direction, and she lifted herself up more. I moved to hold her there until I bent to place her on the bed.

She worked to undo my buttons, and I helped her remove my shirt.

I lifted her hem up slowly, taking her shirt off. I kissed her neck and trailed kisses down to the top of her breasts.

She murmured. After I took my time to work my way back up, she arched her back, tilted my head, and kissed me. She ran her hands through my hair.

The movement sent tiny bolts of delight down my head to my dick. I undid her bra and slid it off her. "Perfect," I told her.

"What is?" she asked. Heat darkened her eyes.

"You are. Everything about you is perfect." I kissed her to stop her rebuttal.

Cobie unbuttoned my jeans, and I helped her out of hers, taking off her underwear. Mine quickly joined hers on the floor.

She slid further up the bed.

I joined her and pushed her legs apart.

"Do you have a condom?" she asked. Her words sounded husky.

I fished one out of my wallet and rolled it onto my dick. Once I brought my dick to her vagina, I stopped myself from entering her. "Are you sure about this?"

"I've never been more sure of anything in my life," Cobie answered.

"Same with me. From the moment you saved me from my fans." I pushed myself inside her and then back out.

She bit her lip as she wrapped her legs around me, pulling me deeper inside of her.

Sweat beaded on my brow as I moved my dick in and out of her.

After a few times, Cobie moaned. She kissed my lips and ran her hands down my back. She moved her hips in rhythm with me.

I positioned myself to hit the spot again and again.

"Jordan," she said.

"Cobie," I copied her. I kept slamming my penis into her vagina, aiming at the spot to make her quiver.

She trembled underneath me, and her vagina wrapped tighter around my dick. She cried out.

I kept going to hear her screams of pleasure from her again.

Cobie yelled, and her body bucked. She ran her hands down my back, and the movement undid me.

I slammed into her once more, coming inside her. I rested on top of her as I tried to get control of my breathing. My heart slammed against my ribcage. I kissed her softly and touched her face.

Her hair matted to her forehead, and she stared at me. She stroked my back.

My dick grew hard inside of her just from her touching me. I'd been able to go a few rounds of sex one after the other, but not as fast as this. I pulled myself out of her.

She growled at me.

"I'm not done with you," I told her. After tossing the condom into the trash, I slid another one onto my fully erect dick.

"How many condoms do you have?" she asked. Her cheeks glowed, and she radiated with pleasure.

"This is my last one. If we need more, I'll get some."

"How?"

"Danny," I answered.

"Will he care that we're together?" she asked.

"He's been rooting for us. My band likes you."

"Everyone?"

"Except for Royal, and I don't give a shit what he says."

"You don't get along with him," Cobie said. Her words didn't sound like a question.

"We'll discuss anything and everything you want later, even another guy, but not when I'm naked in front of you." I pushed her legs apart and moved on top of her. I nipped at her earlobe. "Unless you want to talk about another guy."

"Not at the moment." She ran her hand through my hair, and the same zap flowed through my body.

I slid inside her and had her panting within minutes. I enjoyed the way she reacted to me.

Cobie screamed my name.

I kept going and brought her to another climax before I followed shortly after.

She lay in my arms and asked, "Why don't you and Royal get along?"

I brought her in closer to me and kissed her shoulder to give me a chance to explain. I should've figured she would want an answer. She technically didn't face me naked. "He's always hated me. In the beginning, it hurt, but then I realized not everyone would like me. Your ex-manager told him to get rid of me."

"They're both fools, so was I. I'm sorry I said I wasn't your fan." She rolled onto her back and touched the side of my face.

"Did you lie?" I kissed her palm.

"I did. You were a bit too smug, and I wanted to wipe the smirk off your face."

"Have you been a fan of my music?" I asked her. My heart leaped into my throat, and tears welled in the back of my eyes. If she said no, I wasn't sure what I would do.

"Yes, especially the songs you're releasing now." Cobie kissed me on the lips.

I wanted to do nothing else but make love to her for hours. I shouldn't have wasted two condoms to hear her scream. "You're the singer I look up to the most. You inspired me to sing and write music."

"I doubt I do now." Pain crossed her face, and she closed her eyes.

"More than ever, you do. Your ex-manager took everything away from you, and you found yourself back on the stage in what? Less than a year?"

"Try four months," she answered.

"You're amazing, and the world knows you are. We need you. I need you, and I'll be by your side all the way." I kissed her on the lips and pulled her into my chest.

"Can we stay like this?"

"We can until morning and then I'll find condoms to make love to you until your rehearsal, which I'll try to watch before someone forces me away. After the concert tomorrow, we'll hang out on the tour bus."

"I may need to return to our city before Monday to sue."

"Then I'll go with you," I told her.

"You have a show, and I won't be the one who stops you from doing the concert," Cobie said.

"I'm not needed until Wednesday. My band and I usually hang out and prepare or decide what we'll do next."

"You should be with them."

"I need to support you, and they'll understand. Now sleep, we'll argue more in the morning."

Cobie closed her eyes and snuggled more into me.

I waited until her breathing turned rhythmic in sleep before I pulled off my covers and crept to the bathroom. Making love to her hadn't simmered the anger inside of me. I now boiled with rage.

After checking the business names of Cobie's ex-manager and old record label, I called Cole.

"Hey, you're awake?" he answered on the first ring.

"Pull any of our songs with RAB Management and Golden Records."

"Why? What's going on?"

"I can't tell you why, but you'll find out soon. Wait a few days, and you'll understand."

"Has the band taken a vote?" Cole asked.

"This is my decision. I have the right to," I answered. I owned the copyright for writing the songs.

"The band could vote you out as co-leader."

"I don't care if they do."

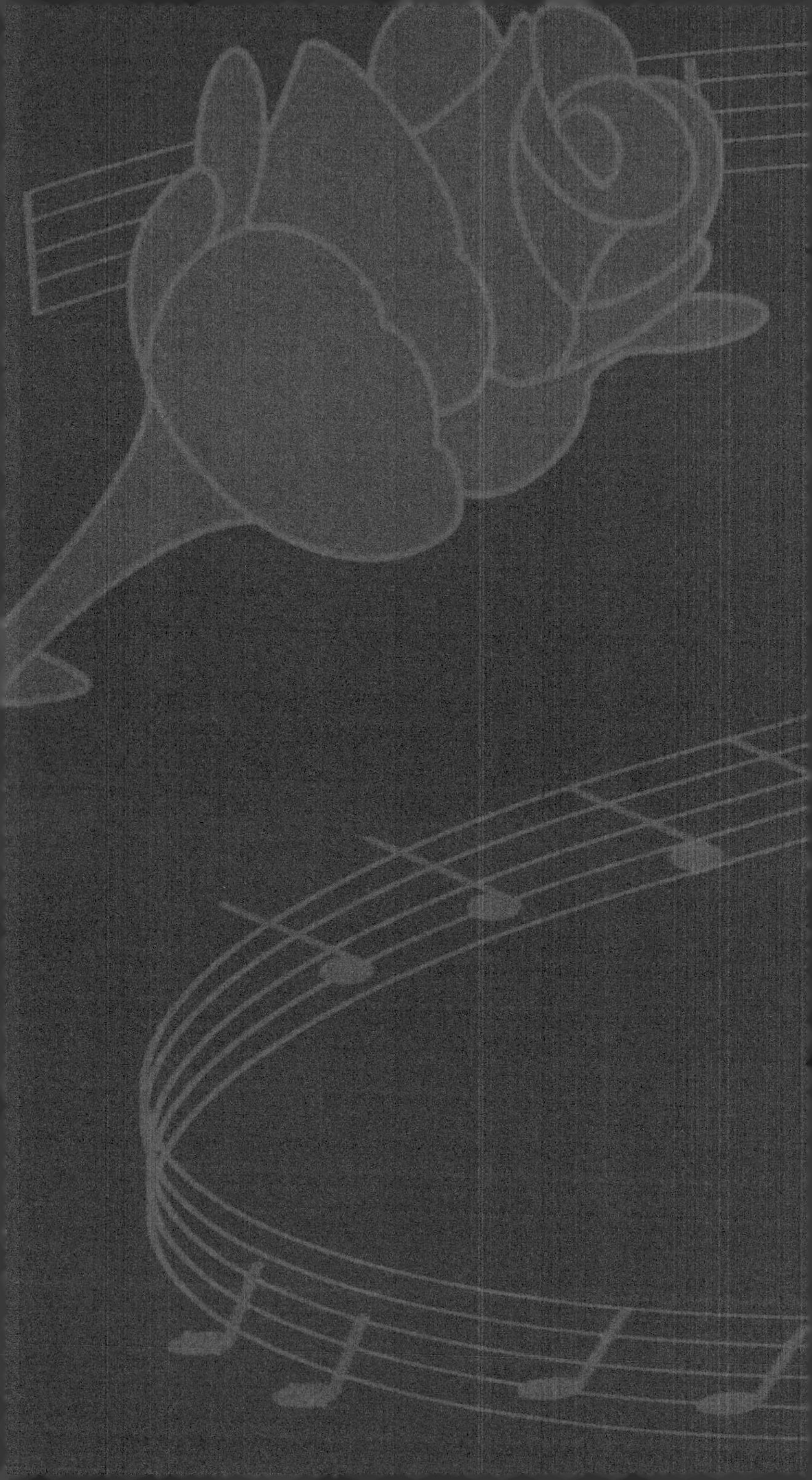

Chapter Twenty-Five

Cobie

I heard Jordan get up, and panic gripped my heart. I had slept with him. Since he got what he wanted, he would leave me. I reminded myself that he wanted to be with me. My fears slowly eased.

He headed to the bathroom, I assumed, to relieve himself. Instead, he argued with someone on the phone.

I tried to sleep, but my brain wouldn't shut off. It ran through every scenario with Jordan and my life. Why would he like me? Why did Megan decide to help me? Given my inability to afford a hotel, did I have any value? What if the lawsuit failed?

Jordan opened the bathroom door.

My phone buzzed with a text, and I read the message from him.

> *Jordan: If you wake up, I went to get con-doms. I'm making love to you in the morn-ing for hours.*

Every doubt I had washed away. I refused to let my former man-ager and record label destroy the years of confidence I had built.

Another alert came across my phone. I glanced at it, thinking Jordan wanted to say something else. Instead, my Cam notification had gone off. The headline said my song—as in me—had taken off and people were demanding to hear it. Everyone who posted it from my concert got over a million views.

I would release the song if I could. I had yet again disappointed my fans, and I doubt Rick would forgive me for singing it. Sleep was far off until Jordan returned to the room and pulled me into his arms.

Jordan smiled at me when I woke up, and my heart definitely throbbed. Damn him for being good-looking.

"Hey," he said. His voice sounded husky. "Did you sleep well?"

"I had a bit of a panic attack, but I got through it," I answered him truthfully.

"Why?"

"When you left the room, not sleeping in a familiar place, and I could go on and on. Thank you for the reassuring text. I needed it last night." I kissed him on the lips.

Jordan embraced me in a tight hug, and his dick was hard. "I'm sorry I left you feeling afraid, and I promise never to do it again. Please tell me what you need."

"This to start and reassurance. I'm not sure where we're going with our relationship," I said.

He stroked my head, and I kissed his bare chest. He had hair right around his nipples with a trail from his belly button to his groin. "I shouldn't say this, but I plan on marrying you someday. I'm not sure what timeline you have, but we can work through both of ours together."

"Why shouldn't you tell me?"

"A stupid guy rule, and we're not supposed to cry or show our feelings. I don't give a shit. You're the most important person to me, and I'll do anything to keep us together. Cobie, I love you."

I lifted my face to stare into Jordan's gorgeous brown eyes. Our combined phone calls and hanging out added up to more time than I spent with all my previous partners. When we're apart, I hurt. If what I felt for him was infatuation, so be it. I would remain infatuated with him for the rest of my life.

"I love you, too," I told him.

Jordan kissed me and shifted us so he was on top of me.

I eagerly kissed him back, running my hands down his back. He quivered under my touch. I wanted him inside of me to keep his promise last night, not with the arguing. Whatever we had disagreed about slipped my mind.

He nudged my legs apart and settled his body between them. I was already wet and ready for him. He kissed me forcefully before sitting up. He pulled a box of condoms from the side table.

I took the condom, ripping it open with my teeth. After I put it on him, I slid my hand down his cock.

Jordan groaned, and heat passed through his eyes. He nipped at my neck while teasing the opening to my vagina with his dick.

I wrapped my legs around his waist to pull him inside me.

He eased himself in all the way, moving his hips around. When he found my G-spot, pleasure filled me and my breath quickened. He pulled out of me and then pushed back in, tapping it again and again at an unhurried pace. He intertwined our fingers on one hand.

I panted, biting back the scream building. I fought the wave of pleasure as it rocked my body. Sweat stippled my forehead. I moaned.

He kissed my lips, trailed kisses to my ear, and nibbled my earlobe before he worked down to my nipple. He tugged it between his teeth. After he switched to my other breast, I lost my mind.

My body jerked as another orgasm erupted. I saw sparks of white behind my eyelids.

He tapped my G-spot again and again as he quickened his pace. Sweat dripped from his body, and he trembled underneath my legs.

I wrapped my arms around his back as he cried out.

His dick jerked inside of me and sent me through another climax. He lay on top of me, not moving for a few minutes.

I touched his finely sculpted body.

"Time to eat, and I prefer you on the menu." Jordan slid out of me and took off his condom. He tossed it into the trash before trailing kisses down my body. Once he got to my vagina, he licked me.

I covered myself up, stopping him. "For real? What time is it?" My stomach growled, and I needed some substance.

He glanced at the alarm on the nightstand. "We have one hour before you're due on stage, which means I have fifteen minutes to eat you out."

"How do you figure? Getting back to the venue will take ten minutes without traffic, fifteen to twenty with. We'll need to order food, and that'll take thirty, if not more. I want a shower." I needed one after what we did last night and this morning.

"Come on, then." Jordan helped me sit up and helped me out of bed. He used the hotel phone to order two of the number one breakfasts.

"What did you order?"

"No clue, but by the time I make you cum in the shower, we'll have food to eat." He definitely made me at least once.

Someone knocked on the door while we dried off.

"I'll get it." Jordan took off naked, and I called after him. He found his pants before heading out to answer.

I shut the bathroom door and finished with the body dryers. I needed clothes to keep myself from wanting him again, or maybe I should ride him. He had gained us a few more minutes without looking at the menu. I wrapped my hair up and checked if we were alone.

Jordan wheeled the cart to the table, setting the silver domes and plates in spots next to each other. "Your food, my lady." He bowed and revealed an omelet.

I sat naked in front of him, taking my fork and ignoring him as he stared at me. I sliced my omelet open. The chef folded in tomatoes, mushrooms, onions, spinach, bacon, ham, sausage, avocado, cheese, and another softened cheese. I took a bite, and the combination tasted divine.

"Are you eating naked?" Jordan kept his gaze on my face.

"Yep, do you have a problem with it?" I drank my OJ and crossed my legs.

"Not at all. I'm enjoying the view."

"If you eat most of your food, I'll ride you after."

His eyes widened. He bit into a sizeable chunk and winced.

"What's the matter?" I asked.

"Not a fan of cooked tomatoes or this green stuff." Jordan picked it out.

"Spinach. You ordered the number one."

"Why did they put mushrooms in it? Isn't the first dish the best?"

"Some people enjoy this." I split open my omelet and fished out the meat, giving him the most.

"You don't have to give me this," he said.

"This is too big for me to finish, and I'm not a fan of ham. If you eat all of my bacon, we will have words," I told him.

"I never will." He removed the stuff he didn't like and polished off his food.

I should take my time, but I wanted to be in charge of the next sex we had. After setting my fork down and napkin, he held out his hand for me to take. He helped me to stand. "Stay here," I ordered him.

Jordan's eyebrows furrowed.

"Sit down." I grabbed a condom from the box and returned to him. I slid his pants off with his help. He slid the condom on, and I climbed on top of him, easing him inside me.

"Fuck," he said as he gripped my waist.

I rode him hard and fast, using the back of the chair as leverage. The towel around my head slipped, and I shook it off my head.

He wrapped his hands around my back as he kissed me. His dick convulsed, and he cried out.

I stopped moving.

"I need to make you cum," Jordan said.

"Not this time." I eased off him.

He got rid of his used a condom before he pulled me into his arms, kissing me and leaving me breathless. "I will make you scream my name tonight."

"If I watch your concert, I probably will."

Jordan smiled, and his shoulders shook as he held in his laughter. "Smartass."

We picked up our discarded clothes around the suite. Until now, I hadn't gotten a look at anything except the bed, bathroom, and table. I wanted to remember where we had slept together.

"You'd better get some clothes on or I'll want you again." He kissed my shoulder.

I dug out a fresh set from my backpack and changed.

He played with a hole in the side of my shirt, inserting a finger. "I'm buying you a new wardrobe."

"No, you're not. Stop trying to give me your money," I said.

"Exactly why I'm buying you clothes and a car. A new phone. A computer or anything you want."

"You're buying me stuff because I don't want it?" His words made no sense to me.

"You should have everything. If you'd invested, you'd top the list of the richest people in America."

"I invested." Dick had my shares, and he probably sold them. Wait, they were under my real name. There was no way for him to sell my investments. "I need to call my lawyer."

Chapter Twenty-Six

Jordan

I showed Cobie the view overlooking the city after she spoke to her attorney. I should've shown it to her at night with the city lights.

If she hadn't lost everything, we wouldn't have met. I pushed the thought away. Considering Royal had insisted on our working together, we would've been together much sooner. Her auditioning to open for my band without my knowledge was merely a crazy coincidence. My bandmate deserved more thanks than I gave him.

My band waited with our manager for our SUVs to arrive off to the side of the doors in a little nook. None of them sat at the tables or on the couch.

I went to Royal with Cobie. After setting my bag and hers onto the ground, I touched his shoulder and said, "I appreciate what you did for me."

Royal shook me off and sneered at me. "What the hell did I do?"

"Getting Cobie to open for us. If you hadn't, I would've never met the woman of my dreams again," I answered.

"I should no longer be on probation then," Royal said. Figures he would turn around my proclamation.

"Not happening. You defied the band's wishes. Cobie and Jordan would've met some other way." Danny squared his shoulders and glared at Royal.

Danny was right. Cobie and I were in the same industry, facing the same problems.

"Why am I getting punished?" Royal asked.

"Because you deserve to," Danny said with a shake of his head.

I felt eyes on me and turned around as two bodyguards and Cobie's attorney walked toward us. "You're not stopping me from holding her hand," I told them as they joined us.

They eyed me as if I were in trouble.

Her attorney chewed on her bottom lip and ran a hand through her dark hair. Didn't Cobie call her Megan?

"Ms. Meine, do you want to hold his hand?" one bodyguard, much larger than the other, asked. I was tall at six foot but he made me small with his height and frame.

"Jordan can Tim," Cobie said. Her voice sounded calm.

"Cobie, when are you due at the venue?" Megan asked.

Cobie glanced at her watch, answering, "Less than half an hour."

"Our SUVs have parked," Tim said as he stepped closer to her. Two black vehicles waited in the loading zone.

"Jordan, are you coming with us?" Jay glanced at me and then back at Cobie.

I hesitated. I wanted to reassure my girlfriend last night was amazing, especially after she had a panic attack.

"You'll see me at the venue in a few minutes. Go with your band," Cobie said.

"I want to ride over with you. Can I come with you?" I asked her.

"You can," she answered. She smiled small at me, and my heart soared.

"We should talk as a band in the van," Cole said.

Noah parked behind the two SUVs. I had given him his jack back last night after thanking him.

"We'll be together soon enough. I want to speak to my girlfriend before we get pulled off in different directions today," I told them. Cobie and I slept together, and we should do something other than eat and work. She deserved so much more.

"Jordan's smitten with her. Give him a week, and he'll be back to his annoying self." Royal leaned against the wall.

"But they never impeded the band," Jay pointed out.

"How is hanging out with Cobie for twenty minutes interfering with us?" I ignored Royal's comment.

"You weren't at breakfast." Jay looked down at his shoes and tapped one against the floor.

"I don't want to cause issues with your band," Cobie said to me. She shifted her weight from one foot to the other.

"You're not. They're fine without me for a meal or two," I said.

"We need to go, so Cobie isn't late." Megan kept glancing at her watch.

"We're going to the same place. Let's split up the vehicles. Cobie and Jordan with her bodyguards. Her lawyer and I can go together, and the rest of you can figure it out," Danny suggested. He had stood taller ever since Megan joined us.

Tim said, "Only Cobie's guests may use my vehicles."

Cobie turned to me and said, "We'll ride together and then you need to meet with your band. We promised to not let our relationship interfere with the tour."

"I want to see you perform," I told her. Did she not want me there?

"You can during my soundcheck or when I open for you. I want nothing more than to hang with you all day, but you have other duties like me," Cobie said.

I studied her for a moment. She wanted to be with me as much as I wanted to be with her. I had never felt more relieved.

Cobie tugged on my hand as she headed to the door with her people.

"Jordan?" Cole called after me.

"After the drive," I told him.

Cobie and I settled next to each other in the SUV's backseat, and she set her head on my shoulder.

"I like this," I told her.

"Like what?" She sounded confused.

"You putting your head on my shoulder and holding your hand. Even if we don't talk, I enjoy being with you."

"I enjoy your company, too." She giggled a little, and then her cheeks heated. I witnessed her exact thoughts as it crossed her face. She had a great time last night and this morning, and so did I, especially when she took over.

"How goes the music writing?"

"I've gotten a few songs done. I need to work on the arrangements to make them better," Cobie answered.

"Can I help you with anything?" I asked.

"Can I borrow your studio after I'm done opening for you?"

"You can, but I plan on asking you to stay longer."

"Between the lawsuit and your band not liking me, I'm not sure I should."

I tilted her face up, and a hurt expression crossed her face. "Only Royal dislikes you, and I don't give a shit. If he is out of line with you ever, let me know. I won't put up with his comments to you."

"You said nothing to him earlier," she pointed out.

"He's right. I am smitten with you, and I'm not denying those words. He made more of a jab at me than at you."

She frowned. "I dislike the way he treats you."

"I'm used to it."

"You shouldn't be. You're the heart and soul of Solar Harmony. Can't he tell?" she asked.

"He doesn't care. Let's discuss something else since we know the truth and he never will." I blew out a heavy breath and switched topics. She had seen the way he acted. Who else had?

"How is your songwriting going?"

"I never wanted to write more than I do now. I couldn't listen to music or eat after the accusation. When we get to the city for the next concert, I plan on writing."

"After rehearsal, Megan will tell me if I need to head back. Hopefully, I can join you later. I doubt my old record label and ex-manager will answer fast and make counterclaims."

"If you can't, we'll talk on the phone," I said.

"Good thing I'll have a new cell tomorrow," she said.

"Did you get a case?" I felt at ease with her and had to see if she needed anything.

"I better because I drop them a lot." She held out her wrist to show me the scuff marks on the protective case on her watch.

"Ms. Meine, we're here." Tim shifted the vehicle into park.

Cobie read the time. "Crap, I'm almost late." She took her bag from me, fished out the staff badge, and put it on. She didn't need it, for everyone knew her.

Tim opened the door for her.

She almost slid out, put her guitar on her back, and then turned around, kissing me on the lips.

"I'll text you," I told her as I slid out.

She waved before she headed inside with two of her bodyguards, and Megan walked slowly behind them.

I waited for my band to pull up a few minutes later.

Royal got out of the front seat, hurrying inside.

Danny and the rest stopped before me, and we followed behind the asshole. My buddy didn't get his wish to flirt with the lawyer. He enjoyed female company, but his affections were unrequited with one.

I patted Danny on the back. "If you need me, I'm here for you," I told him.

"What are you saying now?" Danny asked. His eyebrows squished together and touched the base of his neck.

"With you and Brittany. I'm here to talk," I answered.

"Let's keep to just one band member dating the staff at a time." Cole opened the dressing room door for us.

"Cobie isn't staff." I sat on the couch and checked the schedule for the day. We had the final mic check in thirty minutes. They never wanted us to play our entire set on the day of the concert. If I arrived early, I could watch Cobie perform.

Royal sat in a chair, playing with his phone.

Someone had brought fresh flowers and set them on the coffee table.

"I wanted everyone here to discuss Jordan's proposal," Cole said.

The calmness I had vanished. "What I said to do wasn't a request. I wrote the songs."

"Wait, what's going on?" Danny took the spot next to me, with Jay next to him. Baylee sat in the back as usual.

"I want to pull any artist we collaborated with RAB Management and Golden Records," I answered.

"Cobie's old companies," Cole explained.

"Why the fuck would we?" Royal asked.

"You'll find out why soon enough. We can't let them get away with what they did to our opening act," I answered.

"You mean your girlfriend? Stop thinking with your penis for once." Royal faced the mirror and shook his head in it.

"I'm not," I said.

"We should put this to a vote," Royal said.

"First off, we need to hear the arguments. For and against," Baylee said.

"Of course, you'd side with him." Royal raked his hand through his black hair.

"I...I haven't. I want to know why we're pulling our songs." Baylee zipped up his sweatshirt and covered his mouth with it.

"As acting leader, we'll hear both arguments for and against. Royal can start," Danny said.

"Losing money is stupid," Royal said.

My phone buzzed with a text, and I glanced at the message, hoping Cobie had sent me something. Instead, Deedee had. What she told me had calmed me for a strange reason.

"Jordan?" Danny shifted on the sofa to face me.

I sat up and glanced at everyone, giving myself a moment to form my words. "Look, I can't share the details of everything with Cobie because I don't know it all. What I witnessed is enough for us not to support anyone who steals everything from an artist. What if it is us next? Where will be when our records no longer sell or we don't fill stadiums?"

"We'll still have royalties," Royal pointed out.

"You won't as much as me or our label. I own the copyright, and they own the masters," I said.

"Will you give us some of it?" Royal asked.

"Why wouldn't I? You're my friends, and I want what is best for us. I will always do what is right." I had almost blurted out the information from Deedee, but I had to keep it in for now.

"We don't even know if the label will go for it," Cole said.

"Tell them if they don't, we won't renew our contract in October," Jay said.

"You're okay with this nonsense, too?" Royal asked.

"Worst they can do is say no," I said.

"Let's vote. Who is for pulling our songs associated with those two companies?" Danny asked.

Jay, Baylee, Cole, and I raised our hands.

"Cole can't vote," Royal said.

"If Cole voted to keep the songs, you'd say he could," Baylee pointed out.

"Keep it up," Royal said in a threatening tone.

Baylee winced and hid his face.

"Never raise your voice to Baylee again. He pointed out the truth," I said to Royal. He had a lot of nerve to act the way he did.

"Baylee did, and my vote won't count, but I can't imagine doing what Dick did to Cobie," Cole said.

"We need to calm down. Who wants to keep the songs?" Danny asked. He and Royal raised their hands.

"I'll see what I can do." Cole took out his phone and left the room.

"This is bullshit," Royal said.

"Do you know what's real bullshit? You getting Dick's daughter to work backstage for us so she can plant evidence to accuse me of harming her father's client," I said. Even angry, I prevented myself from saying her accusation.

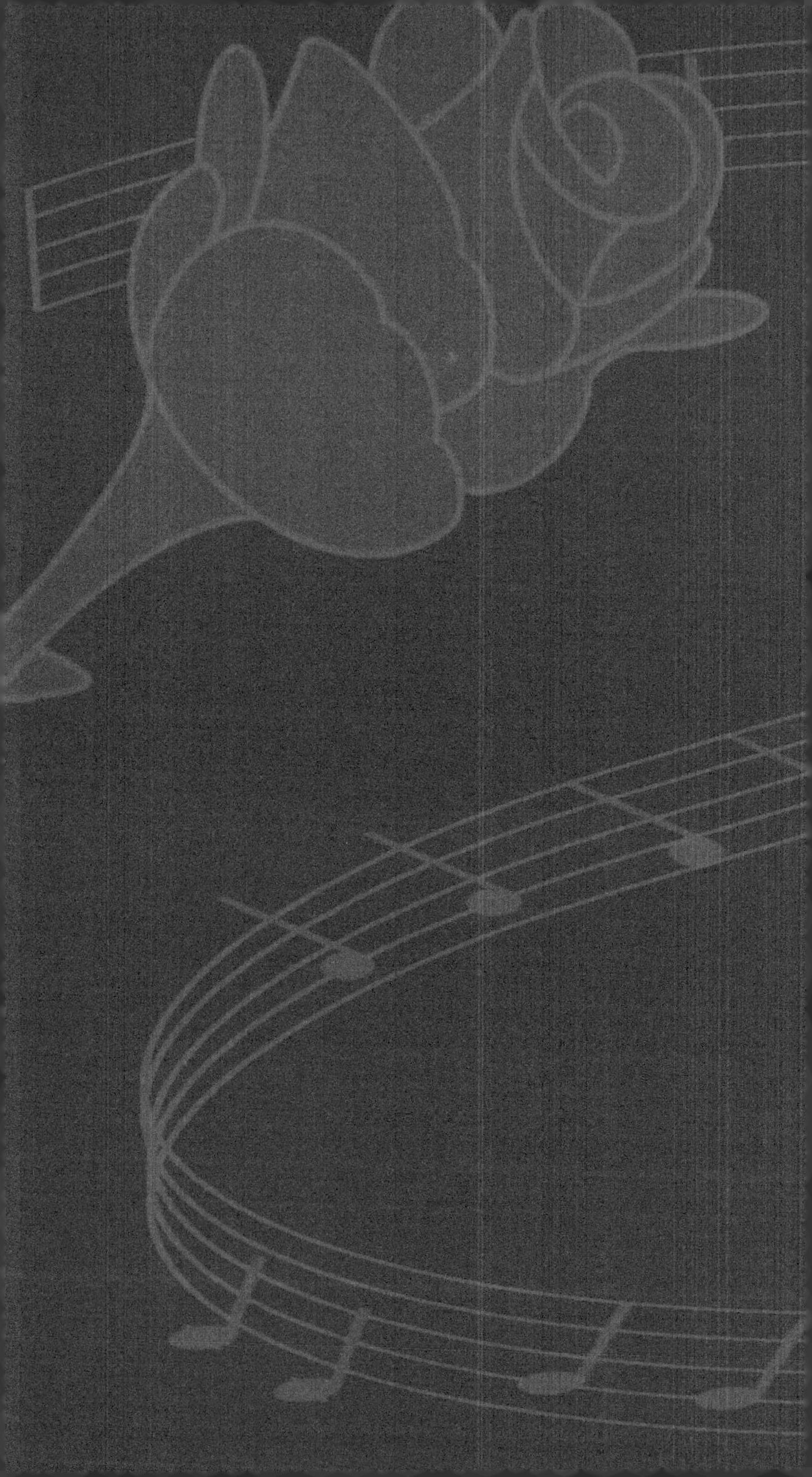

Chapter Twenty-Seven

Cobie

Monday

Despite my plans to be with Jordan post-concert and Sunday, Megan had demanded we return home to get ready for today. The courts weren't open, so I could've stayed another day. She had work and more questions for me to answer. She was also the one paying for my ride. At least I needed to be in the next tour city on Wednesday.

Jordan hadn't sent me a text this morning. He had told me last night he wanted to finish the lyrics he'd been working on after I had gone to bed. How late had he stayed up?

I sent him a message, like he normally did.

After I showered, I headed to breakfast. Megan had paid a courier to serve my former manager and record label, and once they succeeded, they'd bring us the proof. I figured I'd get a meal or two before they finished. The record label would have staff present today, but Dick hated to pay people for jobs he deemed unnecessary. He had found out quickly why custodians existed after he fired them.

The dumbass.

Megan's mom had made another spread. She sat down to eat and looked over the newspaper.

Her daughter busied herself with some paperwork. They shared similar expressions, with their furrowed brows and pursed lips. Their resemblance was close. Megan had definitely gotten her eyes and complexion from her mother. Why hadn't I noticed this before?

I made my plate, enjoying eggs with sausage on a biscuit. When I needed a quick meal, eggs were an excellent source of protein for cheap, unless the bird flu outbreak happened. I hadn't bothered picking any up during the months I'd lived in my apartment.

After I ate, I finally checked the news about myself. I'd been avoiding it since I revealed my identity to the world. Every article stated the same thing. I was the alleged Cam. Even the information about my lawsuit got out.

"How is our lawsuit get in the press?" I asked.

"I leaked it." Megan sipped her coffee. I called it tar water, since it was black. I preferred mine with cream, sugar, and cold.

"Why would you?"

"Companies like to claim they didn't get the paperwork. Besides, our lawsuit is public knowledge."

Someone had already published a video explaining the details of my case and my side. At the end, they asked why I hadn't come forward before and why I didn't reveal myself much sooner.

"Am I allowed to post anything about the lawsuit?" I asked.

"Nope. You're under a media blackout." Megan held her hand as if she wanted my phone.

I hugged my new cell to my chest. She could pry this from my cold, dead fingers since I needed it to contact my friends and my boyfriend. "I won't post anything."

"You'd better stay off social media if you won't give me your phone. I'll charge you an exorbitant fee if you do."

I held out an empty hand to her.

She looked at it and frowned.

"Here's my down payment," I told her.

Her mother and I laughed while Megan scolded me.

"What? I have no money. Actually, I should have some," I explained. My payment from last week should've hit my bank on Friday. Man, I should've stayed with Jordan and flown or taken a bus back.

"From the tour?" Megan asked.

"Yes, do you want some money?" I asked.

"Give me a dollar, and I can say you're officially paying me." Megan held out her hand.

"I'll be right back." I had some change in my bedroom, so I didn't need to ask her for her account with a finance app. After retrieving the money, I gave it to Megan.

She set it next to her on the table.

"What does everyone do all day?" I set my plate in the sink and rinsed it.

"I usually go to work, but I'm working from home today. Tomorrow I'll go into the office. I have to brief others on my cases if we get a response," Megan answered.

"Will we?" I asked.

"You never know," Megan answered in her lawyer style. She always left things open until they happened, unlike salespeople and managers. They promised the world despite not owning it. I preferred dealing with those who represented facts and truth.

I turned to Wilma and asked her, "What will you do?" What would I do until the drive tomorrow? Probably write. I had no life except for music and Jordan, and I wouldn't change it.

"Clean and watch TV shows," Wilma answered.

"If you want to go somewhere, I'll plan with your bodyguards," Megan told me. "If I'm on a call, my mother will plan it instead."

"Why don't you give me the number and I can?" I asked.

Megan slowly shook her head and returned to reading.

"You're a guest. You don't cook, clean, or wash your clothes," Wilma explained.

"Thank you for this meal. I'll be in my room if anyone needs me." I pushed in my chair before Wilma did it for me. Even when I stayed at the record label's mansion, I'd handled my own things. I usually bought new clothes because I was often too tired to do the laundry.

Jordan called me after lunch. "Hey, beautiful. Sorry I didn't text you this morning. I was asleep. How are you?"

"I'm good. How are you?" I answered.

"Exhausted. I slept too long. What are you doing today? How did the lawsuit go?"

"Paperwork got served, and I saw the proof. Megan says I have to wait for their response and can't tell me when it will be. I'm working on another song."

"Can I hear it?"

"Soon," I answered.

"Whenever you are ready, I'm here," Jordan said.

"What are your plans for the day?"

"I'm eating breakfast with the band soon."

"Don't you mean lunch?"

"Nope, the first meal of the day is breakfast, the second is lunch, and the third is supper," Jordan answered.

"You'll have two more meals today?" I asked.

"I wish I could have them with you."

"Same."

"When can you come here?"

"I will be at rehearsal on Wednesday, no matter what. I planned on driving down tomorrow morning," I answered.

"Fly, baby. Fly. I want you in my arms much sooner, and I'll book you a ticket or I'll come get you," Jordan said.

My heart throbbed. *Damn him and his smooth words.* He meant everything he had said, which warmed me.

"You'll have to speak to my lawyer." I took a deep breath. "This song I'm working on is about letting go of the things you can't control."

"Go on," Jordan said.

"And accepting, we push through everything until the end of the day."

"Sing it to me. I want to hear your voice."

After I opened my mouth, the words flowed out. "Please give me a moment. I don't have time to be depressed. I don't have time to be sick. I don't have time to be in pain. Because I need to get things done." I finished the song with more about how I lay on the bed at night once the day finished for a moment, and I would be fine tomorrow for the chorus.

"What's the song called?" Jordan sounded sad.

"*I Need a Moment.* What do you think?"

"That was the most beautiful song I have ever heard."

Clapping sounded behind me, and I jumped.

Megan and her mother stood in the doorway of my room.

"You all need to knock." I touched my chest to stop my fast-beating heart.

"Sorry," Megan said as she ran over to me. She wrapped me in a big hug.

"Come here, child." Wilma gave me a mother's embrace I hadn't felt in years.

Tears spilled from my eyes, and I swiped them away.

"When will you release that song?" Megan asked.

"I need to finish the melody first, tweak the lyrics, and get a recording studio to record it," I answered. Some verses needed to be fixed to create a better flow.

"Start working on what you need, and I'll give you my credit card."

"Cobie? Are you okay?" Jordan called.

"I'm fine. Hold on a second. Megan and Wilma heard and watched me sing," I answered.

"I'm jealous," he said.

After covering the mic, I told Megan, "Put your credit card away. I'm not ready for anything. Thank you for the hugs." My heart felt fuller than it had in a long while.

"Let me know when you need it." Megan stuffed it back into her wallet, and her shoulders drooped.

The doorbell rang.

"I'll leave to answer the door, but I would love to hear more of your music sometime." Wilma didn't wait for me to agree or not and took off.

"I would love for you to sing again, too. The club hopping me would get jealous of my private concert with Cam," Megan said. Her eyes danced with merriment.

"I'll sing one more song tonight. I need to rest my voice," I said.

She glanced at the phone in my hand.

"We're finishing up our call," I answered her unasked question. Besides, singing strained my voice more.

"Megan?" her mother called from downstairs.

"I'll tell my mom about tonight." Megan smiled as she took off.

"Sorry," I told Jordan.

"Can't blame them for listening to your concert. I've been a fan for years and still am. Who is Wilma?" he asked.

"Megan's mother. She's nice and a superb cook."

"I'm glad Megan is treating you well."

"More than well." I sat on my bed.

"You should have a throne and people to do everything for you, my queen," Jordan said.

"Whatever," I told him.

"For real, you've done so much, and that's why I pulled all of Solar Harmony songs with your ex-manager's company and old record label."

"You did what?" His words came as a complete shock to me.

"I pulled all of Solar Harmony songs with your ex-manager's company and old record label."

"I heard you. Why?" I gripped my phone, and my mind raced with the potential lawsuits.

"They wronged you. I won't stand by and let them get away with it. I already pulled the titles, and they won't be up again until you have everything back," Jordan said. Muffled sounds came from his end before he returned to the conversation. "I just sent you a link from Baylee. Check it out."

"What does he say about pulling your songs?" My phone dinged with a message.

"Most of my band agreed. Your situation could be ours some-day. I hope you understand I did this as a musician, not as your boyfriend."

Not like he gave me much choice. We'd never discussed this, but I didn't have the right to dictate his music, like he didn't for me.

Megan waved at me from my door.

"Check the link and get back to me. My band wants breakfast, and I'll talk to you later," Jordan said.

"I've got to go, too," I told him.

"Have a good day, amazing woman," Jordan said.

"You too, amazing man," I told him with a laugh. He made me smile.

"Rick Davis is here to see you," Megan told me as soon as I ended my call.

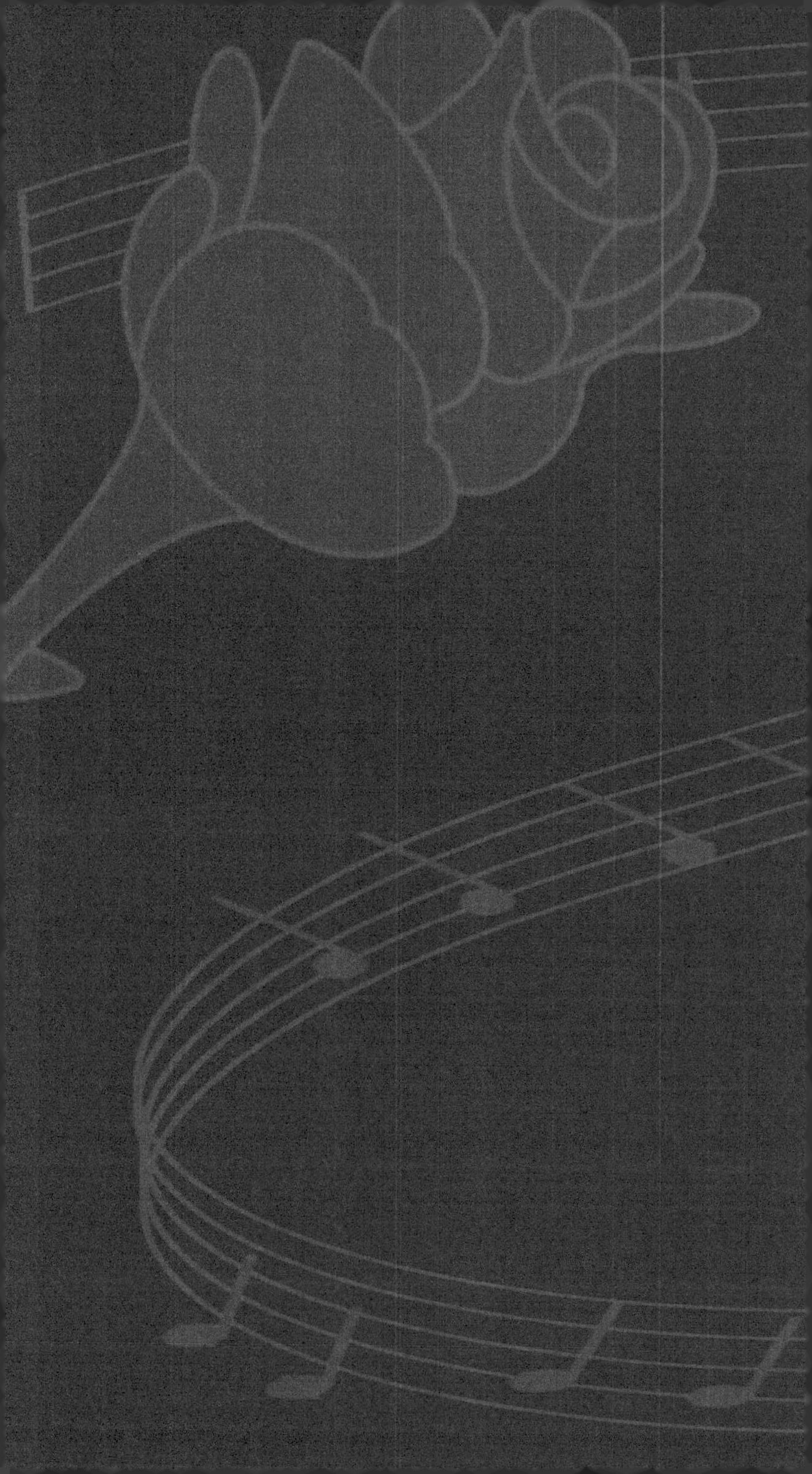

Chapter Twenty-Eight

Jordan

I told Cobie, "Have a good day, amazing woman."

"You too, amazing man." She giggled a little before she hung up.

"How did Cobie take the news of us pulling our songs?" Baylee asked.

"She's not happy, but it's our music," I answered. Hopefully, the link would make her understand. Another singer spoke up in favor of Cobie's situation. I bet once they found out what my band and I did, they would join us.

"I understand why you did it. One slip of the tongue and the fans can turn on us fast. Musicians need to stick together."

"Wish our other members would understand." Everything felt like it slowed down, but nothing had. Cole kept his promise, and by lunch, our songs were off the market. I couldn't be the only one in the band who wondered how he had accomplished the task so fast, but he did his job of keeping us happy, and he did it well.

"Jay's on our side. He's waiting for us to get him for lunch."

Not my best mate, Danny. I didn't say those words to Baylee. Instead, I said, "We'd better not keep Jay waiting."

We exited the typical hotel suite and headed to Jay's. After the fallout with Royal, I was glad we got hotel rooms after being stuck on the bus for twenty hours with him. He had somehow turned my accusation against him into helping another manager whose daughter needed to learn the value of money.

Give me a break. I contained an eye roll as Jay opened his door.

"Did you see our fans are noticing we pulled certain songs and wondering why?" Jay adjusted his collar on his black shirt with our band name across the chest.

"Should we make a statement? The lawsuit Cobie brought against her manager and record label is out," Baylee said. He also wore a sweatshirt with our band name. Someone must not have given me the memo.

"If they don't figure it out by tomorrow, we can. Our fans are pretty bright." I walked next to Jay, and Baylee trailed behind us.

"They're still fighting over the girl you took to the hotel," Jay said.

"Let them argue." I would scream I was with Cobie from the top of our hotel, but she needed to focus on her lawsuit. Afterward, we could go public with our relationship.

My phone chimed, and I glanced at the message, hoping it was from her. No such luck. My ex-girlfriend had slid into my DMs. I blocked her instead of responding.

"What's with the face?" Jay asked.

"Bree messaged me." I shook my head and pressed the button to call the elevator. She was another one who had never reached out to me until now. Most of those who I thought were my friends apologized and said they knew I was innocent. Did they? Probably not, but at least they didn't send me any hate messages. Whenever a celebrity had a legal issue, we waited for the results before we acted. If we sided with them and they were guilty, we would lose everything, too. Despite knowing this and doing this, I was still mad at them.

"What does she want?" Jay asked. His upper lip curled.

"Don't know; don't care. I blocked her," I answered.

The elevator dinged, and we stepped inside.

"Is that a good idea? Word could get out, and her fans will hate you." Baylee covered his face again, and I realized he did it whenever he wasn't too sure of his statement. He was dead right most of the time.

"You're right. Her people can fight my people," I said with a laugh. I was more than sure Bree had dated me to get work, and I no longer cared enough to check.

"Hers wouldn't win," Jay said.

"Has the hotel stopped our fans from coming inside?" I gave up a long time ago on keeping our location a secret. With social media in everyone's life, they found out fast.

"So far. Royal had an incident yesterday," Jay answered.

"What happened?" I asked. If he got some much-needed karma, I would be happy.

"A bunch of girls snuck past security and surrounded him," Jay answered.

"Did he lose his clothes?" I asked Royal always escaped justice, and I felt disappointed.

"They asked for autographs, not his clothes," Jay answered.

We stepped out, and they led me to the attached restaurant. I hadn't come here until now.

The hostess immediately told us to follow her. She proceeded to the rear with the customers, observing our progress. Most of them were also celebrities, so they would let us eat in peace. She stopped by the table reserved for VIPs and asked while she handed out the menus, "Will anyone be joining you?"

"Maybe one more," Jay answered, to my surprise. No way would Royal join us. Had Danny forgiven me? He'd barely said two words to me, and I doubted he would until he got over the decision we made. Cole would come. Although I didn't want to see him, since I had avoided telling him I had torn the NDA and refused to get Cobie to sign it.

The hostess set another menu on the table before saying, "Your server will get your orders."

The menu fit the current state where we performed for the next two weeks, which included bigger portions, brisket, hamburgers, and chili, to name a few. I decided on a rare, big cut New York Strip, baked potato topped with chili and cheese, and loaded mac & cheese. My mouth watered in anticipation of bacon added to the latter. I also planned on eating their blooming onion since it had the best sauce for dipping.

Danny pulled out the chair next to me and sat. "Hey," he said.

I acknowledged him before checking the drink choices. Our server made her way over to us.

She took our drink orders and left.

"Have you talked to your mom?" Danny asked me as he lifted the menu.

"Nope. She hasn't called me," I answered.

"She called me," Danny said.

I waited for him to tell me more. For a guy who hated 'chick moments', he liked to draw out emotional conversations more than any woman.

"She wanted me to ask you to call her," Danny finally said.

The server brought our drinks and asked, "Are you ready to order?"

"Not yet," Danny said.

I waited for her to leave before I said to Danny, "Give my mom my new number." I had to change it after the fake Cam released it into the world.

"Your mom told me what happened to her. She's sorry she didn't reach out to you," Danny said.

"And that's why I'm mad at her. Why would I harm anyone after seeing her reaction?" I asked. My mom had certain triggers, like a smell, that sent her into a deep depression. I never wore cologne near her, fearing one would set her off.

"Find out for yourself." Danny set his menu on the table.

"Nope, she needs to call me first," I said. Yeah, I was being an asshole, but the pain of knowing my mother believed I was a monster wasn't something I would soon, if ever, forget. Excessive saliva filled my mouth, and I swallowed.

"Can you stop being an ass and talk to your mom? You're ignoring everyone reaching out to you," Danny said.

I took a pull of my beer and set it on the table. "I'm cutting out the people who betrayed me. Until you go through what I did, you'll never understand."

"Come on, you didn't have a hard time," Danny said.

I bent closer to him and whispered, "My life would've been over if the police hadn't dropped the charges. If I can't sing or write music, I have nothing."

"You have me, the band," Danny whispered.

"You would've left me, too." I blinked back the tears in my eyes. "I'm angry at the people who didn't stand by me. Tell them I need space, please, for me."

"We will." Jay slung his arm over me and gave me a side hug.

I desired Cobie to embrace me, but I wouldn't turn it down from our youngest band member. "Thanks, man." I hugged him back.

"We're here for you, whatever you need, even if you make stupid choices," Danny said. With those words, he forgave me.

We chatted for a bit about life until the server came and took our orders. Everyone except for Baylee ordered some type of steak. He liked to try different foods, while I preferred sticking to meat and potatoes.

I texted Cobie once we'd almost finished our meal. She had to go like me, but she didn't give me a reason. I worried a little over what and reminded myself she had four bodyguards to protect her. Unless Megan didn't require them at her place. What kind of home security did she have?

My phone rang with Cobie's reply, and my anxiety rose.

> Cobie: I'm meeting with Rick Davis now. I'll text you when we're done.

Rick was one of the top songwriters and producers in the country.

I felt too hot and too cold at the same time. I'd given her the terrible advice to sing a song that proved she was Cam.

"What's the matter?" Danny asked me. He must've noticed my fidgeting.

"Cobie's meeting with Rick Davis," I answered.

"So?" Danny ate his last piece of steak dipped in sauce.

"Isn't Rick the producer you told to push through to you if he called?" Baylee asked. The drawback of his sharp mind was his perfect memory.

"He is, and Cobie sang the song they wrote before its release," I answered.

Danny cursed.

"Doesn't Rick challenge his co-writers where they want to leave the music industry?" Jay asked.

"A lot do, but his work breaks sales records and wins awards," I answered. Nausea rose in my stomach, and I wanted to throw up my steak. I tossed my cloth napkin onto the plate.

"What are you doing? You're paying for lunch and our next meals for the rest of our lives, since you have something to fall back on," Danny said. His tone sounded half-joking, and I didn't care.

"I'm heading to Cobie. She needs me." I pushed in my chair.

"We have a concert, practice, and sound check this week. You can't throw away your responsibilities," Danny said.

"I'm not. We have practice on Wednesday, and I'll be back before then." I tossed five hundred bucks onto the table, turned around, and then faced my friends again. "Cobie's not some chick. She'll be my wife someday."

Danny opened his mouth, shut it, and did the action again. He looked like a yellow tang.

Baylee said to me, "You never said those words about a girlfriend before."

"Cobie's different. I promise I'll be back and we'll eat supper together." I took off before they said anything else. Near the door, I looked at the hostess. "Money is on the table," I told her. I didn't wait for her reply and entered the hotel. If a dinosaur had sat in the restaurant's corner, it would've gone unnoticed by me.

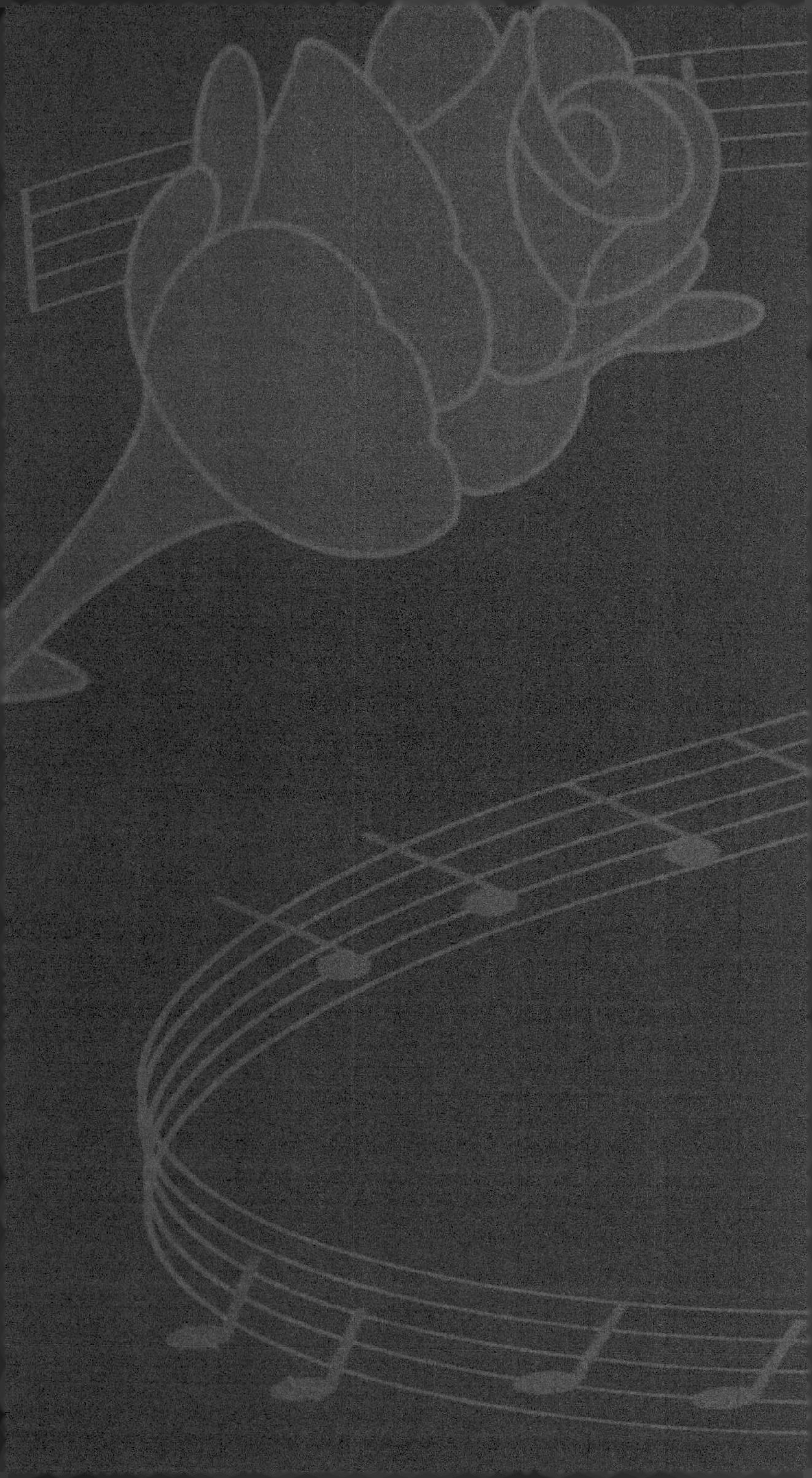

Chapter Twenty-Nine

Cobie

"Rick Davis is here to see you," Megan told me again. Her words hadn't quite reached my brain the first time.

"Did he say why?" I shifted my weight between my feet and looked toward the window. If I jumped out, I might break a leg. My bedroom was on the second floor. I could hang on like I used to do when I left my childhood home for auditions.

"He didn't. I'll be at your meeting just in case you need an attorney to represent you." Megan hadn't liked my singing the song Rick and I wrote. I had to explain to her how copyright worked for musicians. He and I shared it. We agreed once we finished the song, I would record it and I could sing it. I had finished the song, so I sang it. Her lawyer ways had rubbed off on me.

She led me through the hall, door after door, and down the grand staircase. "I placed him in the parlor," Megan explained. Why did her mansion have so many rooms for just her and her mom?

We entered a closed door off to the side of the entrance.

Rick stood when he saw me, and his face held no emotion.

"Rick," I said. The bubble of nervousness boiled over, and I almost stubble as I made my way to him. I held out my hand for him to take.

"Cam," he said. Had he asked a question? His tone of voice gave me no sign of his intentions.

"My real name is Cobie Meine. You can call me Cam or Cobie."

"Cobie, you understand why I'm here?" Rick not calling me by my stage name wasn't a good thing. He didn't accept me.

"Not really. You said I could sing the *Heart to Heart* once I finished it," I answered with ease.

"Sing it for me then." He took a seat.

Megan remained quiet and sat in a chair facing me. She would object if he said or did anything wrong.

My mouth ran dry. Rick was someone I respected. I cleared my throat and sang. "I wear my heart on my sleeve. I gave you all I've got, and I need you to talk to me. Can't you see I cherish you? Why do you keep ignoring me?" I continued singing until the song ended.

Rick stared at me; stone faced.

Megan had tears in her eyes and smiled at me. My song was about having the hardest conversation in life, and I had definitely had a few of those since everything happened.

Rick stood. "I heard everything I needed." He held out his hand to Megan, telling her, "It was a pleasure meeting you."

"What do you mean? Will my client be able to sing the song?" Megan shook his hand.

Rick faced me next. "About time you showed up. You can have the song, Cam. It's yours. I prefer to call you Cobie, if you don't mind."

I released the breath I hadn't realized I held onto. "Some people do."

"I'll let the record label know. Can I give you a hug?" Rick asked. After I nodded, he wrapped me in a hug, and I returned the quick embrace.

"Wait, what are you telling Cobie's former record company?" Megan asked.

"That they'll lose your lawsuit. I saw the video of Cobie performing, and every suit at Golden Records was in a tizzy after. They weren't sure what to do against your claim. I came here to see Cam with my own eyes. Your mannerisms are the same. On land you're like a fish, but once you sing, your confidence soars higher than any bird in flight," Rick answered.

"So, you came here to check on Cobie? I knew I shouldn't have let you in." Megan glared at the man, and she stepped toward me. A furious protective aura radiated from her. Despite her being only ten years older, she acted like my mother. Mine had better things to do than notice me. Shoot, she hadn't realized I'd left for auditions across the country until I returned with a contract and Dick.

"Actually, Golden Records wants to meet with Cobie and her lawyer to discuss how much they owe. They want to join your lawsuit against RAB Management, which you should get a countersuit soon." Rick undid the top button of his light blue dress shirt. He wore tan slacks and black shoes. He had never worn clothes like he did now and told me on more than one condition he would quit music if he did.

"Why are you in a suit?" I asked him. Granted, he didn't wear the jacket.

Rick's brown eyes widened for a split second. "Because of you. The lawyer for Golden Records said I need to look presentable representing them," he answered.

"Why did you come? And how did you come? Wouldn't the label want one of its lawyers instead?" I preferred him to most attorneys, except for Megan. She was great.

"I told them I'm producing our song, and if they didn't let me, I'd never write another for them ever again." Rick appearance relaxed, and his tone filled with warmth.

"Sounds like something you'd do." I smiled at him. He worked musicians hard, but always shared kind words if he noticed we faltered.

"Hold on, Cobie won't be producing anything until she gets paid. Also, when is RAB Management suing?" Megan held up her hand like it would do anything to stop Rick and me.

The doorbell rang.

"The answer to your second question is most likely now," Rick said.

"I'm getting it." Megan turned to me. "Don't agree to work on anything with Mr. Davis, not even a song until I'm back." She hurried away before I agreed or not.

Rick extended his hand out as if to say we should sit on the maroon leather couch.

I took a spot and said, "I've been working on an album." Until Rick had given me permission to record our song, I had no plans to add it.

"Tell me more," Rick said as he sat next to me.

"I need to work on the melody."

"You always saved the notes for last, and I never understood why, since they're in your head." Rick tapped his temple.

"I can't seem to get them out and onto paper."

"We can work on that."

Megan returned and heard the tail end of our conversation, saying, "Cobie isn't working on anything with anyone yet." She carried an envelope.

"Glad you got the bulldog on your side," Rick said to me.

I raised an eyebrow and glanced at them. I didn't like the nickname he used for Megan, but he had never spoken badly about anyone in front of me before.

"Bulldog is my nickname in court, and I hope your record label doesn't forget it." She sat on the leather chair she had earlier.

"Did I get sued?" I asked.

Megan glanced at the paperwork, answering, "Yes, you're being sued for what I suspected—false accusations."

"Please reach out to Golden Records. We're on Cobie's side." Rick handed Megan a card. He touched my shoulder and said, "If I had known what Dick did to you, I would've found you and protected you myself."

"Thanks, Rick," I said. My cheeks heated. I had more friends than I thought in the industry.

Someone knocked on the door before they entered. Wilma brought in three tall glasses of water with ice and a pitcher. "I thought Cobie would need a drink after singing." She set the tray on the coffee table in front of Rick and me.

I thanked her and drank half of my glass.

"Thanks, Wilma," Megan said before her mother left.

"What do we do about Dick?" I asked.

"We'll go to court," she answered with a glance at Rick.

"Talk in front of me or ask me to leave the room. All I know is I want to work with Cobie on her album." Rick held his hands up.

"She hasn't agreed to do an album, has she?" Megan stared at me.

"No, you told me not to," I answered.

"I would love to hear more details, and Golden Records is anxiously waiting to meet with you," Rick said to me.

Megan frowned and then set my latest lawsuit on the coffee table in front of her. Her eyebrows twitched as the wheels in her head spun. "We'll go, but Cobie will need her bodyguards."

"I'm glad you got our message to protect her," Rick said.

"My law firm got death threats, too, and most are subsiding," Megan answered.

"Ours are slowing down as well. Once we announce Cobie is Cam in an official statement, we hope they end," Rick said.

My phone alerted with a text, and I apologized to Rick and Megan. He hated when anyone he worked with got distracted. I read the message and stopped myself from putting my phone on silent.

> Jordan: Is everything okay?

I'd forgotten to tell him what I would do today. We checked in with each other, and it felt good. I sent him a quick reply before shutting it off.

"You're not sorry enough to turn your cell off while we're talking," Rick pointed out.

"Some things are more important," I told him.

Rick smiled and took a sip of his drink.

The meeting with the attorneys and Golden Records executives exhausted me. Megan had taken them on to make sure I got paid well and sealed the deal

"Should we check out the studio?" Rick asked as we left.

Energy returned to me like I'd gotten a shot or drunk a whole can of pure adrenaline. "Let's go."

Megan asked me, "How are you so bright-eyed?"

"Anything with music awakens Cobie," Rick whispered, even though I had heard him. He led us down the modern hall with gray carpet, windows, and meetings rooms. The bright LED lights shone since night had fallen. He called the elevator and pressed the button for the second-highest floor once we boarded.

"We'll get the best studio?" I asked. The president of our label had his office on the top floor.

"They're rolling out the red carpet for you," Rick answered.

"Nah, it's gray." I tapped the floor with my shoe.

Rick laughed and sobered the next second. "Have you seen the views on the videos posted about you singing your song?"

"They got a million views," I answered.

"Try a billion views on several of them. If they're added together, you hit the most-viewed video ever," Rick said.

"I checked them out, and everyone is speculating on whether or not you're really Cam. People just love drama," Megan explained.

I would never win over everyone, but so far, I had my record label back, and, with Megan's help, a better deal. I re-signed with them using my real name. If Dick won his lawsuit against me, he'd get to keep my stage name. I read the crap he put in the legal paperwork on the way to the studio, and it gave me a massive headache. He claimed he had never met me. My parents would side with him for money. He stated I was an opportunist looking for publicity and caused the fake Cam emotional stress. I'd like to show her some mental pressure for what those two had put me through. I tried to remind myself she might be a victim too, but after a year? I doubted it. How many people could he manipulate?

The recording studio had two separate sections. The biggest had a music adjuster at least eight feet or more. Every instrument imaginable, some unfamiliar and unpronounceable, sat inside the recording booth. What sound did they make?

"What do you think?" Rick asked.

"It's beautiful," I answered. Everyone signed with Golden Records strived to earn a chance to create their song here, including me.

"And about time you finally get to record here," Rick said.

"I had a lot of growing to do. Still do," I said.

"No, you were supposed to come here ages ago. You're our top-selling artist and have been for years. Your ex-manager refused to let you," Rick said.

Figures Dick would keep me out of here. I didn't understand why, since he would gain more money if my songs had more clarity with the best equipment in the industry. Jordan would love to see these rooms, and he probably knew what everything was and the name of every instrument.

Crap!

I hadn't texted him since I had spoken to Rick. Guilt washed over me. Everything had distracted me too much to even think about Jordan, and I'd silenced my phone. I hoped he would understand. His last message said his flight landed in thirty-one minutes.

Chapter Thirty

Jordan

Cobie hadn't answered my texts or phone calls before I boarded my plane, and none would come through until I landed. I feared what the hardass Rick would do to her. Megan wouldn't let him harm her, but hurtful words cut deep into a person's soul, lasting a lifetime. My girlfriend had gone through more than enough in her life, and I vowed to keep her safe from now on.

After I disembarked, my phone rang with messages upon messages. I found hers between the ones from my bandmates and sighed with relief. She apologized for not contacting me, but her meeting had ended. She planned to pick me up at the airport. I canceled the ride I had ordered, leaving them a tip to make up for the no-show.

I glanced around the terminal and spotted a cute brown-haired beauty with a white baseball cap next to four large bodyguards. Cobie waited with a sign and my first name on it. She was adorable.

I walked past the other passengers as they met with their people or headed toward the door. My gaze remained steady on my girlfriend, and when I got to her pretty brown eyes, my mood brightened. "Hey," I told her.

She smiled before wrapping her arms around me.

I embraced her back and enjoyed the feel of her in my arms. She would never learn how much I needed this. I kissed her. "Did your meeting with Rick go well?" I asked her after our hug ended.

"Let's talk in the car." Cobie glanced around.

People pointed at us. They had to recognize her, not me. I wore the blond wig, glasses, and the hat she had gotten me. She stuck with a baseball cap.

She took my hand and led me out of the airport. Her bodyguards followed close to us. People had to notice four enormous men in dark suits.

Inside the SUV, she explained everything. I had no words other than, "I'm happy for you. Are you happy?"

"Extremely. I can't stop smiling." Cobie rubbed her face and continued. "You got to put the music you made with Golden Records back up. They're helping me."

I hesitated. Companies made promises every day they didn't keep. "I'll wait until they sue your former manager's company."

She frowned. "Okay." She leaned against my shoulder and squeezed my hand. "I can't believe you returned for me."

"I believed you were in trouble when you texted about meeting with Rick. He has a terrible reputation."

"He's a teddy bear in the studio. Yeah, he's infuriating, especially when he's right, but he truly wants what's best for the singer and the music," she said.

"Where's your lawyer?" I asked her. Two bodyguards sat in the front seats. Since they didn't talk, I forgot they were there.

"She returned home. I'm exhausted and need sleep. Tomorrow I'll work on the song to release before flying out with you." Cobie stifled a yawn. Her day had been longer than mine, even though I had stayed up later. Contract discussions drained me, and she had spent half the day doing it. What an ass I was for having her come pick me up?

"Do you want to go to my place or Megan's?" Did she hear the hope in my voice?

"Your place."

My heart soared with her answer.

The chief bodyguard asked for the address, and I gave it to him. He didn't ignore Cobie and my conversation, which was part of his job to keep her safe.

"Are you still getting death threats?" I asked her.

"Some, but they've lessened. I hope once we go to court, my fans will realize I'm Cam," she answered.

"They're fools for not seeing it."

"You're not mad at me for keeping the truth from you?"

"I...I don't blame you. You spent years wearing a mask, and have had to fight even harder to keep it off. We all have secrets."

"Do you have some you won't tell me?" she asked.

"Nope. I'm an open book, and Danny has more than once wanted to close me," I quipped.

"How are they taking the pulling of your songs?"

"We voted and agreed to pull them. They'll be happy to have them back on the radio and for sale."

"You should put them back on now. Why are you waiting?"

"I don't trust that your record company will sue. If they do and side with you, the artist, I will. I'm tired of seeing singers taken advantage of, and I'm in a place where I can help."

"We should do it together," Cobie said. Music executives and managers couldn't stop us if we joined forces. With her, more singers would take a stance. They loved her.

"Have you heard from your friends?" I asked her.

"I didn't have any besides Deedee and Brittany now." Cobie ran a hand through her hair and rested her head against my shoulder again.

"You intimidate other singers, but if you reach out, they'll respond. They would love having you in their life like I do." As we drew closer to my home, something dawned on me. "We need to stop for supper and breakfast."

Cobie looked up at me.

"I doubt I have any food. We usually give it to the cleaning staff or toss it out when we start a tour," I explained.

"I'd like a burger," she said.

"You'll get one. Anything you want for breakfast?"

"You pick."

I moved my shoulder, and she sat up. Before she asked me anything, I whispered in her ear, "I'll have you in the morning."

She said nothing for a moment, and I didn't need to see her face to know it had become bright red. She giggled.

"We'll pick up bagels and cream cheese. Are you okay with that?" I asked. If she hated it, I'd change it.

"Works for me," Cobie said.

I pulled her back down onto my shoulder and watched the lights outside the window as we drove by. This was the life I wanted and would fight to keep. I read the texts from my band, surprised they supported my choice to leave. I told them Cobie was safe and everything worked out.

The next morning, I woke up next to the most beautiful woman in the world. Her eyelids fluttered, and she murmured in her sleep. What did she dream about?

Cobie said, "No, get away from me."

I shifted from her to give her space.

She had a nightmare the first time we slept together. Her life had been more challenging than I had realized.

I wanted to wake her, but everything online said I shouldn't. Instead, I told her, "I'm here for you."

She slept for another five minutes before her eyes opened. She stretched and asked, "What time is it?" Did she realize she had nightmares?

"Around 6 a.m." I handed her a room-temperature bottle of water. Cold water made me lose my voice much faster.

"Thanks." She drank half and set it on the nightstand.

"Are you ready for breakfast?"

"Not yet. I rarely eat until I'm fully awake," Cobie answered.

"Me neither, but I am hungry for something else." I kissed her cheek.

"You weren't joking about that?" She leaned her head back, inviting me to nip at her neck.

"Not one damn bit." I shifted to be on top of her and kissed my way down her body. I helped her out of her shirt before I sucked her tit.

Cobie gasped.

Every sound she made caused my dick to harden, and I ached to be inside of her. I planned to take my time with her. Last night we were too tired to make love. Our relationship was much more than sexual.

I nipped at her other tit, and she bit her lip. I trailed kisses across the perfect size to fit in my hand, massaging one as I moved down. Her underwear had to go, and she lifted her hips as I pulled it off. The way she synced with me felt like we'd been talking and making love for years.

I rubbed her clitoris with my thumb.

Cobie called my name in a husky voice and ran her hand through my hair.

I dipped a finger into her vagina before taking it back out. I wanted to hear my name on her lips repeatedly. When she did once more, I inserted two fingers and moved them around. She was wet. I kissed her vagina before licking her inside.

Her breathing became ragged.

I tasted her juices and kept lapping at her. Her body stiffened, and she screamed as her orgasm shook her. Once she finished, I sat up and stuck on a condom, sliding into her. She wrapped her legs around me to get me deeper. She came once more, and then so did I.

I lay on her, unable to move even if I had wanted to.

Cobie rubbed my back and unwrapped her legs. Her heart beat wildly in her chest.

We stayed with me inside of her, and her touching me for half an hour. I slid out of her, tossing the condom into the trash. She edged closer to the edge of the bed, and I helped her to her feet. We showered and ate in time for her bodyguards to take us to her studio.

Rick waited for Cobie in the lobby. He said nothing about my being there and brought us to the best recording studio on the planet. I would have given my kidney in order to own that giant mixing board.

"What do you think?" Cobie asked me.

"Can I live here? Thank you for bringing me." I gave her a quick hug. She had asked me last night to come with her to watch her record, and now I understood why. I felt like this could be my second home.

Rick sat in a chair and turned a few knobs. "Ready for you whenever you are, Cobie," he told her. He moved out a chair, indicating that I should sit by pointing at it.

When he didn't ask me to do anything, I moved back to give him space.

Cobie entered the booth and did her vocal warm-ups. "Testing," she said after.

"Ready," Rick said. He played a track of music the concert band had played.

She sang the song they wrote together, and he touched nothing on the mixing board.

I closed my eyes to listen to her, realizing something I had heard in tall tales.

Cobie finished and asked Rick, "Do I need to go again?"

"Nope, as always, you're perfect," he answered with a smile. He played the song and questioned any changes she wanted.

"Everything sounds great. What do you guys think?" she asked.

"If you're happy with it, I am," I answered. She needed to decide everything for herself, and I found nothing wrong. I doubted I would even if I listened to her song multiple times a day.

"Perfect, like always, the one-take wonder," Rick answered.

Cobie set the headphones on the stand.

"Does Cobie have a golden voice?" I asked Rick.

"A what?" she asked as she stepped into the room.

"A golden voice means you have a perfect sound," I answered.

Cobie asked, "Isn't perfection subjective?" Her tone sounded flat, and she pressed her lips into a line.

"Everyone would say you have a golden voice if it existed," Rick answered her.

"But it doesn't," she said.

"If only it did. What exists is your unique form of chromesthesia," Rick said.

"Is it rare?" she asked.

"Extremely. Sound for me doesn't have color," he answered.

"Not for me either," I said. Every day I learned something new about Cobie, and I couldn't wait to learn more.

We chatted for a bit until the musicians came. I sat on the couch watching her work with them, and when the guitar player didn't show up, I volunteered. I had to read the sheet music a few times to get it right. Cobie didn't need to. By lunchtime, she had her song ready for release.

Rick and she chatted about her next plan. He turned to me, asking, "Can you help Cobie get the melody out of her head and onto paper?"

"Sure," I answered. We had time between concerts. We could figure out a way that worked best for her.

"I don't want to cause you any issues with working on your music," she said to me.

"Once we're done with your song, we'll work on mine," I told her.

"Deal." She held out her hand, and I shook it. Her small hand was missing one thing: a ring.

Rick hugged us before we left. He had to do the final touches to the song to get it to the label. If I told any of my bandmates he had embraced me, they would never believe me. I felt comfortable leaving Cobie in his hands.

Megan waited for us outside the studio. She covered her face with her hands and pulled them away. Her unhappy expression signaled something bad had occurred.

Chapter Thirty-One

Cobie

Megan handed me a court document, and I read the first few lines. "I can't appear in court tomorrow. I have to rehearse three states away," I told her. My flight took off today.

"The next paperwork is the motion for a continuance. Having a contract to work in another state will show good cause," Megan said.

"Why is the court date tomorrow? Lawsuits have to go through a lot of back and forth before the court will let the case proceed," Jordan said.

"Mr. Bronson must've pulled some strings," Megan answered. She frowned afterward.

"Don't you need a jury?" Jordan scratched the back of his head and shifted his weight between his feet. What he asked made sense. How did this happen so fast?

"The case will be before a judge. I requested a jury, but the court denied my request," Megan answered.

"Do they usually deny you?" I asked.

"Depends on the judge. Ours is a no-nonsense which will help with your case. We have the facts on our side. I suspect your ex-manager decided on a speedy trial as a tactic, but he doesn't know me well. I'm great under pressure. You and your record label are being sued, and I'm already talking to their attorney. They seem to want what's best for you, and we'll cooperate with each other," Megan answered.

"They want to keep Cobie. She's an amazing singer, and they know it," Jordan said. His voice filled with happiness.

"Let's get a room to sign the paperwork, and then I need lunch," I said.

"I'll treat you both. Your bodyguards will take you to the airport. I already packed you a bag," Megan said.

"Thanks," I said to her. What had she packed for me?

"Don't worry. I didn't forget your guitar." Megan found us an empty conference room, and we reviewed the paperwork.

I sent her the copy of my contract I had stored digitally, just in case my bag got stolen. I wouldn't be a fool again.

Once we finished the paperwork, Megan asked, "What should we eat?"

Jordan and she turned to me and waited for me to respond as we walked out of the building.

"Why are you asking me? Jordan likes meat and potatoes. Megan hates anything that is not healthy. Of the three of us, I'm the least picky. Where can we go with a salad bar and steak?" I asked.

"I know a place," Tim said. I hadn't heard him approach.

"Take us there, please." I climbed into the first SUV and scooted over for Jordan.

Megan got in along with Tim and Brad.

I looked forward to the day I wouldn't need them anymore, and I regretted not attempting to get to know them better. When I worked with people, I liked to learn something about them. I intended to resolve this matter immediately.

"Tim, are you from here?" I asked.

"Born and raised. I spent some time in the military before starting my bodyguard business," he answered as he drove.

"If you run the company, why are you watching me?" I asked. He had better things to do.

"I come out for VIPs," Tim answered.

"I'm not a VIP," I said.

"Sweetie, you are. You're adorable, not realizing how much of a queen you truly are." Jordan touched the tip of my nose before he kissed my cheek.

Tim said to me, "You're the biggest client I've ever had. My daughters are huge fans."

"I'd love to meet them sometime," I said.

"You would make me the best father in the world if you did," Tim said.

"Can my wife meet you, too?" Brad asked.

"Of course," I answered.

Lunch with my lawyer, Jordan, and the bodyguards was awkward in the beginning. After we ordered, we had a good time. I learned the other bodyguards' names were Hugo and Dew. Megan dropped off my boyfriend and me at the airport. Calling Jordan that one word felt great and unbelievable. He was much more than the playboy singer I thought he was when we first met.

I woke up the next morning to Jordan missing from our bed. The flight, meeting, and recording messed up my days like being on the road had. I typically slept to synchronize my schedule, but the urgent need to compose my songs often prevented me from doing so.

Jordan must've heard me, for he came into the room and handed me a cup of cold coffee. "Tell me whether you prefer more or less sugar and cream."

I sipped it, giving him a thumbs up. "How long have you been up?"

"Around an hour. I went to the living room to work on my music."

I hung my head. "Sorry for taking up your time last night."

He sat next to me on the bed and kissed my forehead. "No apology is necessary. We're a team, and your former manager failed to get you better music writing training." Jordan's eyes darkened, and his voice rose. He sipped his straight black coffee. He had never called Dick anything but his name, 'ex', or 'former'. I was technically still under contract with Dick, and part of me knew he would pull that string soon enough. How soon? I had no clue.

"I have a better teacher now." I kissed Jordan on the cheek and asked him, "What time is it?"

"A few minutes after 8 a.m., I promise to have you at the venue before your practice time at 10," Jordan said.

"Why are you so good to me?"

He winced and touched the side of my face.

I kissed his hand.

"Why do you ask such a question? I want to spend my life taking care of you. I'm ready with the next step of you meeting my friends," Jordan said.

"Haven't I met them already?" I asked.

"Officially, as my girlfriend."

"I'm ready whenever you are. They won't be as bad as meeting my parents."

Jordan frowned.

"Don't worry. You won't meet my parents. They're not in my life, and I prefer them to stay out," I said.

"Someday I hope you can tell me why." Jordan took my empty cup and set it on the side table.

"They didn't notice when I left and let me sign with Dick. They got paid, so they didn't care until they didn't. They kicked me out. My sister is their golden child, and they don't acknowledge me." I rubbed my face and realized my heart no longer ached. I wasn't angry with them anymore.

"What's your relationship to your sister?"

"We have none, and I prefer it that way," I answered. She loved to gloat.

"My mom didn't call me and believed I did what the fake Cam said," Jordan said. His eyes welled with tears.

I set his coffee next to mine and hugged him.

"Danny, my best friend, told me to call her. If she wanted to speak to me, why didn't she call me?" Jordan asked.

"She might not know what to say. I had proof you didn't do what fake Cam had claimed. Your mom didn't," I answered.

"Please don't be on her side. My mom should never have believed I was capable of such a thing." Jordan pulled away from me and headed toward the window. He pulled back the curtain.

I went to him and wrapped my arms around his waist. "I'm always on your side. If you want her to call you, I'll make sure she does. If you don't, I'll make sure she doesn't."

Jordan thanked me and then kissed me enough to make my toes curl. "For now, I'll wait. We have bigger things to keep our minds occupied with your song releasing, your court, and our tour. If you need to leave for your trial, I'll let you out of your contract."

"Nope, I'll stay and open for you. Not sure what I'll do after my contract is up."

"You should headline your own show, but if you want, I'll put in a good word with the lead singer." He smirked at me.

"Please do. Did you get your songs back up?" I asked.

"Yeah, for your record label only. My fans understood why we pulled them, and a few artists removed their work from your ex-manager's company." His eyes widened. "Did Dick move up your trial because of my actions?"

"You heard Megan. He moved it up so that he could win his lawsuit. The artist in me says thank you for your support." I kissed Jordan on the lips. "And the girlfriend will thank you later."

"You don't need to. I wish there were more I could do for you."

"You've done more than enough." I rummaged through the expensive luggage bag Megan gave me, pulling out an outfit I had never bought. She hadn't mentioned she added to my wardrobe. At least she folded my bag neatly at the bottom. My contract with her and Solar Harmony rested in plastic covers with a note for placing inside a fireproof safe. Not like I could carry one around with me.

Jordan led me to the shower, and we ate breakfast after. "For supper, I'd like you to meet my band," he said. The suite was like our last one, with a bedroom, kitchen, table, and I bet a view.

"Supper with them sounds great." I didn't tell Jordan that I didn't want to see Royal.

"I'll plan it."

My phone rang, and I showed Jordan who was calling. "Hello," I said when I answered Megan. I glanced at the clock on the wall. It read almost 9 a.m. I didn't expect to hear from her until after rehearsal.

"Hey, our court date is Monday," she said.

"What about next Wednesday and next Friday?" I had one week left with Jordan's band after this week, and I had events on those dates.

"We'll have court on Monday and Tuesday and then break for the following week. The judge stated he won't be lenient again."

I read between the lines. He wouldn't let me continue with Solar Harmony even if I wanted to. Opening for them brought me back to when I started out, and I didn't want to miss the feeling or those days again.

We chatted for a bit before hanging up.

Jordan asked for the update, and I told him.

"I'll let my manager know to find a replacement," Jordan said.

"Will this cause issues with your band?" I asked.

"We have openers leave all the time. Getting a two-week notice, Cole will be happy, and he'll attend our dinner, too."

"Can Megan come? She's flying out soon to join me here. She wants to prep me for court when we have time."

"Yeah, and your bodyguards. I can't wait until they're no longer needed." I must've given him a strange look, so Jordan continued. "When they leave, no one is threatening your life. I want you safe."

"Fans can get overzealous." They wouldn't rip off my clothes since I was a woman—at least, I hoped they wouldn't.

"That day was the best day of my life."

My mind froze and then thawed as I asked him, "You like when you get chased?"

"Not at all. I got to meet you, and you changed me. My songs will remain unreleased until I'm happy with them. My band can't decide anymore," Jordan answered.

"As long as you're happy, because they'll never be perfect. Nothing ever is."

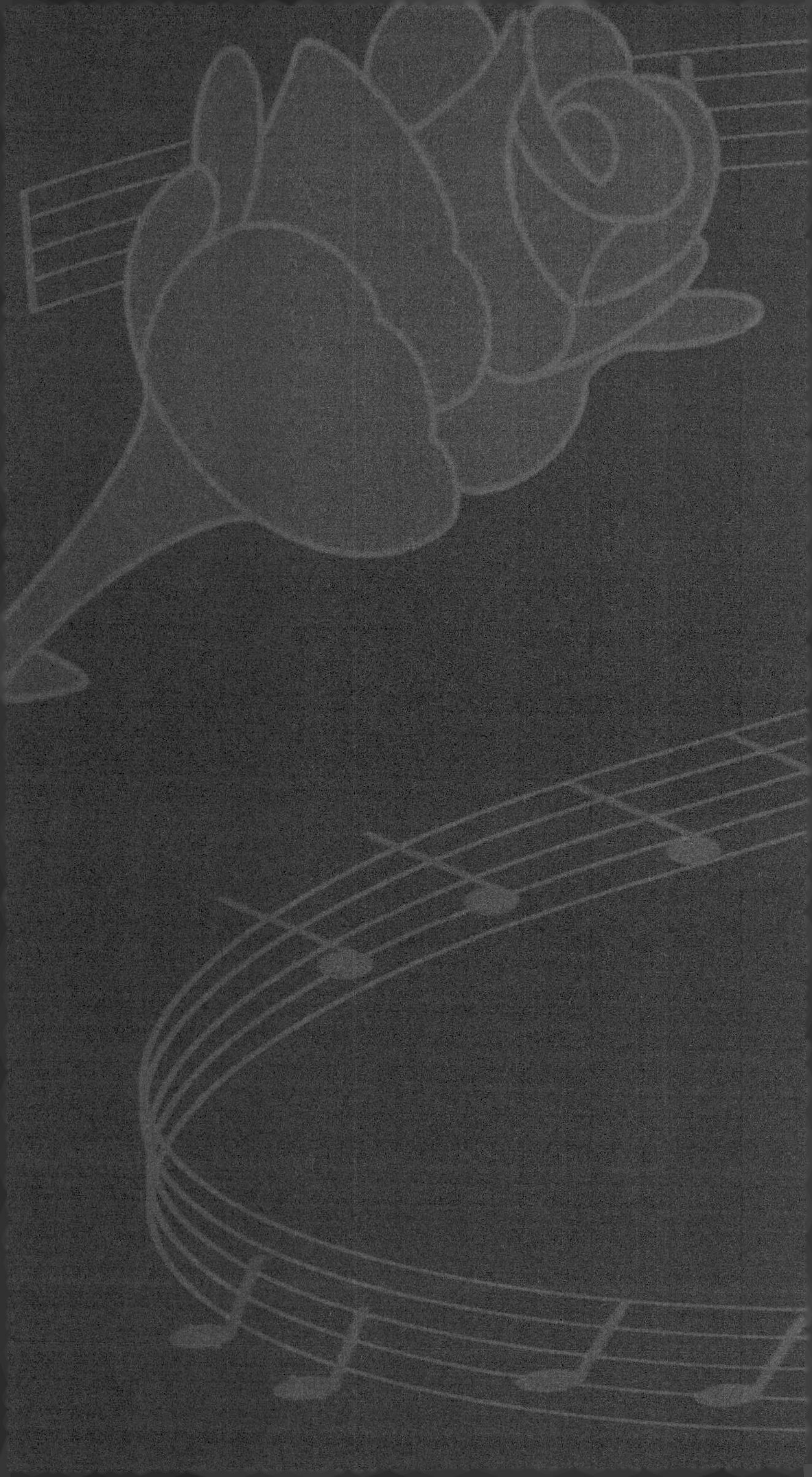

Chapter Thirty-Two

Jordan

Cole asked me for options to replace Cobie after her contract ended.

I silently groaned, since my band would want to meet right away, I couldn't watch her rehearsal. "Do you know a singer who would open for my band?" I jokingly asked Cobie.

She chewed on her bottom lip, and her eyes widened. "I met someone." She showed me a profile on social media.

Blaire Gunn had the typical celebrity no-smile image, and he was bald with a goatee. He needed more followers for Royal to agree for him to open for our band.

Cobie played a video of his singing. He hit the high notes unlike anything I'd ever heard from a guy.

"How did you meet him?" I asked. Jealousy rose inside me, and I pushed it back down. She had the right to have friends, male friends.

We should discuss whether we were exclusive. I planned on being, and I hoped she would, too.

"During *America's Next Big Star* auditions. I wonder how far Blaire got." Cobie ran a search online and found out he had lost in the live quarterfinals. If he sang like in the one video, the judges were idiots.

"Send me his profile link, and I'll check the songs as I ride back to the hotel."

"You're not staying to watch me?"

"Can't this time because my band and I have to find an opener. We usually do three, and Cole signs one of them."

"Why are you coming with me to the venue if you're returning to the hotel?" Cobie asked.

"I get a few more minutes with you," I answered.

"You're adorable." She kissed me on the cheek.

"Are we exclusive?"

Cobie winced, and her tone became flat. "I don't plan on sleeping with any except you. Do you think I am?"

"Hell, no. I had to check because I don't know what kids do nowadays," I said.

"Kids? You're what? Two years older than me," she said.

"Hey, being in the industry ages us."

"I must be super old then, especially after this year." Cobie sighed.

"Everything will get better soon." What else could I tell her? She might lose her court battle because the judge didn't understand she was Cam. I hadn't told her I planned on being with her on Monday, another reason I wanted to meet my band.

After the SUV stopped, we climbed out.

Fans already waited for us. Some held signs for her and others for my band. I hadn't worn my disguise and waved at them before we headed inside. I pulled her into my arms and pushed her hair out of her face, kissing her.

She kissed me back.

"I have rehearsals at one, so I'll text you when we're done with the details for supper." I hugged her before checking outside. The problem with heading to the venue with Cobie, her bodyguards stayed with her and parked their vehicles.

Noah pulled up in a van, and the fans screamed.

My cell dinged. I glanced at the message and headed to the vehicle.

Danny opened the door with a grin. "You didn't think about returning, did you?" he asked.

"Move over," I told him as I climbed inside. My face heated, and I sat next to him. Yeah, I'd forgotten.

"How is everything with you and Cobie?"

"Great. We should have supper together with her and Cole." I wanted to hide, but inside a van I had nowhere to go except for the front seat. Danny had to tease me.

"Please say Baylee and Jay can come. They're getting on my nerves. I told them you had a girlfriend."

"Of course, they're invited along with Royal, though I doubt he'll come." I couldn't keep the bitterness out of my voice.

"You're still mad at him," Danny said. His words didn't sound like a question.

"Wouldn't you be? He let the woman who accused me into the venue. I don't buy his BS story of helping her father." I held back from saying more and then decided I shouldn't. Deedee and Brittany had gotten nowhere with their investigation. I hadn't checked who did at the mansion, since I was busy with the tour and Cobie.

"Royal explained it as a favor."

"How did she know my password?"

Danny shrugged. "The staff knows. I knew."

"I did, too," our driver, Noah, called.

For a second, I forgot he was there. I needed to wait to tell Danny about the culprit texting fake Cam from my phone at our home.

Noah dropped us off at the door of the hotel a few minutes later.

"Thanks," I told Noah. Once Danny and I entered, I pulled him to the side. "I have to tell you something."

"What's up? You and Cobie didn't get married, did you?" Danny raised an eyebrow and glanced around the room.

"Stop teasing me about her."

"But you make it so easy. I've never seen you this serious about someone before."

"I'm getting annoyed with it."

"Can't I have a little more fun? I'll stop after," Danny said.

"Never mind," I told him. I stuck my hands in my pockets and headed toward the elevator. His inability to handle a simple request made me question how he'd react to a betrayal.

"I'm sorry." Danny chased after me.

The elevator opened, and we waited until the guests got out before we stepped inside.

Someone tried to get on, and Danny asked, "Please take the next one?"

They looked at us and nodded, saying nothing.

"What did you want to tell me?" Danny asked once we were alone. The awful music played through the speakers. The hotel needed to update its playlist. Even a country song would be better than what they were playing.

"We can't prove Dick's daughter sent the texts to the fake Cam when I was at the venue," I finally answered.

"Is that why you're mad? She no longer works for us and won't ever again. You also got more creative with your password."

"Someone sent the messages when I was at home."

Danny blinked at me and opened his mouth before shutting it.

"I can't prove who did it there, either. I have a suspect," I said.

"So, one of our band members framed you, too?" Danny asked. His voice squeaked.

"Or staff. I doubt they did because it wasn't always during hours they could."

"If I had to guess, I'd say Royal. He's always hated you and wants you out of the band."

"My thoughts exactly."

"What are we going to do?"

"Not a damn thing. I don't have proof, but Royal will eventually get himself into trouble that he can't explain. When he does, I'll call for a vote to get him out."

The band agreed on two names and a band to open for us after Cobie's contract ended. Blaire made it to the top of the list. I wouldn't tell her unless he accepted the offer. Most of the band agreed except for Royal until Cole pointed out we would use the publicity from the hit TV show as promo. I doubted we needed anything, since our tickets for all of our upcoming shows had sold out in record time.

I reserved a room for supper at a restaurant, not fine dining. Cobie and my friends wouldn't like it. She and Megan promised to meet us there since they had been busy prepping for her hearing on Monday.

The owner and head chef met us at the door, ushering us to the room away from the other patrons. They apologized for the hassle and the condition of the restaurant.

"This is great. Thank you for having us," I told them. I enjoyed the beams overhead and the large windows instead of a ceiling and walls.

"Is anyone else joining you?" the owner asked as he closed the window.

"Six more," I answered.

A server handed out menus and set more on the table.

"This is my daughter," the owner said. She sounded proud.

"Nice to meet you. I'm Jordan." I held out my hand to her, and the girl blushed.

She shook my hand and asked, "Can I get a picture with you?"

"I told you not to ask," her mother scolded her.

"Actually, bring out your staff before we leave, and we'll take pictures." I enjoyed meeting fans, and I also liked not being bugged during a meal. If I promised later, the staff would.

leave us alone.

"Okay!" the girl squealed.

"Sorry," the mother mouthed as she pulled her daughter away.

I suspected the teenager would let her friends know, and we'd have a circus outside the restaurant fast. At least Cobie would stay safe with her bodyguards.

"When's your girlfriend getting here?" Royal asked. He had come once he found out Cole would join us.

I read a new text from Cobie and answered, "They're pulling up now."

Cole handed me a hat.

I put it on as I headed out the door.

Cobie entered, and her gaze flittered across the room. We met halfway.

I gave her a kiss on the cheek and said, "Hey, Megan."

"Hi, Jordan," Megan said. She crossed her arms and looked around the room.

"We have a private room in the back. The restaurant vowed to keep others out," I told her.

"We'll station ourselves by the door," Tim said.

I led them to the backroom, and my band moved over for Cobie to sit next to me. Most of them said hi to her as she sat.

Megan took the open chair on Cobie's either side.

"This is Megan, Cobie's lawyer," I told my band and manager. I also introduced everyone else to her.

"What's good here?" Megan asked.

I winced, for I had forgotten she liked more of the leafy food. I glanced at the menu, spotting salad and soup options. Not going to a place for Cobie's friend to eat would make me a horrible boyfriend.

We had some beers and good food with light conversation. I enjoyed spending the downtime with everyone here, even the bodyguards and Royal. They seemed like good people. Besides Royal.

The staff asked for pictures after we had finished most of our food.

I put my arm around Cobie, and she leaned into me. Photos of us had already leaked as went to the venue today. They didn't get a good shot of her at the hotel the first night we slept together. Now the world would know we were together, and I couldn't be happier.

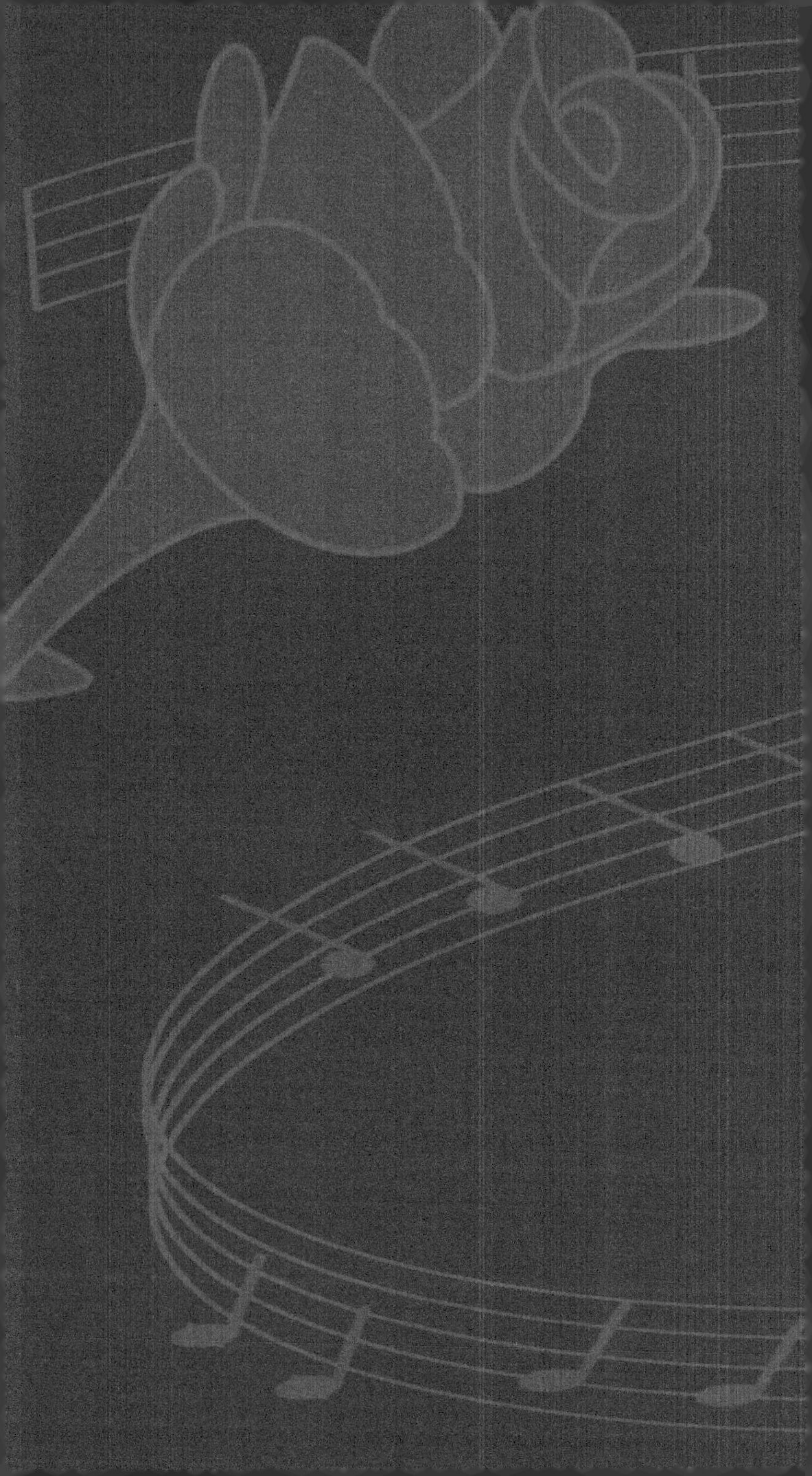

Chapter Thirty-Three

Cobie

Monday Court

Megan had bought me suits and helped me put on makeup. "Your mom never helped you with this?" she asked me the morning before court.

"My mother was too busy with her perfect daughter." I rolled my eyes.

"Wait, you have a sister. Can she sing?"

"Nope.

"How much money did you pay your parents?"

I shrugged.

"Do you have an account? Can you get access to those records?" Megan pressed her lips into a thin line, and her eyes moved back and forth. She had to plan something.

"I'd have to check if the account is open. My parents probably closed it," I answered.

"They had access to your bank?"

"Yeah, I couldn't open one at twelve."

"You never started a new one?"

"I never had time to," I answered. When I started out, I handed out flyers and played at any place willing to host me. After I made a name for myself, I spent about ninety-five percent of my time away from my parents. Once I turned eighteen, I didn't see them for a year.

"Close your eyes," Megan instructed. She applied eyeshadow to my eyelid, the crease, and my brow bone. She emphasized a subtle look but with a dark red lipstick for fierceness. The colors matched well with my tan skin and light brown hair.

I pressed my lips together.

"Stop touching your face and pressing your lips together. You'll smear the makeup. If we need to, we do it in front of the mirror." Megan checked her face in front of one and removed a small clump of mascara. "Perfect. My hands will never touch my face, and besides, it makes you look guilty."

I got yelled at a lot for messing with my hair and rubbing my eyes whenever a makeup artist worked on me. I'd never realized just how often I touched my face until I couldn't anymore.

Wilma knocked on the doorframe. "How are my girls? Ready to battle?"

"I'm always ready." Megan placed her hands on her trim waist and puffed out her chest.

We laughed and headed downstairs to the waiting SUVs. Soon I might not need my bodyguards, and I would miss them. They,

Megan, and Jordan made me feel safe. Something I hadn't felt most of my life, not even with my parents.

Wilma waved at us until we drove out of sight.

"I like your mom," I told Megan.

"She likes you too and wants to adopt you. I told her that, as a lawyer, she can't adopt adults." Megan smiled and tapped her fingers against the briefcase next to her. Despite knowing everything about my case and the lawsuit, anything could happen in court, according to her.

Reporters lined up as we parked.

"Don't speak to them, and Tim will get you inside. Cobie's safety comes first," Megan reminded my top bodyguard.

"Always, ma'am." Tim handed the keys over to his partner before they left the vehicle. He opened Megan's door, and she slid out.

I followed behind her. A nervous energy rose inside me, and I pushed it back down. I hated being the center of attention unless I was on stage. The walkway before the courthouse was the backstage, and I needed to go up the steps to perform.

"Are you Cam?" a reporter asked me. They shoved a microphone in my face.

"No questions," Megan answered.

"Excuse us." Tim positioned himself between me and the reporters.

I held my head up high as I walked past the crowd, paying them no attention.

My actual fans lined up and screamed my name behind a barricade. Some said unkind words to me. Why didn't the reporters wait behind the established boundaries with them? The police and security granted access closer to the courthouse to anyone with a media badge.

Someone hurled something at me.

Tim grabbed me by the waist, pulled me into his body, and pushed the reporters away at the same time. He knocked the glass to the ground with his other hand.

The bottle broke, and white smoke poured out.

"Don't breathe in," he told me.

I covered my mouth and hurried inside the building, where I took a deep breath. "What did they throw?" I asked.

"My men will find out. They're controlling the crowd, and the police have already arrested the culprit. How is everyone feeling? Any symptoms?" Tim covered his ear as he listened to his men.

"I'm fine," I answered.

"I'm good, too," Megan said.

More security guards came rushing toward us. One guy asked us to move aside.

Megan handed me a bottle of water from her briefcase. "Drink this."

I quenched my thirst. I was extremely nervous, and I wanted to text Jordan, but he'd probably pull some knight-in-shining-armor bullshit to be here with me. He had already flown to me at the first hint of trouble.

Tim spoke to us, "We're still confirming, but dry ice was inside the object." No wonder it exploded on impact. How long had it been inside?

"We can ask for a continuance with the court after this incident," Megan said.

"No, I'd rather get it over with. Dick probably organized it all," I said. I wouldn't put it past him. What better way to make me look like a fool than to stage something stupid like this?

Megan nodded, and we headed to the metal detector.

The guards motioned us through. Even Tim and Hugo didn't buzz as they made their way through the scanner. They were deadly enough without guns.

Tim opened the door to the courtroom, and Dick's annoying voice drafted through.

"Your Honor, we should call for judgment. One plaintiff isn't coming," he said.

His words made my skin crawl.

"Sorry, Your Honor. There was an incident outside of court that threatened my client's life." Megan walked up front, and I followed behind her. My bodyguards stayed back.

Jordan and three of the four other members of Solar Harmony sat in the pews on my side.

My heart swooned at the sight of them.

The attorney and owner of Golden Records stood for us as Megan and I joined them.

Judge Roy Russo raised an eyebrow, but didn't ask for more details.

"What did this Cobie person stub a toe or something?" Dick asked.

His attorney cleared his throat; a clear sign for my former manager to shut the fuck up.

I forgot Dick liked to talk. We could use that against him. I glanced at the table with him, and he had Cam. Well, fake Cam. She wore a mask next to him.

"No matter. You're here now, and I will learn about the situation later," the Judge said. He sounded unhappy. "Please be seated."

I settled into my spot between the two lawyers. I had met the owner of Golden Records a handful of times while employed at Cam. He had been at the new contract signing and insisted we work together. He had apologized for Dick's behavior toward me even after his council told him not to.

"The plaintiff may proceed with their opening statement," Judge Russo said.

Megan walked to the podium and spoke into the microphone. "Good morning. My client is Cobie Meine. We're here because Cobie used the name Cam until last year. She signed with RAB Entertainment and owner Dick Bronson to represent her when she was twelve years old.

"They decided she should wear a mask because she had stage fright. When she wanted to remove her mask, Dick left her by the side of the road with nothing except the clothes on her back and the money in her pocket. He took her identification and her stage name, Cam. We're here to prove Cobie is Cam and get the money she never received from being the top singer in America, maybe even the world. We will also prove she did not sign away the investments she had bought in her real name for Mr. Bronson. Thank you for your time."

Megan's last words got my attention. I didn't read everything in the lawsuit because the lawyer's speech made my eyes blur.

The attorney for my record label gave our second opening statement, presenting facts in our case.

"Mr. Rover," the Judge said once he finished.

"I am Blaine Rover, and I represent Richard 'Dick' Bronson, the owner of RAB Entertainment. Dick has never met the plaintiff, Ms. Meine, and he bought the investments without ever meeting the seller. She is not Cam. Cam is sitting next to him in court. We'll focus on the evidence in this case to prove Ms. Meine is not Cam. You're being asked to decide if she is. We will prove the counterclaim against Ms. Meine and Golden Records is true. Thank you, Your Honor," the lawyer said.

We had a recess and then returned to the courtroom. I hadn't had time to speak to Jordan or text him. His support meant a lot to me.

"All rise, Honorable Judge Russo presiding," the bailiff said.

The courtroom rose and sat at the Judge's command as soon as he entered.

"Plaintiff may call its first witness," Judge Russo said.

The attorney for my record label stood and said, "We call Rick Davis to the stand."

Rick came forward wearing another suit, but this time, he wore a jacket. I definitely owed him for yet again dressing uncomfortably. He stated his name and occupation for the court, swore to tell the truth, and answered the first question of how we first met. The inquiry continued into how he realized I was Cam.

"I was working with another client who needed more time before we continued. Once she left, my assistant entered the room with the news of Cobie's performance earlier while I was in session. I don't like being interrupted. As soon as I heard her sing the song we created together, I knew she was Cam," Rick answered.

"Who knew this song existed?" Megan took over questioning to eliminate coaching allegations from the record label's attorney.

"Only Cam and me," he answered.

"Why not your record label?" she asked.

"They don't hear any of my music until it's finished. The song wasn't finished," Rick answered with ease.

"How did Cobie sing it if you hadn't finished it?" Megan asked.

"She completed it," he answered.

Megan asked, "How do you know Cobie is Cam?"

The defense tried to object, but the Judge squashed it and ordered Rick to answer.

"I've worked with Cam, and she is incredible with music. Look at the articles published by other producers and songwriters. They will say the same thing," Rick answered.

"These articles?" Megan pulled up the first one. A highlighted portion showed another producer saying I was a one-take wonder.

"Yes, as you can see. Cam is a one-take wonder, meaning she sings the song the correct way on the first and only take. She has an instinct for it. Next article, please," Rick answered.

Megan brought it up.

"Cobie has perfect pitch for identifying notes played after hearing them once. She has a golden voice as well. You won't find it in any articles. Having all three things is astronomical. I've only met one person who has them, and that person is Cam. Cobie has it, too. They're the same," Rick answered.

"Have you met this Cam?" Megan pointed at the woman next to Dick.

"Yeah, she's not Cam. She's so unprofessional that I almost gave up on her singing the song we were working on together," Rick answered.

"No more questions," Megan told the Judge.

The defense tried, but they never got Rick to admit anything in their favor. Too bad the judge didn't moonlight as a musician; he'd be able to understand our world more.

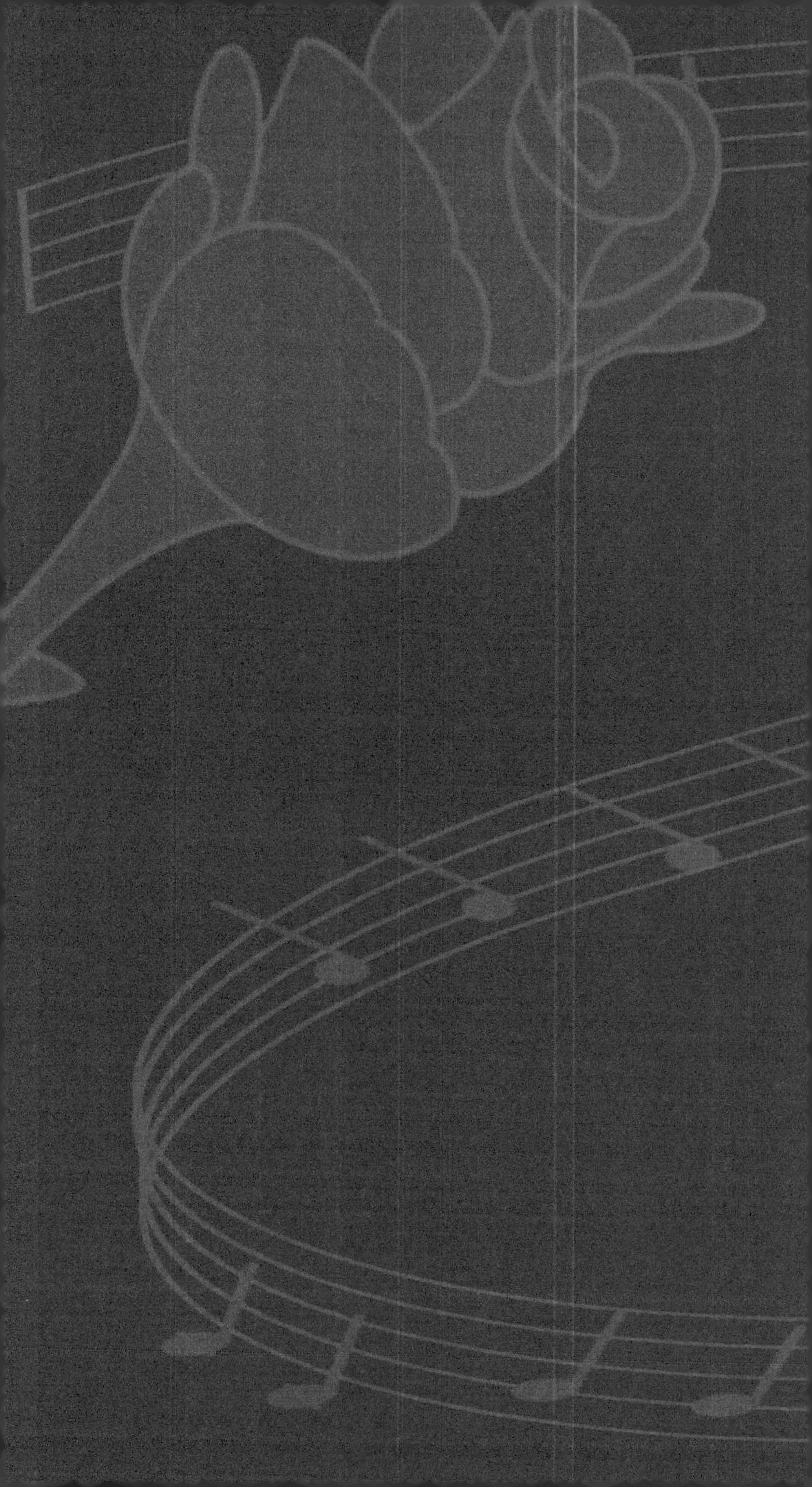

Chapter Thirty-Four

Jordan

Megan finally called Cobie to the stand.

Cobie swore to tell the truth before she sat in the witness box.

"Cobie, why did you wear a mask?" Megan asked.

"Performing in front of people I had never met made me sick. I had severe stage fright. Time passed, and the mask became a security blanket. I worked to become less afraid. I let Mr. Bronson know I was ready to shed the mask, and he wouldn't let me," Cobie answered.

Megan asked her more questions about what happened to her after Dick left her.

Cobie entered excruciating detail.

Danny placed a hand on my arm and whispered, "Get in line to punch him." He motioned his head at Baylee, who sported sheer hatred across his face.

I had balled my hands into fists, and the urge to punch swept through me.

"Where did you live after you couldn't afford your apartment?" Megan asked Cobie.

Cobie's eyes flickered to me and then back to Megan before she answered, "On the streets, if the shelter didn't have cots."

"You, the richest signer in the world, lived on the streets?" Megan asked. Her tone reflected her disbelief. Everyone in the courtroom heard it as she faced the judge.

"Yeah, I had a blanket I hid at night to keep it safe," Cobie answered.

"Why didn't you return to your parents?" Megan asked.

"I did, but they kicked me out after Mr. Bronson stopped paying them," Cobie answered.

They spoke about more proof that Cobie was Cam, with certain things that happened through her life only the mega pop singer would know. Megan sat down when she finished. Why didn't she have Cobie sing? Once the judge heard, surely he would understand she was Cam.

The defense asked questions and tried to get Cobie to stumble. She held her own rather well. For a second I thought Megan had coached her, and then I realized Cobie acted like she was on a stage. Off-stage, she was a little timid and kind, but once she sang or discussed music, she brightened.

The Judge called for a recess until tomorrow, with the defense starting with its case.

I waited with most of my band to see what Cobie would do. The rest of the court shuffled out until only she, her bodyguards, us, and her lawyer remained.

"Thank you for coming," she told Baylee. She proceeded down the line until she reached me and embraced me. "I'm so happy to see you."

"I had to come, since I can't be here every day," I told her as I embraced her back. She felt good in my arms despite the connection being brief.

"You shouldn't be here at all," she said.

"Stop it. I'm here for you, and if I can't be, I'll watch your trial online as much as possible." I nodded at the camera stationed on the wall. The view eliminated the empty jury boxes and people watching. None of the Solar Harmony fans would see us. If they did, the trial would become more of a circus, and I would have to stay away for Cobie's sake.

"What happened when you came to court? Why were you late?" Baylee asked. He had left his usual dark-colored hoodie at home for a black suit. He and Danny had ditched a tie. They had better plan on wearing one at my wedding, whenever that might be.

I was relieved he asked my girlfriend, instead of me. The thought of her pain if I asked would end me.

Cobie hesitated before answering. "Someone tossed a container of dry ice at me. Tim protected me from it." She lifted her hand and stopped herself from touching her hair. She made a fist as she brought it down.

"Why would someone throw it at you?" Jay fiddled with his bowtie.

"To cause Cobie harm," I answered. The anger in my voice seeped out, and I wanted to do something a celebrity should never do. We had to maintain control, but no one should attempt to harm us or treat us like possessions. I loved my fans, and I enjoyed singing with them, but I was a normal human who sang a little better than the masses.

"The police arrested the criminal and want a statement. I can let them know you need another day," Tim said.

"No, let's get it over with." Cobie turned to me and said, "And we have music to write after." Her eyes sparked with mischief. She wanted to do much more, and I was down for whatever she had planned.

I had never worked on so many songs in such a short amount of time until I met her. I loved every minute. Writing a song and then making love to her was the best way to end the night. I wanted to repeat it for the rest of our lives. Of course, tours and court dates would get in our way.

"We'll take Cobie to the police station and then let's eat supper together, my treat," Megan said.

"Where should we meet?" Danny sounded a little too eager. His crush on Megan had yet to subside, and I should warn him she might have a thing for my lawyer.

"I know a place," Tim said. Afterward, he told us the name. He glanced at his watch before committing a time for us to meet there.

"If we get there first, we'll save the spots." Danny clapped his hands together.

I kissed Cobie on the cheek before heading out. Somehow, our fans realized we were at the courthouse, and they lined up. We waved at them and then our driver pulled to the curb. One of our band members must've told him we were done.

"How did it go?" Noah asked after we piled in.

"Hard to say," I answered. Danny and I sat next to each other on the way back, with the other two taking up the seat in front of us. Funny how, despite Royal not being here, we never claimed his spot in front.

"We should invite our manager to dinner," I said.

"Noah can come too," Baylee said.

"Yeah, man. Thanks for flying back with us and for taking us to court. We appreciate it," I said.

"I like Cobie too. She's the secret member of Solar Harmony," Noah said. He asked us where to go.

"I need to get out of this suit. Do I have to wear one tomorrow?" Danny played with his collar and loosened a button.

"If you plan on coming to court tomorrow, you do," I answered him.

Cole picked up after the first ring and agreed to come.

"We had better invite Royal to supper." Jay turned around in his seat, and his lower lip trembled.

"Do we have to?" Danny asked. Ever since I told him about someone in our band sabotaging me, he had been extra mean to Royal.

"We can ask, but he might not come," I answered.

"He won't come if you ask," Danny said with a grin.

"Fine, I will," I said.

Noah parked at our place and climbed out of the van with us. "Need to take a piss," he said as he hurried inside.

"I'll open the door." Jay followed our driver.

"Why don't you like Royal anymore? I get why Jordan doesn't," Baylee said to Danny.

Danny glanced at me and then shrugged. He shoved his hands into his dark navy dress trousers before entering the mansion.

Baylee turned to me as if he expected me to answer. How much did I trust him?

I ran my hand through my hair and told the truth. He and Jay would never betray me. Jay was loyal to a fault, and Baylee never kept a secret. I hoped he'd keep this one. "Because Royal sabotaged me. I don't have proof, but I've built a timeline of the planted text messages to fake Cam. Some line up with when I was home."

Baylee opened his mouth and snapped it shut. He touched his clean-shaven chin as if he were thinking of something. "How did Royal get hold of your phone?"

"Not sure. He never hung out with me, and he stayed out of my side of the mansion."

"Jay wouldn't do anything to you. He idolizes you."

"Exactly, and you speak your mind. Never change."

"Royal tells me to watch what I say in public," Baylee said. His eyes filled with sadness.

"Because people will take what you say the wrong way. You make an innocent comment like we're working on an album. Next thing, everyone wants to know when it's coming out. Best to keep our answers open," I said.

"Are we working on an album?"

"Have you heard any songs lately?"

"No, you haven't been sharing."

"Exactly," I said.

"That doesn't answer my question. Are we releasing another album?" Baylee asked.

"We'll release another album in the future."

Baylee gave me a dirty look, and I grinned back at him. His eyes widened. "I see what you did there. I want to know when we'll release an album soon."

I hurried inside the mansion.

He chased after me and asked, "When are we releasing an album?"

"When are we releasing our next album?" Royal asked me.

"We did a few months ago, and I'm working on the next," I answered them. Every day, I grew a little closer to completing the songs necessary for an album.

"Our Christmas album doesn't count," Royal said.

"Our sales say it does," I pointed out.

As I was about to ask Royal, Jay asked him instead, "We're having supper together with Cobie and her people. Cole's coming too. Are you joining us?"

"I could eat something." Royal scratched his chin and leaned against the counter. Who in the hell did he try to put a show on for? Our band should be the only ones here, other than Noah.

"Do we have a guest?" I asked.

Royal curled his upper lip, rejecting my question with one look.

"Why are you acting like this?" I wagged my pointed finger around him.

"Like what?" he asked.

Danny laughed from the couch and explained, "Royal's trying to get a certain member to idolize him. I can read Royal like a book."

"Like you ever picked up one in your life," Royal muttered. He didn't deny it, so he must be.

I felt like he had an ulterior motive. When didn't he? "I'm changing and meeting you in twenty minutes," I told them.

Noah said he had enough time to gas up. I felt a little bad about him driving us to supper, even when he was coming along. We paid him well, though. He drove and hit no paparazzi, no matter how much they got in the way.

Dinner with everyone gave us time to relax. The staff freaked out, and we told them they could take pictures with us after. Once Megan had paid, I took Cobie back to my place. I had cleaned my room. We never got around to making more music.

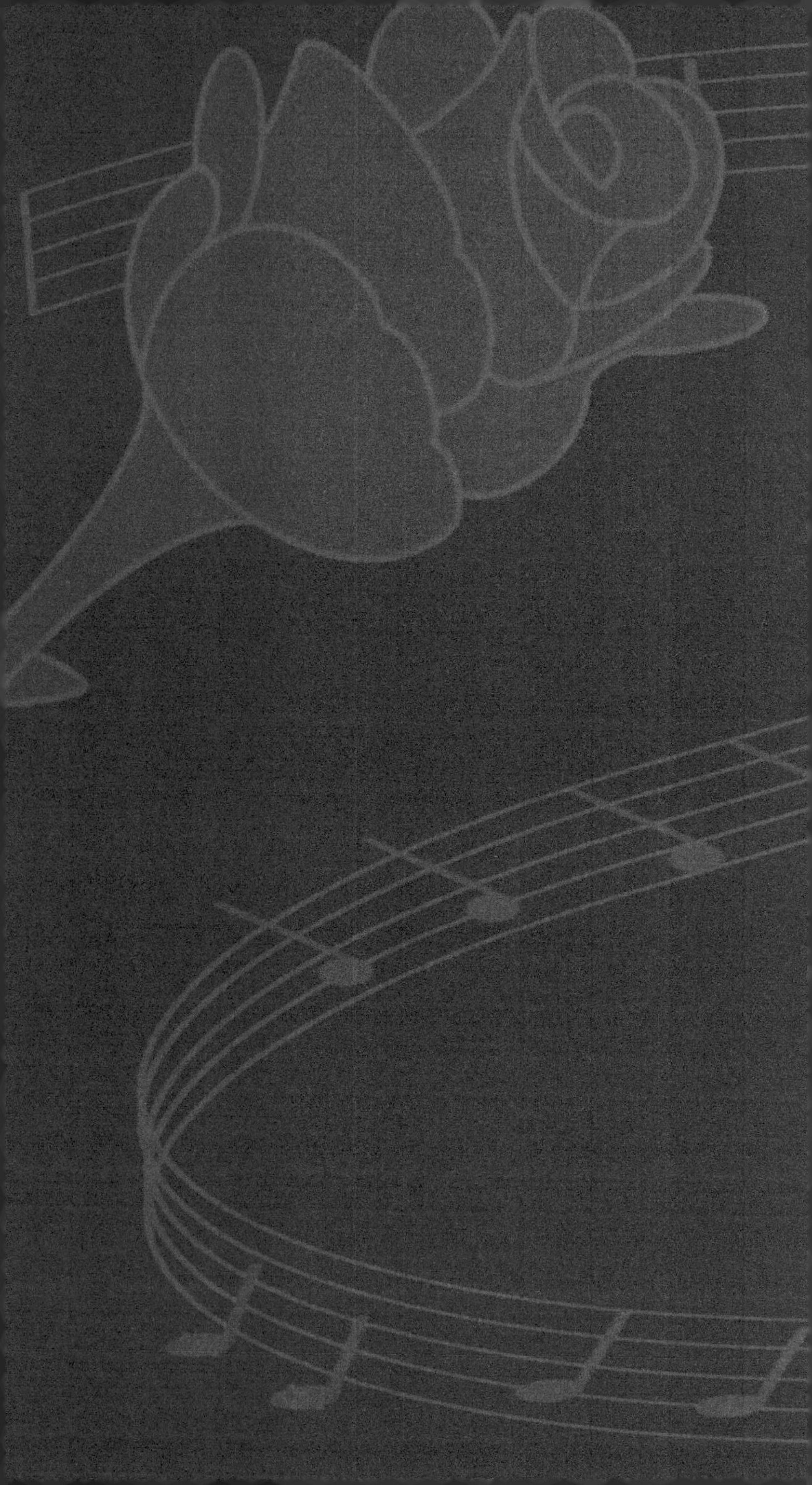

Chapter Thirty-Five

Cobie

The Next Day

The following morning, my alarm sounded far too early. I felt like I hadn't slept.

Jordan pulled me into his arms and said, "Five more minutes."

"Can't this time." I hadn't grabbed my suit for court, and I had to shower, dry my hair, and do my makeup. The latter was easier when someone else did it for me, like when I had a concert or some event. I had never learned how to do my own because of them. For today, I'd do the basics. I should try contouring after the trial.

Jordan peeked at me with one eye and grinned. He kissed me, leaving me breathless. "Do you need to get up now?"

"Unfortunately, I do." I kissed him back before finding my clothes strewn around his room. He had it picked up until we'd tossed other things everywhere. When did he have the time? He either took a bus back to show up yesterday or he flew.

"At least let me make you breakfast. Have you had a home-cooked meal lately?"

I zipped up my pants. "Megan's mom cooks for us."

"Lucky you." Jordan pulled out clean clothes from his dresser and closet. He handed me one of his shirts. "I might've destroyed the buttons on your blouse." He hung his head sheepishly.

My cheeks heated as I put on his shirt. I took my hair out of the collar, running my fingers through it. I needed to brush it. Sex hair and bedhead made a bad combination.

"What's for breakfast?" I asked.

Jordan held out his hand, and I took it. He led me to the kitchen, where most of his band had already cooked. The smell of sausage and bacon made my mouth water.

"Where do you want me to help?" I asked them.

"Guests sit and relax. Do you prefer orange juice or apple juice?" Jordan asked me.

"The first," I answered.

Baylee set a tall glass in front of me. He had a dusting of freckles across his face I'd never noticed before. He hid his mouth with the sleeve of his hoodie, like he normally wore whenever I saw him.

I thanked him for the drink, and the cold tang gave me a bit of a toothache.

Danny flipped a pancake. He wore an apron with frilly edges around it, and he looked adorable in it. I swear if any of his fans saw him like this; they'd blow a gasket.

Jay took a piece of crispy bacon out of the pan and put it on a plate.

Jordan toasted bread and spread some butter on the slices.

They worked with the same rhythm they exhibited when singing their music.

"When did you find the time to learn to make breakfast?" I asked them.

"Jordan's mom had a fit when we said we couldn't cook. She taught us how, even Royal." Danny glanced at my man.

Jordan's shoulders had tensed at the mention of his mom, but he said nothing. He still hadn't worked out their issues. I hoped he would soon, but I wouldn't pressure him into it. If anyone tried to force me to speak to my parents, I would flip out. They stole my money, and his mom didn't believe him. Which one was worse? His. Money was replaceable, but lost trust wasn't.

Baylee continued to pour more drinks and take items out of the fridge. Where did Royal fit in their setup? He would never wear an apron like Danny and Jay.

While we ate breakfast, Royal joined us. Now I understood where he fit in. I should give him a chance, even though I held a grudge for the way he treated me when we first met and the way he acted toward Jordan. His fans claimed I tried to flirt with him. He wasn't my type. Neither was Jordan in the beginning, but I was wrong about him. He was sweet and caring, not a player. He loved music more than me.

"Are your bodyguards coming to get you, or can I give you a ride to Megan's?" Jordan asked me after we finished the meal.

"Does Cobie have to leave?" Jay asked.

"I have court, but we can hang this week since I'll still be opening for you during the tour still. Sorry I can't continue after I'm done," I answered.

"Jordan mentioned you'd apologize for something not under your control," Jay said.

"We already found a replacement." Danny stared at Jordan.

"We did?" Jordan asked.

"Yeah, Cole tried to call you, but you were busy last night," Danny answered.

Jordan nodded and never asked who their new show opener would be.

My face heated, and I turned to Jordan, asking him, "Can you give me a ride to Megan's, please?" The chance of me being a car owner soon was slim. The lawsuit stopped the royalty payments from my record company directly to me instead of my ex-manager. They wouldn't pay me for the current song until after the quarter ended. I was still broke, and I owed a lot of money to Megan.

"I wish you could stay on longer," Baylee said to me.

"Why? Her music doesn't go with ours." Royal glared at me from across the room on the couch.

"You're an idiot. Cobie has a golden voice and can sing anything," Jordan told his roommate. He patted my leg. "Let's go."

Royal said something, but Jordan ushered me out of the house.

He opened the door of his Lambo for me. Once he climbed in on his side, he sighed. "I'm sorry my bandmate is such an asshole. You deserve way more respect than he gives you. I'm talking to him after I drop you off."

"You don't have to," I said.

"Yeah, I do. You're my girlfriend, and he needs to stop being a royal pain in the ass." Jordan started up his car.

I gave him a kiss he wouldn't forget and stopped myself from laughing at his words. Damn, he was so cute.

"I'll see you in court," he told me after dropping me off.

Jordan showed up for my court hearing with his manager and his band, even Royal. Their talk must've been interesting, but I suspected the real reason the royal pain in the ass attended was because his fans stood behind the barriers at the courthouse.

At least I made it to court on time and without another incident. I had to ask Megan to find out if the police had caught whoever posed a threat to my life. I needed to be more involved rather than just coast along. If I didn't, I'd end up in another situation with lawsuits.

Judge Russo called the court to order, and Dick's attorney started with their side, their lies. They had witness after witness to poke holes in my lawsuit. Megan had warned me they'd use this tactic, and I shouldn't get angry. My face needed to remain neutral.

"We call Cam to the stand," the defense attorney said.

I stood.

Megan set her hand on mine and shook her head.

"I said, Cam," the defense attorney said in a snide voice. He glared at me.

Fake Cam came made her way toward the witness box.

A few people in the courtroom chuckled.

Jordan cleared his throat behind me, and I felt the anger coming off him in waves.

I sat down with a shrug.

The Judge pressed his lips into a line and asked fake Cam to state her name for the court.

"Will Cam do? I want to keep my anonymity." She laughed nervously and ran her hand through one of the many wigs I wore throughout my career. Her voice sounded familiar.

"You may," the Judge said.

"My name is Cam," the faker said.

The Judge swore her in, and the defense attorney approached her.

"How long have you been Cam?" the defense attorney asked fake Cam. He paid no attention to us.

"Since I was twelve. I had my parents sign a waiver for me to join RAB Entertainment," she answered.

Holy shit! I knew who she was, so I tapped Megan on the shoulder, whispering to her. Dick using her made a lot more sense than anyone else.

"Have you met Ms. Meine?" The defense attorney pointed at me. In attending law school, he had never learned it wasn't nice to do the gesture.

"Never." Cam gave a nervous giggle. "I'm sorry. No one sued me."

That was her first lie. Megan had uncovered something I never realized. Someone had sued me, and Dick kept it from me.

His gaze hardened, and his lips flattened. He clearly wasn't too happy with his little princess. He could testify that he had never told Cam, me, about the lawsuit. Doubted the idiot would realize it.

The defense and fake Cam continued with more fabrications regarding her time as me. Once they finished, we had a recess.

Thirty minutes later, the court session continued, and I anxiously awaited my team's reaction to the new information. Using the bathroom prevented me from talking to my attorney or Jordan.

"The cross-examination of Cam will continue," the Judge said.

"Judge Russo, please refrain from calling this person Cam. We're in a lawsuit for my client to prove she is the real Cam," Megan said.

"What else would you call her?" Dick asked. Venom filled his words.

"I'm the one deciding who Cam is in this matter," Judge Russo told Megan.

"How did you determine to use the pseudonym?" Megan asked fake Cam. Her asking questions surprised me because she told me this morning on the ride over she wouldn't cross-examine. My label worked with me and understood my music better than she did.

"I'd rather not say," fake Cam answered.

"Answer the question," the Judge said.

"If I do, I'll reveal my identity, and I'm not ready," fake Cam said.

"I'm fine with that, Your Honor." Megan turned back to the girl in the witness box. "But using C.A.M. is specific. Is it your initials or something special to you? You can at least tell us why you chose the three letters."

The other girl looked at her attorney before saying into the microphone, "Um, they're my initials."

"Interesting. How does Talia Mary Bronson, your real name, become Cam?" Megan asked.

The courtroom gasped.

Dick climbed to his feet and shouted a few seconds later.

"I'll have order in my courtroom," Judge Russo yelled. He banged his gavel. Once everyone settled down, he faced my attorney. "I won't have another outburst."

"Sorry, Your Honor. I'd like Ms. Bronson to answer my question," Megan said.

"Objection, Your Honor," the defense attorney said.

"On what grounds?" the Judge asked. What excuse would the defense attorney use?

The defense stumbled over his words and rubbed his chin as he sought an answer. "This is a sensitive matter, Your Honor. Whether or not Cam is Ms. Bronson, we can't have speculations over the identity of my client's client."

"You're right. I'll ask everyone to leave the courtroom, including the bodyguards. We'll stop recording here also," Judge Russo said.

The bailiff ushered everyone out.

I waved at Jordan before he left and turned to face the front. The red light on the camera stopped flashing.

"Cam, answer the question. Are you Ms. Bronson?" The Judge stippled his hands in front of himself, and his voice sounded calm.

Talia covered her masked face with her hands. She nodded her head.

"Please take off your mask so we can speak to you," Judge Russo said.

She lifted her head, pulled off the mask, and crocodile tears rolled down her cheeks. She always knew how to cry on command. Her wig caught on the back of the examination box before it fell to the floor.

"State your name for the court," the Judge said.

"Talia Mary Bronson," she said with a squeak.

"Objection, Your Honor. My client doesn't want her name known to the public. She'll get harassed like Ms. Meine has," the defense attorney said.

"Strike it from the record," Judge Russo told the court reporter.

He did something on his stenotype machine.

The Judge told Megan to continue her questioning.

"Ms. Bronson, how old are you?" Megan asked.

Talia glanced at her father and muttered a word.

"We can't hear you," the Judge told her. His voice grew soft.

"Eighteen," Talia answered. She moved down in her chair as if she wanted to hide.

"How have you been recording music for ten years?" Megan asked her.

She glanced at her father and then faced Megan again. "I started at eight?"

"Are you asking a question?" Judge Russo asked Talia.

"I am not. I started working at eight," Talia answered. The confidence in her voice grew, and she squared her shoulders and straightened her posture.

Dick had given her the money hand sign and lowered his hand back down. He would no longer pay her if she messed this up.

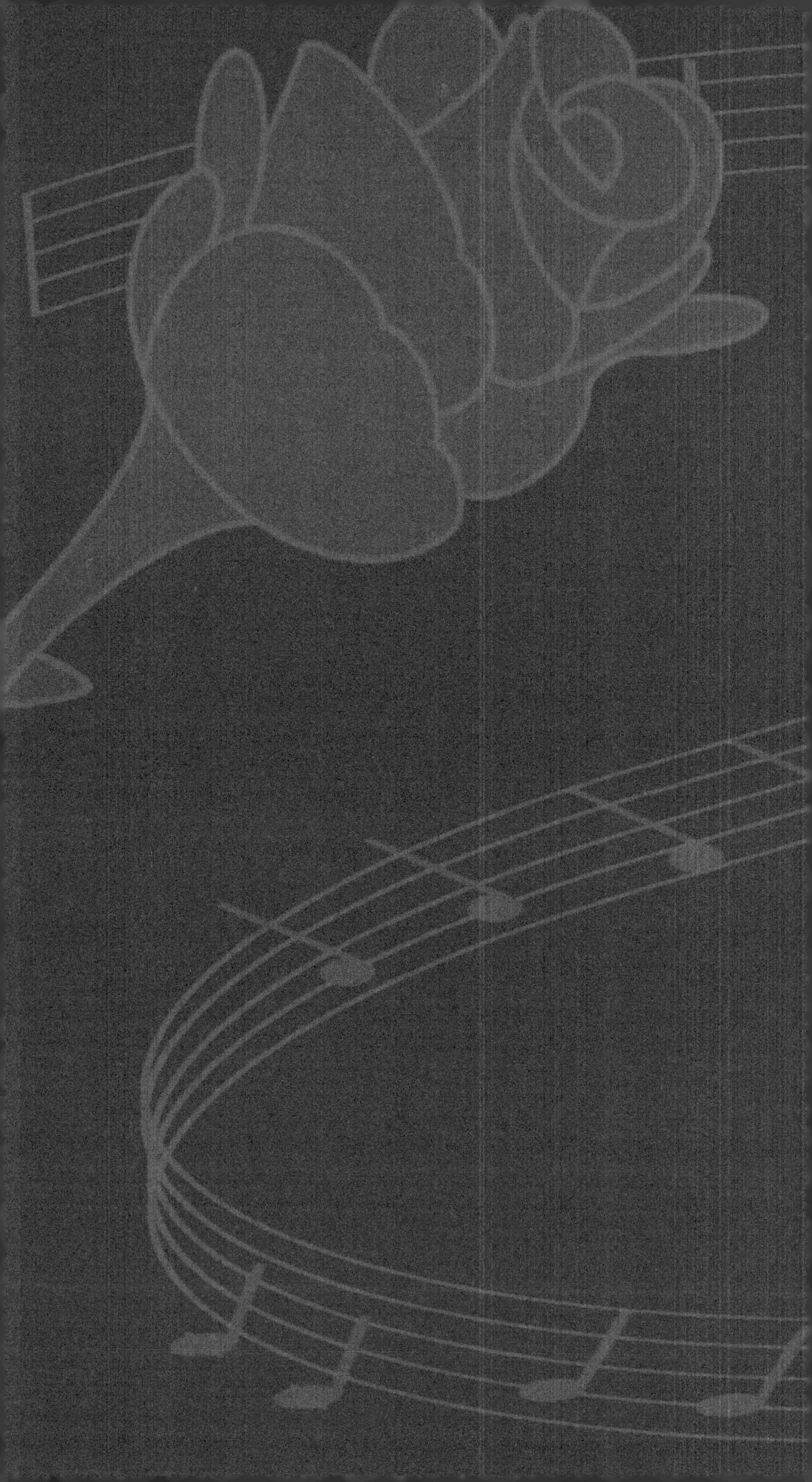

Chapter Thirty-Six

Jordan

Leaving the Courtroom

I wanted to tell Cobie something before I left, but after a second, I decided against it. She had a case to focus on, not me.

She waved to me as I left.

I waved back before joining the crowd.

Once everyone was out of the courtroom, they spoke. They all wanted to know if Talia was Cam or if Cobie was.

Jay tapped me on the shoulder and said, "I need to tell you something."

"Yeah, sorry, we couldn't talk. Give me a few more seconds so we can get away from people," I said. He had begged me to speak with him on the ride over, but Danny had been asking questions about the show opener. Cole had made my best friend the point of contact.

"We need to find safety for you," Tim, Cobie's chief bodyguard, said to me and the rest of the band.

A few of the people looked at us and whispered.

"Lead the way," Cole said as he noticed the situation.

Two bodyguards moved us away from the crowd into an empty room.

"We should be fine in here," Cole said as he checked another door.

Tim also checked it out and said, "Toilet."

"I call it first," Royal said as he headed toward it.

"Jordan, I have to tell you something." Jay glanced at me and then back to the closed-door Royal had entered.

"Go ahead, or do you want to speak alone?" I asked.

"Did Cobie tell you fake Cam was Dick's daughter?" Danny asked me.

"She said nothing after supper or breakfast. We were focused on other things," I answered. My face warmed once my words reached my brain.

"Jordan!" Jay yelled.

"Sorry, man. What did you want to tell me?" I asked.

"Royal asked me to grab your phone a few times since you left to meet the fake Cam. He had told me he deleted the schedule, and you refused to resend it to him," Jay blurted out.

"What did you say?" Cole asked Jay.

Jay repeated himself after he took a breath.

"I'm killing him," I said about Royal. Now, I had my evidence. Although he might get out of this too.

Royal stepped out of the bathroom.

I ran at him and slammed my fist into his face.

Somebody pulled me off of him, but not before I got a few more decent hits in.

"What the hell, man," Royal said. He sounded pissed.

I gave up struggling and told Tim, "Let me go."

"If you want me to handle the situation, I will," Tim said to me. He released his hold on me.

"No, my band and I will take care of this," I said.

"What's going on?" Cole asked as he glanced between Royal and me.

Danny sat in a chair at the conference table, and he opened his mouth to say something, but nothing came out.

"I vote for Jordan to be removed from the band for assaulting me." Royal demanded as he wiped the blood off his split lip.

"We don't need to go there," Cole said. He raked a hand through his hair.

"We agreed to never fight, and if we did, we would throw them out of the band. Look at me." Royal pointed to his face, and his left eye had already swollen shut.

"You fucking deserve it. Why did you set Jordan up for a sexual assault allegation?" Danny glared daggers at Royal.

Baylee punched Royal in the other eye. "You made me believe I caused my favorite person to lose his dream job."

"Thanks, Bay," I said to him.

"Fuck. Stop punching me." Royal covered his eyes.

"Explain to me what's happening," Cole said as he glanced at everyone, even the bodyguards.

They held no expression on their faces except for Tim. Royal was the object of his hard, tense stare.

I told Cole everything I had learned, and Jay filled in that he had borrowed my phone after Royal asked.

"Is this true?" Cole asked Royal. My manager's voice rose, and he scowled at my bandmate.

"I...I hate Jordan." Royal sat on the ground. "Jordan has everything I want. I wanted to take him down a peg or two, not get him barred from music. Dick's daughter and I hatched this plan after Jordan dissed her."

"Is Dick's daughter Cam?" Cole asked.

"No. She told me her dad kicked out the real Cam and made her perform as the famous singer instead. Tabitha grew tired of doing everything, but she feared her father would cut her off financially if she stopped." Royal set his head against the wall.

"What does this have to do with me?" I asked.

"You're the dumbass that figured out Tabitha wasn't the real Cam. Then the brain kid over there blabbed it to the world." Royal pointed with his thumb at Baylee.

"First off, stop being a dick to Baylee. You won't ever say anything mean to him again. Do you hear me?" I didn't wait for an answer from Royal as I continued. "Second, the daughter's name is Talia, not Tabitha. Why can't you ever keep the names straight of the people you've slept with?" I demanded, automatically assuming that she and Royal had indeed slept together.

Royal shrugged, confirming my suspicions.

"We should vote to remove Royal from the band," Danny said. My best friend seethed next to me as he raised his hand. He was even more upset than I was at the incident. I understood jealous people did a lot of crazy things. Didn't mean I accepted it, but I understood it.

The blackness had entered my heart on more than one occasion, like how Royal looked better behind a camera with his dark style than me, or how Danny excelled at any sport without trying, but I never would've crossed the line Royal had.

"I second it." Jay lifted his hand into the air.

"Wait, I have evidence that Talia isn't Cam, and she planned everything. I recorded her a few times during our planning." Royal wouldn't look at anyone, and his posture sagged. At least he had the decency to appear defeated.

"You'll give us the proof for what? To remain in the band? How can any of us trust you after this?" Danny asked.

"We should see the evidence," I said. My mind buzzed with the possibility of Cobie getting her life and money back. She belonged in a mansion or in her own home. After she had told me she lived on the streets, I vowed she would never again. Every time we had texted about music, our dreams, and our lives, she never mentioned how badly she struggled. I had never met someone I admired more than her.

"Hey, man." Danny patted my back and pulled a tissue from the box on the table.

I hadn't realized I was crying. I muttered thanks to him and wiped away my tears, blowing my nose.

"You made Jordan cry, asshole," Danny said to Royal.

"I didn't think the accusation would get this serious," Royal said.

"Accusations of sexual assault against celebrities never end well." Danny shook his head.

"When one person makes a compliant, the police side with the celebrity. Jordan is such a mama's boy. No one else would have come forward against him," Royal said. He had thought his scheme through. None of it impressed me or stopped anything from happening. My presence at the mansion and with Cobie kept me out of jail.

"Not when the celebrity is Cam. She's the biggest singer in the world," Cole said.

"I didn't think it would blow up," Royal said.

"Your problem is that you haven't thought about anything except yourself since you were a kid. I can't save you this time," Cole said.

"I'm sorry. I was jealous of Jordan. He can make music, and anytime I try, he destroys my songs." Royal tapped his head against the wall.

"Nothing comes easy for Jordan. Do you know how he learned to write great music? He worked with better writers and kept learning. He never stops breathing and living the music." Cole bent close to my soon-to-be ex-bandmate.

"Show us the evidence," I said to Royal.

"We won't keep Royal no matter what he shows. There is no coming back from what he did!" Danny said.

"We're in the middle of a tour, and we need to think of the repercussions on our careers. Royal fucked up. I won't deny what he did. But he did it to me. I want to see the evidence he has," I said.

Royal opened his phone and played a video. Talia and he discussed how to get back at me for the issues I had caused them. Seeing two people hating me sucked. She devised the plan and explained it.

He asked, "What if my music life ended?" At least he half-assed tried to protect me.

She promised to save it.

"You knew the risks and took part in this foolish plan?" Danny asked, even though he already knew the answer.

"Play the next video," I told Royal.

This time Talia admitted she hoped to ruin Cam's reputation, so she no longer had to play the role. The fans criticized everything she did. If she lip-synced the wrong song, they would notice. She yearned to shed her disguise and be herself, not a celebrity. Afterward, she and Royal proceeded to another part of the plan, setting up the sexual text messages to her.

"Send me these two videos," I told him.

Royal nodded, and my phone pinged twice with his messages. He played the next three videos as more details formed after they happened. He took off his trench coat about midway through reading off the text exchange between Talia and him. Sweat beaded on his forehead, and his skin paled.

I sent the second video to Cobie with a simple message of proof Talia wasn't Cam. I hoped she could present it in her case. Sometimes the law never worked in favor of the righteous.

"What's the verdict?" Cole asked us after Royal finished.

Royal broke down and cried. Tears rolled down his cheeks.

"He needs to speak to a psychologist before we vote or do anything," I said. His reaction wasn't normal, like he had a mental break or something.

"I have someone I can send him to." Cole helped Royal to stand and led him out of the room.

"Was Royal faking?" Baylee asked.

"Not sure. Royal isn't getting out of this," Danny answered.

What I wanted to do most was talk to Cobie and get a drink. She had other problems to worry about. I hoped the video would at least prove she was indeed the real Cam and end her legal troubles.

Chapter Thirty-Seven

Cobie

Judge Russo called a day to review the evidence. Talia was only eighteen and hadn't been singing since she was eight. The timeframe didn't add up.

I waited for my bodyguards to return while my lawyer and my label's lawyer packed up their things. I decided at that moment to take charge of my life. "Are there death threats against me?" I asked once we were alone in the courtroom.

Megan paused and placed her files back in her briefcase.

Dick and his attorney had already left with Talia. Her dad would most likely cut her off if he lost the lawsuit. Like she was to blame for his poor decisions.

"My law firm has gotten none in a week," Megan answered. She picked up her briefcase.

"We've received phone calls, but they arrested our major concern. We sent everything to your attorney," the other lawyer stated.

"Everything will come to me, and you'll let me know if any more arrive," I told them.

Megan and the other attorney glanced at each other.

"This is not negotiable. I should know if my life is in danger, and I'll let Tim decide the amount of protection I need," I informed them.

"As you wish," Megan said.

My lawyer at my label nodded his head.

Tim walked into the courtroom with an apology about the situation he had to handle. He had secured my ride out of the courthouse. Hopefully, the incident didn't involve Jordan and his band.

My phone buzzed with a text from Jordan, and I watched the video he had sent. "Megan, we have to stop." I showed her the confession.

"How did he get the footage?" Megan asked.

I messaged Jordan, and he called me instead of answering my text. We spoke briefly until I put him on speakerphone because repeating Megan's questions was getting annoying. I thanked him once she had no more questions.

"Send me the video, and I'll present it to the judge. Hopefully, with this proof and Talia's confession earlier, he'll rule in our favor." Megan glanced at the watch on her wrist.

"I have to get to the airport soon," I reminded her. I had to practice with the concert band tomorrow.

My bodyguards and I exited into the crowd at the courthouse. No wonder they had issues getting to me once court had ended. They pushed their way out, and everyone moved out of their way until we were outside.

"Cobie Meine?" someone asked me.

Tim had already stepped forward to stop the guy in a bicycle helmet from coming any closer to me.

My heart picked up speed, and I stepped back into Hugo. "Sorry," I told him.

"All good, Ms. Meine. After yesterday, I can't believe you're not a little jumpier." Hugo smiled down at me. I would miss him and his coworkers, but I really wanted not to be in danger anymore.

The bike messenger sent a furtive glance at me and shifted his weight between his feet.

"What do you need with Ms. Meine?" Tim asked. His voice sounded calm, but his shoulders tensed, and he balled his hands into fists at his sides.

"Please give this to Ms. Meine. She has been served." The messenger handed a letter over to Tim before he took off.

"May I?" Tim asked me.

"Go ahead," I answered.

Someone called my name, and I recognized that voice anywhere. Jordan and his band, except for Royal, made their way to me. He wrapped me in a hug.

"This is clear. Ms. Adams will want to know about it," Tim said after he handed the envelope to me.

I pulled the papers out as we headed toward the SUVs, reading them over. My anger rose.

"What's the matter?" Jordan walked next to me with Hugo next to him, and Tim on my other side.

I handed him the lawsuit with a shake of my head.

Jordan swore more times than me.

"What's going on?" Danny asked behind us.

Jordan looked at me, and I nodded for him to tell them. Everyone in the world would hear soon enough, anyway. "Cobie's parents are suing her for guardianship."

"On what grounds?" Baylee asked.

"They say because of Dick taking my money and my career, I need someone to manage my personal and financial affairs. I can't do it on my own," I answered. My heart pounded loudly in my ears, and I was so pissed off I couldn't even cry.

"Cobie?" my mother called to me behind my fans, anti-fans, and Solar Harmony's fans. She stood next to my father. "We're doing what's best for you."

I froze, and all thoughts and feelings I had also stopped.

"Cobie?" my mother called again. She gained the attention of everyone around her and the reporters. They filmed me and then switched to her.

"Are you okay?" Jordan asked me. His brown eyes shone with concern.

"I need to go," I told him.

He took my hand and gave it a squeeze before he hurried me over to the first SUV. Tim opened the door for us as we slid inside.

"Where to?" Tim asked from the driver's seat.

"Anywhere but here," I answered.

"My place. No one can get to you there." Jordan pulled me to his chest and held me.

Tears streamed down my face. Why did my parents care about me now? Last year, they got rid of me. The obvious answer struck me, and I wanted more than anything to block them out of the rest of my life.

Fuck them.

Jordan said nothing as he hugged me tighter.

I muttered an apology and swiped at my tears as I typed a message to Megan about the latest development in my life.

She called right away and told me to send a copy of the paperwork to her to work on a game plan.

My hands shook badly, and Jordan took over taking pictures of the pages of the lawsuit. I wanted to burn it, but that wouldn't make it go away. "Do my parents have a case?" I asked Megan.

"They'll try. I'll do my best to get it thrown out," Megan answered.

"Is there anything I can do?"

"Get the information about your finances they stole from. If we can prove they swindled your money, no judge would give them guardianship."

She gave me an update on my other case and said the judge would reach a verdict soon. Soon meant anything from later today to tomorrow to next week. We hung up after I promised I would try to get the bank information.

Jordan pulled me into his arms again and said, "I'm sorry you're going through this. Tell me what you need."

"Sleep in your arms, and I need to get into my old bank accounts," I told him.

"We can use my laptop. I have a new one you can have." He swept the hair out of my face and gave me a kiss.

"If you can't get the information online, I know a person," Tim said.

"Is it legal?" I asked.

"Depends on your definition of 'legal'," Tim answered.

"Megan will want to use it in court," I pointed out.

"My offer will stand up to scrutiny. This gal is good," Tim said.

"Let me try getting into my accounts first. Can she get the information if the account is closed?" I doubted my parents kept anything open with my name and theirs on it once they drained it. Did they need my permission to close it?

"She should be able to," Tim answered.

At Jordan's place, I found my closed bank account and requested the information. The bank had issues until I proved I was of age. They would mail the information to me, so I gave them Megan's address.

Jordan patted his bed. After I sat next to him, he pulled me into his arms. He kissed me on the lips.

I kissed him back.

Jordan pulled us apart and asked, "Are you still tired?"

"Exhausted," I answered.

"Sleep. I'll wake us up when we need to leave for the airport." He wrapped me in his arms.

I closed my eyes. "Thank you for getting me away from my parents." The sight of them made me want to scream.

"You're welcome. You can decide whether or not you want to see them again. Like you told me, I'll call and yell at them if you want me to. I'll keep them away from you, or I'll reach out to them for you. Whatever you want or need."

"I love you," I told him.

"I love you, too. Now sleep, woman. I'll wake you up soon enough," Jordan said.

Jordan woke me up what felt like mere seconds later.

"What time is it?" I sat up and stretched. My throat felt raw from the crying and sleep.

"We have three hours before our flight. I figured you missed lunch and needed something to eat. I know I do."

My stomach growled in agreement with him, and my face heated. I covered it to hide my embarrassment.

"Time to get my woman fed." Jordan held out his hand.

I took it, and he helped me out of bed. I straightened my clothes. My hair needed a good brushing, and I found a brush in the bag I had grabbed before coming to Jordan's. I had given Megan the original lawsuit copy. She promised me to add it to the fireproof safe in her home with my other two documents.

"We should leave some of your items here," Jordan said as he kissed my shoulder.

"Is our relationship ready for this step?" I asked him.

"I already cleaned out space in my closet and drawer for you." He opened up the second drawer, showing me it was empty, and he brought me to his walk-in closet next. "This side is for you."

The black wood against the white floor and ceiling made the space much bigger than it appeared. I touched a suit jacket on his side.

"If you want, I can move my stuff," Jordan said.

"I have nothing to leave at your place," I told him.

"We'll need to go on a shopping spree. How does Paris sound?"

"I prefer a mall." I hated shopping and would rather have someone pick something out for me. If I gave Brittany my credit card after I got paid from the lawsuit, she would totally get me a wardrobe and spend money on herself as payment.

"Why are you grinning?"

"I hate shopping," I answered.

"You're smiling because?" Jordan lifted an eyebrow and rubbed my arms.

I shivered in the small room without realizing it. "I have a solution."

"To me, spending money on your clothes?"

"I'm buying my own."

Jordan sighed. "Can I get you something?"

"I need a brush here."

"Done. Do you like my suggesting leaving your things here, or is it too much?" He hugged me, and I embraced him in return.

"I like it. My hair needs a lot of maintenance." I ran my hand through the thick strands, and I had already tangled it. I had done nothing more than walk into the closet with Jordan.

"We'll get your favorite products then, too."

His band had ordered a meal before the flight.

"How are you doing?" Danny asked me after I sat between him and Jordan to eat.

"Pissed off," I answered truthfully.

"Sorry, your parents are trying to pull you into a guardianship." Danny bit into his slice of pizza.

I shrugged. I should've figured they would pull something, especially when I had a new song at number one on the music chart. Rick loved to send me updates.

"Guardianships happen a lot with celebrities." Baylee told us who had to endure it and why.

"How do you know about this?" Jay asked him. They sat together on the couch.

"I started researching after hearing Cobie is getting sued for it," Baylee answered.

"Thanks, Bay," Jordan said. He put an arm around my shoulder.

My heart warmed at the notion of his friends accepting me, except for one. "Where is Royal? Hasn't he eaten yet?" I asked.

"He had a mental breakdown." Jordan filled me in on the details.

I hugged him. He was loyal to the people he cared about. Royal's betrayal must've crushed him. "What will you do?" I asked Jordan. I took his hand in mine, giving his hand a squeeze.

"We're not discussing it until Royal is better. Right now, I'm pissed off and never want to see him again, but he gave me the video to save you. I can't hate him completely. He also, in a roundabout way, brought you into my life," Jordan answered.

"Please don't keep him if you don't want to. I won't use the video if he tries to stay in your band because of it," I said. Guilt rose inside me. I should've asked Jordan more questions instead of immediately presenting it to my lawyer.

"That's why you're an honorary member of Solar Harmony." Danny embraced me with one arm.

"Hey, keep your hands to yourself." Jordan grinned, and I always wanted to keep a smile on his handsome face.

Chapter Thirty-Eight

Jordan

Cobie's phone rang shortly after we finished our food. The time read 3 p.m. We needed to leave in ten minutes for our flight. Even famous people had to wait in line.

"He's already decided?" Cobie asked. Her voice rose, and she touched her face.

I heard only her side of the conversation, but the main thing hanging over her head was the lawsuit. If the 'he' in her conversation wanted her back in court, she had to go. I brought up our tickets and searched for the next available flight. Luckily, more than one airport served our city.

Cobie ended her call and sighed. She never did the latter unless she was upset.

"What's the matter?" Baylee asked before I did.

"The judge wants me back in court. He has made a ruling. He didn't let Dick's side finish, so hopefully, the judge rules in my favor," Cobie answered.

"I already switched our flights," I told her. I booked two leaving before eight tonight, and we'd get in around one in the morning.

"You don't have to come with me," Cobie said.

"I am, and I'm heading to court with you, too," I said.

"Hey, what flight should we switch to?" Danny asked.

Cobie frowned and glanced at me and then at my best friend.

"Do you need to change your clothes?" I asked her.

She nodded.

"Go do that, and I'll deal with my band," I told her.

After she left, Danny said, "We're going with you and her. This isn't negotiable."

"You're making this harder for Cobie. We'll meet you at the hotel tomorrow morning," I told him.

"I want to go to court," Baylee said.

"Same. I need to change my clothes first." Jay climbed to his feet and hurried to the door.

"Flight?" Danny said with a smile.

I gave him the details and thanked them all.

Inside my room, Cobie dug around in her suitcase, flinging clothes as she emptied it. Tears glistened in her eyes.

"What's the matter?" I asked.

"I can't find a suit. Should I wear a new one or an old one? I didn't pack one. What did I do with the one from earlier today?" Cobie asked.

"Take a deep breath." I held her hands, and she took a breath, letting it out slowly.

Once she calmed down, she thanked me. "I freaked out."

"A little. I stuck your shirt and jacket into my dirty laundry." Her behavior had more to do with the verdict than the apparel.

Cobie made a face.

"Let's see what we have here before we fish anything out." I leafed through her items and found a white blouse.

She pulled out a black suit jacket and skirt. "I don't wear skirts. Why did I pack this?"

I checked her suit pants for dirtiness. After smelling them, I handed them to her. "I have spray in the bathroom for getting the stench out, but these smell fine."

She kissed me on the cheek and headed to the bathroom with them, anyway.

I put on a fresh suit. "Beautiful," I told Cobie once she stepped out of the bathroom.

"I need to brush my hair," she said.

"Still beautiful." I handed her a brush.

She touched up her makeup and packed her bag. She left her skirt out.

"My band is coming with to support you for the trial like me, and we have nothing until tomorrow afternoon." I added the last part to take the worried look off her face.

"I'd rather have them on their flight," she said.

"So would I, but they won't listen to me. They've officially adopted you into the band. You're stuck with us now."

Cobie's lips stretched into a smile, and my heart soared.

"Where do you want me?" I tucked her brown hair behind her ear.

"I want you right here." She wrapped her arms around me and kissed me.

Someone cleared their throat behind us, breaking us apart.

"Noah brought the van. We should get Cobie to the courthouse," Danny said.

"Did Noah switch flights, too?" I asked as I took Cobie's hand.

"He already had a later flight planned," Danny answered without elaborating. Noah had to give the van back to Cole's company.

"All rise, the Honorable Judge Russo presiding," the bailiff said. Was it presiding or residing? The bailiff's heavy southern accent made it hard to tell.

I climbed to my feet with my band and the rest of the courtroom. We had a packed room with every major news network and entertainment news station in attendance. The courtroom was so full that it was literally standing room only.

Cobie stood between both of her attorneys.

I wished I could be next to her. Instead, I had to stand behind her to show my support while her former manager smiled. Unease grew inside me as I watched him. Did he know something we didn't?

The Judge came into the courtroom. "Please be seated except for the defense and the plaintiff. I'll get straight to my ruling. Ms. Meine has proven she is, in fact, Cam." He read off every part of the lawsuit and ruled in favor of Cobie, tearing apart her ex-manager's countersuit. He awarded her nowhere near enough money for the years she had worked. "Ms. Meine, you need to take control of your assets."

"Yes, Your Honor," Cobie said. Her voice filled with warmth.

"Court is adjourned." Judge Russo banged his gavel.

Cobie hugged her lawyers and then turned to me.

I embraced her over the barrier, and my band each gave her their congratulations. If anyone had any doubt she was Cam, I hoped it ended today.

The news people left to write up their stories and release them. Some would wait on the courthouse steps for a statement. Had Cobie or her lawyer planned to speak?

The court cleared out except for us, Dick, and his lawyer.

Dick had a smirk on his face. Why did he? He lost a lot of money.

His attorney walked over to Cobie, and Tim stopped them. Relief washed through me as he handed the much bigger man an envelope, but the feeling didn't last long. "Tell your employer, Ms. Meine, she has been served."

Cobie ripped the paperwork out of Tim's hand before he inspected it. The bodyguard didn't take it from her. She shook her head as she read over the paperwork. A tightness sprang to her eyes. She took a deep breath and handed the papers to her lawyer.

Megan snatched them and read it. "Really, Mr. Bronson, you're suing my client for failure to comply with her contract with you? You stole her money, and no way in hell is she obligated to tour with you."

"If she doesn't, I won't have money to pay her. I'll claim bankruptcy," Dick said with a shrug.

I saw red; I was so furious. My brain didn't comprehend what my body did until I couldn't move. I had raised my hand to punch Dick, but one of Cobie's bodyguards stopped me along with Danny, Cole, and Jay.

Baylee stepped in front of me. "Don't," he said.

His one word calmed me down more than anything.

"Not a good idea," Cole told me.

"Seemed like a good idea," I said. Anger flowed through me, and I reined it in.

"Calm your brute of a man down. Cam, we can work together like old times. I've always been good to you," Dick said to Cobie. Was he a fucking idiot?

"I'm not stopping Jordan from doing anything because I fear for my life," Cobie said.

Tim spurred into action. He stepped forward and told Dick, "You need to leave or let us go, sir. I won't have you threatening my client."

Cobie took my hand and rested her head on my shoulder. "Let's get out of here. After my verdict, no way a judge or jury would rule in his favor."

"We have a contract!" Dick called after Cobie as she steered me out of the courtroom.

She paid him no attention and kept her hand on mine. Her body trembled next to mine.

"You're amazing." I kissed her forehead and wrapped an arm around her. She used words to defeat the man, and I chose violence. No one had filled me with so much rage in a short moment, besides Royal and his confession.

We climbed into the back of the SUV. Had her bodyguards changed their flight plans? I didn't know if they were coming with us or not? Was she still in danger? My next thoughts ended as Cobie kissed me.

She broke us apart and said, "Thank you for defending me."

"I shouldn't have lost my temper." I would hate myself forever for showing her a side I never realized I had.

"My grandma said I need to find a man willing to help me whenever I need it. A man who keeps me laughing. A man who makes me smile. She was wrong about one thing."

"What was she wrong about?"

"Those three men can never learn each other existed. You're all those things and more. I'm so glad I met you and that we're together."

"Same, beautiful." I pulled her into my arms, giving her a kiss she would never forget. I needed to go ring shopping, so I entwined our fingers to get her size. In my mind, I already envisioned what she would like—something simple with history. Had any rings been a part of music besides the chains in hip-hop?

Our fans waited for us outside the airport. Cobie waved to them and thanked them for their support.

I used one hand to wave without letting go of her. How I carried my carry-on bag with me for the trip at the same time had to be a pro move.

Cobie wheeled her bag behind her because she wouldn't let me take it. "How can you hold my hand and my bag at the same time?" she had asked me more than once.

I set our bags in the overhead bins and settled in next to her. "Do you need anything?" I whispered.

"A drink," she answered.

I waved down the flight attendant and asked her for something strong.

"We don't give out anything until after takeoff," the flight attendant said.

"I'm nervous about flying," I told her. The lie rolled off my tongue.

"This time I'll get you something if you'll sign something for me," she whispered.

"Of course." I smiled at her and glanced back at Cobie.

She frowned at me.

"Here you go." The flight attendant handed me a piece of paper.

I signed my usual with thanking her for being a fan and took the little bottle of liquor from her. I handed it to Cobie.

"Did you have to flirt with her?" Cobie asked. Jealousy filled her tone.

"Did I?" I thought I had talked to the flight attendant. Did I do something more? I hoped not, since Cobie was the only woman I cared to flirt with.

"You used your smoldering smile. I bet her heart throbbed."

"I'm sorry if I did. Sometimes I don't think before I act."

"He's too friendly," Danny said behind me. The jerk was of no help.

"You got me a drink." Cobie downed it and breathed out heavily.

"Did you want water instead?" I asked her.

"As long as you don't have to flirt to get it," Cobie said.

I handed her the bottle I had snagged while the flight attendant grabbed the liquor. "I'll be more conscientious in the way I act toward other women. Please forgive me."

"All I ask." Cobie rested her head on my shoulder again.

I definitely needed to stop flirting. My exes had mentioned I did it also, but I never stopped for them. For Cobie, I would.

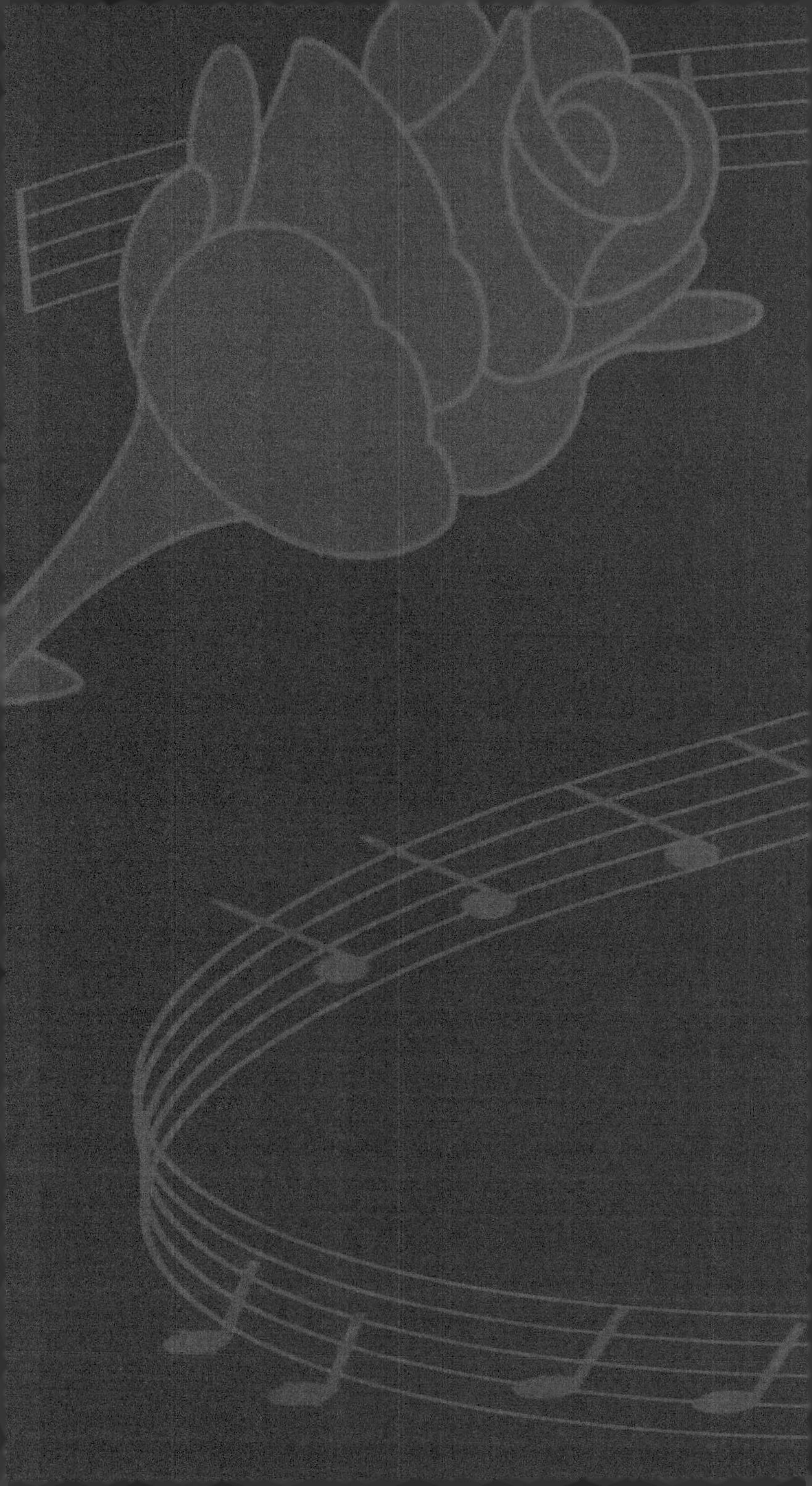

Chapter Thirty-Nine

Cobie

The Following Monday

J ordan returned with me for my trial. He wouldn't let me face my parents alone, which I was thankful for. He had to sit behind me, though.

I wanted to hold his hand. This was another court case that got moved up on the docket. How many favors did everyone have? How did I get one?

The court started before another Judge. We rose, and he told us, "Please be seated. I'm presiding over the docket of Mr. James and Mrs. Mary Meine for an adult guardianship of their daughter, Cobie Meine. The plaintiff will start with their opening statement."

My parents' lawyer told the court how I had failed to handle my money and how I lost everything. They used the recent lawsuit I won as evidence. I ended up tuning them out after a few minutes for my sanity.

Megan spoke to the Judge and played me as the innocent victim. How I came back from nothing to have the number one song on the charts. My parents had done nothing until then. They had also kicked me out instead of helping me. The way she described me, I sounded like a saint.

"The plaintiff will start with their case," the Judge said.

"We call Mary Meine to the stand," her attorney said.

My mother sat in the witness box and got sworn in.

"Tell us about your relationship with your daughter, Cobie," her attorney said.

"Cobie has always been difficult and not good with money. She would always spend every penny she made the second she got it." My mother glanced at me as she spoke next. "Baby, we love you and want you back home. You need help. Let us help you."

"Objection, Your Honor," Megan said.

"On what grounds?" the Judge asked.

"Relevancy," Megan said.

"I believe a parent loving and wanting the best interest of their daughter is relevant," my parent's attorney said.

"Not if they're not acting in the best interest of their child," Megan said.

"Sustained," the Judge said.

My parent's lawyer kept on asking questions about how bad I was with money and how much I needed help. Once they finished, I swore lightning should strike my mother for the lies she had told.

"I have exhibit A to submit," Megan said on her turn.

The other lawyer objected, but because of the fast pace of the court case, the Judge allowed it.

"This is Cobie's account with her parents' names on it. I highlighted the deposits and withdrawals of enormous sums." Megan handed copies out to the Judge and the other attorney. "What was this amount used for?" she asked as she gave my mother her copy.

"We bought our family a home," my mother answered.

"With Cobie's money?" I asked.

"Yes, Cobie agreed to it," my mother lied.

"Where is her bedroom in this home?" Megan asked.

"She has her bedroom painted pink in the basement," my mother answered.

"I'd like to enter exhibit B, the floor plan to this house, along with exhibit C, photos from Mrs. Meine's social media account of the basement." Megan loaded the images onto the television. "Where is this pink bedroom? I see a workout room and your other daughter's room."

The image of the pink workout room flipped onto the screen, and three seconds later it was replaced with the video of my mother entering Kelsey's room to give her a car played on the screen. I had probably paid for that, too.

"My workout room is upstairs," my mother said. She shifted in her seat. "I don't post photos of Cobie's bedroom online, since she's famous."

Megan flipped back to the workout room and zoomed in on the window. "This is an egress window with a window well. Only the bedrooms on the basement have this setup. According to your homes floor plan, you have two bedrooms in the basement."

"You must be mistaken," my mother said.

"I'm not. The window is big enough to escape through in case of an emergency. You can climb out of the window well." Megan flipped the video through the other bedrooms upstairs, including my parents, my dad's office, and a guest bedroom. Even people staying over got a bed in the place I bought.

"This is Cobie's bedroom," my mother said in the last photo of a bed.

"You don't post images of Cobie's online. Why is this here? Where is anything of hers in this room?" Megan asked.

"James?" my mother called to my father. She had to feel overwhelmed to ask for him. She could answer on her own, but she liked to play the helpless stay-at-home mother, clueless without her husband.

"Answer the question, Mrs. Meine. Your husband may have his turn next," the Judge said in a gentle tone.

"Cobie stays in the guest room when she visits," my mother answered.

"When was the last time she stayed in the house she bought?" Megan asked.

"Last year," my mother answered.

Megan dismissed her, and my parent's lawyer called my father to the stand. He answered the questions similarly to my mother until he spoke about my mental health. He would know nothing about it since he never hung around me. He was always busy with his golfing buddies.

"Breakdown? When did Ms. Meine have a mental breakdown?" the Judge asked.

"Shortly after she left the care of Mr. Bronson. I have documentation from her shrink," my parent's lawyer answered.

"Objection, Your Honor. The plaintiff hasn't sent these documents to us. Also, HIPPA prevents them from having these files," Megan said.

"Your Honor, these prove the state of Ms. Meine. Here you go," the other attorney dumped the paperwork on the desk.

Megan leafed through the information.

"Put me on the stand," I whispered to her.

She nodded as she read the information presented in court. The psychologist had spoken nothing but lies. I lost access to healthcare after Dick abandoned me.

As my parent's lawyer read off dates, I visited and summarized what happened. I wrote the information down. Funny part was the first visit happened when I had spoken to the police about getting identification. They had to contact my hometown, and it took hours. The second visit had happened when I was stuck on a bus for three days as I headed back home. The third had happened when I returned on the bus.

"We're done with this witness," the other side said.

I handed the notes to Megan.

She looked it over and smiled at me before turning around.

"Mr. Meine, when did your daughter return home?" Megan asked.

"I'm not sure." My father stared forward with no emotion on his face.

"Your daughter remembers last year in January. Does that sound correct?" Megan asked.

"Could be," my father said.

"How could she meet with a psychologist when she was in another city?" Megan asked.

"Well, then Cobie didn't return home in January," my father said, as if his words explained anything.

Megan turned to the Judge and said, "Your Honor, please allow us a quick recess."

"What for?" the Judge asked.

"With the proof of when Cobie returned home, we'll prove she didn't attend three visits to this so-called psychologist," Megan asked.

"I'm game for it. You have ten minutes." The Judge left before the other attorney objected.

I pulled up my bus tickets and sent them to Megan. My parents didn't let me live in the house I bought for even one week.

Megan called her assistant and asked for the police report I had filled out back then.

Court was called before I had time to go to the restroom. Megan presented the evidence.

"This happened. Cobie needs to be at home," my father said.

"Why? She's an adult," Megan said.

"I am her father," my father pointed out.

"Who forced your daughter to pay for your house, who kicked her out of said house when her manager abandoned her, and who is suing her to get access to her money?" Megan asked.

"Objection," the other lawyer said.

"For what?" the Judge asked.

My parent's lawyer stumbled on his words.

"Overruled," the Judge said. He faced my father. "Answer the question."

"I am her father," my father said instead.

The Judge frowned and shook his head. "I've seen and heard enough. Mr. and Mrs. Meine have no grounds to file for adult guardianship. This case is dismissed." He banged his gavel.

"What? What does that mean?" my mother asked.

"The judge ended our case. We'll appeal," her attorney answered.

"Stop wasting the court's time, Mr. and Mrs. Meine." The Judge called my name next. "Cobie Meine, you need to take care of yourself and not appear in court cases like this again."

"Yes, Your Honor. I learned my lesson," I said, and I had. Only I decided when I held a concert, released a song, or hired bodyguards, if I was in danger. No one else would anymore. Well, I would ask for advice on the latter because Tim and his associates were good at their jobs.

The Judge nodded and left the courtroom through his door.

"Cobie?" My mother rose to her feet and moved toward me.

Tim stepped forward, blocking her from me.

"Cobie!" my mother yelled.

"Young lady, you stop being a brat," my father spat.

Jordan touched my shoulder. "Is there anything you want to say to your parents?"

I thought for a moment, and the words popped into my head. "Tim, please move aside."

Tim did as I asked.

"Mother, father keep the house. After this, we're done. I am not your piggy bank, and you will stay out of my life. Any kids I have will never know you. If you contact me, I will get a protective order against you. Pay attention to the daughter you actually care about. We're through," I told them.

My mother opened her mouth to say something, but I stopped her.

"I mean it. We're done. Let's go." I turned to my associates, and we headed out of the courtroom with the rest of the crowd.

My parents called after me, but I ignored them.

Jordan took my hand, giving it a squeeze.

"One trial left, and you should be clear. Please stop getting sued," Megan said to me. She walked on my other side.

Something in my brain clicked into place. "Does Dick have a case against me?" I asked her.

She hesitated. "He could with the right argument and judge."

I had won two cases, technically three, with Dick's counter lawsuit. My luck had to run out, eventually. I came up with a plan to avoid another trial.

"Can we reach some type of agreement with my former manager?" I asked Megan.

She waved her hand for me to follow her, and we entered an empty courtroom. "What do you have in mind?" she asked me.

"Give Dick what he wants." I explained my plan.

"Are you sure?" Jordan asked me. He opened his mouth to speak, but he closed it again.

"I'm tired of courts. I'm tired of not being able to be myself. If this gets Dick off my back, I can stomach a tour with him," I answered. A three-month concert was preferable to the remaining six years of my contract.

"I'm on your side, but I don't like the idea of you being alone with him." Jordan kissed me on the forehead.

"She won't be," Cole said.

I'd forgotten that he and the rest of Solar Harmony had followed us into the little conference room except for Royal. We had taken up most of the room.

Baylee, Jay, and Danny sat in the back, watching and not saying anything. They loved Jordan a lot and wanted to be close to him. We would spend many meals and time together in the future, which was fine by me. I had already grown to love them. They were the brothers I'd never had. Now, if they got rid of Royal because of what he did for Jordan, I would be happier. Even if they didn't, I would be on my man's side always.

"Cobie is looking for a new manager. My firm will sign her if she wants, and I have someone I trust for her to work with," Cole said.

"I need to get back to lawyering," Megan said. Despite her words, she had done a great job of helping, like a manager would, and she had loved every minute. She had her life, and I needed to take charge of mine.

"Who?" I asked Cole.

"My sister," Cole answered.

I looked at Jordan.

He nodded at me and said, "I trust Cole completely. If he says his sister is up to the task, she is." His manager had been fair to him and always looked out for his best interest, even if the idea wasn't the greatest, like with pulling his music.

"Okay, but I'm deciding the terms of any new contract," I said.

"I agree completely. Range C Entertainment will be happy to have you." Cole held out his hand for me to shake.

For the first time in my life, I felt like I had made an excellent decision. I shook his hand.

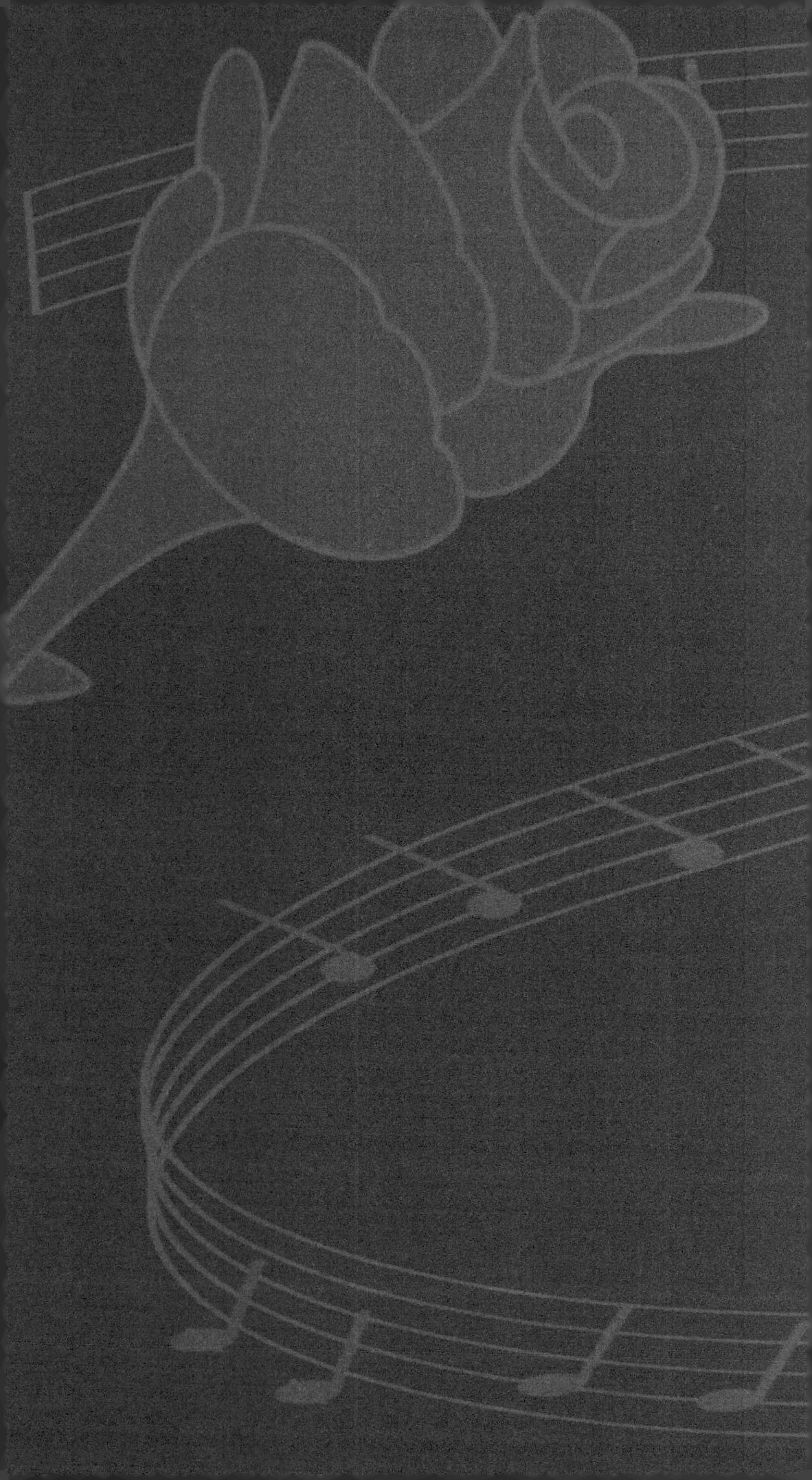

Chapter Forty

Jordan

Almost Three Weeks Later

I'd been searching for a ring since Cobie's soon-to-be ex-manager accepted her proposal of her last tour under his management if she began immediately. We had spent seventeen days apart so far, catching each other on video calls and texting. I hated not being with her, but I understood why she did the tour. I did a countdown to the day we'd reunite. Her first concert started tomorrow.

"How many more jewelry stores are we hitting up?" Danny complained for the umpteenth time.

"Every single one until I find the perfect ring," I answered him.

"We've been to every place on the East Coast." Danny searched for the next shop and read off the address despite his words.

"Punching it in now. Keep them coming," Baylee said in the front seat of the bus we had rented for our excursion.

Noah parked at the next location a few minutes later. "This is the closest I can get you," he said.

"I feel good about this one," I said.

"You've said those words for every single shop," Jay pointed out.

"This one is different." I put on my blond wig, hat, and sunglasses. The rest of the band and Noah did the same. Our fans had yet to figure out our disguises because they didn't realize we were in this city, nearly three hundred miles away from where our concert would be held tomorrow.

"How?" Jay snapped. He took a deep breath and let out a heavy sigh. "Sorry. I didn't mean to get angry."

"You need to let the whole thing with Royal go. He did everything, and he's in therapy to help with his issues," I told Jay.

"If I didn't tell you—" Jay said, but I cut him off.

"I would've figured it out, eventually. He had texted vile things to Dick's daughter as me. Someone at our place did it, and I knew you didn't and Baylee didn't," I said.

"And not me?" Danny asked.

"Obviously not you. Royal had done it, but I couldn't prove it. Besides, if this didn't happen, our arguing would've torn our band apart." I opened the van door and climbed out.

My band followed me as I headed toward the next shop with a spring in my step. Cobie had already called me this morning, complaining about Dick. He had tried to add more tour dates, but thanks to Cole's sister and the ironclad agreement Megan drew up, he couldn't. She would be in my arms soon. Since she toured instead of practicing, I planned on catching a redeye back to her after my concert on Saturday.

The bell above the door rang as we entered. This shop had the typical layout of counters with glass cases and jewelry inside. The customer stood on one side and the jeweler on the other.

The jeweler looked up from her station in the middle, and a smile appeared on her face as she asked, "How can I help you?" Despite the wigs and expensive sunglasses, we wore mostly designer clothes. Baylee loved his ratty pullover. He had many brands begging him to be an ambassador, but he turned them down.

"I need a simple, unique, and expensive engagement ring," I answered. To prevent any form of flirting, I had to be direct in what I wanted. No more smiling or leaning in closer when I didn't get my way.

"You have a tall order. I'll see what I can do. Your woman or man is special?" the worker asked.

"Woman, and she is. She deserves the best," I answered. I realized I show my love by buying expensive items. Cobie hated my spending money on her, but I would with this ring. Also, if the tabloids found me skimping on it, I would never hear the end. None of this should matter except to her. But because I was a celebrity, I had to worry about the rest.

The jeweler pulled out tray after tray, setting them on the counter.

"What are you looking for?" she asked.

"I'll know when I see it." I picked one up and held it up to the light. The prongs appeared like a rose holding the four-carat, pear-shaped diamond center and two-carat diamonds on the side stones. If I pushed the carat bigger, Cobie would hate the size.

"You have good taste. My most expensive ring in the shop," the jeweler said.

When she told us the price, Danny faked a heart attack.

"Is he okay?" she asked.

"Yeah, he's just being dumb." I refrained from rolling my eyes and played with the ring in the light. My brain worked on something, and I worked to figure out what.

"Get up. You're embarrassing us." Jay toed our comrade.

"The money. Why does it have to be so much?" Danny asked.

"Why do you care? You're not paying for it," Baylee pointed out. He helped Danny to stand.

"Yeah, Danny doesn't have the balls to settle down with anyone," I said. To the worker, I continued directly. "Can you engrave the outside?"

"With what?" the worker asked. Her gaze flickered to Danny and back to me.

"I have balls," Danny muttered.

"Music notes." I penned on her notepad the first verse.

"We can put this amount on one side and this on the other." She circled a few of the notes.

"Can you duplicate the sides?" I asked. The notes covered the two words I wanted to say to Cobie after I played her my new solo song.

The jeweler and I discussed the final details. For a huge fee, she would have it done by Saturday. Noah volunteered to come get it for me. I agreed since I had planned on rollerblading at the park with Cobie to ask her the next day.

Danny caught up with me on the way to the van. "I have balls, man."

"Do you? You've had a crush on Brittany since she started working with us," I said.

"I've asked her out, and she told me no. She doesn't date people she works with," Danny said. He sounded annoyed.

"If you really liked her, you'd figure it out," I pointed out.

"I'm not quitting the band, and she loves her job." Danny had given their relationship some thought, and I didn't know what he could do to change her mind.

"Can't you help Danny and Brittany?" Baylee asked me inside the van.

"How?" I buckled next to Danny in the back.

"Brittany wants to be a designer. Didn't Cobie have an offer to design her own clothing line?" Baylee asked.

"How do you know?" I asked, a bit annoyed. I doubted my friends would listen in on my call with Cobie.

Jay pursed his lips and stared at me with the *'really'* look. "You tell us everything having to do with Cobie."

"I do not." I shifted in my spot and played a few memories through my head.

"You do, too," Danny said.

"I'll talk to Cobie." I ripped off the wig and set it next to me. For spending a lot of time on the phone with her, I had been over-compensating with my band. I had most likely told them things I shouldn't have.

I pitched Baylee's idea to Cobie last night, and she squealed at the idea. This was the first time I had heard her so excited. She planned on asking Brittany after she ironed out the details of the deal. My woman was deciding her fate, and I couldn't be happier for her.

As Brittany did my makeup for the concert, I had to bite my tongue to keep from telling her. I had kept Cobie agreeing to Baylee's idea from my band. They were bigger blabbermouths than I.

"Ready?" Royal asked everyone.

"I am," I answered curtly.

Royal snarled his lip and asked me, "When will you get over what I did? My therapist says you're projecting." Pretty sure the person had said he did.

"When you get accused of sexual assault and didn't do it," I answered him. My anger rose inside me, and I took a deep breath to calm myself. We had a show to do. I was a professional and needed to act like one. Too many times, I had allowed my emotions to get the better of me.

"No one is getting accused of anything, and everyone is signing an NDA when they get into a relationship," Cole said.

Royal opened his mouth to say something, and I glared at him. He shut his mouth fast. For now, he performed with us, but we'd decide as a group after the tour was over whether or not we'd keep him.

I wanted him out, but Solar Harmony wouldn't sound the same without him. I had created our songs for the five of us. Would four work instead? He had a lot of work to do before I would even think about forgiving him. Which reminded me, I had one more person to call.

The stage manager announced over the speakers, "Ten minutes to the start of the concert."

"Am I good?" I asked the replacement for Deedee. She had given birth to her son a little over a week before. Her husband had left to take care of their children with her.

"You are," the woman said.

I thanked her and headed out the door.

"Where are you going?" Danny called after me.

"To make a phone call," I answered.

"Cobie's at a concert," Danny pointed out.

"I'm not calling her," I told him before leaving. I went to our dressing room before I chickened out.

My mom picked up on the first ring, saying, "Jordan? I'm sorry, my son shine." She always called me that nickname with sun spelled like son and as two words instead of one.

"Ma, I'm at a concert, and I don't have a lot of time before I go onto the stage. I'm still pissed off at you for believing I would ever hurt a woman, not after everything you taught me," I told her. My body tensed, and I gripped my phone tighter.

"Oh, Jordan."

"Let me finish. I will forgive you in time, but I need you to understand how hurt I was. Why didn't you call me? Why didn't you stand up for me?"

"I...I can't." My mom's voice sounded weak.

"You can, Ma. You're the strongest woman I know besides the woman I plan to marry. She's amazing. I called you to tell you I found someone who will always be by my side, and I'll be by hers. Give me some space for me to forgive you." I pulled out the ring Noah had picked up.

"If you need space, I'll give it to you. I love you, and I'll always be waiting for your call."

"I love you, too." After I hung up, I let out a breath. I took another one in and then out, calming myself down.

The stage manager called five minutes.

I headed to the stage, and my band waited for me. Someone handed me a microphone. After thanking them, I made my way to the center of the stage.

The new lead guitarist started the first chords of our top song. Well, second. *Best for You* had broken our sales record and kept climbing the charts.

"This song goes out to the one special woman in my life," I told the crowd as the lights popped on. The ladies here would believe they were it, but I didn't look at them. I stared at the open space next to me where she should be. "Hey, girl. I see you dancing alone. I walk past everyone on the dance floor and start making my moves."

Chapter Forty-One

Cobie

My watch buzzed as my alarm went off. I silenced it and told the concert band, "Let's go."

The lead guitarist started, and the keyboardist joined her.

"You know this song. I know you do," I told my sold-out audience. "Hey, boy. I see you dancing by yourself. I walk past the men hollering at me, and start making my moves. The way you dance makes me want to take you home with me." I swayed my hips to the music. I was always a fan of this song and the band that made it. They had stumbled, but their recent releases had me listening again. I felt glad Jordan had taken my advice the first day we met.

After the concert ended, Dick spoke to me, but I ignored him and headed to my soon-to-be manager. She looked a lot like Cole, with black hair, dark eyes, and a sharp nose. Their major difference was that his hair was already speckled with gray. They could be twins.

"You were great," Abby told me. She handed me a bottle of water.

"Thank you for coming along with me," I said. Her being here stopped me from being uncivil to my former manager. I kept counting down the days until I put him behind me for good.

"I can't have Dick try to steal you back." Abby nodded her head at someone behind me before we headed to the back door.

I glanced back to see Dick glaring at us. He had lost me as a client and owed a lot of money to me. Rumors floated around as other singers wanted to leave him, too. He could've avoided his current situation if he had paid me and allowed me to reveal to the world I was Cam. I didn't feel bad about him. Because of what he did, I had met Jordan. I dismissed the thought. He and I would've met him a few days later when we worked together. Would we have fallen in love? I believed so.

Abby and I climbed into the back of an SUV and headed to the hotel. She had made the arrangements for me to sleep and get to the venue. "Tomorrow night, I'm flying to another city after my concert," I told her.

Her shoulders hunched, and she pressed her lips into a tight line. "As long as you are in the next city by rehearsal, I'll keep Dick off your back. Where are you going?"

"To see Jordan. I miss him. Being dragged away from him to get ready for this tour sucked, and I can't go another three weeks without being with him."

"I'd tell you the time would go quickly, but I get it. My hubby is flying out and taking a week off to be with me next week. Do me a favor, though?" Abby ran a hand through her hair.

"What's that?"

"Call Jordan and tell him you're coming. He might get the same idea as you. What am I saying? I've met him, and he will," Abby answered.

I laughed. "I'm calling him after his concert tonight. He would fly to see me, and then I would, and we would miss each other. This isn't a movie, so I'm finding out his plans first."

"Good." Abby grinned at me, and she asked how finding a house was going. She had put me in contact with a realtor.

"Nothing feels like home to me. Do my words make sense?"

"You've lived on the streets for months and in someone else's place for years. Your record label will gladly give you back the mansion you used before anytime."

"I want my place," I said. So, no one could kick me out of it. Dick's company had paid nothing yet, and he would drag it out as long as possible. I should threaten to leave the tour if he didn't fork over some cash. What did he do with the money I had made for him?

Abby walked me to my hotel room. I had gotten it not to overstay my welcome at Megan's. My new manager had a room next door.

I showered, dried my hair, and checked the time. Three hours until Jordan's concert was over. He had left me a text during my show, and I read it. He missed me. I sent him a text back saying the same thing. I wanted to stay up, but I felt too exhausted to try.

My phone rang at 10 a.m. the next morning, right when I planned to get up. I checked the caller ID before answering. My heart soared. "Hey," I answered.

"Hi, honey. I miss you," Jordan said.

"Why are you up so early?"

"I had to call you to wish you a good day and to break a leg at your concert."

"Thank you, sweetie. I miss you, too." I pulled the blankets off and climbed out of bed.

"Have you seen the videos from our concerts? Our fans have figured out what we did." Jordan sent me a link.

I played the video, and tears welled in my eyes. Someone had overlayed the videos of us singing *Hey Girl* together, making it look like we sang next to each other on stage. Even our movements appeared as we danced together. "This is incredible."

"I can't wait to do it again."

"I already set my alarm." Dick would throw a fit if he learned what we did. Even if he did, I had no plans to change it. He was lucky I agreed to the tour. Which reminded me, I had to find out Jordan's plans. "Where will you be at 11 p.m. your time tonight?"

"Finishing the concert and catching a redeye back to you."

Happiness swelled inside of me, for he and I agreed. "I'll stay at your place, then."

"Please do. How is finding a home going?" he asked.

"Not good. I keep getting sent links, and I visit when I can, but nothing is calling out to me."

Jordan grew silent on the other end, and I waited for his piece of advice. "Why don't you design your home, then? You know what you want, right?"

"A studio to work in, a kitchen, a bedroom, an enormous bathroom, a pool, and more." My cheeks heated when I listed off the third item.

"I like how you mentioned a studio first. Tell your realtor what you want, and if she can't find it, build it. You can always stay with me until you find a place."

A soreness settled inside the back of my throat. "I need a home to call my own. What if I get kicked out again and wind up on the streets?"

Jordan's voice softened. "I would never kick you out, and I'll give you every reassurance you need. A room of your own? Done. Just tell me."

I thanked him again and brushed the tears off my face. "I need to see you."

"You will in less than twenty-four hours. I'm catching a red-eye at 1 a.m. tomorrow morning."

"Give me the details, and I can pick you up."

"You got a vehicle?"

"Yes, I did."

He told me when to meet him.

We chatted for a few more minutes before needing to rest our voices for the night. I couldn't wait to see him the following morning.

I worked out the details of working with Brittany. She wanted to stay with the Solar Harmony for the rest of their tour before she took the leap. It worked out great for the brand wanting me. Once I finished, I headed to the concert.

Blaire sent me a text about breaking both legs, and I sent him the same message back. My man and his band had him open for them, and I was happy for him. They suggested some openers for me, but Dick decided, and I didn't care.

The concert was a success since I was still riding the high from Jordan's call this morning. We had texted until I hit the stage.

Dick waited for me at the end of the encore. "The tour bus is waiting for us. We need to discuss the first song you've been playing in the encore."

"No, we don't. You have no say in the music I sing, and I'm not going with you," I told him.

"I'm still your manager, and you'll listen to me, young lady." Dick's voice rose, drawing onlookers.

"Former manager soon enough, and I won't be taking advice from you. The last time I did, you took all of my money. By the way, where is the payment for my judgement against you?" I placed my hands on my hips as I glared up at him. He used to make me afraid, but now I saw the pathetic, manipulative man he truly was.

"We're still doing the concert," Dick said.

"Are we? You need to pay me. If not, I'll walk," I told him.

"You'll be in breach of contract if you do." Dick gave me a smug smile.

"If you don't pay me, you've broken the contract. I'm giving you a formal notice of my intent to withdraw—" I said until Dick cut me off.

"Fine!" He huffed away.

"Sorry," I told the staff and bowed. Megan's lessons had really helped me out.

Abby stepped up next to me, and her arm brushed mine. "Ready to go?" she asked me.

"I am. Sorry you had to witness the entire exchange between him and me." I was too angry to even speak his name at that moment.

"You handled him beautifully. Keep blowing him off and putting him in his place." She hummed as we headed to the SUV.

Not having my bodyguards with me felt weird, but I was glad no one wanted me dead. I also got to meet their kids, wives, and husband. I placed Tim's company on retainer to review any threats against me, which happened a lot more than I had realized.

I set a few alarms to meet Jordan at the airport, not wanting to miss his flight. I put on a red wig and made a sign with his first name on it. People stared at me as they passed, and nervousness rose inside of me. According to Tim, the threat against me had ended, but I still needed to be aware of my celebrity status. The guy pleaded guilty in attempting to harm me once the truth of the court outcome came out. He loved me a little too much. I placed a restraining order against him despite the piece of paper not doing anything to stop those who ignored it. I hoped he didn't.

Jordan searched the crowd for me. He wore the blond wig I had got him and sunglasses. He was adorable.

I held my sign up higher for him to spot.

He came to me and wrapped me in a tight embrace. "I missed you," he said.

"I missed you, too. Let's get out of here before anyone figures us out." I tugged on his hand, and we walked to where I parked my car.

"Nice car." Jordan set his bag on the back and climbed in next to me.

"I wanted something I could put the roof down on. At the car lot, I told the sales associate I'd pay it off then and there. He didn't believe me. Apparently, people don't pay for cars all at once." I shrugged and started the engine.

"Not for this price tag."

"He also wanted me to build my own." I made a face before pulling out of the parking. Another took my spot.

Jordan chuckled. "Are you happy with it?"

"Completely. What should we do today? Did you sleep on the plane?" It had all-wheel drive and space in the trunk for groceries, not a massive box.

"I am ready to go. We should rollerblade in our park."

"We'll have to stop by your place to get our rollerblades."

"Fine by me. How did Dick act when you told him you wouldn't go with him to the next tour location?" Jordan asked.

"Dick blew a gasket. I also told him, pay me, or I'm walking," I answered.

"Would you walk away from the tour?"

"I wouldn't disappoint my fans."

Jordan placed a hand on my shoulder and gave it a squeeze. "I swear I won't tell him."

"You'd better not, or I won't see a dime." I already figured I wouldn't.

We chatted for a bit until I parked outside his mansion. Jordan opened the front door for me. We grabbed our rollerblades and headed back out.

The light traffic on the road to the park made arriving there much faster. I parked a block away. On Sunday, we shouldn't see too many people until after noon.

Jordan and I rollerbladed hand in hand, wearing our disguises.

"Someone will figure you out in this wig," I told him. He needed to switch off.

"Not today, though. Let's go underneath the bridge near where we first met," he said.

I steered us onto the path that didn't require us to walk down the hill. Out of everything we could do today, I didn't think Jordan would want to rollerblade. We had met here, though.

He let go of my hand.

I rolled forward and flipped around when he didn't follow me. I was about to call to him, but he had pulled out a ring.

Jordan glided to me and bent down on one knee. "Will you marry me?" he asked.

"Yes!" I didn't need to think.

He put the ring on my finger and pulled me into his arms, kissing me.

I kissed him back. I would love this man for the rest of my life. Our different career paths, fans, and goals would pull us apart, yet we'd always find our way back to each other.

The End

Acknowledgments

This book means a lot to me. It helped me with my frustration with fans, especially the overzealous fans. They know who they are. I wish the singers happiness, and their fans to realize they are people too. They deserve love, personal space, and our encouragement. Thank you for the music you wrote.

Thank you to my family for putting up with me. Thank you to my friends for their support and love. I appreciate you so much. Thank you for my editor, who I wouldn't be able to release so many books in a year without her. Love you!

Dear reader, thank you for giving my book a chance. I appreciate you!

About K.A. Meng

K. A. Meng lives in North Dakota, in the same town she grew up. Her love for the paranormal started at a young age when she saw her first ghost.

Today, she spends her time writing paranormal romance, fantasy, and everything in between. When life drags her away from it, she hangs out with her son and friends, goes to movies, watches TV, plays board games, walks her dogs, and reads books. She is actively involved in one writing group and wishes to some day visit Disney World.

Social Media Links

Website: http://www.kamengauthor.com

Facebook: https://www.facebook.com/KAMengAuthor

K.A. Meng Books:

https://www.facebook.com/groups/kamengbooks/

(Secret word is Mask.)

Twitter: https://twitter.com/KAMengAuthor

Blog: http://www.kamengauthor.com/blog

Instagram: https://www.instagram.com/kamengauthor/

TikTok: https://www.tiktok.com/@kamengauthor

Email: kamengauthor@gmail.com

Books by K.A. Meng

HELP ME SOLVE MY MURDER

After failing every pitch, podcast host Kaya Fortune has one last chance when a Play Me audio file appears on her computer. She plays it in front of the only sponsor willing to give her a chance after a scandal, and the voice of the dead girl asks Kaya to help solve her murder.

The sponsor loves the idea and gives Kaya a contract with the stipulation her co-host is dead. Kaya has never met the girl and isn't certain if she's dead. Kaya must determine why the deceased girl reached out to her from beyond the grave.

Along for the investigation is Kaya's hot producer, Tobias Carr, who dislikes Kaya because of the scandal and insists on being involved in every process, including the research. The more they dig into the dead girl's murder, the more suspects they cross off.

With the help of an odd computer whiz, tension turning steamy with Tobias, and a wacky cat, Kaya may solve her co-host's murder.

https://mybook.to/HMSMM

A TOWN OF MURDERERS BOOK 1:
THE FIRST SCHEME

An intruder breaks into Joann Fields home in the middle of the night and kills her husband, David. The evidence, like blood on her clothes and GSR on her hands, piles up against her. She's arrested for David's murder.

Mike Carroll is a reporter, who wanted nothing more than a story, and he gets one when Joann asks him for help. The deeper Mike digs, the worse things are for her. Joann may not be the innocent victim she portrays herself to be.

https://getBook.at/TFS
BOOK 2: https://getbook.at/TSP
BOOK 3: https://getbook.at/ATOMs3

A PORTER FAMILY ADVENTURE BOOK 1:
DESTINATION BERMUDA TRIANGLE

Alexandra Porter was never an adventure TV show star, unlike her parents. Her life takes a drastic turn when her father, Dax Porter, goes missing in the Bermuda Triangle. Less than one month, the search for him is called off, and five months later Alexandra stands on the deck of the Tranquil Seas filming her own reality TV show to solve the mystery of the Bermuda Triangle, hoping to find her father.

Five different experts join Alexandra and work as the ship's crew. No one except for the captain and her has experience. The Bermuda Triangle expert can't get along with the conspiracy theorist. When she sneaks away to search her father's last known location, she gets close to a shark.

The crew and TV show executives are mad at her and threaten to cancel the show, but nothing will stop Alexandra from finding her father.

https://mybook.to/DBT

THE WAYWARD STATION

A tornado whisks Kayla Stark into The Wayward Station, a realm between life and death. This special place is in trouble from a ghost with a bad attitude, Jacoby Marone. He has been stealing a precious commodity. If she doesn't stop him, she and The Wayward Station may disappear forever.

http://getbook.at/WS

SUPERIOR SPECIES BOOK 1:
SUPERIOR SPECIES

Ivory Ames isn't special. She's like everyone else until she moves to Los Roshano for college. Now Ivory's caught the attention of the "Models"—the upperclassmen who are supernaturally beautiful.

Ivory tries to concentrate on school, but she's surrounded by mysteries. Every freshman she meets is an orphan. The town has a strict sunset curfew because wild animals have killed several people. She's asked out by the most popular "Models".

Nothing makes sense, but to keep her friends safe, Ivory must figure out the truth behind the town before it's too late.

https://mybook.to/SSB1

BOOK 2: https://mybook.to/SSB2

BOOK 3: https://mybook.to/SSB3E

BOOK 0.5: https://mybook.to/SSB05E

BOOK 4: https://mybook.to/SSB4E

BOOK 5: https://mybook.to/SSB5E

BOOK 6: https://mybook.to/SSB6E

BOOK 7: https://mybook.to/SSB7E

BOOK 8: https://mybook.to/SSB8E

Extra

Here are the set lists for what was played at the concerts. I never figured out Solar Harmony's set list for day 7 and 8, or who opened for Cobie. Oops.

Cobie's set list for day 1 of the tour.
1. Time After Time by Cyndi Lauper

2. All of Me by John Legend

3. Love Yourself by Justin Bieber

4. Hey, Girl by Solar Harmony

5. I Wanna Dance with Someone by Whitney Houston

Cobie's set list for day 2 of the tour
1. Heartbreak by Cam

2. Hold Onto You by Cam

3. Let You Go by Cam

4. Never Stop by Cam

Solar Harmony's set list day 1 and 2
Show Openers (4)

1. Hey, Girl (Lead signer Jordan)

2. Bad Boys (Lead singer Royal)

3. Loner (Lead singer Danny)

4. Sorry, I Can't Love You (Lead singer Royal)

Main Set Closers(3)

1. I'll be There (Lead singer Jay)

2. Best for You (Lead singer Jordan, and Royal day 2)

3. Don't Want to Stop (Lead singer Baylee, and day 2)

Show Closers (3)

1. What I do for You (Lead singer Danny)

2. Last Breath (Lead singer Jay)

3. Slowly (Lead singer Baylee)

Encores Played (1 or 2)

1. Home With You (Lead singer Jay)

2. Take me Home (Lead singer none added for day 2)

Cobie's set list for day 3 and 4 of the tour

1. Fuck You by CeeLo Green

2. Against All Odds (Take a Look at Me Now) by Phil Collins

3. Born This Way by Lady Gaga

4. Heart to Heart by Cam (unreleased)

Solar Harmony's set list day 3 and 4
Show Openers (4)

1. Best for You (Lead singer Jordan)

2. Sorry, I Can't Love You (Lead singer Royal)

3. You're my One and Only (Lead singer Royal, originally Danny)

4. I'll be There (Lead signer Jay)

Main Set Closers (3)

1. Sins we Love (Lead singer Baylee)

2. Hey, Girl (Lead signer Jordan)

3. Loner (Lead singer Danny)

Show Closers (3)

1. Bad Boys (Lead Signer Royal)

2. Break Everything Down (Lead singer Danny)

3. Slowly (Lead Singer Baylee)

Encores Played (2)

1. Take me Home (Lead singer none)

2. Home With You (Lead singer Jay)

Cobie's set list for day 5 and 6 of the tour

1. Born This Way by Lady Gaga

2. Fuck You by Cee Lo Green

3. Against All Odds (Take a Look at Me Now) by Phil Collins

4. Heart to Heart by Cam (released now)

Solar Harmony's set list day 5 and 6
Show Openers (4)

1. Hey, Girl (Lead signer Jordan)

2. Loner (Lead singer Danny)

3. You're my One and Only (Lead singer Baylee)

4. My troubles (Lead Singer Jay)

Main Set Closers (3)

1. Best for You (Lead singer Jordan)

2. I'll be There (Lead singer Jay)

3. Don't Want to Stop (Lead singer Baylee)

Show Closers (3)

1. What I do for You (Lead singer Danny)

2. Last Breath (Lead singer Jay)

3. Slowly (Lead singer Baylee)

Encores Played (1 or 2)

1. Home With You (Lead singer Jay)

2. Take me Home (Lead singer none)

Cobie's set list for day 7 and 8 of the tour

1. Hold onto You by Cam

2. Let you Go by Cam

3. Never Stop by Cam

4. Heart to Heart by Cam (released now)

Blaire Gunn Set list for day 9 and 10

1. Locked out of Heaven by Bruno Mars

2. I am Me by Blaire Gunn

3. I Love It by Icona Pop

4. If I were a Boy by Brandi

Solar Harmony's set list day 9 and 10

Show Openers (4)

1. Hey, Girl (Lead signer Jordan)

2. Bad Boys (Lead singer Royal)

3. Loner (Lead singer Danny)

4. I'll be There (Lead singer Jay)

Main Set Closers (3)

1. Best for You (Lead singer Jordan)

2. What I do for You (Lead singer Danny)

3. Don't Want to Stop (Lead singer Baylee)

Show Closers (3)

1. You Have Me (Lead singer Danny)

2. Last Breath (Lead singer Jay)

3. Slowly (Lead singer Baylee)

Encores Played (1 or 2)

1. Home With You (Lead singer Jay)

2. Take me Home (Lead singer none)

Cobie's set list day 1 and day 2

Show Openers (4)

1. Love Will Get us Through by Cam

2. Heart to Heart by Cam

3. Cool it Down by Cam

Main Set Closers (4)

1. Hold Onto You by Cam

2. Let You Go by Cam

3. Let's Rock by Cam

4. I Can't Stop Loving You by Cam

Show Closers (3)

1. Never Stop by Cam

2. Work by Cam

3. Heartbreak by Cam

Encores Played (1 or 2)

1. Hey, Boy (Remake) by Solar Harmony

2. You're Mine by Cam